Children of Nemia

Nym
Homestead
Western Forest
Desert
Mt. Falkrist
L. Nymera
Seat Mercura
N

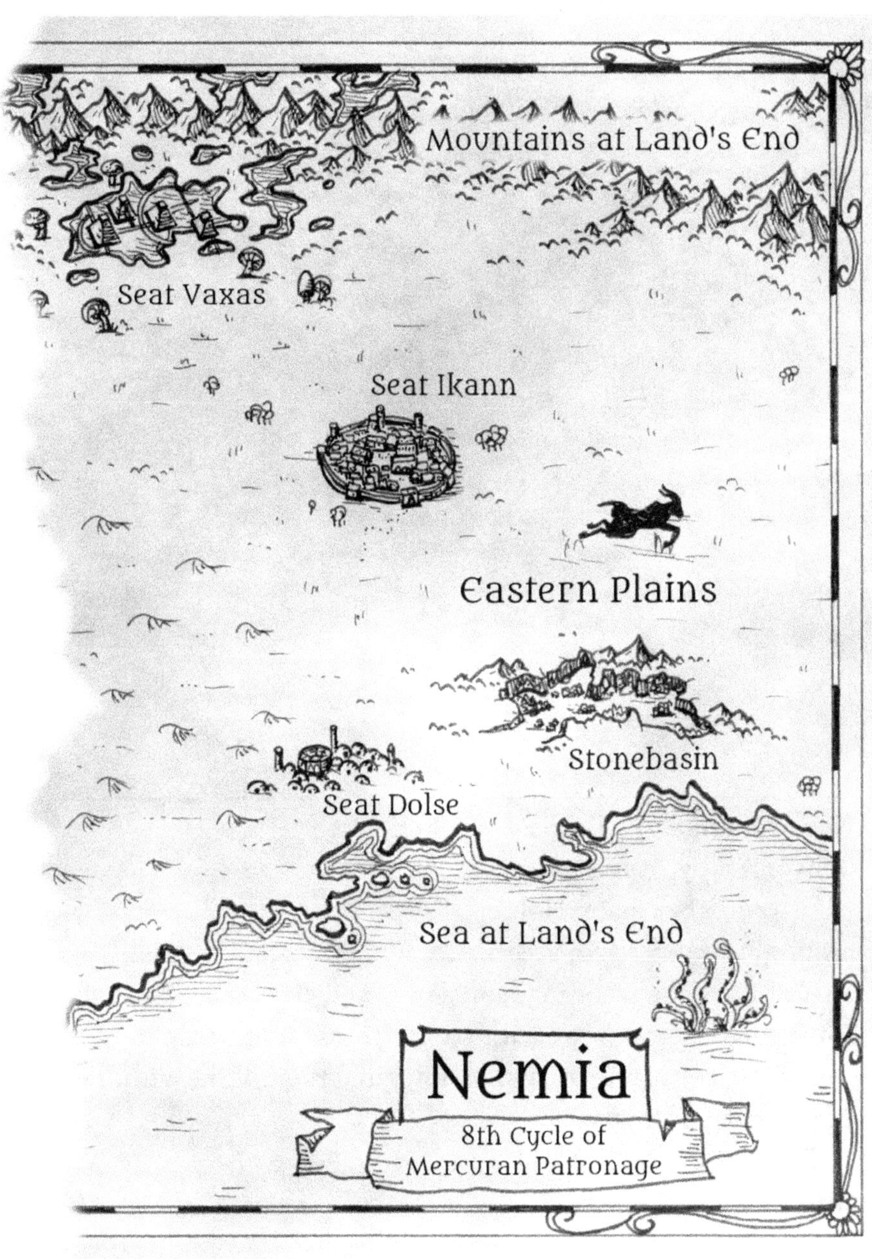

Mountains at Land's End
Seat Vaxas
Seat Ikann
Eastern Plains
Stonebasin
Seat Dolse
Sea at Land's End
Nemia
8th Cycle of
Mercuran Patronage

MICHAEL GOE

CHILDREN OF NEMIA

1 Seat Dolse

"Do you remember how to tell your stars?" asked Farseer Daz. "And strip a carcass?"

"Yes, Father," answered Van.

They sat together on a rocky bluff up the beach, watching the sun dip low over the ocean. The familiar vista was a privilege reserved only for Nemians of tribe Dolse, as no other tribe made their home near the sea. For Van and his father, it was a mere hour's walk to the cliff-studded shoreline, though in recent years, they made the trek only on warm, dry days when Daz's joints were merciful. Soon, the seasons would change and the rains would come, which meant fewer trips to the beach—but Van would be gone by then.

Glancing at Farseer Daz, Van reflected that he had finally surpassed him in height. It was a recent change, and even as it filled him with a swell of pride, it brought with it an uninvited awareness of his father's mortality. Van now stood at nearly six feet, while according to rumor, Daz had shrunk an inch in the last year.

"If you remember, you will do fine," said Daz, his eyes fixed on the pastel bloom of the horizon. "But beginning tomorrow, you must remember to say, *yes, Chieftain.*"

"People have died on the Journey of Patronage!" blurted Van, his strained voice jumping between a child's shrill and a man's baritone. He ignored the resultant twitch at the corner of Daz's eye.

"People die in all manner of places, for all manner of reasons," Daz observed. "In my youth, I witnessed a man slip and die at our fishing pond, simply because he forgot how to place his foot on a wet stepping stone. And your mother died in our own home simply because she forgot how to wake up."

"I want to succeed," Van plowed on. "I want to bring honor to the tribe. To you."

"You daydream of bringing honor to yourself," Daz hissed.

Van hung his head, stung. After barely a moment, the chieftain rested a hand on his shoulder and sighed.

"I promise you, Van the Scribe, so long as you do not become overproud, you will return home safely. Be nothing more or less than your truest self."

Van wanted to brood, but knowing he'd soon leave, he chose to smile instead. He helped his father up, and they prepared to return to Seat Dolse. As they ambled down the bluff, Van noticed Daz smirking, and he cocked his head.

"And so long as you watch where you put your feet."

Daz winked at him, and Van stifled a laugh.

They arrived home after nightfall. Van led the way with a torch fashioned from driftwood and oilcloth, in part to help them navigate the darkness, but also to aid the Seat's rangers in distinguishing Van and his father from encroaching wildlife. Striking fire from the knife and flint he now carried was another new skill, but Van had been practicing, knowing it would prove useful on the pilgrimage.

He held his torch high as they crossed into Seat Dolse, the tribe's oldest and largest community. Before them lay hundreds of communal buildings and clay huts, the favored architectural style in southern Nemia owing to the abundance of soft earth near the sea. Among the larger structures, all illuminated by bonfires, was a webwork of dugouts framed with wood or stone. Dolsers gathered in these shallow coves to share meals and teach crafts. Some were in use even at this late hour.

Men and women stood and bowed to the chieftain as Van helped him through the streets to the house they shared. There, Daz shed most of his clothes and allowed Van to assist him into bed.

"Before you sleep, see that our guests are settled," said Daz, shifting in his hammock as Van pulled a fur over him.

Van grimaced. "I checked on the dark girl before we left. She was asleep," he said. "But Father, I don't like Simon of the Mists. He cares only for drink and sexmaking."

Daz waved a hand dismissively. "You'll soon be a man by rite of pilgrimage. You should care a little more for sexmaking yourself."

Van gave his father an exasperated look, but Farseer Daz only chuckled and rolled over. He knew Van would obey and look in on the foreigners.

Their "guests" had arrived just under a year ago, only a few weeks apart. Van was the one that had found Simon of the Mists, washed up on the beach wearing flamboyant, colorful garb that looked far too heavy and—by Van's estimation—poor for swimming in. He was frail with a sickly pallor like tanned rabbit hide, and his curiously long ears ended in sharp points. The elders of the tribe couldn't believe such a person had survived childhood until he demonstrated his skill with magic. After being nursed back to health, the stranger expressed no desire to return to his own lands. Instead, in exchange for regular meals and a hammock to sleep in, he assisted the Seat's laborers using his spells.

"Where did you come from?" Van had asked the man from across the sea, the day his alien eyes first cracked open in the medicine hut.

The foreigner had stared at him before tracing a pattern in the air that seemed deliberate and murmuring, "Try again."

"Where did you come from?" Van repeated patiently.

Simon of the Mists narrowed his round eyes. "Better you don't know."

"What are you called?"

"Simon," he replied hoarsely. "Although, I think you can call me *Mister* Simon."

"What happened to you?" asked Van.

"I *died*."

Simon of the Mists never seemed exactly happy or exactly sad. Some of the more adventurous young women of the Seat did sexmaking with him.

Despite what he might try to convince his father of, Van actually *was* curious about it. For some time, he'd felt occasional stirrings when he chanced upon girls washing or working in the public baths. He'd felt similar stirrings when looking at some of the men. But this was the year of his pilgrimage, and sexmaking was not a skill that would serve him in his coming trial. Instead, he chose to learn the blade and the bow.

Their second visitor was found by rangers on the outskirts of Ikanni territory, alone and naked in a scorched field. Physically, she was the inverse of Simon, with skin the color of fired charcoal and hair white as alabaster—though she had the same pointed ears. The tribe's shamans had begged Farseer Daz to send her away or have her killed, even more urgently than when Simon had turned up, but just as with Simon, the chieftain commanded she be taken in and cared for.

Outsiders were forbidden in Nemia by law, but the chieftain's word was final, at least to other Dolsers. Even Van had confronted Daz, terrified of what might happen should the other tribes discover his father harboring foreigners. But his pleas fell on deaf ears.

"All is as it should be," Farseer Daz had said. "Trust in your chieftain."

After helping his father into bed, Van wandered to the hut his tribe had gifted to Simon of the Mists. As he drew near, he was surprised to see not the foreigner, but his friend Otep Acrearms emerging from the dwelling.

"Otep!" Van called, brightening. When his enormous friend lifted a finger to his lips, he lowered his voice. "I mean, First Ranger!"

Otep smiled. "When it is just the two of us, I think I still prefer Otep. What brings you here, Van the Scribe?"

"Father sent me to see that Simon of the Mists was looked after."

"It is already done," said Otep. "I fed him moon's milk and shared stern words with him regarding tomorrow's ceremonies. He understands there will be no time for shiftless rutting in the days to come."

"Then come to the bonfires with me," Van begged. "I was talking with Father about the pilgrimage, and he told me—"

Otep Acrearms patted him affectionately on the head with a hand the size of a potter's wheel, interrupting him. The champion of Dolse was the son of human rangers of normal height and girth, but it was believed the blood of giants was in his ancestry, which was known to skip a generation or several. Looking at him now, it was hard to challenge the claim. Otep was seven feet tall with skin the color and texture of sandstone. It was said his hide was so thick it could turn a blade.

"I would enjoy nothing more, Van the Scribe. It is already late, however, and we will all be very busy come morning."

Otep was right, of course. Reluctantly, Van bid his friend goodnight after congratulating him for what felt like the hundredth time on becoming the tribe's champion for that year's Journey of Patronage. He'd run out of ways to tell Otep how proud he was to be his friend. But he hadn't yet found the words to tell him he was also scared—scared that while they would be leaving home together as peers, Otep's role as First Ranger somehow meant he was leaving Van behind.

Retiring to his bed of furs in the chieftain's hut, Van listened to his father's rhythmic snoring in the neighboring chamber, hoping it would lull him to sleep. Late as it was, the nearness of the opening ceremonies had his blood pulsing. Sleep refused him. Outside, Seat Dolse grew dim and quiet— yet strangely, not completely dark nor entirely silent. Still wide awake, Van let his curiosity get the better of him. He slipped his sandals back on and crept outside, following the murmur of voices.

Rather than a group holding conversation, Van discovered a lone speaker orating in a dugout where a bonfire still flickered. It was the Teaching Circle, Van realized. He wandered over and dropped into the dugout unceremoniously, startling the sleep-addled children gathered within. Seeing Van, the speaker paused his lecture to glower disapprovingly in his direction.

"Why, if it isn't our chieftain's own son," said Ghan Mudcatcher, elder of Dolse and that year's Pilgrimage Guide. "Why have you come to my Teaching Circle?"

"What are the children doing awake, Ghan Mudcatcher?" Van said, crossing his arms over his chest. "It is late, and we will all be very busy come morning."

Van hoped to impress his childhood teacher with the same appeal to reason Otep had used on him. This proved foolish.

"Because, boy," Ghan said, pointing an accusatory finger at the gathered youths, "the mothers of these fools came to me two nights ago and told me they were caught sneaking out of bed."

Van tilted his head to one side, confused.

"These ones all came of age this year, and they will soon embark on the Journey of Patronage. This will be the second night I deny them sleep, that they might better appreciate its benefits and the importance of its schedule."

He punctuated his words with a loud hiss—an unnerving sound in any circumstance, but particularly effective coming from the drawn lips of Ghan Mudcatcher, who was wildborn. The elder looked much like a snake the size of a man. The children recoiled, an untested self-preservation instinct cutting through their drowsiness. Tired as they were, they would not close their eyes in proximity to the snake-man.

For Van, such childhood mysticism was a thing of the distant past. He knew Ghan was kind, if terse. As an elder of the tribe and their Pilgrimage Guide, it was also his sworn duty to protect the aspirants, young and old alike. Van understood that in this moment, that meant keeping them awake and frightening them.

"I will stay and listen as well," Van declared, settling in with the children.

Some of them seemed thankful for his presence, but Ghan only snorted indignantly. "If you are awake at this hour on the eve of such an important day, then I suppose you'd better."

Ghan resumed his lecture from where he'd left off—a chronology of the Eighth Cycle of Mercuran Patronage and the Cycles that came before it. Van assumed he'd chosen the topic offhand, the only point being to keep the children from dozing, but one young listener surprised Van with a question.

"How many times has Dolse been Patron?" asked an inquisitive girl of about twelve, with long brown hair and chestnut brown eyes.

"Not once in remembered history," affirmed the elder, grinning as if he were proud of the fact.

The children exchanged looks of disbelief. Van, knowing his histories, could only fold his arms and look at the ground.

While countries across the sea waged war on one another and held so-called "elections"—a word learned from Simon of the Mists—the four tribes of Nemia engaged in no such trivialities. They merely undertook the pilgrimage, as they had for generations, as a peaceful means of deciding which tribe would lead the others.

Patronage was almost always awarded to tribe Mercura, the Stewards of the Forest and the River Nym. Owing to the good relations between Dolsers and Mercurans, Cycles of Mercuran Patronage were felt as times of plenty for tribe Dolse, which Van could attest to, having lived his life to the day under Mercuran Patronage. But many years before he was born, there was a Cycle of Ikanni Patronage. While it had lasted just nine years, that era was said to have been a time of strife and hardship.

Farseer Daz had told Van much about the Ikanni and their time as the Patron tribe. He'd been in his prime then, newly appointed as chieftain, and he'd made great sacrifices to keep his people safe and fed under the abuse and extortion of their near neighbors, the Stewards of the Plains and Highlands. Even now, under Mercuran Patronage, rangers returning from the borderlands told tales of violent confrontations with outriders of Ikann.

"Otep will change things," Van muttered.

He wasn't sure if Ghan heard him, for he offered neither acknowledgment nor rebuttal. Soon, exhaustion caught up to Van, and he found he had no more appetite for the self-deprecating tone of the elder's histories. Leaving the dugout, he made his way home and climbed back into bed, but anxiety continued to roll in the pit of his stomach. Try as he may, he couldn't reconcile his faith in Otep Acrearms with his childhood teacher's visible confidence that tribe Dolse would once again serve as attendant to another Patron—and perhaps always would.

The next day, Van slept through morning assembly, earning himself extra chores as punishment. Seat Dolse would soon have many mouths to feed, so Van was put to work in the kitchens. He'd garnered a reputation for being useful there—he could skin a rabbit faster than most, and he knew a good trick for pitting cherries. He had no sense for spices and flavor balance, however, so those aspects of meal preparation were left to others.

Finishing his extra shift in the labor dugouts, Van emerged to find the community crowded to bursting with unfamiliar faces. These were his visiting kinsmen, he realized—the aspirants of Dolse, come to the Seat from far and wide to receive their chieftain's blessing. Most were human, like Van, but he also saw giantkin like Otep Acrearms—only a few of whom rivaled the First Ranger's impressive stature—wildborn like Ghan, and even startouched that resembled the gods of the land themselves.

The youngest of them were only twelve years old, having come of age that very year. Meanwhile, any unfortunate enough to have been *eleven* during the last pilgrimage would today be grown men and women—in every way except the one that mattered.

Van was caught gawking, and for his impropriety, he was punished with further chores.

For the next hour, Van carried out pails of refuse from the Seat's bonfires, and hauled in firewood from the storehouses. He found no time to eat, or even wash himself, before a horn was sounded. The sustained note summoned the residents and guests to the grand amphitheater, where the opening ceremonies for the Journey of Patronage would begin. He shouldered his way through the crowd as it moved and managed to find a seat near the stage. From here, he had a clear view of the chieftain's throne.

His father hadn't arrived yet, but several rangers in bone masks and fur mantles flanked the throne, standing still as statues. Van contemplated the old throne in silence, waiting for the gravity of the moment to feel real while eavesdropping on the excited conversations of his kinsmen.

He'd seen his father on his throne only once before, at the commencement of the last pilgrimage. Van was just six years old then, too young to leave home with the aspirants of his tribe. But nine more years had come and gone, and this time, he would go with them.

A hush fell over the crowd. Farseer Daz marched toward the stage wearing his mask of bone and crown of antlers, Ghan Mudcatcher and Otep Acrearms in tow. He offered a blessing here and a prayer there as he strode through the crowd, some of the aspirants reaching up to touch the beads and feathers around his neck. Daz gave Van a blessing, too, but there was no familiarity in it—only the same impersonal warmth offered freely to all.

He took the stage and faced the congregation, and when he flung his arms wide in greeting, Van found he barely recognized him. This was not his aging father, with his bent back and stiff joints. Today, the chieftain looked like some mighty bird or restless spirit, ten feet tall and moving with the graceful vitality of a stalking cheetah.

"Children of Dolse, soon to be blooded kin," began Farseer Daz, "welcome to my Seat. As guests here, you may share the warmth of my fires, partake of my larder, and rest your heads unafraid under the protection of my rangers. But know that two sunrises hence, I will cast you out, and I bid you not return until you can call yourselves men and women of Dolse."

A susurrous murmur rippled through the crowd.

"While you are outcast, remember that the Journey of Patronage is no mere private ordeal. You shall honor the traditions of your tribe, and you shall learn the values of your cousins from the tribes of Mercura, Ikann, and Vaxas. It is in this way that we find our next Patron, and strengthen the bonds of trust and friendship among ourselves."

More thoughtful whispers, the nervous shuffling of feet.

"Your First Ranger will be presented tomorrow, with the arrival of his peers," said Daz, gesturing to Otep. "But many of you already know him well. Lend him your support as he tests himself against the trials of Nemia's chieftains, and whosoever wins those games, you shall recognize their tribe as your Patron and stand proudly beside them for the next nine years."

Just don't let it be Ikann, Van prayed.

As the son of the chieftain, he knew he shouldn't cling to old prejudices, but he had his doubts that friendly bonds between Dolsers and Ikanni would be strengthened that year —or on any other. Sitting to his left, Van recognized the girl from last night's Teaching Circle. She frowned and pursed her lips, as if struggling to internalize Daz's wisdom.

"Feast now!" Daz shouted, startling Van back to attention. "Exalt the gods of the land, our Emissaries, and be joyful tonight. We shall reconvene here tomorrow, when we greet the arrival of our esteemed cousins."

The stage was quickly vacated, and an energetic drumbeat was taken up. Masked rangers roved through the crowd, offering flasks of the tribe's ceremonial wine to even the youngest aspirants. Many accepted the drink with uncertain deference, but Van didn't partake. He had no fondness for the smell of alcohol, or the impairment of reason he knew accompanied the indulgence. But he was hungry, so he decided to explore the notion of a feast.

Slipping away from the thronging crowd, Van followed his nose to a dugout where fresh bread, stewed meats, and savory vegetable mashups were being heaped into serving bowls. He ate heartily and washed his bowl, hoping to linger in the kitchens again to avoid the raucous festivities overtaking the Seat. Unfortunately, the transparency of his motives betrayed him.

A group of youths found his hiding place and hauled him back outside. He was made to dance for a time with several boys his age, all laughing and reeking of wine. Overstimulated, he escaped again at the first opportunity.

He didn't bother to look for his father or Otep. They would be where it was loudest, at the center of the chaos, and Van avoided those places—at least, to the extent he could. He didn't find true reprieve until after nightfall, when he ventured into an alleyway between a few huts in the village outskirts. The light of the bonfires didn't reach here. It was quiet. Or… almost quiet. Strolling through the shadows, he thought he heard someone crying close by. Worried someone was hurt, he sought the source of the sound.

She was curled up alone in the dark. Unharmed, thankfully, but sobbing with a force that shook her whole body. It was the brown-haired girl from the Teaching Circle again. Van approached noisily, hoping not to surprise her, but she was so entrenched in her own turmoil, she was blind to the world. She didn't notice him at all until he placed a hand on her shoulder.

The girl yelped and recoiled, but she recognized him quickly. She calmed for just a moment, then started weeping again.

"Girl," Van said softly, "why do you cry?"

"There are too many people," she choked out between helpless sobs. "And it's too loud."

"I dislike it as well," Van said with a sigh. "This is a good place you've found to pass the time. May I share it with you?"

She nodded, tears still streaming down her cheeks as she pulled her knees up to her face. As many doubts as Van still had about his own capabilities in the face of the pilgrimage, he saw it must be even worse for her.

"Girl," he said again, when her sobbing began to make him uneasy, "what is your name?"

"Lilim," she said with a sniff.

Van waited, but she spoke no further.

"Your earned name, I mean," he prompted.

She shook her head. "Mama and Papa never gave me one. I'm just Lilim."

"What!" blurted Van.

He'd never heard of such a thing. He had earned his own name at five years old, when he'd demonstrated an affinity for written language. According to local legend, Otep had earned his at age two, having grown to the size of children twice his age.

Van worked his jaw, thinking. On a whim, and partly in hopes of stemming the fresh wave of tears he sensed coming on, he said, "From now on, you are Lilim the Brave!"

Her crying ceased. She grew still, staring up at Van in profound confusion. As the moment stretched on, her expression warmed and her eyes brightened. Van held her gaze, willing a sense of confidence and security to flow from himself to her. Eventually, she tore her gaze away.

"I don't feel very brave." She spoke in a small voice, but one no longer interrupted by the pitiful hiccups of a child's weeping.

"You must be the bravest girl I've ever met," Van insisted. "You face the pilgrimage at only twelve years of age, and you are unafraid."

She nodded slowly, her expression dreamlike. Van sensed she was deciding whether to trust him. Weighing his next words carefully, he decided against filling her head with notions that she was clever and courageous. Instead, wanting to understand her better, he asked her to tell him of herself. A more complete picture formed as he listened to the things she told him—and the things she didn't. Details about her life and upbringing she didn't want to share, or couldn't.

Just like Van, Lilim was born and raised at Seat Dolse, but because of their age difference, their paths had never crossed. She shared a dreary account of her home life, which consisted mostly of chores foisted on her by her parents—tasks that generally required little skill or physical stamina. She told him that her earliest memory was of her mother scolding her for ruining a dress while washing clothes.

She spoke of no fondness from her mother and father. No special birthdays or favorite bedtime stories. No teachers, mentors, or childhood friends. And nothing whatsoever of learning crafts and survival skills under the tutelage of the tribe's elders. As far as Van could tell, she'd been afforded no opportunities to explore and experience the world around her.

From a young age, Lilim had been fragile. Common foods enjoyed by many Dolsers upset her stomach, and she had a habit of getting lost even in places that should be familiar. Contact with plants and animals considered harmless might make her break out in a rash or develop sores. Despite all these problems—any one of which Van thought warranted attention—she spoke of no efforts made by the village healers to provide advice or care.

Van shifted uncomfortably while he listened. As the chieftain's son, he'd enjoyed many advantages in life. His father hadn't spoiled him, raising him to know humility, but it was still a basic fact that he'd grown up wanting for nothing. It seemed a grave injustice that this talkative, earnest girl had received so little by comparison.

Sitting in the darkened alleyway, Van saw at last how he would honor his father and his people as an aspirant on the Journey of Patronage—and he made a choice.

"Lilim the Brave," he said, when her long and winding story gave way to restless silence, "thank you for sharing this space with me tonight. It has grown late, and the virtues of sleep are many. May I see you home to bed?"

"I don't know your name," she said blankly.

Caught off guard, Van probed his memory and realized he'd never introduced himself.

"I am Van the Scribe," he replied. "And beginning tomorrow, if you would have me, I will walk with you."

2 Journey's Eve

Van made certain he didn't oversleep again. After escorting Lilim home, he'd returned to the chieftain's hut and brewed himself a mild tea from berries that were *technically* poisonous. The resulting irritation of his bladder, precisely five hours later, spurred him out of bed before sunrise. He crept outside, careful not to wake his father, and urgently urinated on a nearby bush. Going back in, he packed for the road and dressed for travel, leaving his rucksack under his hammock. He would come back for it before the procession departed.

Being scolded yesterday wasn't Van's only reason for playing such a mean trick on himself. Before heading to the great amphitheater, he wanted to leave ample time to speak with Otep Acrearms.

In the misty twilight before dawn, the First Ranger of Dolse greeted him from the entrance of his family's home, rubbing his eyes and clad in nothing but a loincloth.

"Otep Acrearms," proclaimed Van, conjuring as much severity into his voice as he could, "I need your help."

Otep listened patiently as he explained his decision to take Lilim under his wing. With a low bow, he then formally asked his friend—as the tribe's First Ranger—to help him ensure her safety on the Journey of Patronage.

"Van the Scribe," began Otep once Van was finished, "I will say to you two things. First, you already know I will be tested to my limits on the pilgrimage. The games of the chieftains, as well as my other responsibilities, will require my full attention. Even if I made it my purpose to safeguard the children of our tribe, many other ill-prepared youths will be traveling with us this year, all just as deserving as your Lilim. But Van, I cannot be in a hundred places at once. I'm sorry. I cannot extend a personal promise of safety to this girl."

Van struggled to maintain his composure. He felt betrayed. Wasn't it a ranger's duty to protect the tribe? And wasn't Otep *First Ranger?* He opened his mouth to retort, but Otep raised an enormous hand to silence him.

"Second, as your friend, I offer you a warning. Abandon your oath. The trial you face is significant, and will require your undivided focus. Look to your own needs, and set aside the needs of others."

Van shook his head in disbelief, stumbling back a step.

"I do not know this girl," Otep continued. "But I can guess a few things from what you've told me. For example, why her mother and father didn't name her. They know better than anyone her chances of returning home this year. They do not expect to see her again. Revisit your own expectations of her, Van the Scribe. I say to you again—for your own good, abandon your oath."

Van felt apart from himself. Otep's expression was strained, and not from lack of sleep. Saying these things wasn't easy for him. Last night, Van had felt so sure of his convictions. Now, he stood before a man greater than himself—someone he loved and trusted—who was urging Van to cast his convictions aside.

"I must go now, Van the Scribe," said Otep. "It is time we prepare for assembly, and what's to follow."

With that, Otep left Van alone in the street. He stood there dumbly for a while, then forced his feet to move. He shuffled along at an unhurried pace, but even still, he had the amphitheater to himself when he arrived. The sun was barely up.

Van stared up at the empty stage. Before drifting off to sleep last night, he'd imagined sharing these moments with Lilim and Otep. His friend would warm to her instantly, just as he had. But now...

On the first morning of the pilgrimage, when he was supposed to be *his truest self*—all he felt was bitterness.

He clenched his fists. *I'll do it on my own if I have to.*

Van wasn't sure whether he'd said it aloud or merely thought it. There was no one there to testify. Either way, his resolve was restored. He promised himself again that he would stand by Lilim the Brave, both during the pilgrimage and for as long as she needed him afterward, with or without the help of his tribe.

The aspirants of Dolse began to trickle in and sit down, and by some miracle Van spotted her. Lilim ducked nimbly past her larger kinsmen, a few times scampering on hands and knees to avoid getting pushed or trampled. Van called to her, and because nobody else yet knew to call her Lilim the Brave, she glanced in his direction and smiled. She hurried over to him and sat in the spot he'd saved.

"You look well, Lilim the Brave," Van said in greeting. "Did you sleep well? Have you packed everything you'll need?"

"I did, and I have," she said, her tone bright and cheery.

The chieftain arrived a short time later with the delegates of tribe Dolse in full ceremonial garb. Otep's cloak of fox furs gave him a regal and imposing appearance, and the gathered Dolsers cheered as he took the stage. Van, though, found it difficult to even look at him.

The ceremonies began in earnest, starting much like any other morning assembly. Ghan Mudcatcher led a prayer to the Emissaries, the day's schedule was reviewed, and the aspirants were reminded what etiquette was expected of them when their cousins arrived.

Van had expected something more on the first day of the pilgrimage, but he also understood that anything said now would only have to be repeated once the aspirants of Mercura, Vaxas, and Ikann reached the Seat. He dearly hoped the Mercurans arrived ahead of the others. They would remain the Patron tribe until the end of the pilgrimage, and if they arrived before the Ikanni, they could act as tribe Dolse's shield if it proved necessary.

Seat Mercura, hidden deep in the Western Forest, was the farthest from the lands of Dolse. The Patron tribe had nonetheless appointed Farseer Daz as first host that year, a concession of great benefit to the Dolser aspirants. Surely, the Mercurans knew as well as anyone how tenuous things were between Dolse and Ikann, and had left their lands early with those tensions in mind.

Once all his kinsmen were gathered, Van took a rough head count. There were a thousand at most, their ranks filling about a third of the amphitheater. Up on the stage, Ghan Mudcatcher selected another prayer from the tribe's book of hymns, leading the aspirants in song to pass the time. The day dragged on, and Van grew restless.

To ease his anxiety, he whiled away the morning hours talking with Lilim. She was chatty, and today she wanted to know more about him. What was his favorite pastime? How old was he? What was it like being the chieftain's son? The torrent of basic questions was a stark reminder that they had only just met. Close to midday, a horn blared in the distance, jarring the aspirants to attention. The gathered Dolsers stood and looked to the horizon.

While traversing the lands of their neighbors, the tribes of Nemia marched with distinctive banners. The heraldry itself would be difficult to make out at a distance, but the banner's color would tell all. Brown for tribe Dolse, blue for Mercura, green for Vaxas, and yellow for Ikann. The moment stretched on in tense silence as those at the amphitheater watched and waited.

As the banners crested the horizon, Van spotted what looked like tiny, shimmering emeralds. Tribe Vaxas had arrived.

He grabbed Lilim's hand and squeezed it, as much for his own reassurance as for hers. Like most Dolsers, Van instinctively feared the Ikanni. But that was a fear he understood—the same fear a child might harbor for a neighborhood bully. Van also had a certain fear of tribe Vaxas, and in many ways that fear was harder to describe.

The Vaxals were the Stewards of the Great Swamp and Marshlands, a domain far to the north said to be virtually uninhabitable. Van had heard stories that the shamans of Vaxas walked in worlds beyond this one, where they traded secrets with alien entities that allowed them to extort bounty from the lifeless earth around them. It was even rumored that tribe Vaxas benefited in mysterious ways from the Journey of Patronage.

Van watched the Vaxals shamble through the streets of the Seat, then file into the amphitheater, where they quietly found places for themselves. They were as diverse a group as the aspirants of Dolse, their expressions curiously sedated.

"Welcome, cousins," Farseer Daz greeted them from the stage. "Please know that we still await tribes Ikann and Mercura. We are gladdened by your arrival and it is our pleasure to host you today. While we wait, we will sing prayers to the Emissaries. Help yourselves to food and drink, for you have traveled long to be here."

As if on cue, refreshments were brought forth, offered to the Vaxals by women of the Seat. Van recognized many of them as mothers of that year's aspirants. He was proud to see them smile warmly and without aversion while attending their visiting cousins.

After another song, the horn sounded again. This time, Van clenched his fists as he stood and peered at the horizon.

Let the banners be blue, he prayed furiously.

The gods of the land heard his prayer and responded with a blessed kindness. Indeed, the arriving group was tribe Mercura. Rangers of Dolse met the Mercurans with genuine fondness as they led them through the streets, some joining arms with their countrymen or stopping to embrace. Van relaxed, breathing a sigh of relief as they took their seats. But his anxiety welled up anew when he noticed a troubling detail. There were only half as many Mercurans as there were Dolsers or Vaxals.

As Farseer Daz repeated his welcome address, Van scanned the faces of the newcomers, wondering which among them was their First Ranger. None seemed to carry the same awesome presence as Otep Acrearms. Nor did any of the Vaxals, decidedly.

Before Ghan Mudcatcher could select a new song, the horn blared for the third and final time. It was no longer necessary to stand up to see who had come. Standoffish silence fell over Seat Dolse as the Ikanni crowded into the amphitheater. Van noted with a sinking feeling that their group was the largest by far. There were so many, those at the back were made to stand, and he worried it would be taken as a sleight, igniting their tempers.

At his side, Lilim whimpered. A quick glance revealed that her cheerful, carefree composure had completely deteriorated.

"Lilim the Brave..." he uttered in a strained voice, putting a hand on her shoulder.

She paid him no attention, simply curling up into a quivering ball.

Van cursed under his breath, finding himself frustrated with her for the first time. Her poor upbringing had turned her into something like an emotional lamprey—she had only Van's strength to draw on, and no inner fortitude of her own. When Van felt safe, she felt safe also. When she perceived that he didn't, she fell to pieces.

Farseer Daz welcomed the Ikanni with arms stretched wide. Now that all of Nemia's aspirants were assembled, the opening ceremonies of the Journey of Patronage could truly commence.

"Countrymen," the chieftain began, "for those who do not yet know me, I am Daz, chieftain of Dolse. I am called Farseer, for it is in my nature to look ahead. I have seen much throughout my life, and what I see before me today fills my heart with hope. If you see the same thing I do, you have no further need for trite speeches about the strengthening of bonds, or the virtues of trust and cooperation. So let us waste no time and instead present the First Rangers of Nemia!"

Ghan Mudcatcher and Otep Acrearms took the stage first.

"Greetings, cousins," said the wildborn elder with a shallow bow. "I am Ghan Mudcatcher, Pilgrimage Guide representing tribe Dolse."

Van clapped a hand to his mouth to stop himself from laughing as the elder drew out the last syllable into a reptilian hiss. He was putting on the same act he'd used with the children at the Teaching Circle.

"Here, before all of you and before our gods, I vow to see us safely across the land," Ghan continued. "Because our journey will be long, I vow also to use our time together to open your minds to the ways of my tribe. It is my honor, next, to present the First Ranger of Dolse. Behold Otep Acrearms, blood of giants, protector of the small, and strongest man living!"

Otep strode forward and took a stance in silence. It was not his moment to speak—only to be observed. Ceremony permitted him to wear his favored weapon when he was presented, but Otep wore none, for his greatest weapons were his powerful body and mighty fists.

As his kinsmen cheered wildly, Van felt a wellspring of renewed pride. It stung just a little, though, to hear Ghan list "protector of the small" among his titles.

The clamor died down, and the stage was vacated. Tribe Vaxas went next.

Two figures stepped forward. Both were startouched, though of different descriptions, as the term could be used for individuals of many racial backgrounds. The older of the two was bald with skin like liquid crystal, a man made seemingly of blown glass. He wore simple green robes, and strapped to his back by a hodgepodge of knotted cords was a stack of leather-bound tomes.

The second figure was a young woman belonging to the more common variety of startouched, who bore resemblance to the Emissaries. Her unblemished skin was a dark red, and the horns on her forehead were petite, their symmetry pleasing to the eye. She was athletically built, though not heavily muscled, with raven hair cascading down her back and piling around her shoulders.

She looked to be a few years older than Van, and he guessed that men her age would consider her attractive. Her attire was simple but well made— leather high boots over cotton breeches and a buttoned tunic, with a dagger sheathed at her hip.

"I am Memnon the Still Pool, elder of Vaxas and Pilgrimage Guide," said the crystal man.

Van struggled to make out his words, not because he was speaking softly, but due to some other ineffable quality of his voice. It was like listening to a person speak while holding one's head underwater.

"I present to you the First Ranger of Vaxas, Brynda Blackblade."

The young woman stepped forward and gave a curtsy, but just as Otep had, she remained silent. Wearing an easy smile, she looked out over the crowd while the aspirants of Nemia appraised her. Van studied her eyes—a pretty shade of red lighter than her skin—and was briefly struck by the sense that she was staring back at him. There were so many faces in the crowd, though, it simply wasn't possible.

The moment passed, and the feeling with it. The stage was cleared again. As they waited for the next pair of delegates, it briefly occurred to Van that elder Memnon had sworn no vows of protection or shared knowledge, nor were any titles listed for his First Ranger.

Farseer Daz summoned the delegates of Ikann to the stage next. Their Pilgrimage Guide was wildborn, and their First Ranger another startouched of the usual pedigree.

"I am Kekrin the Nose of tribe Ikann," shouted the wildborn, an ugly little man with a face like an anteater. "I am the Nose because I can smell danger coming from leagues away, and I am your Pilgrimage Guide because I can smell the lies you tell—not just to one another out of petty vanity, but to yourselves, believing you are safe from harm!"

Van glanced around at his neighbors, relieved to see mostly confused expressions. He was worried he'd missed something. Kekrin's bizarre diatribe soon gave way to the more sensical introduction of his companion.

"Before you also stands Galdur Goldeyes, First Ranger of Ikann. Witness the undefeated champion of the arena—master of the blade and slayer of great beasts!"

The young man came forward and swept his defiant gaze over the crowd. He was hairless, with one horn longer than the other—not uncommon for startouched. His lithe physique and fierce yellow eyes conjured the image of a coiled viper. Galdur Goldeyes wore belted leather armor over a fine tunic, a shining pauldron affixing a scarlet half-cape over his shoulder. Sheathed at his hips were twin longswords.

The chieftain dismissed the Ikanni delegates with further words of thanks and welcome, then finally called the Patron tribe forward.

Another wildborn and startouched duo mounted the stage, both of them young. Once more, it was the wildborn who stepped forward and addressed the aspirants. She carried a staff carved from the wood of the Western Forest's giant sequoia tree, and she held it aloft as she spoke.

"I am Riverspeaker Gheela of tribe Mercura," she declared. "Though I am untested compared to my peers, I swear here and now to extend the full measure of your Patron tribe's protection to each and every one of you. It is my profound honor to serve you as Pilgrimage Guide—and to present to you my First Ranger, Sol Starfletcher."

The startouched stepped forward, lowering his head and closing his eyes. He was a breed of startouched Van had never seen—thin lips, almost no nose, and skin that was gray-green like the algae-rich water of a tide pool. His hair was tied back into a long braid, and across his shoulder hung a magnificent longbow.

"Our champion has already earned many titles in his short life, but he has asked me not to list them today. Instead, I invite you to come to know him in your own way, and in your own time."

Van considered Sol Starfletcher, his eyes drawn to the bow he carried. Curiously, there were just three arrows in his quiver—one with blue fletching, another with red, and a third with black. Van favored archery himself when it came to hunting, so he privately resolved to make Sol Starfletcher's acquaintance at the first opportunity, as Riverspeaker Gheela had suggested he should.

Lilim's mood seemed to improved as she watched the Mercurans excuse themselves from the stage. Regaining her attention, Van offered her a smile.

With all of Nemia's delegates now formally introduced, the next order of business was the presenting of gifts from the visiting delegates to their host. Brynda Blackblade took the initiative, approaching the stage first with a book in hand, chosen from among those carried by elder Memnon.

It was then that Van the Scribe first heard her speak. Her voice was enchanting—eerie, almost musical—and so clear. If elder Memnon's voice was a fog, hers was the light that cut through it. Van shivered.

"My thanks for your hospitality, chieftain Daz." She took a knee and lifted the tome. "Many scholars have risen to prominence among my people in recent years, their principal craft the written word. Please accept this anthology representing their collected achievements, the accomplishments of more than a dozen great minds. May you find it worthy of a place in your renowned archives."

Daz accepted the heavy book, taking it under his arm.

"Thank you, cousin," he said. "Your gift is well received."

Brynda Blackblade stood and bowed, then returned to her seat with her Pilgrimage Guide. It was a good gift. The sincerity of the gesture and her visible respect for the chieftain softened Van's attitudes toward her—and by extension, tribe Vaxas itself.

Galdur Goldeyes pushed through the crowd next, bowing hurriedly to Daz before facing the spectators. He lifted a hand and snapped his fingers, initiating some prearranged action. The gathered aspirants parted to admit two more Ikanni dragging a horse behind them. They led the animal to where Galdur stood, tugging roughly at its bridle.

"Chieftain of Dolse," began Galdur, addressing the congregation rather than Daz. "We of Ikann pride ourselves in rearing beasts of burden, and we would entrust one such beast to your care."

One look at the horse told Van its days as a ranger's steed were long passed. The beast was emaciated, its legs trembling. Its sparse coat was mottled and unclean, as though it hadn't been brushed in weeks, and its mouth foamed from dehydration.

"It was no easy task to find an animal that might prove your equal," Galdur said, a grin twitching at the corners of his mouth. "But we believe we've found you the perfect match."

Van's stomach rolled with repulsion. He dared a peek at the aspirants of Ikann, and he was sickened to see most of them choking back laughter.

If the chieftain was offended, he gave no sign.

"Thank you, cousin," said Daz. "The talents of which you speak are well known to us. We accept your gift in the spirit of friendship."

Galdur bowed flamboyantly and returned to his seat while Farseer Daz ordered the horse taken to the stables, where it could be fed and watered—or more likely, simply put out of its misery.

Sol Starfletcher approached the stage last, pulling a drawstring satchel from his tunic pocket.

"Farseer Daz," began the First Ranger of the Patron tribe. "For hosting us today, my kinsmen have entrusted me with a small token of our gratitude, which I now gift to you. I'm afraid you may find it a mere frivolity, but I hope it affords you a few moments of entertainment, should you find time for such diversions."

Daz set Brynda Blackblade's book aside to accept the satchel, then drew on its string to open it. He fished something out that was so small Van had to squint to see it—a tiny piece of carved wood.

"There are fifty-two pieces within," Sol Starfletcher explained, gesturing to the satchel. "I'm told that if they are put together in a particular way, they will form a perfect sphere. I am also told this is not an easy task, and requires a degree of cleverness and patience."

Daz turned the puzzle piece over in his hand, examining it. At length, he returned it to the satchel and drew it closed.

"Thank you, cousin," he said. "Your gift is well received."

Van couldn't see his father's face beneath his ceremonial mask, but he guessed he was smiling. Those who knew Daz well, who in truth were few in number, understood he had a childlike fascination with puzzles. Sol Starfletcher bowed low to the chieftain and returned to his seat.

With all gifts now bestowed, Farseer Daz stood from his throne and held his hands high.

"Cousins," he bellowed. "We will soon announce the first game of the Journey of Patronage, which I will use to test the First Rangers of Nemia."

Van leaned forward in anticipation. He had no idea what game his father had planned—he'd managed to keep it secret even from his son. The Patron tribe would make an announcement as well, because it was their privilege to pose not one, but *two* challenges of equal worth, one of which would span the full length of the pilgrimage—to be judged only when the aspirants reached Seat Mercura, their final destination. Five challenges in total. At journey's end, whichever champion had emerged victorious in the greatest number would win Patronage for their tribe. The highest honor a Nemian could achieve in life.

"First, I must ask that you tolerate an interruption to these proceedings," said Daz.

Van stilled, surprised by the turn of speech. Something was wrong.

"It has fallen on me to explain an unusual matter to you, my esteemed countrymen, but I will make an effort to be brief."

Daz clapped his hands once, and Van's excitement drained from him, replaced by nervous dread. Four rangers of Dolse came forward, leading two figures behind them. When the aspirants of Nemia caught their first glimpse of the foreigners, they gasped and scrambled to clear a path. Simon of the Mists and the dark girl were prodded onto the stage for all to see, dressed in chains and manacles.

"These outsiders hail from lands beyond our own," Daz proclaimed. "I have offered them sanctuary, and today, they have lived among my people for nearly a year. They have helped us in our labors and have made efforts to learn our ways—everything expected of an aspirant in fealty to their tribe."

The chieftain paused, letting his words sink in. Some in the crowd cast glares of condemnation toward the stage.

"What I ask of you is this. Allow these two foreigners to undertake the Journey of Patronage alongside you. In this way, let them earn the right to call these lands their home, should they choose to remain. Consider them aspirants of Dolse, and number them among your peers. View them as equals, and I promise you, they will become invaluable comrades."

With his gambit laid bare, the chieftain fell silent. Van could only stare at his father with his mouth ajar, wondering to what fate Farseer Daz had just doomed himself. And to what fate tribe Dolse was now just as doomed.

3 The Games Begin

"Heresy!" cried a voice from the crowd.

It was Galdur Goldeyes who spoke, and when Van craned his neck, he saw others leaping to their feet with him. The crowd might have turned violent were it not for Riverspeaker Gheela thumping her staff against the ground.

The aspirants quieted, and the young Mercuran Pilgrimage Guide spoke with the authority of the Patron. Prior to that moment, the wildborn woman had reminded Van a little of a stuffed doll. Now, her ursine countenance seemed threatening, like a mountain grizzly preparing to defend its cubs.

"Farseer Daz, I am obligated to remind you that contact with foreigners is forbidden. What you have done is against our laws, and what you request is impossible."

She paused for emphasis, furrowing her brow.

"Additionally," she continued in a measured tone, "if they have been among us as long as you say, merely sending them away may be impossible as well. Though it saddens me to do so, I must remind you that the consequence of the actions you've confessed to is exile. In the case of the foreigners, death."

"And I must remind *you*, cousin," countered Daz, towering over her on the stage, "that I am a chieftain of Nemia on the year of the pilgrimage. As such, I would exercise my right, here and now, to demand the matter be put to a vote."

Van swallowed in a dry throat. His father meant to put up a fight, but in doing so, he was stretching the very limits of Nemian law. Under any other circumstance, he would be stripped of his titles and sent into the desert or across the mountains to waste away and perish. But because senior representatives of all four tribes were in attendance that day, the matter could instead be debated—at the discretion, of course, of the Patron.

All eyes fell on Gheela, who hesitated.

"Memnon the Still Pool, Kekrin the Nose," she called out when she found her voice. "With me."

Ghan Mudcatcher wouldn't be permitted to join their session, as it was his tribe that was on trial. Van could easily guess how tribe Ikann would vote, and he could only hope that as friends of Dolse, tribe Mercura would side with them. Which meant the vote that would spare his father's life—or end it—would be cast by elder Memnon of Vaxas.

The three Pilgrimage Guides departed to find someplace private where they could decide the chieftain's fate. As for Farseer Daz, he watched them retreat, then sat back down on his throne to await their verdict in silence. All throughout the great amphitheater, Van's kinsmen wore expressions of bleak resignation, while the aspirants of Ikann had begun gossiping excitedly. They buzzed around their First Ranger like bees at a hive, and Galdur Goldeyes drank it all in with a smirk.

Unlike his father, Van couldn't simply sit and wait.

"Lilim the Brave," he said, turning to gauge the girl's mood, "would you wait here a moment while I speak to my fa—to the, um, chieftain?"

She nodded obediently, and Van decided she would be all right on her own for now.

He stood up and fought to the stage, all the while eyeing his father, who sat stoically on his throne. Van made it only halfway before his path was blocked by Otep Acrearms.

"Van the Scribe," the First Ranger said sternly, "I must ask you to remain in your seat."

Taken aback, Van drew himself up and puffed out his chest. "I would have words with my chieftain and father. As is my right."

Otep didn't budge.

"On any other day, I would not refuse you that right," he said. "But I have been given careful instructions regarding this day. Farseer Daz is to be approached by no one. He wishes to be left alone and offered no counsel."

Van dug his fingernails into his palms. Refused by Otep for the second time in a day… There was still a chance he could be heard, though, so he reined in his outburst.

"Then beseech him yourself, on my behalf," Van pleaded. "Have him recant his foolish request. If he orders the foreigners put to death, here and now, he might be pardoned for the mistake of meddling in their affairs!"

Van took no pride in making such a heinous request. All life was sacred—he'd learned that from Otep—but in that moment, he would have said anything to save his father.

"No," said Otep, raising his voice. "I will not disobey a command from my chieftain."

Van's face flushed with heat. He moved to walk past Otep, but the First Ranger grabbed him by the collar and shoved him back a step.

"Comply with your chieftain's will, and return to your seat," he growled. "Do not make me use force."

Escalating the argument into a physical confrontation would have been foolish indeed, but Van found himself ready to scream his throat hoarse—to call his friend a coward and a fraud. Before he could, he noticed the tears welling in Otep's eyes, and his anger turned to shame.

"I'm sorry," Van choked. "I'm sorry, Otep Acrearms."

They stared at each other in silence for a long moment before Van dragged himself back to Lilim and sat down, feeling small. She seemed to recognize his distress, and this time, it was she who tried to comfort him.

"Van the Scribe," she said tentatively, resting her hand on his, "it'll be fine, you'll see."

Whatever meager skills the girl might be hiding, reassuring others in times of doubt was not among them. Van stewed quietly, already grieving for his father.

A full hour crept by. Farseer Daz never budged from his throne. The foreigners, on display like captive animals, waited anxiously. At least, Simon of the Mists looked anxious. The dark girl looked simply bored.

The sun touched the far horizon when Riverspeaker Gheela and the other Pilgrimage Guides returned at last. The aspirants bristled, a few of the younger ones stirring as if from sleep. The delegates took the stage and faced the crowd, not sparing a glance at Farseer Daz. Standing at the fore, Gheela thumped her staff again, and the sound carried far.

"Countrymen," she shouted. "I have heard my peers, and our deliberations are complete. Before I speak further, know that we are of one mind in our decision, and seek no further discord over these matters."

Van leaned in, his heart hammering in his chest.

"First, regarding the apparent disregard for Nemian law demonstrated by Farseer Daz," she announced, "we decree that he shall remain chieftain of Dolse, for as long as his spirit resides in this world. He will not be stripped of holdings, nor will he face exile."

Van breathed a deep sigh of relief, thanking the gods for their beneficence. A smile spread across his face, which he shared with Lilim. She smiled back with a hint of *I-told-you-so* twinkling in her eye.

A cheer rose from the crowd, Dolsers and Mercurans alike applauding and whistling. Gheela thumped her staff once more to quiet them.

"Second, in the matter of the foreigners," she continued, "none among us can comprehend the chieftain's decision to grant them refuge, nor do we understand his desire for them to join the pilgrimage, which for centuries has been a birthright of Nemians alone."

Death after all, then, Van thought bleakly.

But Gheela's words took a turn.

"Nevertheless, we grant the chieftain's request. Let us trust that there is wisdom in his choices, and make an effort to know these outsiders, so we might find ourselves less disoriented by the prospect of sharing our home with them."

Van's jaw dropped. He'd thought his father lucky just to have been spared, but now, he felt almost foolish for having doubted him. Everything had gone in his favor. Had he predicted all of it?

"Farseer Daz," continued Gheela, finally turning to face the chieftain, "our announcements are thus concluded. Would you continue in your duty to lead the day's proceedings?"

"Thank you, cousin," said Daz, standing from his throne. "It would be my honor."

With that, the delegates exited the stage, and the rangers released the foreigners from their bonds. Simon rubbed his wrists where the manacles had left marks on his tender flesh, smiling nervously at his captors. Meanwhile, the dark girl slipped off the stage with a look of nonchalance. Watching her, Van wondered if she could have slipped her bonds at any time, and had merely chosen not to.

Across the amphitheater, Galdur Goldeyes was fuming. Van tried his best to ignore a sinking feeling that the First Ranger of Ikann yet intended to make tribe Dolse pay.

"Aspirants," called Farseer Daz, "the hour grows late. I was a young man once, if you can believe it. Though my years have taught me patience, I remember well what it was like to sit in your place. I will therefore conclude the day's ceremonies by announcing the first game of the pilgrimage."

The crowd tensed in eager anticipation, the dreary atmosphere from just minutes ago quickly lifting.

"But first," Daz continued, "I will turn the stage over one last time to our esteemed Mercuran cousins. As our Patrons, they have a challenge to explain as well."

Sol Starfletcher and Riverspeaker Gheela returned, and Gheela yielded the floor to the First Ranger.

"Countrymen," called Sol Starfletcher, "are you familiar with the bird known as the Phantom Nighthawk? You needn't answer aloud, for you surely are. The creature has garnered no small amount of notoriety."

Van thought back to his days at the Teaching Circle. Crossing paths with the Phantom Nighthawk was considered a good omen. Once, Ghan Mudcatcher had demonstrated its call for him—one of the elder's many esoteric talents. Van had also studied illustrations of the Nighthawk, so he would recognize the bird should he ever chance upon one. Which, of course, he never would. The Phantom Nighthawk was extinct.

"Our challenge is this—let us hunt the Phantom Nighthawk as we travel the land. Whosoever gathers the greatest number of the bird's pinion feathers will be declared winner. You may hunt with the technique of your choosing, for as long and as often as you deem worthy of the task. The feathers you collect will be counted when we reach my chieftain's Seat."

Van blinked, dumbfounded. He saw no logic in Sol's choice of game. Common sense dictated any contest devised by tribe Mercura should award some advantage to their own First Ranger. It was true that Sol Starfletcher, a man of the bow, would be better equipped than his peers to take down a bird in flight. Galdur Goldeyes appeared to be a man of the blade, a tool comparatively useless for the job, and Otep Acrearms couldn't simply strangle the animal out of the air. Brynda Blackblade was still a mystery, though Van had to believe a man called Starfletcher was the better archer of the two.

But none of that mattered if their prey no longer existed. Why choose a game that could have no winner?

"Thank you, Starfletcher," said Farseer Daz. "I look forward to receiving news of the outcome."

He waited for the Mercurans to vacate the stage before he continued.

"I will now announce my own challenge. Mine is a contest of skill, and one my tribe holds dear—the treasured pastime of fishing!"

A sly grin crept across Van's face. Strong as Otep was, he was no mere brute. Fishing was a favorite hobby they shared, one of the ways in which they'd grown close. Van's luck at the sport was touch and go, hit or miss, but Otep was a natural. He wasn't just good at fishing—he was superb.

"Whoever fishes best is the winner, simple as that," said Daz. "Because the light of day will soon fail us, we shall begin tomorrow at dawn. Let us assemble again at my tribe's fishing pond, which any of my rangers can direct you to. We will fish until midday, at which time we will weigh your catches to see who has won."

Daz surveyed the crowd and noticed Sol Starfletcher raising a hand politely.

"Yes, Starfletcher? Is there some aspect of my game I can clarify for you?"

"Indeed, Farseer," he said. "Is your game won by catching the greatest number of fish, or merely the single largest specimen?"

"Thank you for asking," said the chieftain. "But I believe I said your catches would be weighed. I meant this rather literally. Scales will be brought forth, and whatsoever fish-meat you suss out of my pond will be piled onto them to determine its value. You might win my game by catching a large number of very small fish, or a small number of very large fish."

Sol nodded in thanks, but Farseer Daz wasn't finished.

"There is one more rule in my game. I intend to give none of you any instruments for fishing. You are to use the time between now and the coming sunrise to fashion these things for yourselves. In this way, I will test not just your skill at the sport, but your familiarity with the tools of the trade."

With that, Farseer Daz dismissed Nemia's aspirants from the amphitheater and invited them to enjoy the amenities of Seat Dolse. They were encouraged to mingle with their countrymen in the spirit of friendship, but for the time being, many abstained. Aside from the Mercurans, who all Dolsers viewed as the heroes of the hour following the chieftain's gamble with the foreigners, the visiting tribes camped in the surrounding fields, preferring the company of their own kinsmen.

Van's rump was sore from sitting all day, and beside him, Lilim was fidgeting. Still, they remained seated, waiting until the more impatient aspirants had all filed out of the amphitheater. The sun slipped beneath the horizon, and the Seat's bonfires flickered to life.

"Would you take evening meal with me, Lilim?" asked Van. "We would do well to eat a little something before bed."

She smiled up at him and nodded.

After they'd eaten their fill, Van walked Lilim home, promising to find her again once the procession was underway. He'd assumed his father would be out partaking in the festivities, but when he entered the chieftain's hut, he found him already settling in for the night. Daz had shed his mask and other finery. He was Van's father again.

"Father!" Van stepped in from the street, grinning wide. "You brought me so much honor today. I am proud of you, especially in the matter of the foreigners. I confess, at first you had me—"

A slap across Van's face stole his words. The hut fell silent, and Van felt tears in his eyes.

"Why?" he asked in a hushed voice.

"Because, Van the Scribe," said Farseer Daz, "I am disappointed in you. You might believe I was preoccupied today, but I observed well how you conducted yourself. Childish superstition gripped you when our Vaxal cousins arrived, and worse, fear clouded your heart with the coming of tribe Ikann. You must reevaluate your attitudes toward your fellow aspirants. Beginning tomorrow, you must do better."

"But, Father," Van pleaded, "it isn't just me. Most Dolsers feel that way about the Ikanni."

"You are not most Dolsers!" shouted Daz. "You are my son, and I'm sure I raised you to know better. Hear me, Van the Scribe—no state of war exists between Dolse and Ikann. They are not your enemy. They can be trusted, relied upon. Treat them with the warmth and respect they deserve."

Van could only nod. He didn't want to argue. Not on his last night at home. Not when just hours ago, he thought he might lose his father forever. At length, Farseer Daz sighed and pulled Van into a tight embrace.

"I love you, son. I wish only for you to face this trial unburdened by animosity. Look always forward. Never back. What's passed is done. If you but remain clear of mind, and generous of heart, I know you'll return to me safely."

Slowly, Van wrapped his arms around his father, trying to be present in the moment and let his love simply wash over him. Daz gave him one more firm squeeze, then released him and stepped back.

"Let us sleep," said Daz, smiling now. "If I have played my cards right, we should have quite the treat in store for us tomorrow. But we will need to rise early if we intend to enjoy it to its fullest."

Van forced a smile, and a short time later, he was lying in his hammock, his father snoring in the next room. Despite the conflicting feelings clamoring within him, he managed a few hours' sleep.

Finding his way to the fishing pond was an unexpected challenge. Farseer Daz was already gone when he woke up, so he set off alone, hiking toward the village outskirts. He'd made the trip to the pond more times than he could count, but today, the other tribes' campsites stood in his way, their tents pitched in the normally-vacant fields north of the Seat.

Van hesitated, mulling over the idea of going the long way around. Recalling his father's words from the night before, he summoned his courage and forged ahead, carving right through the middle of the crowded field. His countrymen paid him no mind. They were busy rousing themselves, sharing breakfast, and packing their gear for the road. It helped that Van, too, was distracted, mentally rehearsing what he'd tell Lilim when he saw her next.

When the pond came into view, his disorientation returned in full force. He wasn't late, but already, there were more people than he'd ever seen at the pond in his life. Seat Dolse's fishing pond was one of his favorite places because of its tranquil beauty and natural quietude, but today, the aspirants of Nemia surrounded it in their thousands.

He spotted his father and Ghan Mudcatcher near the water's edge, a cluster of youths competing for their attention. Van decided to hang back, pondering where he might sit that he could enjoy relative privacy and still watch the game.

"Van the Scribe!"

Van glanced over his shoulder and saw Lilim.

"I waited for you outside Mama and Papa's house, but you never came."

Her hands were propped on her hips, and an imperious look clouded her face. Van probed his memory. Hadn't they agreed to meet on the road?

"I'm sorry, Lilim," he said out of courtesy. "I must have been in a hurry. Will you forgive my negligence?"

She frowned at him a few seconds longer, but then smiled and took him by the hand.

"I forgive you," she said cheerfully.

As she dragged him toward the pond, Van felt a pang of worry that he might truly have his work cut out for him over the coming days. Together, they found a spot to themselves beneath the shade of an old jackalberry tree and sat down.

The First Rangers arrived when the sun was half risen, escorted by their Pilgrimage Guides. Farseer Daz and Ghan Mudcatcher met them partway, and on closer inspection, Van observed that only Sol and Otep carried rods. The contestants had traded their ceremonial attire for heavy boots and loose clothes better suited for outdoorsmanship—except for Galdur Goldeyes, who was dressed as before.

"Welcome, First Rangers." Farseer Daz spoke loud enough for the crowds to hear. "We will begin momentarily. Be reminded that we will play from now until the sun's zenith."

Daz clapped his hands, ordering a pair of the Seat's rangers to bring a set of scales forward, massive and ornate. They left the scales near the water where all could see them, then departed, returning again with a sleigh piled high with counting stones.

With the sleigh came four oaken barrels, into which, it was explained, each contestant would place their catch. The barrels were set on the scales in turn, and each was weighed empty against two stones to prove that there were no hidden advantages.

The aspirants, along with the other residents of the Seat who'd come to spectate, were then asked to step back, to give the contestants space and—presumably—to keep the fish from scaring.

"Without further delay," announced the chieftain, "you may begin!"

Otep Acrearms and Sol Starfletcher squatted to begin baiting their hooks while the First Ranger of Vaxas threw her own burden on the ground. Rather than a fishing rod, she'd brought her rucksack. Galdur Goldeyes, meanwhile, simply folded his arms and glared.

"Galdur Goldeyes," said Farseer Daz with a hint of curiosity, "I see you've not brought a rod today. Do you intend to jump in my pond and catch fish with your bare hands?"

The chieftain spoke in a voice meant just for Galdur, so Van had to strain his hearing to make out what was being said.

"I do not *intend* to participate at all," sneered Galdur. "Fishing is a game for children, or the work of servants. Such things are beneath me. I assume your offer to make ourselves at home in your Seat still stands? If so, I will find something better to do."

Daz studied him for a moment, then gave a shallow bow. "Of course. Do as you will."

Galdur Goldeyes turned on his heel and stalked off, the stunted Kekrin scurrying after him. Why would a First Ranger give up their chance to win one of the very games that decided Patronage? Van had no idea what Galdur could be thinking—and he almost didn't care. Whichever way he looked at it, this was good news for tribe Dolse.

Otep and Sol had finished setting their lines and were wading into the shallows. Brynda, meanwhile, produced something entirely unexpected from her pack—a heavy woven net.

"Brynda Blackblade," said the chieftain with interest, stepping over to question her just as he had Galdur. "I see you've brought a net to my pond today. Would you care to explain yourself?"

She blinked and cocked her head.

"I didn't realize my actions warranted explanation," she said. "I intend to cast my net in your pond and catch fish thereby."

Daz raised an eyebrow.

"Yesterday you used the term 'instrument of fishing,' " said Brynda. "There was no mention of rods in particular."

The chieftain nodded slowly. "Then you've broken no rule. Best of luck, cousin."

She bowed to him, then followed after the other fishermen, brandishing her net.

The contest was slow going. Sol Starfletcher and Otep Acrearms played the more patient game, casting their lines and waiting for bites, while Brynda threw her net, cinched it closed, and pulled it in. Each time, it came back empty. Only after several of these failed attempts did Sol and Otep share a private glance of relief.

The first catch of the day went to Sol Starfletcher. He pulled in a perch no bigger than the palm of his hand, and walked it to his barrel to applause from the crowd. Otep's first bite came later, but in his case, he landed a weighty sturgeon. All the while, Brynda walked along the water's edge, casting her net time and time again without success. She took frequent breaks to catch her breath and sun herself, looking out over the pond with a serene smile despite her dwindling odds.

And so began the first game of the Journey of Patronage.

4 Strengthening Bonds

It wasn't long before Van realized that, as a spectator sport, fishing left much to be desired. He turned to Lilim, who was lying on her stomach in the warm grass, her chin cupped in her hands.

"Do you have any predictions as to who will win my father's game?"

"Otep will win," she said with the casual confidence only a child could flaunt.

Van nodded sagely, then cleared his throat to make sure he actually had her attention.

"Lilim the Brave," he began, "we'll be leaving Seat Dolse in just a few hours. If you'd like, we can walk together today. Regarding tomorrow and the days that follow, I have been considering how we might make the most of our time on the road."

Her eyes locked onto his.

"What I propose is this: every morning, in the hour before sunrise, I will visit your tent and tutor you in the skills familiar to me. You might give up a little sleep this way, but I doubt I could focus on the task while hiking. Does this arrangement suit you?"

"It does," said the girl, beaming.

Van smiled back. They watched the First Rangers a while longer, but Lilim soon began kicking her feet.

"What if we started now?" she suggested.

Van looked at her.

"They'll be at it for hours yet," she complained, sitting up straight. "Teach me something."

Van rubbed his jaw, thinking. He'd planned to instruct her first in reading and writing, because those were his favorite subjects and he was best at them. But he didn't have any of the tools on hand. More than anything, he needed a way to gauge Lilim's current skill level. An idea came to him then.

"Very well. Let us start by having you spell out your name."

She closed her eyes and furrowed her brow. For a moment, Van was truly worried, but she eventually recited the letters of the Nemian alphabet that spelled "Lilim," and then, she decided to impress him further by spelling out her new earned name, "Brave."

Van heaved a sigh of relief. The fact that she had to stop and think confirmed his suspicions that she was developmentally behind, but she had a foundation. That gave Van a place to start.

With her first task complete, he quizzed her on the spelling of various other common words, stopping to provide anecdotes about daily life that the words applied to and watching her reactions. They spent the whole morning drilling her spelling, quickly losing track of the events at the pond.

"Enough!" shouted Farseer Daz, startling Van out of his conversation with Lilim. "I bid you, contestants, cease in your efforts and assemble beside your barrels. It is time to determine a winner."

Van glanced up at the sky, surprised to see the sun directly overhead. It had been over an hour since he'd last tried to guess who was in the lead. Near the water, Farseer Daz congratulated the three First Rangers on their work before examining each of their barrels in turn, starting with Brynda Blackblade.

"First Ranger," said the chieftain, "it appears your barrel is empty."

"So it would seem, Farseer," replied Brynda Blackblade.

"You will excuse me, then, if I forgo the weighing of its contents."

"I see little sense in attempting to do so," Brynda agreed.

Daz and Brynda bowed to each other, and the chieftain moved on to the next in line—Sol Starfletcher. Unlike Brynda, the First Ranger of Mercura did have a catch to weigh, and no time was wasted in moving his barrel to the scales.

"Seventeen stone," Daz announced when the last stone was placed and the scales settled. "An impressive catch."

Sol bowed to the chieftain, and then waved at the crowd as they applauded.

Last was Otep, and Van held his breath as his father's rangers piled stones onto the scales, counting each one. *Fourteen. Fifteen. Sixteen...*

"Twenty stone!" Daz shouted triumphantly, at which point the crowd erupted into cheers. "I declare my own champion, the First Ranger of Dolse, the winner!"

The men and women of Dolse—and even most of the Mercurans—surged forward to congratulate Otep Acrearms on his victory, singing his praises.

With a full heart, Van stood up and brushed the grass from himself. He wanted to relish the moment, too, but when he glanced at Lilim, he sensed her need for quietude. She tugged gently at his sleeve, rubbing her eyes with her free hand, so he walked with her back to Seat Dolse, where they shared their last meal at home together.

The aspirants of Nemia began their northward march a short time later. After reconvening at the amphitheater, the chieftain's final blessing of farewell was kept brief. Even then, Van barely had time to double back home for his rucksack, where he made a few last-minute changes to his packing list.

He carried his tent, spare clothes, and survival gear as was expected of every aspirant. He also wore his knife and bow, the tools of the hunt. For Lilim, he made a snap decision to bring two books, a few rolls of parchment, and a quill with a single jar of ink. The books were bulky and fit awkwardly into his pack, but he would manage.

Van hoped he might share a private goodbye with his father, but this proved impossible. Their moment together the night before would be his last memory of Farseer Daz that was his alone.

Van would recall little from that first day's travel, for in truth, it was uneventful. He remembered only the feeling of Lilim's hand in his, the warmth of the sun on his shoulders, and the smooth dirt of the road beneath his feet. When the procession made camp after sundown, he sat at a bonfire while he ate his modest supper, his imagination alight as he gazed into the flame. And later, when he pitched his tent and lay down on his bedroll, he closed his eyes, hoping to dream. On that first night, though, he didn't.

The dreams would come later.

An hour before sunrise, while the delegates of Nemia conferred in private, Van made good on his promise to Lilim.

"Come in," she called when he announced himself outside her tent.

Stepping into the confines, Van was unsurprised to see she hadn't yet dressed for the road. Privacy was a rare commodity in most Dolser communities, so one grown accustomed to seeing one's kinsmen in various states of undress. Lilim was barefoot, still in her sleeping gown.

"I thought we might pick up where we left off yesterday," he said, crawling forward and sitting down next to her.

Producing his writing tools, he arranged them on the floor. Because writing called for a firm surface, he'd also brought one of his books—a hefty thesaurus.

Van unstoppered the ink and picked up his quill, smoothing a fresh roll of parchment across the book in his lap. He wrote his name in a slow, deliberate script so Lilim could see.

"Van the Scribe," he said, pointing to each letter and naming it. "Can you do the same with yours?"

Scooting closer, she reached for the quill, but she hesitated when holding it over the ink jar.

"I shouldn't," she mumbled. "Ink is precious."

Van drew his eyebrows together, crafting his response carefully.

"These things are gifts," he said. "In the spirit of pursuing new skills, it would honor me to share them with you."

Lilim bit her lip. Cautiously, she dipped the quill in the ink, then moved it to the parchment. Noticing her grip was faulty, Van caught her by the wrist before she could apply pressure and snap the quill's tip.

She whipped her head to face him, startled, so he relaxed his touch.

"It's fragile. Hold it like this."

Without letting go, he guided her hand across the page, and together they wrote her name, "Lilim the Brave."

Next, they revisited a few other vocabulary selections from yesterday's impromptu quiz. Van had to correct her spelling only once or twice, but her handwriting was another matter. For now, he decided not to comment on it. She would improve with practice, and there was no sense in making her self-conscious in the meantime.

"Do you need help packing your things?" he asked after collecting his writing supplements, the sun cresting the horizon.

"I can do it myself," she said, already tying up her bedroll.

They bid each other farewell and agreed to meet again on the road. As Van left her tent and wandered toward the center of camp, he considered a new problem.

The light was weak in the hour before dawn, and building a fire would be time-consuming and wasteful. For now, Lilim seemed unbothered by it, but Van could only hope she wasn't straining her eyes too much in the dark.

At assembly, Otep Acrearms and Ghan Mudcatcher, fresh from their private conference with the other delegates, greeted the aspirants of Dolse. It would be exciting to imagine they'd been discussing secrets of dire import, but in all likelihood, they were only reviewing travel logistics. Since there was no grand amphitheater on the road, the aspirants sat cross-legged on the ground while Otep made the day's announcements.

"Good morning, kinsmen," greeted the First Ranger. "First, please know that we will march until midday before making camp. In the afternoon, we will hunt, but I ask that none of you solicit a place in my party today. Our journey will be long, and I will make myself available to any of you that would call yourselves rangers. For this first hunt, though, I have chosen my companions ahead of time."

The aspirants sulked, Van included. He'd looked forward to showing off his skills for Otep on the pilgrimage, but he supposed he could wait his turn like everyone else.

"Regarding our route, our first destination is Stonebasin to the east, where we will pray, as is custom, at the Temple to the Emissaries and resupply our caravan."

While the procession was largely expected to provide for itself on the Journey of Patronage, subsisting on hunted game and foraged goods, they'd left Seat Dolse with a dozen oxen-drawn carts laden with supplies in case of emergency.

"We should arrive three mornings hence," Otep continued. "From Stonebasin, we travel north toward the lands of Ikann."

Morning assembly was thus concluded. Van stood up with a heavy sigh, dusted himself off, and pondered how he might spend the day. As the others dispersed, however, Otep Acrearms marched directly up to him.

"Van the scribe, will you hunt with us today?"

Van blinked. "But you said—"

"Only that I had chosen my company ahead of time." Otep chuckled. "Quite some time ago indeed, in your case. It would honor me if you joined us."

Van brightened. "Of course."

Otep smiled, instructing him to meet up with the other rangers after mealtime, when they'd reconvene at the center of camp. Van was warned not to tarry, as their plan for the hunt involved a degree of timing.

Promising he'd be the first to arrive, Van parted ways with Otep to break down his tent. He packed quickly, shouldered his rucksack, and took to the road again with the aspirants of Dolse.

Lilim was quick to find him, and they walked together again that morning.

"Congratulations on being invited to hunt," she said, giving him a once over before nodding at his new leather boots. "You look handsome in those."

Van examined his travel attire. Everything he wore—his boots, his tunic, the bow on his back—had been a gift from his father, still barely broken in. He wanted to return the praise, appreciating how nice offhand flattery felt at times, but he couldn't find much about Lilim that drew notice. Her plain clothes were little more than threadbare rags compared to his. As much as he enjoyed her company, Lilim looked plain in general.

"Thank you, Lilim the Brave. You carry yourself well," was the best Van could come up with on the spot.

"Thank you!" she replied, beaming.

Soon after they set out, Van had his first unexpected encounter of the day. He was approached by a man that was an aspirant of his tribe by technicality only.

"Hey, kid," said Simon of the Mists, "we need to talk."

The foreigner easily caught up to him where he walked with Lilim, in part because he wasn't carrying a rucksack. His pack simply bobbed through the air after him, floating along seemingly of its own accord.

"Uh, hello? Is this working?" Simon prodded impatiently.

"I hear you, Simon of the Mists," Van said warily, keeping himself between the foreigner and Lilim.

"Okay, good," said Simon. "So hey, what's happening right now, and where are we going? I get that your dad almost got me killed the other day. So I'm happy to be here, I guess. But now we're—what, on some kind of road trip?"

"We have embarked on the Journey of Patronage," Van said blankly. "To prove ourselves blooded men and women of tribe Dolse."

"Wow," said Simon. "That sounds like a pretty big deal. Hey, listen to me for a second."

He stepped in front of Van, halting him.

"I can only understand you people for about an hour a day, and up until now, I've had to more or less guess when it would be a good time to switch the spell on. The thing is, I have some questions. So, let's make a deal."

Van bristled as the foreigner put his hands on his shoulders. Lilim glanced between them in confusion.

"After we set up camp, and things settle down, let's you and I talk. I'll find you, and I'll do this."

Simon moved a hand close to Van's face and pinched his first two fingers to his thumb repeatedly.

"That's code for 'let's talk.' If you do it back, we'll go someplace private, and I'll start up the spell. For every question you can answer, I'll let you ask one of your own. Anything you want to know about the outside world you people try so hard not to be a part of, just ask. That's our deal."

Van hesitated. "Very well. But please know that today I have promised my time to First Ranger Otep Acrearms."

"Doesn't matter," said Simon with a dismissive wave of his hand. "Spell's already about to wear off. We'll start tomorrow."

Van nodded. With a sigh, the foreigner stepped out of his way, apparently satisfied. Van and Lilim began walking again, Simon lingering alongside.

"One other thing," murmured Simon a few minutes later. "Who came up with 'Simon of the Mists?' "

"You told me yourself that was your name," Van replied.

The foreigner frowned and shook his head. "When have we ever even talked? You don't mean—?" He deflated. "Oh. Wow."

After pitching his tent at midday, Van practically inhaled his food when the procession distributed meals from the supply carts. He then hurried to the center of camp, remembering his promise to Otep, and swore under his breath when he saw the First Ranger and the rest of his party already waiting for him.

"Well met, kinsman," said Otep, standing up and stretching. "We will explain our strategy on the way. Come."

The hunters left camp at a brisk pace, striking out across the Eastern Plains of Nemia. There were thirteen of them, all carrying bows except for Otep. The First Ranger's strength was wasted on a bow, so he instead wielded a sling, using stone discs roughly the width of Van's torso as ammunition.

"What will we hunt?" Van asked after they'd walked for a time.

"The gazelle of the plains," replied Otep. "The nature of the pilgrimage leaves us no time to set traps, and I'm sure you know that no ranger living can simply run down a gazelle— but because we have Orum the Mutable with us, we can shepherd them."

Otep gestured to the hunter at his left. The boy was close to Van's age, but with fairer skin and longer hair. Orum the Mutable offered a wide smile, holding up his hand, and Van's jaw dropped as he watched it transform into a wolf's paw.

"A skinchanger!" blurted Van. He had no idea any had been born to the tribe in recent years.

"The gazelle in our lands are not typically hunted by the wolf," mused Otep. "But they will recognize one as a predator all the same. More importantly, Orum's howl will serve as our signal to strike."

"So, we just have to find the gazelle," Van supplied.

"Orum's nose will find them easily enough," said Otep. "All we are looking for is a suitable place of ambush."

It wasn't long before they found one—a ravine just deep enough to conceal them all, including Otep, if he hunkered down. The hunters turned their backs to Orum to give him privacy as he disrobed, and moments later, a great white wolf leapt from the scar in the earth where the hunters hid. The creature shook out its coat, acclimating to its new anatomy, and then bounded off across the plains in search of prey.

The hunters waited.

Van's hands shook as he crouched in the ravine, his knuckles turning white against his bow.

"Patience, Van the Scribe," whispered Otep. "When the time comes, leave everything to instinct."

Just as the sky overhead began to turn orange and darken, a howl pierced the air. The sound was louder and closer than Van anticipated, and when the hunters emerged from the pit with bows drawn, the gazelle were right in front of them.

The beasts scattered when they saw Otep and his rangers, some rearing up and snorting, a few tripping over themselves and tumbling in the dirt. Arrows flew. Van had time to make three shots before even the slowest gazelle vanished in a cloud of dust across the tundra.

When it was over, fifteen gazelle lay dead on the field, most of them large bucks. Otep Acrearms had slain three with bone-breaking discs hurled from his sling. *Those will be hard to clean,* thought Van as he examined their ruined bodies.

Impressively, one ranger had scored five kills in the skirmish. Van watched with envy as the ranger retrieved his arrows—a tall wildborn with pronounced avian features.

"You do not disappoint, Wilm," said Otep as he stowed his sling.

The young hunters clapped one another on the back and celebrated their success before rounding up their quarry. Each of them would carry a gazelle back to camp, and because there were a few extra, Otep would carry three.

Van brooded on the return trip, because none of his arrows had met their mark.

"You hunted well today, Van the Scribe," said Otep, likely noticing his mood.

"I didn't take any down," Van muttered.

"But your accuracy and reflexes have improved," Otep said. "That is worth taking pride in."

Van forced a smile, not wanting to pout in front of his friend.

"Will you hunt with us again tomorrow?" Otep asked, smiling back.

Van faltered, feeling self-conscious again. "Many want to hunt with you, Otep Acrearms. Don't give me special treatment just because I am the chieftain's son."

Otep surprised him with a laugh.

"If I am giving you special treatment, it is because I enjoy your company." His smile faded. "But if you do intend to join us again, know this—our future hunts will be carried out in partnership with the other tribes."

Van tensed. "Even Ikann?"

"Even Ikann," Otep confirmed. "But we will take things slow, and perhaps start by sharing a hunt with tribe Mercura. Provided Sol Starfletcher is amenable, of course."

Van clenched his teeth, his hands trembling again. "Then I will hunt."

Otep's party was excused from the chore of cleaning their kills when they returned to camp. As was custom after a successful hunt, the gazelle were left with their younger kinsmen to skin and dress.

Free to do as he pleased with the rest of the day, Van recalled the clearwater brook that ran nearby. Opportunities to clean his clothes and gear would be rare on the road, so he went to his tent—where he was surprised to discover some of his belongings missing.

Bewildered, he wandered to the stream, where he chanced to see Lilim washing her clothes in a shallow eddy. All of Van's were piled beside her.

"Lilim the Brave," he said carefully. "May I ask what you're doing?"

She didn't look up from her work.

"You were out hunting," she said, "so I am doing this for you."

"Um," Van mumbled.

"Mama and Papa do it for each other all the time," she explained.

"I'm sure they do," Van said. "However, your mother and father have… a rather different relationship than we do."

She paid him no mind, scrubbing dutifully at his spare linens with a rough soapstone.

Van let the matter go, and when dusk fell, they had supper together around a bonfire. Venison from the day's hunt and porridge brought from the Seat. Ghan Mudcatcher had taken the younger aspirants to forage, evidently with some success, as there were fresh nuts and berries on offer as well.

Lilim, for her part, was hungry only for attention. She bombarded Van with questions again that day, asking about the hunt, and what it was like to be friends with Otep, but her expression fell when he informed her he would be out hunting again tomorrow.

"I know you wish to spend time together," Van said, keeping his voice calm but firm. "But remember that this is the pilgrimage. In the coming days, you should make an effort to spend time with your countrymen while I'm away from camp."

"I will," she promised, looking at her feet.

As she went on to regale him with the particulars of her afternoon, Van stared into the fire and let his mind wander. With a suddenness that should have been suspicious, the other Dolsers stood as one and left. Now alone with Lilim, Van was caught off guard when, a moment later, a voice called to him—and for the second time, it made him shiver.

"Pardon the interruption, but are you Van the Scribe?"

Van turned slowly to see the First Ranger of Vaxas approaching flanked by two rangers, a pair of stunningly gorgeous human girls.

"I am Van the Scribe," he heard himself say.

"It's an honor," said Brynda Blackblade. "I confess, cousin, I came here to ask a favor. Would you hear me out?"

Van swallowed, nodding. Brynda sat down next to him, seemingly at ease. On his other side, Lilim moved in close, as if to defend him from attack. The Vaxal rangers remained standing, scanning their surroundings warily.

"I understand you have a talent for writing," said Brynda. "To be honest, I've looked forward to meeting you. If it's not inconvenient, I would ask you to demonstrate your skills for me. And for a friend of mine, who is rather lacking in that area."

"How do you...?" Van stammered.

"You find it strange that I know you?" said Brynda. "Very well, I'll tell you a story."

She leaned back to rest on her elbows, gazing up at the stars.

"Nine years ago, our First Ranger was something like a mentor of mine. She raised me, really. Or, more so than my parents did. When she returned from the pilgrimage, she had much to say about her visit to Seat Dolse. She found time to speak privately with Farseer Daz, who'd boasted about his son, a boy that even then was reading and writing as well as any elder."

Van rubbed his eyes. It was all too surreal.

"I grew curious about that boy. I didn't know him, but I discovered I admired him. And I knew that one day, we'd be on the pilgrimage together."

"I, um," Van coughed. "What's the name of your friend? The one who needs help with reading and writing."

She locked eyes with him and smiled prettily. "Galdur Goldeyes."

Van recoiled, nearly pushing Lilim into the dirt.

"You want me to—?"

"This is the Journey of Patronage," said Brynda Blackblade. "We are each of us charged with sharing our knowledge freely."

So, there it was. He'd just been called to task by a First Ranger on the pilgrimage. Refusal wasn't an option, but perhaps he could still save himself. He thought hard.

"Of course I accept, on the condition that I be allowed to invite Otep Acrearms and Sol Starfletcher to join us."

"Agreed," Brynda said without hesitation. "My tent should be spacious enough. I'd hoped to invite you there for an hour or so. What time of day would be best? In the morning, perhaps? Before we resume travel, of course."

Van shook his head.

"I am conducting sessions of a similar nature with Lilim the Brave, and I have already promised that time to her."

He grabbed Lilim's hand and squeezed it for emphasis, making sure Brynda could see.

"That won't do, then," murmured Brynda. "How about when we make camp, after midday meal?"

"I have promised to hunt with Otep Acrearms," said Van.

"I see." Brynda grew pensive. "Before evening meal, then. When you return from the hunt."

"Yes, that would be fine," said Van. "I will... Oh."

"Yes?"

"I promised I would talk to someone for a while."

Brynda giggled. It made her seem girlish, the mystique of Vaxas shattered once more.

"You are very popular, Van the Scribe," she said, wiping a tear from her eye.

Van frowned and blushed as she composed herself.

"*After* evening meal, then," suggested Brynda. "Whatever time you can make before bed."

"Very well," said Van. "I will look for your tent after evening meal, and I'll do what I can for…" he cleared his throat, "you and your friend."

Brynda stood up and dusted herself off.

"Thank you for your time, Van the Scribe. I look forward to seeing you. In the meantime, I hope you have pleasant dreams." She favored him with her already familiar smile before departing with her ranger escort.

Van the Scribe slept poorly that night.

5 The Bull and the Snail

Van had a surprise in store for Lilim in the morning.

He'd brought two books from home. The first was the thesaurus, an invaluable resource for expanding one's vocabulary, but not the best choice for introducing long texts to a new reader. Van wanted Lilim's first book to be something she could enjoy reading cover to cover. Something that engaged not just the mind, but the imagination.

His second selection, which he took to her tent before sunrise, was his favorite picture book—a collection of stories called *The Bull and the Snail.* Like most good books, Van would happily reread it any number of times, so long as he had someone to share it with for whom it would be new. He was especially eager to re-experience it through the eyes of Lilim.

The book was written for children, with a comedic slant. Each short chapter explored an implausible interaction between the two titular characters, accompanied by funny drawings, and usually conveying some readily digestible moral. Most young readers were quick to recognize that the oafish Bull as a stand-in for a ranger of Ikann, while the Snail —always appearing in the nick of time to rescue the Bull with his sharp wit—represented a worldly, level-headed Dolser.

As the son of Farseer Daz, Van found his favorite chapter was the one others usually scoffed at. The chapter where the Bull helps the Snail. The tiny mollusk finds himself cornered by a rattlesnake, unable to formulate a plan of escape. The Bull then arrives, takes stock of the situation, and simply tramples the hissing predator to death. The Snail is forced to admit that there are some problems the Bull is better suited to solving.

Privately, Van hoped to one day author some final, unifying chapter of the story, and add it to the original work. It had always seemed to him that the Bull and the Snail should team up, combining their strength and cleverness to accomplish impossible things together. As it stood, no such chapter existed. Because it was a picture book, Van would need to partner with an artist if he ever meant to pursue his secret ambition, having no talent for illustration himself.

"The Bull and... the Snail," Lilim enunciated, sitting next to him in the gloom of her tent with the book in her lap.

So far, so good, thought Van.

They managed to finish the first chapter together before assembly. Lilim laughed with glee at the artwork, and Van laughed along with her. She tried to hand the book back to him when they ran out of time, but he smiled and shook his head.

"I am lending it to you," he explained. "You can read some on your own, if you want, while I'm out hunting and... seeing to things."

She hugged the book to herself and beamed at him. Van had never seen her so happy.

In the afternoon, Van learned that their party would share the hunt with tribe Mercura. No fewer than twenty-four aspiring rangers of Dolse were present this time.

"Will we hunt gazelle again?" Van asked with a spring in his step as he followed Otep to the spot where they'd agreed to meet Sol Starfletcher.

"I will leave that up to the First Ranger of Mercura," said Otep. "But most likely, yes."

"And will Orum be our strategy again?"

"No," uttered Otep with a meaningful glance over his shoulder. "And I ask that you not reveal Orum's abilities to our cousins when we convene."

Van stared back in confusion.

"I want to see how the Starfletcher hunts," Otep explained.

Sol Starfletcher stood waiting for them on the outskirts of camp, sweeping his gaze across the vastness of the Eastern Plains. He had only four rangers with him.

"You brought a large party," Sol observed by way of greeting. "That will come in useful."

The rest of their exchange was brief and businesslike. Otep asked Sol if he had any ideas as to how they should hunt, and Sol asked Otep about the gazelle, listening with interest as Otep confirmed the creatures were plentiful in these lands— and that they should be migrating this time of year. Finally, Sol asked whether there were likely to be any watering holes nearby, where animals might congregate.

"Very possibly," said Otep, peering at the scattered rain clouds in the distance. "To the north, I think."

"Lead on, please," Sol gestured forward.

They all walked northward, the Dolsers and Mercurans at ease with one another, swapping tales to pass the time. After an hour, a ripple appeared on the horizon—the sun's heat reflected by standing water.

"How many are there, do you think?" asked Sol Starfletcher, narrowing his eyes at the distant body of water.

"It is difficult to say," said Otep. "Thirty, perhaps."

Van squinted. His vision was generally considered good, but the gazelle were leagues away. He could make out tiny shapes near the watering hole, but he didn't trust his eyes enough to hazard a count. He glanced around at the other members of Otep's party and recognized the avian wildborn named Wilm. Van suspected he had better eyesight than any of them, but when Wilm caught Van looking at him, he only shrugged.

"Thank you, cousin," said Sol. "I will take it from here."

The First Ranger of Mercura unshouldered his magnificent bow and took a stance. Reaching for his quiver with practiced fluidity, he selected his blue-fletched arrow.

The Dolsers shared skeptical looks, perhaps assuming they were being made the butt of some joke. No marksman living —or who ever had lived—could place a shot at that range, much less could any weapon send an arrow over the horizon. The Dolsers shook their heads, cracking smirks at each other, except for Van and Otep. Van's intuition told him he should pay attention.

The First Ranger of the Patron tribe loosed his arrow, and it flew far—though nowhere near far enough. It arced toward the ground after seventy yards, but Van kept his eyes on it, and it began to glow with an intense blue light.

With a flash, the arrow changed into a shining azure bird, beating its wings once to launch itself through the air. In another moment, it vanished entirely, and seconds later, the crash of thunder boomed over the plains. Sol Starfletcher watched his arrow fly until he couldn't, then followed after it at a leisurely pace. Otep's hunters, dumbfounded, followed in turn.

It took them forty minutes to reach the watering hole, where they discovered the bodies of twenty gazelle. Each had a similar wound on its midsection, as though something had bored clean through—bloodless, the flesh cauterized at the point of contact.

"Twenty kills," remarked Otep, surveying the scene.

Sol Starfletcher smiled and chirped at the blue falcon preening itself on the nearest carcass. The bird jumped to his hand obediently, and after it shrank into an arrow again, Sol returned it to his quiver.

"I exercised some restraint," he explained. "No sense in overhunting."

Otep ordered his rangers to pile up the fallen gazelle. His countenance was composed, but Van knew him too well. His friend was shaken.

"Twenty is a fortuitous number, is it not?" said Sol, taking a moment to stretch. "Given we hunted together, I propose we split them evenly. Ten and ten."

"I think it may be a mischaracterization to suggest this hunt was a joint effort," said Otep, eyeing the dead gazelle.

"Of course it was," said Sol. "Were it not for your help, I wouldn't have known where to look. And as I suggested, we'll need the extra hands to deliver our quarry to camp."

Otep said nothing. Marching up to the giantkin, Sol patted him on the elbow, being far too short to clap him on the back.

"Do not worry, cousin," he said. "The aspirants of Mercura are few in number this year. Ten is more than enough for us. I would be honored if you took the rest, to commemorate our first hunt together."

Van was so stunned, the party was almost back to camp before he recalled his other order of business.

"Otep Acrearms," he blurted. "As it happens, I was solicited by the First Ranger of Vaxas last night. She invited me to introduce a, um, friend of hers to the subject of reading and writing this evening. Would you join us?"

"I'm afraid I cannot, Van the Scribe," said Otep distractedly. "I am to go with Ghan Mudcatcher to visit the campsites of the other tribes, in an effort to share the traditions of Dolse with them. We hunt with tribe Vaxas tomorrow, so I will have other chances to come to know Brynda Blackblade."

"Sol Starfletcher," called Van in desperation, whipping his head around. "I would extend the same invitation to you."

"I must decline as well, young Van," Sol adjusted his quiver. "For the remainder of the day, I plan to test my skill at tracking the Phantom Nighthawk."

Van almost slapped himself on the forehead. He'd completely forgotten about the ridiculous Nighthawk business. Had Brynda anticipated this outcome when she agreed to his concession? Thinking it through, Van supposed he would have to be foolish indeed to believe he could outwit the First Ranger of Vaxas.

Resigned to his fate, Van walked in moody silence the rest of the way to camp.

After the hunters left the gazelle at the edge of camp, Van looked for Lilim. He grew anxious when he couldn't find her, but he wasn't given much time to search. Simon of the Mists found him first, and the foreigner once again seemed impatient.

"Straight talk only, no bullshit," said Simon once he traced the pattern that activated his language comprehension spell. "That's our deal."

Van nodded as they huddled in Van's tent, facing each other.

"For starters, tell me about this 'journey' we're on. Try to be thorough, but remember we have a time limit."

Van frowned. It was difficult, not to mention inappropriate, to speak tersely on the subject of the pilgrimage. Conveying its full gravity required significant explanation, and a degree of shared experience. But he sensed Simon's needs were, at least for now, of a more practical nature, so he kept strictly to the facts.

Simon listened, nodding as Van explained the rite of passage and how the next Patron was decided. As Van spoke, he was surprised by how quickly he was able to review the key points. He even had time to list the Pilgrimage Guides and First Rangers, as well as their various accolades, as he understood them.

"Well, I guess I knew most of that already," muttered Simon. "I just didn't think you'd drag *me* into it." He raised his eyebrows. "So, who do you think'll win? Mercura again?"

Van tensed. It was expected of any Nemian that they express pride and confidence in their own tribe. Doubly so between aspirants on the pilgrimage. But remembering to whom he was speaking, he took a breath.

"I believe that to be the most likely outcome, yes."

"Anybody but Ikann, am I right?" teased Simon, smiling casually.

"Indeed, Van sighed. Then, growing curious, he studied the foreigner. "If you can only understand our language for an hour each day, how…?"

Simon laughed. "Honestly? Your politics are pretty basic. It's kind of fun, actually, like watching a four-way game of rugby."

Van didn't know what rugby was, but sensed that Simon was making light of the Journey of Patronage. "This is serious!"

"Sorry," said Simon. "That was insensitive of me."

An uncomfortable silence fell over the tent, and even Van understood that to say nothing would be the absolute worst use of their time.

"Tell me of your homeland," he prompted.

"Your turn, huh?" said Simon. "Fair enough."

The foreigner thought for a moment.

"I'm from a country called Gnosos. A peninsula off of Titan's northern ice cap. We don't have as much land as you guys do here, and only a portion of ours is habitable. So, for a long time we relied heavily on foreign trade. More than half of all the world's latent sorcerers are born in Gnosos. In Megalomemoria, in my case. The capital—most magically advanced city in the world."

He paused, giving Van a few seconds to process the statement. Van could tell it was supposed to sound impressive, but the foreigner might as well be a peacock fanning its tail feathers. With no frame of reference, his boast was meaningless.

"What's Titan?" asked Van.

"That's the name of the planet you live on," Simon explained patiently.

Van considered how he might tie the conversation back to the Journey of Patronage.

"How do you choose your leaders?" he asked.

"You don't pull your punches, do you?" Simon grimaced. "That's a tough one. If I'm being honest, I guess we don't."

Van drew his eyebrows together and crossed his arms, waiting for Simon to elaborate.

"It's like this. We have four Quarters of government. Legislative, Economic, Military, and Foreign Affairs. The presidents of each Quarter are all publicly elected. But here's the catch—above those *Quarters,* we have the Inner Circle. All the presidents really do is micromanage. They keep the country running—day to day operations, that type of stuff. It's the Inner Circle that lays out the big picture when it comes to state policy, issuing directives to the Quarters."

Van leaned forward. "Then, who or what is the Inner Circle?"

"Couldn't tell you."

Van rolled his eyes.

"No, really." Simon held his hands up plaintively. "Nobody knows. It could be a group of people, or maybe it's just one person. Some supremely powerful sorcerer, pulling the strings from behind the scenes. *Nobody knows.* It's a little scary if you think too hard about it, but it's also what makes Gnosos work."

"And no one is bothered by that?" said Van, no longer caring whether he was casting aspersions. "That no one knows who actually rules Know-sis?"

"Sorry, but that's three questions for you. My turn again."

Van opened his mouth to protest, but Simon spoke over him.

"Something you said got me thinking. This caravan we're with, are you telling me this accounts for everyone in Nemia between the ages of twelve and twenty? A few thousand kids, and that's it?"

Van nodded hesitantly.

"If my country did this, rounded up all our adolescents into one place and took a head count," said Simon, "we'd have hundreds of thousands. Maybe a million."

Van's eyes flew wide. "What!"

"And keep in mind what I told you about Gnosos. We have significantly less arable land and fewer natural resources than you. So that begs the question, why aren't there more of you? Some kind of asymptomatic disease? Something in the food? There are plenty of things that could cause widespread sterility and go unnoticed for a few years. Or…"

He touched a hand to his chin, thinking.

Van swallowed. "Or?"

"Or, your civilization is engaged in some form of population control."

"What does that mean?" Van asked, lost.

"For example," said the foreigner, "do you guys have any weird rules about when you're allowed to have kids?"

Van forced himself to consider the question. "When Nemian couples form a union, it is customary for them to seek their chieftain's blessing before bearing and raising new members of the tribe."

"Bingo," said Simon—another word without meaning to Van. "Wow, though. I wonder why…"

Awkward silence settled over them again. This time, Simon was the one to break it.

"I might have to reevaluate how we go about these conversations. Part of the reason I picked you was because I thought you'd have the inside scoop, being the chief's son and all. But now, talking to you, it seems like I might've been wrong."

The foreigner stiffened, noticing the guarded look on Van's face.

"Don't get me wrong," Simon clarified. "I still want to talk to you. I get the sense you're making an effort to be honest with me. I appreciate that. And you did save my life, which I guess scored you some points."

He stood up.

"Anyway, let's call it a day. We can try again tomorrow, or whenever you're feeling up to it. If you need a day off, just shake your head when I give you our signal."

Van nodded, then left the tent with Simon to say goodbye.

"Enjoy the remainder of your day, Simon of the Mists."

Simon attempted a smile. "You too, kid."

Van still had one more obligation to contend with that day —the one he was dreading the most.

He felt naked as he meandered through the campsite of Vaxas, scanning the field for the First Ranger's tent. His tunic was a fleck of brown against a canvas of green and turquoise. Fortunately, the two rangers he'd seen with Brynda the day prior spotted him, and guided him to her tent themselves. It would at least be easy to find again, if he needed to. Hers was the largest tent in camp.

"Come in," chimed Brynda, once Van declared himself.

When Van stepped into the tent—which was spacious compared to his own or Lilim's—he found Brynda Blackblade sitting on her knees, alone. The makeshift room was even furnished, a short wooden table atop a bear skin rug in the middle, and a small chest of drawers near the far end by Brynda's bedroll. She watched him enter, sipping tea from a ceramic cup.

"Galdur Goldeyes appears to be running late," she said. "While we wait, please make yourself comfortable. Are we expecting Sol Starfletcher and Otep Acrearms?"

Van sat down across the table from her, clearing his throat nervously. "Both have prior engagements."

"What a shame," said Brynda, smiling. "Can I get you anything? Tea?"

Van sucked in a breath and looked her in the eye. "There is one thing, I suppose. You could tell me what game your chieftain has planned for our First Rangers at Seat Vaxas."

She chuckled politely. "All I can say is that you might find yourselves quite surprised."

Just then, Galdur Goldeyes barged in unannounced, startling Van so badly, he almost tipped the table.

"*This* is who you found?" snarled the First Ranger of Ikann, glaring down at him.

"I have it on good authority that he is the best there is," said Brynda, scooting over to make room for Galdur. "And I think he'll make for a patient and attentive teacher."

Galdur scoffed, but he sat down next to Brynda and waited. Van realized they expected him to begin without delay.

He coughed into his hand. "Brynda Blackblade, you've asked me here tonight to discuss reading and writing. Regrettably, I have no written works I might share, nor any supplements we might use to practice our form."

Van told himself it wasn't a lie. Everything he'd brought from home was already promised to Lilim.

Brynda turned to her chest of drawers, producing two rolls of parchment and a new jar of ink. She then set a quill on the table next to Galdur, and fetched a second one for herself.

"Oh," Van mumbled. "Um, thank you. A second problem occurs to me, though. It's rather dark, and without a proper light source—"

Galdur Goldeyes reached into his tunic and pulled out a smooth metal cylinder, no larger than the quills. He pinched one end and released it, as if to drop it on the ground. Instead of falling, the contraption floated into the air and fixed itself by his shoulder. It was glowing now, casting clean, clear light across the interior of the tent.

Van stared at the curious little object. "What is that?"

"A magical trinket of some kind," said Galdur Goldeyes. "I didn't bother over the details."

"Where did you...?"

"I am the First Ranger of Ikann," he snapped. "I am given whatever I want."

Clearing his throat again, Van started the session in earnest. Just as he'd done with Lilim, he asked the First Rangers to begin by writing their names.

Brynda held her quill with obvious familiarity as she completed the task. Reviewing her work, Van noted that her calligraphy was professional in quality.

Brynda Blackblade

Unfortunately, Van was watching Brynda when he should have been watching Galdur. The First Ranger of Ikann picked up the quill in his fist, sloshed it about in the ink jar, and before Van could stop him, pushed it through the parchment. Its tip snapped against the table.

"Oh, my," murmured Brynda, casually retrieving a replacement from her drawer.

Rather than guiding Galdur's hand as he had Lilim's, wanting under no circumstances to lay hands on the First Ranger, Van showed Galdur the correct way to grip the quill by modeling the task himself. Galdur watched and tried again, this time destroying neither quill nor parchment. But Van grimaced when he saw his handwriting.

GALDER

For Van's next assignment, he asked the First Rangers to write a brief self-description. He told them not to overthink it, as he only wanted to measure their abilities in vocabulary and grammar. This time, he kept his attention fixed on Galdur Goldeyes.

GALDER STRONG IN FITE   CHAMPEON OF ARENA
MASTER OF BEAST   FEARS NO DEATH

A pattern was beginning to emerge with Galdur's choice of words, making Van a little nervous.

"Well done," he said. "Next, please draw each letter of the Nemian alphabet."

Van watched them scrawl on their parchments, and as he suspected, Galdur's alphabet was short by several letters. He swallowed, knowing his next task would be a tricky one.

He walked around to the other side of the table and asked Galdur for his quill, then wrote in the missing letters so they formed a complete set. He pointed to each letter, named it, and provided examples of words it could be used to spell. By some miracle, he accomplished all this without offending the First Ranger or challenging his competence.

"Next, please list all the animal species found in the Eastern Plains," said Van.

He didn't miss how Galdur sagged his shoulders, but the First Ranger voiced no complaint. He picked his quill up anew and set to work. Satisfied that Galdur could proceed for a time without further supervision, Van turned his attention back to Brynda's parchment and reviewed her work.

Brynda Blackblade is an average seventeen-year-old girl. She projects confidence for the benefit of her tribe, but in her heart she harbors doubts as to her adequacy in the face of the pilgrimage and her worthiness as a champion to her people. Despite her uncertainties, she has already accomplished many of the goals she set for herself a very long time ago.

Van's lips parted as he read. "Brynda Blackblade, you…"

"Yes?" she said pleasantly, looking up.

Van coughed to hide his sputtering. "You are performing admirably."

He returned to his side of the table and sat down, feeling tired. The assignment he'd given them would keep anyone busy indefinitely, and he'd chosen it principally because he needed a break.

Several minutes passed in silence. Just as Van was beginning to consider telling his students to stop for the evening, Galdur's patience ran out.

"This grows tedious," he muttered, setting aside his quill and rubbing his temples. "There are obviously more beasts in these lands than can be counted. Perhaps this was a poor choice for my time after all. To begin with, why must I sit here and be lorded over by some Dolser whelp?"

"Galdur, be useful," replied Brynda impassively, not lifting her eyes from her parchment.

Van braced himself for the explosion of anger he knew must be coming, but it never came. Galdur fell silent, utterly cowed. Van tried to wrap his mind around what he'd just seen. It was as though he'd intruded on something private, accidentally glimpsing the true order of things. When he found his voice, he told them to stop.

"Both of you did well this evening," said Van. "Brynda Blackblade, I assume you mean for me to return around the same time tomorrow?"

She smiled. "Just so."

Suppressing a sigh, Van forced himself to smile back. Somehow, he'd guessed as much from the start.

"Regarding our lack of written works to study," Van said, "I had a thought. Your Pilgrimage Guide, elder Memnon, does he not carry books with him?"

"He does," said Brynda, stowing the quills and parchment. "But those, I think, would be poor selections for the task at hand."

"I see," said Van, deflating. "In that case, I will try to procure something myself, if I find the opportunity."

Galdur stood up and stretched while Brynda walked Van outside to bid him goodnight. He bowed to her, then made the trek back to his tent where he collapsed on his bedroll, completely spent.

6 Lethal Prey

A wave of relief washed over Van when he ventured into Lilim's tent the next morning. Her company was relaxing compared to his other new commitments, and he'd been worried when he couldn't find her yesterday.

"Ghan Mudcatcher taught us how to mix dyes!" she gushed, when Van asked how she'd been getting along.

"That sounds engaging," said Van. "Did you leave time to visit with the other tribes?"

"Um," she fidgeted. "Mostly, I was reading."

"Oh?"

She pulled *The Bull and the Snail* out of her rucksack, and he winced when he saw she'd bent the corner of a page to mark her place. She settled in beside him, smiling, and once he recovered from his minor spasm of anxiety, they read another chapter together.

It was the rattlesnake chapter, and as Lilim eagerly read the story aloud, Van listened, correcting her pronunciation when necessary or helping her with words she didn't recognize. She didn't laugh at the illustrations today, and her mood quickly soured.

"Are you all right, Lilim?" asked Van when she closed the book and fell silent.

"That one wasn't as good," she said. "The Snail should have solved the problem on his own."

Van nodded, studying her.

She sighed "I've figured it out, anyway."

"What have you figured out?"

An uncharacteristic hint of arrogance crept into her voice. "The Snail's one of us, but the Bull is from Ikann."

"I do see how one could draw that comparison," said Van. "Do you want to work on something else for today?"

"No," she said stubbornly, opening the book again. "I want to finish it."

Lilim soldiered through the book's remaining few chapters, which were a return to form after the rattlesnake story. Her mood had improved a little by the time they turned the final page. She returned the book to him, thanking him again for lending it to her. Filing out of the tent, they hurried to assembly.

Van didn't hear most of Otep's announcements that day, instead mulling over what other skills he might teach Lilim. He hoped to take her foraging soon. Since leaving Seat Dolse, he'd been waiting for the procession to camp near woodlands, but thus far they'd stuck to the arid plains.

He was snapped out of his woolgathering when he heard the First Ranger say, "Today, we hunt with tribe Vaxas."

Van admired the beauty of the Eastern Plains as he walked side by side with his excitable young tutee that day. In particular, he surveyed each stand of trees they passed as they followed the old wagon road from the Seat to Stonebasin.

Luck was on his side—they made camp a short walk from a copse of forageable woods. While helping Lilim pitch her tent, he explained his plan for the coming morning, asking her to be packed and dressed before he came calling. She lit up, overjoyed at the prospect of exploring the woods together, and promised him she'd be ready and waiting.

Shooting her one last smile, Van left to join up with Otep. Though he was pleased at the chance to provide Lilim this opportunity, he knew it would cost him. He would have to ask a favor of someone he dearly wished not to be indebted to.

Brynda Blackblade and her rangers met Otep's group in a cleared field north of camp. The woods here had all been cut down to provide lumber to nearby Stonebasin. Van counted himself doubly lucky, therefore, that some trees still stood closer to camp. Curiously, the Vaxals had brought an unladen sleigh, the sort used to haul logs or masonry stones.

The First Ranger was perched on a stump, juggling her dagger idly. She tossed it with a flick of the wrist and caught it by the tip. The motion seemed unconscious, as simple for her as breathing. The blade, made of sparkling obsidian, drew Van's gaze.

"Well met, cousins," said Otep Acrearms to the Vaxals. "Brynda Blackblade, had you any thoughts as to how we might hunt today?"

She stood and slipped her blade back into its sheath. "Only that we stroll west, away from Stonebasin, and see what there is to see."

Otep nodded in agreement. "Lead on."

They walked west through the clearcut field, venturing into the tundra. All the while, the two parties maintained an impersonal distance from one another.

Van watched the horizon for the telltale shimmer of a watering hole, hoping to make himself useful and speak up if he spotted one. He failed to notice when the others stopped ahead of him after a half hour's hike, nearly colliding with one of the Vaxals.

"This hunt is called off," Otep said from further up the line. Van stepped around to see what the commotion was about.

The First Rangers had found tracks. When Van wandered closer to study them, he instantly understood the trepidation in Otep's voice. They were not the imprints of a gazelle's hooves. These belonged to the hornbeast of the plains.

"We must return to camp," said Otep. "To warn the others, and send warning ahead to Stonebasin."

There was strange a twinkle in Brynda's eye

"Why go to the trouble?" she said. "Didn't we come for a hunt? It seems to me we've just picked up the trail of our quarry."

"You cannot be serious," said Otep flatly.

"I won't force you to accompany me." Brynda signaled her team back into formation. "But this is the pilgrimage, and I for one am grateful for the chance to test myself. You may do as you will."

With that, the Vaxals struck out, undaunted. Otep hesitated, glancing at each of his hunters in turn. These were the aspirants whose lives he was responsible for. But Van could tell he was intrigued by Brynda's daring proposal. All he needed was a push.

"I want to see," he whispered with confidence, when the First Ranger met his eyes.

Otep set his jaw and nodded.

Mustering their courage, they followed the hornbeast's trail, quickly catching up to Brynda's party. They became a single unit, all vestiges of childish disinclination cast aside. They would be rangers now, because that was what they needed to be.

Van felt it before he saw it. A tremble in the ground beneath his feet. Regular, building steadily. When the creature lumbered into view minutes later the hunters froze. The hornbeast in the distance was charging straight toward them, as if some preternatural instinct had alerted it to their presence in its territory. The cloud of dust kicked up by its massive hooves looked like a landslide in motion.

Otep and Brynda took front and center. The First Ranger of Dolse had brought both his axe and sling that day, and it was the axe he chose as he stepped forward. The weapon was fashioned of a single piece of dense metal—impossible to lift for anyone of normal strength and stature. But Otep held it comfortably overhead, taking a stance and readying himself.

Van wondered if even a mighty swing of Otep's axe would halt the oncoming seven-ton predator. Brynda leapt into action simultaneously, wielding her dagger free in hand. She whistled to her rangers—the same two girls who'd accompanied her before—and they unshouldered their longbows. One stood behind Brynda, a few paces to her left, and the other behind Otep, a little to the right. Nocking their arrows on their bow strings, they took aim.

The remaining hunters stepped back, Van among them. The avian wildborn Wilm caught Otep's eye for just a second, tensing as they exchanged a meaningful glance, but Otep shook his head. Whatever was about to happen, it would be over within seconds.

The monster was now just seventy yards away, within range of the Vaxals' longbows, but an experienced hunter would want their target even closer—perhaps fifty yards—to reliably hit a vital area and kill with a single shot. In this case, however, Van wasn't sure it made a difference. He wouldn't even know where on the creature to aim for.

At sixty yards, Brynda's rangers loosed their arrows in unison, and Van watched them snap harmlessly against the beast's hide. The hornbeast didn't slow as it lifted its head to examine them, looking annoyed, as though it was deciding which one to trample first.

The lifting of its neck created an opening, exposing a small space under the hornbeast's jaw where its underside was briefly visible. Van's heart jumped into his throat as Brynda tumbled forward, vanishing beneath the colossal apex predator.

Otep raised his axe as the creature thundered toward him, but he never had to let it fall. The tyrant of the plains shuddered to a halt no more than five yards in front of him, and its belly exploded in a geyser of mutilated innards.

Brynda emerged from behind the fallen beast, not a drop of blood on her red skin. She was holding not a dagger, but a whip. The weapon slithered back into itself, becoming a simple black blade again, which she returned to its sheath. Van didn't know if anyone else had even seen it—all onlookers stared transfixed at the hornbeast—but in that moment, Van had eyes only for the First Ranger of Vaxas. She smiled serenely at the dying animal, silhouetted by the setting sun.

The hornbeast gave a baleful moan as its life ebbed away, and a cheer rose up from the ranging party, Dolsers and Vaxals alike exalting Brynda's accomplishment. For Van, it was a culminating moment. Since her arrival at Seat Dolse, he'd been curious about the nondescript but charming young woman from the mysterious northern tribe. After witnessing her today, though, he felt nothing but sincere admiration for her. He recalled then that he would see her again soon, in a more private setting, and unlike last time, he found himself looking forward to it.

The sleigh proved useful after all, hauling the enormous creature back to camp. Because the hunt was a success, the riddle of field dressing a hornbeast was for others to solve, leaving Van free to attend his appointment with Simon of the Mists.

"So, how's it going, kid?" said the foreigner when they sat down in Van's tent.

Van sighed. "I wish you wouldn't call me that. I'm soon to be a man, blooded by rite of pilgrimage."

"Operative phrase, 'soon to be.' Until you finish this thing, you're still a kid. Your rules, not mine."

"In that case, you are also unblooded," Van retorted. "I would be within my rights to call you a child just the same."

Simon chuckled. "Nemia doesn't get to tell me when I'm grown up. I was paying bills when Farseer Daz was in diapers."

Van rubbed his eyes, sure he'd misheard. "You were what? How old are you?"

Simon narrowed his eyes and grinned. "You really don't have elves here, do you? I'm a hundred and three." He paused, then. "So? How's it going?"

Despite his sarcastic tone, Van chose to believe his question was a genuine inquiry as to his well-being. They'd agreed to be honest, so perhaps this was just Simon's way of "talking straight," as he put it.

"I... suppose I'm exhausted, actually," admitted Van. "Keeping pace with the demands of the pilgrimage has been surprisingly difficult. I did not expect to be so busy this early on."

Simon nodded. "Well, the point of this whole thing is to test you, right? If you'd said that to the big guy or Ghan, wouldn't they just politely tell you to pony up and deal with it?"

"Indeed," said Van, his shoulders slumping.

"What else have you been up to, besides hiking in the morning and hunting in the afternoon?"

"Before sunrise, I have been teaching a friend how to read and write. Her name is Lilim the Brave. I'm sure you've seen her with me."

He bobbed his head. "Okay, that doesn't sound too bad."

Van smiled. "It is actually quite fulfilling, though it does require waking up earlier than most others. I suppose it's my evening obligation that concerns me more."

He cocked an eyebrow. "All right. What's the story there?"

"At the request of Brynda Blackblade, I have also been sharing my skills with her and Galdur Goldeyes."

"Holy *shit*," said Simon, leaning in. "Both of them?"

Van nodded.

"How'd she talk you into that? You got a crush on her?"

Van blushed. "She is a First Ranger!"

He held his hands up in surrender. "Sorry, I was joking. Seriously, though, what's that like?"

Van fidgeted. "Brynda has been reading and writing at an advanced level for some time, that much is clear. Tutoring Galdur has been… challenging."

"*Challenging?* Come on, kid. Give me the dirt."

Van knew it was inappropriate, but he couldn't help wondering if expressing himself freely would make him feel any better. Perhaps with Simon, he might be forgiven for ignoring the principles of social conduct Nemians were expected to uphold.

"He has a toddler's mastery over written language. He becomes easily frustrated, and his attention span is miniscule. He insults me to my face and openly insults my tribe, even as I try to render myself useful to him. I shared his company only briefly last night, and already I have no idea how I'll keep my promise to Brynda."

Simon grinned. "Bet it felt good to get that out. Man, though, that is *rough.*"

"A strange thing happened at one point," Van mused. "Just as Galdur was getting himself worked up, Brynda snapped at him. She was very terse."

"Did it set him off?"

"That is the strange part," said Van. "Rather than lashing out, he stopped talking altogether. From then until the end of our session, he focused on his task as though his life depended on it."

Simon scratched his chin. "Weird. That might be worth paying attention to. Keep me posted on any further developments along those lines."

Van went on, now feeling decidedly talkative. "Otep and I hunted with Brynda today, actually. She was most impressive. I have never seen such a… what's wrong?"

Simon's expression had hardened. He was staring at Van in a way that made him nervous. "I was messing around before, but I might not be anymore. You sure you don't have a thing for this girl?"

"Simon, please." Van rolled his eyes.

"Say it with a straight face, and I'll drop the subject."

"I simply admire her gallantry," Van said levelly.

Simon's countenance remained judgmental, but he eventually relaxed.

Van rubbed the back of his neck. "So how is it, um… going… with you?"

"Aw, you do care," said Simon. "I'm actually working on a little side project, but there isn't much to report yet. I suspect we'll talk about it soon."

"Side project?" asked Van.

"The only hint I'll give you is this: I'm not the only one that got dragged along on this year's road trip."

"The dark girl," Van said quietly.

Simon nodded. "She hasn't called me out yet, but if she's feeling anything like I was, it's only a matter of time. She's seen me use my translation spell. It's safe to say I've gained her attention. If you got pulled into it, there's a lot I would need to tell you about dusken ahead of time, and I'm not in the mood to go down that rabbit hole right now. Nothing's happened yet, anyway."

"If she did approach you, would you help her?"

Simon grew pensive. "I guess so. Shared circumstances and all that. But don't worry about it. There are a hundred other Dolse kids I can set her up with who can bring her up to speed on things."

"But when you were in her position, you came to me."

"Well, yeah."

"If she came to you for help, and you made an effort to give her the best help you could, who would you suggest she talk to?"

Simon furrowed his brow. "I'd tell her to talk to you."

"In which case, going forward, our sessions would be a three-way affair."

"Phrasing, kid."

"You might as well tell me now," said Van. "Everything you deem prudent to know of her people before making conversation with her."

"All right," said Simon, sounding tired. "Where to start..."

The foreigner cleared his throat, and his demeanor changed. His speech became formal, like that of an elder giving lessons at the Teaching Circle.

"The dusken live in cities deep below Titan's surface, only accessible through a buried maze of unmapped cave systems. They call it the Twilight World—a societal matriarchy. For better or worse, those of us living on the surface have virtually no contact with them."

A considered pause stretched between them.

"The main problem is their religion. They call their god the Twilight Prophet, and her principal tenants include the glorification of murder for pleasure, and the myriad virtues of slavery. Dusken are instinctively deceitful, taught from a young age to take advantage of anybody weaker or dumber than they are if they stand to gain the smallest thing by doing so. Acts of cruelty and subjugation are second nature to them, sometimes on a grand scale." He shook his head as if to clear it. "Man, I told you I didn't want to do this..."

Vans throat had gone dry. "That's not possible. An entire people can't just be inherently evil."

"It's called indoctrination," said Simon. "They believe that personifying their goddess brings them closer to the divine. A perfectly circular self-justifying spiritual morality. You might as well ask why a spider spins its web."

Simon shrugged, then. "But it's not like I've ever met a dusken. Depending on how things go, maybe we'll get the chance to form our own opinions."

Van meditated on that for a moment. "How much time do we have?"

"We've still got a little," said Simon.

"May we return to the subject of Gnosos?" Van suggested, careful to get the pronunciation right this time.

"Sure. What specifically?"

"I'd like to know why I found you half drowned on the beach near Seat Dolse."

"Okay," said Simon. "I was the commanding officer of a dreadnought—that's a type of large boat—stationed off the south coast of Nemia. A storm hit us, and the swells pushed us into some reefs, where we tore our hull. Went down pretty fast. The rest you already know."

"Would there not have been other survivors?" asked Van.

Simon shrugged. "There were only four sorcerers aboard, so I guess the other three were just unlucky. For the most part, dreadnoughts are crewed by constructs—magically animated service automatons."

"What was the dread-not doing there?"

"All I know is that, around that time, there was a policy change. The Military Quarter decided to keep a closer eye on Nemia. Most likely, the Inner Circle picked up some intel that changed their attitude toward you."

"Very well…" said Van, thinking. "But why did your country send *you?* You told me your country has people whose job it is to attend to foreign affairs."

"Wasn't a Foreign Affairs issue," said Simon.

Van wrinkled his brow. "How could it not be?"

"Because no state of diplomacy exists between Gnosos and Nemia. No state of diplomacy exists between *anyone* and Nemia."

"Then, what could your Inner Circle have learned that changed their attitudes toward us?"

"That's what I'd like to know," said Simon, throwing his arms up for dramatic effect. "That's why we're having these conversations."

Van paused to think it over, and to give Simon a turn if he wanted one. He didn't seem to.

"Why didn't you ever try to go home?" asked Van at length.

"Who knows?" said Simon, his tone detached. "Maybe I was starting to feel disillusioned. You asked me before if it bothered anyone, the whole Inner Circle thing. The answer is yes—it bugs us. Especially those of us who work for the government. But even setting that aside, getting back wouldn't have been easy. Without the dreadnought, I had no way of sending a message to the mainland. If I was really clever, and convinced your dad to help me, I probably could have come up with something. At this point, though, I've been sitting around deciding what to do for so long, they'd probably just put me on trial for desertion if I ever did make it home."

Van nodded as he listened. Simon seemed more at ease this time, like he was starting to open up. Perhaps sensing the same thing, the foreigner changed the subject. He asked Van about the weather, mentioning something called "snow." Van told him no such thing occurred in Nemia. Simon was in the middle of some anecdote having to do with Gnosian dress fashion when his spell gave out.

When the foreigner's words became gibberish, Van made the talking gesture and then drew a finger across his throat. Simon laughed, and they both got up. Van left the tent with him and bowed to bid him goodbye, and today, he was pleased to see the foreigner return the gesture. Van watched him go, realizing only then that he'd forgotten to mention their impending arrival at Stonebasin.

Van had just enough time to share evening meal with Lilim before departing again to the campsite of Vaxas. Because she'd finished *The Bull and the Snail* so quickly, he took it with him tonight alongside the thesaurus. He could explore other topics with Lilim over the next few days, so he may as well put the books to use with Galdur and Brynda.

Just as before, the three of them arranged themselves around the table in the First Ranger's tent. Brynda fetched their writing tools while Galdur produced his luminous trinket and squeezed the end. Van watched the object anxiously this time as it floated up and settled in the air.

"Today, I thought we could discuss synonyms," said Van.

"Synonyms?" Galdur folded his arms.

Van wasn't sure if it was a request to elaborate, or if he was unfamiliar with the word itself. Van explained his assignment, asking the First Rangers to review their previous work and list alternatives to words they'd used that held significance to them. While they worked, he placed his books on the table, thinking over his plan.

Rationality dictated the thesaurus should go to Brynda, as the more advanced learner. The picture book, then, would be lent to Galdur—an easier assignment for the struggling novice. On the other hand, *The Bull and the Snail* was Van's favorite. Surprising himself, he did the irrational, and switched the two.

Galdur eyed the thesaurus suspiciously as Van handed it to him. After explaining its function, he turned to Brynda and offered her the picture book.

"You, um," Van stammered. "You may not find this a particularly challenging text, but as a work of cultural significance to the people of Dolse, you might at least find it interesting."

"Thank you, cousin." She smiled absently as she turned a few pages.

Their lesson was soon underway, and when it was finished, Van told his students they could keep their books for the time being. He ignored the way Galdur kept glancing at the thesaurus—like a fish head he'd found in his stew.

While Brynda cleared the table, Galdur reached up to snatch his trinket from the air. Van knew it was time to ask his favor, and he steeled himself, coughing to gain the First Ranger's attention.

"You may find this presumptuous, Galdur Goldeyes, but I'd hoped you might let me borrow that device of yours. I have some important business before assembly tomorrow morning that would greatly benefit from having it on hand. I can bring it back to you at our next appointment—if the arrangement suits you, of course."

Galdur stared at him and cocked an eyebrow. A cruel grin crept slowly across his face.

"Why *shouldn't* I lend it to you? It's satisfying to know that some Dolser wants to go snooping around in the dark. It tells me I was right in my initial appraisal of you."

Galdur tossed Van the metal cylinder and he caught it, willing himself to forget the flagrant insult.

"Just remember to bring it back," Galdur said. "I'd prefer to be wrong just once, in my appraisal that Dolsers are also clumsy and forgetful."

Brynda got up, dusting herself off. "Considering we arrive at Stonebasin tomorrow, I propose we resume two nights hence. Everyone will be quite busy exploring the community, I'm sure."

They all agreed it would be so. Outside, Van said goodnight to Brynda, and she favored him with her smile, which he'd decided he was fond of.

7 Stonebasin

Van woke up feeling out of sorts. As much as he was looking forward to foraging with Lilim and showing her around Stonebasin later that day, he was preoccupied with a troubling notion. He was in love with Brynda Blackblade.

As promised, Lilim was dressed and ready outside her tent, a carefree bounce in her step as they made the short trip to the woods. Evidently, the problem of visibility hadn't yet occurred to her.

When they stepped into the thick undergrowth, she immediately caught her foot on a gnarled root and fell forward. Van had been expecting it and was ready to catch her. She clung to him, startled, then worked herself free.

"It's too dark!" she complained.

"Well observed, Lilim," said Van. "Foraging is an activity best saved for the daylight hours. I'm sorry I didn't caution you ahead of time, but I wanted you to come to the conclusion on your own. As it happens, I do have a solution, just for today."

He fished out Galdur's trinket and squeezed the end. Nothing happened. He frowned, flipped it over, and squeezed again. It came alive this time, drifting up to hover by Van's shoulder. Their surroundings were now illuminated, as if by the sun.

"What's that?" marveled Lilim.

"A magical device of some kind," said Van. "I didn't ask for the details."

"Where did you get it?"

"I borrowed it from a friend," he answered, starting forward again.

With the trinket lighting their path, they trudged deeper into the woods. They had less than an hour before assembly, but in that time, they found a good variety of plant species. Van pointed out ivy that should be avoided, as well as mushrooms never to be consumed. But they found the fun kinds of plants, too.

"Look there, Lilim," he said, pointing. "That's a blackberry bush. See?"

"Can you eat them?" she asked, cocking her head.

The idea of a twelve year old girl that had never tried a blackberry was positively heartbreaking.

"They're quite healthful, actually," he said. "Some prefer them rendered into a jelly or a jam, but they can also be enjoyed fresh."

In demonstration, he popped one into his mouth and smiled. Lilim approached the bush, taking her time selecting a berry that looked dark and juicy. Plucking it, she chewed it reverently, with her eyes closed.

"It's delicious!"

They picked a few handfuls each, wrapping them in cloth squares Van had quietly requisitioned from the supply carts before stowing their bounty safely in Van's rucksack. Looping through the copse of trees, they made their next discovery halfway back to camp, and it was an important one—another berry bush. Its gold-flecked leaves set it apart, and it was laden with tiny red fruits.

"Do you know the sparkleberry?" asked Van as he called Lilim's attention to the berry bush.

She stepped closer. "Is that the one used for medicine?"

"It is indeed," he said, genuinely impressed. "Do you know its characteristics? The things that make it unique from other, similar berries?"

She furrowed her brow in thought. "It's sparkly?"

"Right again."

He plucked one at random, and held it where she could see.

"A true sparkleberry has little gold spots inside. Do you see them?"

Lilim squinted at the berry, its flesh illuminated by the steady white light of Galdur's hovering trinket.

"I don't know," she said hesitantly.

Van studied it himself. They were faint, but he could see the golden flecks buried deep in the fruit's flesh. It was probably true that in some sparkleberries, they weren't visible at all. He dropped the berry on the ground and squashed it underfoot.

"We will discard it, then, because there is another berry, the trickster's hawthorn, that is very poisonous. It is identical to the sparkleberry in every way, except that it doesn't sparkle. If you can't see the sparkles, you throw the berry away. Understand?"

Lilim nodded.

Van avoided mentioning how heavy sleepers could use the hawthorn to swindle themselves out of bed early. It wasn't a survival skill, strictly speaking. The real lesson was to err on the side of caution, because distilling medicine from those false berries could have lethal consequences.

As with the blackberries, they picked a few handfuls apiece, keeping only those that Lilim could positively identify. The sun crept over the horizon, and seeing it, they hurried to assembly, snacking on berries and chatting as they went.

The sun was nearly overhead when the procession reached Stonebasin. The community was built deep in a canyon, and its population rivaled that of the Seat. Many of its dwellings and civic centers were cave-like; dug from the living earth of the canyon wall. The largest of these was tribe Dolse's Temple to the Emissaries, its heavy stone doors adorned by rock sculptures.

Van had visited Stonebasin many times with his father, but this year was different. Today, he'd come as an aspirant, and he would beseech the Emissaries for their blessing before leaving the lands of his tribe for the first time. Additionally, Van intended to take Lilim to see the Great Kiln and the Scriptorium, two of the great wonders of tribe Dolse, as he suspected she'd never ventured this far from home. The Scriptorium in particular held a special place in Van's heart.

"Will we go down?" asked Lilim, standing at the lip of the canyon with him to watch their countrymen file down the wide trail into the basin.

"We will," he said. "But later, I think. Once the crowds have had their fill and moved on."

Lilim nodded agreeably. She didn't like crowds, either.

Van assumed it would take hours for the procession to resupply, during which Stonebasin would be busiest. It wasn't yet mealtime, and he didn't see Simon anywhere. He'd been excused from his obligation to Galdur and Brynda, as well. For the first time in days, Van had free time on his hands.

He parted ways with Lilim, promising to find her again that evening. As he watched her leave, his exhaustion caught up to him, and he decided that—improbably—the best use of his time might be to simply have a nap. He pitched his tent, lay down on his bedroll, and fell asleep within seconds.

"Van the Scribe, wake up!"

Van roused awake to the sensation of being shaken by a small intruder.

"Lilim the Brave," he mumbled, "it is customary to announce yourself before entering your kinsmen's chambers."

"I did!" she protested, crouched on top of him in the tent. "You were sound asleep."

Outside, Van could see the sky turning colors. He'd slept much longer than he'd intended, and he realized he'd needed it.

"Will we go down now?" asked Lilim. "Everyone else has already come back up."

He forced a tired smile, and got out of bed. But as she slid off of him, he noticed something alarming. Lilim yelped in surprise when he caught her by the wrist.

"When did this happen?" he inspected the skin of her calves above the ankles. Both her legs were covered in blistering sores.

"I don't know," she muttered, sounding embarrassed. "When we got back from the woods, I suppose?"

Van furrowed his brow. He was sure he'd been careful not to lead them through any ivy. "We'll get you something for it in Stonebasin. And Lilim, take your rucksack back to your tent. You won't need it."

She moped, cradling her pack

Van sighed. "I know the idea of bartering for souvenirs is exciting, but you wouldn't want to carry the extra weight along for the whole pilgrimage, would you?"

She shook her head, still visibly disappointed. He put a hand on her shoulder.

"We'll come back to Stonebasin one day, you and I. As blooded members of the tribe, many new opportunities will be available to us. On our next visit, we can indulge ourselves a bit."

She brightened, and obediently returned her rucksack. When she came back, they set off down the trail together.

Their first destination was the Great Kiln, but Van's stomach began growling before they reached it. He hadn't eaten anything all day except for berries. Lilim was also peckish, so they took a detour to an open kitchen where there was still food being offered to hungry aspirants—stewed vegetables, cooked in celebration of the pilgrimage, and Van's favorite, buttered oatcakes. After eating their fill, they thanked the kindly woman at the kitchen for the warm meal, then struck out again.

Van pointed out the Great Kiln as it came into view, and Lilim's eyes widened in awe. Rather than a solitary structure, it was made up of several, each one joined to the others by a webwork of colonnades, so that passersby could look in from the street.

They stopped to watch the men and women of Stonebasin as they worked, hunched over their potters' wheels. Occasionally, the craftsmen stood to convey something in or out of one of the great ovens, where shaped clay was fired into finished products—art pieces like vases for the most part, but also ceramic tools and handiworks.

A giantkin was at work in the Kiln tonight who Van immediately recognized.

"Telgrim Earthshaper!" he called.

The older man looked up, and when he spotted Van, he grinned.

"Van the Scribe," the giantkin wiped his wet hands on the smock he wore and lumbered over to them. "When I didn't see you come down the trail, I worried some ill fate had forestalled you leaving Seat Dolse on your pilgrimage year."

Van shook his head, very much hoping Telgrim wouldn't clap him on the shoulder or pat his head with his enormous muddy hand. "I was only waiting for the crowds to depart."

"Well reasoned," said Telgrim. "And who is this little lady?"

Van pushed Lilim forward so she couldn't hide behind him. "This is Lilim the Brave, a dear friend. We have been sharing the road. I don't believe she's been to Stonebasin, so I am showing her around."

"Well met, young Lilim," said Telgrim, squatting down to get closer to her eye level. "I am called Telgrim Earthshaper, and I am headman here. I hope you enjoy your time in Stonebasin, and I invite you to help yourself to anything you need. You have my compliments on your choice of friends, for you must be very clever to have ingratiated yourself with young Van."

The headman managed to restrain himself from tousling her hair, merely nodding at her before standing back up.

"Where will you go next? The Scriptorium?"

Van only smiled. His love of books was infamous to anyone who knew the first thing about him, and it was no secret that the place where they were made was somewhat sacred to him. His expression hardened, however, when he remembered the errand they needed to see to beforehand.

"First I'd like to get some medicine for Lilim." He knelt and lifted the leg of her trousers slightly. "Though it occurs to me I didn't bring anything to trade."

Telgrim winced and sucked air through his teeth when he saw the blisters.

"I will write you a note," he said. "Take it to the apothecary, and when he sees I sent you, he'll give you ointment, free of charge."

Van smiled up at him appreciatively. "Thank you, Telgrim."

Before the headman turned to leave, an idea came to Van. He cupped his hand to Lilim's ear, ignoring the scarlet blush that spread across her face.

"Lilim, why not ask Telgrim for some more ink and parchment?" he whispered. "We could use it for our lessons, and he did say you should help yourself to anything."

"Headman Telgrim, um," she managed awkwardly. "Might we also have some parchment? And ink?"

Telgrim searched Van's face, and Van met his eyes without comment.

"A moment, please," Telgrim said in a businesslike tone before vanishing into the Kiln.

When he returned, he carried two written notes. One, he gave to Van, for the apothecary. The other, he offered to Lilim directly, kneeling in front of her.

"When you go to the Scriptorium, present this to whoever is on duty. They will be happy to furnish you with whatever you require."

Lilim accepted the note with both hands and a formal bow. "Thank you, headman."

Van felt pleased with himself, and with Lilim. Introducing herself to new people was a skill she needed to practice, and she would benefit from growing accustomed to being treated with respect and kindness by them. He trusted Telgrim to help with that lesson, knowing how much faith his father put in him. Farseer Daz had appointed Telgrim headman of Stonebasin in his early days as chieftain, when Ikann was Patron. He had proven himself a reliable leader and confidante in the years since. Van had known the kind giantkin from birth, and he trusted him with his life.

They bid farewell to Telgrim Earthshaper, departing next for the apothecary's workshop.

A little while later, with a jar of ointment in hand, Van beckoned Lilim to sit on an old stone bench while he gingerly rubbed the medicine onto her skin. He sincerely hoped she wasn't getting sick as he noticed her face flushed pink once again.

When he was finished, they made for the Scriptorium. Lilim didn't need to be told where to look this time—it was the largest freestanding structure in the community. The dedication above the entrance read, *"Preserve Knowledge, That It May Become Wisdom."* The adage resonated with Van, like everything else about the place, and he hoped that in time, Lilim would come to appreciate it, too.

The Scriptorium housed several expansive work areas where books were drawn and bound together, but Van took Lilim straight to his favorite station—the row of desks where scribes worked on illustrations.

There weren't many artists there at present. It was late in the day, and most of Stonebasin's residents were celebrating outdoors with the aspirants. Van had hoped to chance upon some young scribe working on a copy of *The Bull and the Snail,* but it was a rare work to begin with, and he'd known the place would be understaffed. He didn't recognize any of the pieces being sketched or colorized that day.

Regardless, they watched for a time. Some of the men and women here were scribes by trade. For them, it was a path chosen, either because they had talent or because they enjoyed the work. Others were acolytes, children of destitute households in most cases. For them, it would only be another chore. As much as Van treasured literature, he had no intention of letting his moniker become his profession. He would live out his days as a scribe only if crippling injury or age-related infirmity prevented him from serving the tribe as a ranger.

Spotting the Scriptorium's duty officer, Lilim approached with Telgrim's note. The old woman wore a plain brown robe with a wooden plaque around her neck, and when she spotted Lilim creeping toward her, she narrowed her eyes.

"I—" said Lilim, holding up the note.

"*Shhh!*" hissed the woman, putting a finger to her lips.

Lilim flinched, almost tumbling backward, but the woman steadied her and snatched the note. She scanned it quickly before departing, and when she returned a few minutes later, she held two fine leather cases, one for each of them. Inside Van's case were two rolls of parchment, two bottles of ink, and even a new quill—considerably more than he'd expected. The cases themselves were made cleverly, with a hook on one side that could be tied to their rucksacks, and firm, flat backs that could be used as a writing surface.

Lilim opened her mouth to thank the duty officer, but when the woman's eyes flashed with annoyance she closed it again, bowing instead. She and Van watched the scribes work for a little while longer, and then left for their next destination—the Temple to the Emissaries.

Though dusk had fallen hours ago, the community was still abuzz, enlivened by the visiting aspirants. Lilim, however, was already rubbing her eyes and biting back yawns. Thankfully, it was only a short walk further.

The Temple's stone doors were always open, allowing visitors to come and go freely. Above the entrance stood the ancient row of sculptures, each heavy stone carved in effigy of a skull. These were not human skulls, nor did they belong to startouched, wildborn, or any other of the noble races that populated Nemia. It was said these skulls belonged to enemies of the Emissaries—alien creatures, brutal and lawless, that had risen against the gods in the early days of creation. Now fallen and extinct, their names were lost to time.

Peering through the mammoth doors, Van saw that his choice to wait had been rewarded. Van and Lilim would have the Temple to themselves.

He walked between the pews to the altar, where he stood beneath another set of statues, these ones carved in the likeness of the Emissaries themselves. The female on the left wielded a longbow of elaborate design, while on the right, a male rested his hands on the pommel of a drawn greatsword.

Lilim's eyes swept back and forth across the hallowed sanctuary, her expression betraying no hint of whatever she was thinking or feeling. Van took a breath and knelt. Closing his eyes, he prayed aloud. It wasn't obligatory to do so, but it was his usual custom. And in any case, he wanted to show Lilim that she could do the same, if she liked.

"Gods of the land, my Emissaries," he began. "It is your humble servant Van the Scribe, come here on the year of my pilgrimage to seek your blessing of safe travel. I won't beg much of you, as I know you've heard many similar pleas today. I ask only that you favor us with opportunities to prove ourselves worthy of your love, and grant us the clarity of mind to choose wisely when confronted with difficult choices."

Van opened his eyes and tilted his head back, meditating in the presence of the statues. He then glanced at Lilim, who stood quietly a pace back from the altar, expression withdrawn. He knew she was tired. Just as he opened his mouth to ask if she wanted to leave, she fell to her knees and shut her eyes, joining her hands in prayer.

Unlike Van, she prayed in silence, a private dialogue between herself and her gods. Van retreated to the first pew, where he sat and waited.

Farseer Daz had made sure that his son was well educated, in matters practical as well as spiritual. While he had never commanded Van to pray, or required him to seek a deeper relationship with religion, Van had seen Daz pray often. He trusted his father, and in matters where he found he had no strong convictions of his own, he tended to emulate Farseer Daz. Thus, from a young age, Van had prayed as well.

He didn't consider himself a particularly spiritual person. He had merely been blessed with good role models. As he watched Lilim pray, he wondered if he was now becoming a role model to her. If it was so, he dearly hoped he was worthy of the mantle. When she opened her eyes, she joined Van on the pew, and they sat together for a time. She was fidgeting, another of her tells, but Van wasn't ready to leave. It was peaceful here, healing in ways he hadn't realized he needed.

"Lilim the Brave, do you think you can make it back to camp on your own? For my own reasons, I would stay a while longer, but I don't wish to deprive you of sleep."

A yawn finally escaped her. "Are we starting up our lessons again in the morning?"

"Of course," he promised.

She smiled at him with glassy eyes, then slid off the pew. Her footsteps retreated. He was alone.

Van slouched his shoulders and reclined against the pew, letting his exhaustion show only when there was no one left to see it, save for the Emissaries, who would always forgive him. He considered offering further prayer, but the only problem still muddling his thoughts was likely insignificant in the eyes of the gods. Even without divine insight, Van needed only to be honest with himself to know how things stood between him and the First Ranger of Vaxas.

He grew melancholy, and his thoughts soon drifted to his own walk back to camp. The padding of footsteps on the stone floor interrupted his brooding, and he turned to see that the Temple had another late visitor.

"Good evening, kinsman," said a boy Lilim's age, with a slight lisp. He smiled shyly at Van as he sat down on the pew across the aisle. His eyes were bright blue, and his front teeth were missing.

"Good evening," said Van, and because he didn't recognize the boy, he added, "Are you an aspirant?"

"I'm not," said the boy. "I just turned ten. But I can tell you are, and I'm excited for you. I hope you and the rest of the tribe find good fortune on the road."

"Thank you, kinsman," said Van, smiling softly. "Your day will come, and you will be better prepared when it does. I am Van the Scribe. It is good to have met you."

"And you," the boy agreed. "I'm Vauna Featherfriend."

Van couldn't help chuckling. "You must be fond of birds."

"They talk to me sometimes," said Vauna.

Van blinked. "What!"

The boy nodded matter-of-factly. "The first one was a horned owl. He was very rude, but he taught me a good trick for catching voles that I put to use right away at Papa's farm."

"You will grow up to be a shaman," Van blurted.

Vauna looked embarrassed, and if Van wasn't mistaken, a little sad.

"That would be nice," he said, his voice barely above a whisper.

They made no further conversation. Vauna prayed, and Van became lost in his own problems again. He wondered if at some point he'd fallen asleep, because he felt his eyes snap open, and he couldn't remember closing them.

Something about the Temple had changed, and it took Van a moment to understand why he thought so. Looking up, he was disoriented to see fine white flakes drifting down from above. His last conversation with Simon came to mind.

Snow.

But that was impossible. According to the foreigner, snow required a cooler climate to form. And it didn't quite make sense that such a thing could happen indoors. Van turned his palm up, waiting for a flake to land in it. When one did, he closed his hand and reopened it, reducing the flake to a dusty residue. Not white, but gray.

It wasn't snow. It was ash.

When he smelled something burning nearby, he looked around in bewilderment. But the temple wasn't on fire. How could it be? The whole place was made of solid stone.

"Greetings, fellow traveler."

Van's eyes fell on Vauna Featherfriend again, still sitting on the pew across from him.

"I couldn't resist the opportunity to meet you like this."

Vauna spoke in a voice that was not a child's. He was covered in ash, with dark pits where his blue eyes should be. Looking back at them was painful, like staring at the sun. It was as though they were shining, not too bright to look at, but neither were they dark. They gave off an intense negative light—not the absence of light, but its opposite. Whatever that was.

"We're going to do such great things together!"

The boy flung his arms wide for emphasis, and one of the appendages detached at the shoulder. It tumbled to the floor, burning away to nothing. Vauna stared at the severed arm with an expression of unconcerned disappointment. Finally, Van registered where the acrid smell was coming from him. The burning smell, like overcooked meat, was coming from inside Vauna.

"This body rots at my presence," said the horrible voice. "What a waste. But that's where you come in, isn't it?"

Van couldn't move or even speak. A gulf had opened between his mind and his body that could be bridged only with immense effort. The moment took on a dreamlike quality, and Van became captive to it.

"It seems I've arrived too early, though. She doesn't trust you yet. In fact, you two haven't even met. Not really."

"Who..." Van managed at last. "What...?"

The boy smiled, or at least, the tone in his voice made it sound like he was. There was little left resembling a human child, more pieces of him falling away by the moment, only to turn to ash on the floor.

"I've had as many names as there are dead stars scattered in the heavens," it said. "But I think the mortals of this world will know me as Anathema."

Before Van could blink, Vauna Featherfriend was gone. Nothing remained on the pew but a pile of clothes and ashes.

Strength returned slowly, and when Van could finally motivate his stubborn limbs to move, he fled the Temple. He shambled like a drunk back up the trail to camp, ash raining down on him all the way. By the time he reached his tent, he was convinced it was all just a nightmare. He crawled shivering into bed, hoping to slip into a different state of sleep, or escape to some other dream.

When morning came, he struggled to remember his time at the Temple following Lilim's departure, and try as he might, he could recall no details of his bizarre dream.

8 Starfletcher

Van awoke to sunlight streaming into his tent, realizing with a sinking feeling that he'd overslept and missed his appointment with Lilim. He dressed and packed as fast as he could, already late for assembly.

Otep was in the middle of his daily announcements when Van crept to the center of camp. He sat down quickly, hoping not to call attention to himself, and it was only then that he spotted Lilim among the gathered aspirants. She seemed oblivious to his arrival, and he didn't dare get up again just to find a new seat next to her.

"Additionally, Headman Telgrim has asked that we be on the lookout for a missing boy as we make our way north from the canyon," said Otep. "Vauna Featherfriend, ten years of age, has not been seen since last night. His family is concerned he may have fled home."

After summarizing the boy's physical appearance, Otep dismissed the assembly, and the procession departed minutes later. If anything else of note was announced that morning,

Van had missed it. He'd never heard the name Vauna Featherfriend, of course, but he committed the boy's description to memory in case he chanced upon him on the road.

Hoisting his pack, Van rushed to catch up to Lilim, then fell into step beside her.

"You look well today, Lilim the Brave," he said, making an effort to sound cheerful.

"Yes," she said simply.

"Did you sleep well?"

She kept her eyes straight ahead. "Yes."

Van adjusted the straps of his rucksack. "I'm sorry I missed our lesson today. I must have slept poorly, as I woke much later than I'd intended. Will you forgive me?"

"Yes," she repeated.

Van breathed a sigh of relief. "Thank you, Lilim. Regarding our studies over the next few days, I wanted to—"

A sniffle sounded beside him, and he clamped his mouth shut, finally realizing the depth of his error. He stopped and knelt in front of Lilim. Placing his hands on her shoulders, he saw that her eyes were shut tight, her cheeks wet with tears.

"I'm sorry," she choked. "I'm sorry for being so selfish. I'm sorry for always trying to keep you to myself. I won't do it anymore, I promise."

"No, Lilim, no..." Van said, shaking his head.

Shame welled up inside him. Not knowing what else to do, he put his arms around her, and she sobbed as she clung to him.

"I made a mistake, that's all," he soothed. "It doesn't mean I don't want you. Never think that. I told you I would walk with you, and I will. You have my word—I will stand by you, always."

He took her by the hand, relieved to see that she could keep walking, albeit with help.

Lilim's mood had only nominally improved by the time they made camp. She'd shuffled along for hours in complete silence, never letting go of Van's hand, sniffing pitifully every so often. But the morning trek gave Van time to concoct a plan that would serve as a proper apology. After helping her pitch her tent, he cleared his throat.

"Lilim," he said, his tone serious.

She looked at him and froze.

"Today, you will hunt with us."

Lilim stared vacantly, not quite understanding. Then, as if by reflex, she blurted out a series of well trodden excuses.

"I don't know how!"

"I will teach you," said Van.

"It's too scary!"

"I will be with you the whole time," Van assured.

"I'll get in the way!"

That one earned her nothing but a stern look. Van held out his hand and waited. After a particularly spirited bout of fidgeting, she took it. They went in search of Otep's party together, her expression a portrait of nerve-wracked anxiety.

Van's only concern was whether they would hunt in tandem with another tribe that day. To ask Lilim to hunt with the Mercurans was one thing, but if it was the Ikanni, that might still be a bridge too far. Thankfully, when they found Otep, they learned that the hunt would be shared only by other Dolsers.

"Well met, Van the Scribe," said the First Ranger, when Van arrived dragging Lilim behind him. "Who is…?"

Van bowed formally. "This is Lilim the Brave, the friend I told you about previously."

Otep bristled.

"With your permission, I would bring her along today," Van explained.

"She has neither bow nor arrows," Otep observed, sizing up the frightened girl.

"She will borrow mine," said Van.

"How, then, will *you* hunt?"

"I will set traps," said Van. "Or practice my knife throwing."

"You are very bad at knife throwing," sighed Otep, scowling down at him. "And I'm sure I told you before that we'll have no time to set traps."

Van straightened his back, refusing to back down. "Then I suppose I am useless. Will you send me away, First Ranger?"

Lilim clapped her hands to her mouth and gasped while Otep wordlessly held Van's gaze.

"Do not slow us down," the First Ranger finally grumbled. With that, he turned on his heel, leading his hunters out toward the plains.

"You will get in trouble!" Lilim whispered urgently.

"No, I won't." Van passed her his bow. "Otep Acrearms owes me some lenience, due to a bit of unpleasantness back home. Put it out of your mind."

He assumed that since it was not a joint hunt, they would again turn to Orum the Mutable to drive the gazelle. But when he inquired as to their strategy, Orum shook his head.

"I'm sorry, kinsman." Orum smiled weakly. "There will be a full moon tonight, which renders my abilities somewhat unreliable."

Unfamiliar with the intricacies of a skinchanger's talents, Van could only accept the explanation as offered.

"There are woodlands further east," said Otep, having overheard the exchange. "We will try our luck there."

Judging by what he'd seen yesterday, Van didn't think they would find much. If they were lucky, they might track down some smaller game animals—rabbits or wild turkeys, perhaps.

Upon reaching the woods, the party split into teams. Otep and Orum led a group north while Wilm continued east with another, deeper into the trees. Van and Lilim—along with half a dozen other undesirables—were left to fend for themselves.

Predictably, the hunting wasn't good. Not in the traditional sense, at least. Van let Lilim carry his bow so she could learn its feel as they picked their way through the brush, but they found no quarry to practice shooting at.

Hours later, when they all reconvened, only Wilm's group had anything to show for their efforts—a single pair of squirrels. Otep seemed ready to call the hunt off when one of the aspirants from Van's team made a surprise discovery. Just ahead, a third squirrel was asleep on a low branch.

The hunters approached cautiously, venturing no closer than forty yards for fear of waking it. The undergrowth was carpeted with a bed of dry leaves that crunched obnoxiously underfoot, but the squirrel remained asleep despite the noise.

The young Dolser who had first spotted the squirrel drew his bow and took aim, but his shot went wide, his arrow vanishing into the brush. Others came forward to test their archery skills, all of them missing their target. One attempt came close. The arrow lodged itself in the very branch the squirrel slept on, mere inches from its head. Still, the creature refused to stir.

Van pushed Lilim forward.

"Obviously, this is a difficult shot even for experienced archers," he whispered. "Don't worry about hitting the squirrel. Aim for the tree, and practice your form. Try without an arrow first."

Awkwardly, she took a stance and pulled the bowstring back partway, gauging the tension against her strength. It was an imitation of the other archers' posture. Though flawed, it showed she had been paying attention. Van adjusted her draw arm, easing her elbow into a more natural position.

"Imagine a straight line starting here." He tapped the elbow again. "It extends through your draw arm all the way to the hand—" he tapped her knuckle, tense on the bowstring, "—and then through to the bow arm." He touched the knuckle of her bow hand last. "Now, pull back as far as you can without losing that line or overexerting yourself."

She did as he asked.

"This is called full draw," said Van. "The last step is to release the string, thus placing your shot. Now, try it with an arrow."

She reached back with her draw hand and pulled an arrow from Van's quiver, fitting it to the string. She kept her bow arm straight and her eyes fixed on her target. Van was pleased to see she required no instruction in that regard. Yanking the string back to full draw, Lilim made a few last-second adjustments, then let the arrow fly.

It flopped sideways in the air, landing a few paces away.

"What did I do wrong?" she said, confused.

"Nothing significant." Van stepped forward to retrieve the arrow. "My first time was about the same, if memory serves."

Lilim made three more tries after a turn order was established. She surprised herself with her final shot, managing to land her arrow on the wide part of the tree near its base. It bounced harmlessly off the bark due to her lacking strength, but it was an encouraging improvement all the same.

Staring at the tree with her lips parted, she jolted when a cheer rose up behind her. The aspirants of Dolse were applauding, some of them whistling and crying her name. Lilim turned red as a beet, bowing stiffly to her kinsmen. The squirrel, meanwhile, slept inexplicably through the cacophony.

While good for morale, the game was becoming frivolous, and it was getting late besides.

"Wilm," Otep said to the wildborn next to him, chuckling as another novice archer missed the squirrel. "Would you kindly put an end to this?"

"I'm not sure that would be sporting," said Wilm, teary-eyed from laughter.

Otep crossed his arms and smirked. "Then do it blindfolded."

The First Ranger's words were heard by all, putting Wilm on the spot. He smiled and stood up, accepting the challenge.

The hunters of Dolse fell on him, tying a strip of cloth around his head twice to ensure he couldn't cheat. They spun him around a few times for good measure, then sent him stumbling forward with a shove. He groped at the empty air to his side until someone handed him his bow. His knees were wobbling as he took his stance. Van and Lilim held their breath.

The woods fell silent as Wilm nocked his arrow. Before he let it fly, he sucked in a breath and pierced the air with a primal shout, finally startling the squirrel awake. The only sound heard in the moment that followed was the scrabbling of its claws against the tree.

Wilm placed his shot.

The hunters laughed joyously as they hiked back to camp, despite having only three squirrels to show for their efforts. While they marched, they sang praise for the man of the hour. It was in this way that Van learned the prodigy marksman's full name was Wilm of the Horizon.

"You honor me, kinsmen," Wilm said after yet another round of applause. "But to be honest, the day's most impressive display came from Lilim the Brave. I don't believe I've ever seen such rapid improvement. With a bit more practice, her skills might rival those of the Starfletcher himself."

"Lilim the Brave!" shouted the aspirants. "Lilim Starfletcher!"

Her embarrassment was so great that she'd grabbed hold of Van's sleeve, seemingly trying to disappear into it.

To anyone who hadn't been there, the hunt was a failure. Otep's party was thus obligated to clean their kills themselves—all three squirrels. Van was quite good at skinning squirrels, so he demonstrated the technique for Lilim, and as always, she paid dutiful attention. With squirrels, most of the carcass was discarded as unusable, the tail included. One tail, though, was kept as a trophy.

"To commemorate your first hunt," said Wilm of the Horizon, offering Lilim the tail of the famous third squirrel, who they'd posthumously nicknamed Dozy.

Lilim accepted the tail with decorum, her eyes sparkling. "Thank you, kinsman."

"We can fashion it into an ornament," Van suggested. "I'll show you how later. You can wear it on your clothes or hang it someplace special back home."

The bonfire they were sharing gained another visitor, then. Otep and his rangers bristled when Simon of the Mists sat down, and because the foreigner remained silent, Van guessed his spell wasn't active yet. Van alone seemed unbothered by Simon's presence, a fact that drew the First Ranger's notice.

"I'd heard a rumor you were spending time with Simon of the Mists," said Otep, eyeing Simon warily.

"I have been," said Van. "He knows a spell that lets him understand us, but it only works for a little while each day. I have been using that time to, um, help him make sense of things."

"I am aware of this spell," said Otep. "He has used it on me in the past, and he has tried to use it on others."

Van frowned. "You speak as though you don't trust him."

"I don't," declared Otep.

"But my father called on us to accept him as an aspirant of the tribe," said Van. "You even defended Father in his ploy to save Simon's life."

"I obey my chieftain in all things," Otep replied simply.

Van narrowed his eyes. "Can I take that to mean you'll also make an effort to accept him?"

Otep spread his arms wide.

"Here I am sharing his company," said the First Ranger. "I believe that satisfies the chieftain's request."

Van fell silent in frustration, while Lilim played distractedly with Dozy's tail. Sensing a lull in the conversation, Simon made the talking sign, and Van nodded. He congratulated Lilim again on her performance, giving her a quick hug goodbye, then withdrew from the bonfire with the foreigner.

"Mind if we eat while we talk?" asked Simon. "I'm starved."

Van took him to the nearest supply cart and waited while he helped himself to the venison on offer. Van took some, too, realizing that Lilim's fit that morning had distracted him from finding anything to eat.

"Not half bad," said Simon, chewing a strip. "Just out of curiosity, what do vegetarians do on the Journey of Patronage?"

"Vegetarians?" asked Van.

Simon smiled. "A tragically common mental disorder, in some parts of the world. So, would I be right in assuming Mr. Acrearms isn't my biggest fan? No pun intended."

"Um," said Van.

"Don't worry about it," said Simon. "Rhetorical question."

Van was starting to think Simon was simply bored, and in the mood to amuse himself at Van's expense. But when he spoke next, he returned to his pragmatic self.

"Two things," said Simon. "First, I'd appreciate it if you kept me in the loop going forward about any stops we're planning on making. I had no idea what was going on yesterday."

Van grimaced. "I'm sorry, Simon. We got so caught up with other topics last time, it slipped my mind."

"Which brings me to thing number two," said the foreigner. "You pretty much called it, kid. Our new friend cornered me when I couldn't find you, and she wants to talk."

"The dark girl?" asked Van uneasily. "You're sure? Should we look for her now?"

Simon shook his head. "I haven't seen her today. But I told her about our arrangement—taking turns, being honest, and all that. She, uh… She said she'd play by the rules."

Van nodded. "If she gave you her word, that is good enough for me."

"I told you before," said Simon, his expression serious. "Dusken are pathological liars. Take whatever she says with a grain of salt, or several."

"You also told me you had never met one," said Van.

"Fair point." Simon rolled his eyes halfheartedly. "I guess it's good that you're open-minded. If you weren't, you probably wouldn't be talking to me."

Van wondered if this was what his father had meant, when he spoke of being generous of heart. "Did you have a chance to explore Stonebasin?"

"As a matter of fact, I did," said Simon with a grin. "Old Ghan took me into town and showed me around."

"Truly?" Van said, surprised. "Ghan Mudcatcher?"

"The very same," said Simon. "Turns out, you're not the only Nemian who can put up with me for more than five minutes."

Van sat back, impressed. "But wait, if you'd already used your spell talking with the dark girl, how did you communicate with Ghan?"

Simon shrugged. "There are plenty of ways to get a simple point across without opening your mouth. That goes double for wily geriatric types like me and Ghan. Clever move, by the way, letting every tribe bring one really smart old guy along."

"What did you think of our Temple to the Emissaries?" said Van.

"I took a pass," said Simon. "I've been in every kind of church there is, and I never exactly feel welcome in them, if you catch my meaning. But your Scriptorium was pretty great. That's an impressive operation you have going down there."

"Truly!" gushed Van, brightening. "You thought it impressive?"

"For sure," said the foreigner. "I mean, I'd already assumed you hadn't figured out the printing press yet, but don't feel bad about that. The West beat us to it, too."

Van wrinkled his forehead. "Printing *what?*"

"Press," said Simon. "It's a neat little invention that spits out book copies about a thousand times faster than the rate you're going now, and it more or less runs itself."

"What!" Van exclaimed.

"Yeah, you'd love it. I bet somebody here will get around to it soon. That's one of the funny things about technology. Most world civilizations tend to come up with the same solution to a problem around the same time, even when they're working independently from one another."

"Is it magic?" said Van, struggling to imagine what such an innovation would make possible.

"The printing press?" Simon waved a hand. "Nah, fully mechanical. It's a little strange, actually, now that I think about it."

"What is?"

"I've seen a lot of books since I got here," said Simon. "Comparable to anywhere else in the world, which shouldn't really be possible."

"What does that mean?" asked Van.

Simon shrugged. "You place a lot of value in the accessibility of information, I guess. That's a good thing. Impressive, like I said."

Van smiled. He had to admit, it was slightly gratifying to hear genuine praise from the foreigner.

They went to another bonfire to finish their meal while they talked, and again, the space was shared by other Dolsers. They stared guardedly at Simon as Van chatted with him, which spurred a strange thought.

"Simon, am I the only one that can understand you right now?"

"Yeah," he replied. "I can only aim the spell at one person at a time. Why?"

"How will we share conversation with the dark girl?"

"You've never had to work with a translator before, huh?" mused Simon. "Let me explain. When I aim the spell at you, you'll talk to me. Pretend you're talking to her, and say whatever it is you want to say. Then, I'll switch the spell to her and repeat your words in whatever language she speaks. Next, I'll listen to her, then I'll switch the spell back and repeat the process."

"That sounds... cumbersome," said Van.

"It'll take some getting used to," Simon conceded. "But if I do my part right, eventually, it'll feel like you're just having a normal conversation with her."

"Did she give any indication of what she wants to discuss?"

"None whatsoever," said Simon.

Van bit his cheek. "That's worrisome."

"Little bit, yeah." Simon nodded.

"You haven't asked for a turn yet."

"We've gone over the important stuff," said Simon, growing pensive. "What's the story with that girl you're always with?"

"Lilim the Brave?" said Van.

"Yeah, her," said Simon. "Seems like she's sort of a passion project of yours. Has she been holding up okay?"

"Yes, very much so." Van smiled. "She joined us on the hunt today, in fact. Otep's rangers were very supportive, and they were patient with her. She does so well, when she applies herself. But I, um."

He looked at his feet.

"I worry that I mishandle things with her, from time to time."

Simon studied him. "You're a pretty impressive kid, you know. You've taken a lot on, and I've barely heard you complain."

Van shrugged. "The pilgrimage calls on us to be our best selves."

"Best selves, huh?" Simon rubbed his chin. "Check out the kid sitting next to you. Don't actually look—he'll know we're talking about him. You want to know what he's been up to while you were out hunting with Otep, hanging out with the First Rangers, and making the world a better place?"

Van cocked his head.

"He takes double rations off the supply carts at lunch and again at dinner. Sometimes, he gets one of his buddies to go back around again and steal a third helping, if he's in the mood. With his free time, he bullies the younger kids into cleaning his clothes and gear for him, then he goes to bed early."

Van stared at Simon, dumbfounded. He didn't think the foreigner would lie about such a thing just to prove a point. "Have you spoken of this to anyone?"

"Who would I tell?" said Simon. "The big guy? Who's he going to believe? Ghan? Ghan's got enough on his plate already."

Van put his head in his hands, ashamed.

"I'm not trying to bring you down, kid," said Simon. "All I'm saying is you're doing a good job. So, cut yourself some slack."

Van nodded, trying to accept the compliment at face value. "Thank you, Simon."

The foreigner smiled. "You want to hit up one of the other carts before your next appointment? I think one of them still has strawberries, and apparently, no one will stop us."

Van declined Simon's invitation, waiting until evening meal before he ate anything more. He met up with Lilim again before sundown, catching her on her way back to her tent after some demonstration Ghan Mudcatcher was putting on for the younger aspirants.

It took him only a few minutes to debone Dozy's tail, scraping out the inside with the tip of his knife and salting the small trophy so it wouldn't start to smell before handing it back to her.

"Dozy was a pretty squirrel," she murmured, turning the tail over in her hands.

"He was," said Van.

"*She,*" corrected the girl.

Van smiled at her, and then unexpectedly, she took on a formal air.

"Van the Scribe, may I use some of our extra ink and parchment before our next lesson?"

"Telgrim Earthshaper gifted those things to you, Lilim," he said, slightly surprised. "You don't need my permission."

Van certainly had no reason to discourage her from practicing her writing in her spare time. If anything, it would save him some effort in planning future lessons. She thanked him anyway. They parted ways, agreeing to meet again in the morning.

A short while later, Van announced himself at the First Ranger's tent in the Vaxas campsite, and Brynda Blackblade invited him in. He found her alone, drinking tea. His copy of *The Bull and the Snail* was left out on the table.

"Punctuality, it seems, is not first among our cousin's virtues," Brynda said. "Please, make yourself comfortable while we wait for Galdur."

"It's no inconvenience," said Van, his gaze flitting to the picture book. "I hope you had ample time to enjoy Stonebasin?"

"I did," said Brynda. "Truly a testament to Dolser ingenuity."

"You honor us, First Ranger. Did tribe Vaxas hunt well today?"

"The hunting was poor," said Brynda, setting her teacup down. "But that is sometimes the case near large and busy communities."

Van nodded. "Ours was a bit of a disaster as well, albeit an unexpectedly pleasant one."

"Pleasant disasters can be good medicine for the heart," observed Brynda, a smile teasing her lips.

She craned her body to return her cup to her chest of drawers, allowing Van a glimpse of her profile—cheekbone, jawline, the nape of her neck. His face felt suddenly warm. He closed his eyes and coughed into his hand to distract himself.

"Was the book to your liking?" he asked.

"I'm grateful to you for lending it to me, cousin, but you were right in that it wasn't a particularly challenging text," said Brynda.

"Oh," said Van, trying to hide his disappointment. "Of course. I apologize for wasting your time with such things."

Brynda studied him quietly for a moment.

"I enjoyed the scene depicting the Bull rescuing the Snail from the rattlesnake. That was a clever change of pace for the story."

Van brightened. "That is my favorite part as well!"

"Taking that chapter into account, the story feels unfinished by the time you reach the end."

"I agree!" said Van. "In fact, I—"

Galdur Goldeyes stormed into the tent, then, muttering under his breath.

"Dolser *shits* took the better campsite again. I swear, the sooner we leave their lands, the better."

Following their nightly lesson, Van made his way back to his own tent. Brynda had returned his picture book, but Galdur made no mention of the thesaurus after Van gave him back his glowing trinket. The First Ranger of Ikann either wanted to make further use of it, or he had forgotten it existed.

In the dark of night, Van spotted a solitary figure as he crossed the empty fields between the campsites, the tall silhouette striking out across the twilit plains at a brisk pace. It took him only a moment to recognize the bow the lone hunter carried.

"Starfletcher!" Van called.

Sol Starfletcher stopped and glanced in his direction, changing course to meet him.

"Van the Scribe, if memory serves," the First Ranger greeted. "Does sleep elude you as well?"

"I was just heading to bed, actually," said Van.

"A shame," said Sol Starfletcher. "I'd thought to invite you to hunt with me when I heard you call, but I suppose you would do well to seek rest."

"It would be an honor to join you!" said Van. "However, I don't have my bow, and, um..."

He fumbled awkwardly with the picture book.

"We can stop by your tent first, if that suits you," said Sol.

"It does," Van said eagerly.

Sol Starfletcher followed him to his tent, where he traded *The Bull and the Snail* for his bow and quiver. The First Ranger seemed withdrawn as they ventured from camp, and Van wondered what he was doing out alone.

"Some would say it is late for a hunt, First Ranger."

"Some would say that," agreed Sol. "But the Phantom Nighthawk was not named arbitrarily."

Van winced, feeling like an idiot. Of course. Once again, he had forgotten all about the Nighthawk. He was too embarrassed to attempt further conversation, so they shambled over the terrain in silence—though that silence was soon broken. Van fumbled for his bow, nearly dropping it in his hurry to nock an arrow, as a mourn's howl pierced the night air. Sol only cupped a hand to his ear and listened, seemingly unafraid.

"Will you not ready a shot?" asked Van. "That sounded close."

"I'm afraid the limit of my ability allows loosing only one arrow at a time," said the First Ranger.

Confused, Van checked Sol's quiver, counting just two arrows in it.

They pressed on, watching and listening. Van kept his arrow fitted to his bowstring, holding it at half draw in case he needed to make a snap shot. It would be difficult to see a mourn coming in the gloom of night until it was practically on top of them. He didn't want to admit to the First Ranger the childhood fear of mourns he'd never quite outgrown, but to keep his nerves from fraying he made another try at idle conversation.

"Have you had any success tracking the Nighthawk?"

"Not as of yet," said Sol. "Perhaps you'll prove to be my good luck charm. Although…"

"Although?" echoed Van, only half paying attention as his eyes darted to every shadow that seemed to move.

"If the Nighthawk appeared before us, right here and now, would you attempt a shot? As I said, I am effectively without a weapon."

Van furrowed his brow, glancing at Sol. "It wouldn't matter if I did. I am not Otep Acrearms."

"There is no rule in my chieftain's game stating the trophy must be claimed by a First Ranger," Sol said casually.

Van probed his memory, realizing with a start that it was true. Interpreting the rules literally, the game could be won by anybody. Why would tribe Mercura open the competition to include every aspirant? It was senseless—but then, nothing about the game made sense in the first place.

Van was still dumbly pondering the revelation when the mourn bounded out of the darkness, fangs flashing in the moonlight. It was barely five yards from him by the time he spotted it.

He lifted his bow, but it was over before he could take aim. A bolt of lightning struck from the cloudless sky, vivisecting the mourn mid-pounce. The creature would have torn Van's throat out in another second, but instead it rolled lifeless in the dirt.

Sol's falcon glowed white hot where it had touched down, and then jumped to the First Ranger's hand to become an arrow again. Van didn't even register that he'd fallen until Sol helped him up, checking him for injury. Seeing he was unharmed, he smiled at him before giving his arm a reassuring squeeze.

"It would seem our true quarry has eluded us," said Sol. "Shall we head back?"

Van's near-death experience left him in a state of nonverbal shock for most of the return trip. So, as a change of pace, it was Sol that offered up idle banter.

"Why do they call you the Scribe, cousin?"

"What?" mumbled Van. "Oh. I believe I demonstrated some affinity for writing when I was young."

The silence quickly grew oppressive again.

"I suppose I don't need to ask why they call you Starfletcher. You're probably the greatest marksman alive."

"I am not the first Starfletcher," said Sol, surprising him by responding sentimentally. "With any luck, neither will I be the last. These arrows are passed down, earned once in a generation, and the title with them."

"With any luck?" echoed Van. "If that's true, then there will always be a Starfletcher. For as long as there are Nemians to take up the bow."

Sol set his jaw and looked to the horizon. "Just so."

9 Sexmaking

When Van entered Lilim's tent the following morning, he recognized right away that she had something on her mind.

"Did you find time to practice your writing?" asked Van, stifling a yawn.

"I haven't finished the, um, thing that I am working on," she said, fidgeting.

"In that case, did you have some other topic in mind for today?"

"Yes, actually," Lilim mumbled, averting her eyes. "Sexmaking."

Van blinked, certain he'd misheard her. "I, uh, beg your pardon?"

She locked her eyes on his, composed herself, and spoke slowly—as if to a child who was bad at following directions, or someone very old and hard of hearing.

"I would like to know about sexmaking."

Van was now fully awake. "Your mother and father might be better suited to teach that subject. They would be more knowledgeable about the, um, particulars of the act itself, and about things such as childbirth."

"I know about that already." Lilim stared straight at him.

"Oh," said Van flatly. "You do."

Was this his cue to be relieved?

"What I'd really like to know is what one should consider when choosing a partner for it."

"Oh." Van stuttered again, shrinking into himself. "Well, I suppose there are two opinions. Views that are common and considered acceptable, I mean. Some believe sexmaking is best reserved for a partner you share a deep bond with, that you've devoted yourself to with the intention of building a life together. Others feel that sexmaking should be sought casually. For the simple, um… the simple pleasure of it."

Lilim nodded attentively. "And which would it be between us?"

"Sorry?"

Lilim spoke as before, enunciating each word. "If you and I were to do sexmaking together, would it be of the former kind, or the latter?"

Van stared blankly. "It would be neither, Lilim the Brave. I don't look upon you that way."

She nodded again, breaking eye contact. "I'm very tired this morning. I think I will go back to bed until assembly. You should do the same."

Van shook his head, bewildered. "If I said something to—"

"Leave, please," she said, already turning over in her bedroll.

Utterly confused, he left her tent, stepping out into the still-dark camp.

It was almost an hour until sunrise, but going back to bed seemed silly and futile. Instead, Van went to the center of camp and simply waited.

Ghan Mudcatcher and Otep Acrearms arrived at dawn, followed by the aspirants of Dolse. Lilim startled Van half to death when she plopped down beside him, but she smiled politely and seemed her usual self.

Van was soon brought up to speed on the announcements he had missed yesterday—most important among them, the procession's route north from Stonebasin. Their next destination was Third Stone, a six days' march. From there, three days more would bring them to Farthest Tree, beyond which lay the lands of Ikann.

Van tried to gauge Lilim's mood as they walked hand in hand that morning, but she was as cheerful and chatty as ever. Because they'd skipped their morning lesson, he quizzed her on history while they traveled.

"Tell me everything you know about the chieftains of Nemia. Start with tribe Ikann, since we'll reach their lands first."

Lilim furrowed her brow in thought. "The chieftain of Ikann is Rhaggo Bullbreaker. He is giantkin, like Otep, and very strong."

"When was he appointed chieftain?" Van prompted.

"Twenty years ago."

"Nineteen," Van corrected. "What about his predecessors, or noteworthy accomplishments?"

Lilim only shook her head, so Van cleared his throat and reviewed the most important points.

"Rhaggo Bullbreaker was preceded by Dorin Ironhand, who was preceded by Gul the Coming Storm. Gul was appointed chieftain of Ikann thirty-six years ago and led the Ikanni for just nine years—the full length of the last Cycle of Ikanni Patronage. It was by Gul's decree that rangers of Ikann were allowed to collect tributes from settlements throughout the Eastern Plains, including those of other tribes."

Lilim's face fell, her pace slowing. He couldn't blame her. It was a scary story, and he remembered reacting the same way when he first heard it.

"The tributes were compulsory, collected under threat of force to provide food and resources to Seat Ikann. Dolser farmsteads and family homes were even burned or raided, out near the borderlands."

Lilim stared up at him. "So they *do* steal from us!"

"Let me finish," said Van. "Gul the Coming Storm was removed as chieftain twenty-seven years ago by decree of tribe Mercura in the first months of the current Cycle of Mercuran Patronage. The elders of Ikann appointed Dorin Ironhand to replace him, and he swore an oath to my fa—"

Van coughed.

"—to chieftain Daz, that the collection of any such tributes would forevermore be condemned as a criminal act. When Dorin Ironhand died nineteen years ago, the Ikanni appointed Rhaggo Bullbreaker to succeed him."

Lilim chewed her lip, pensive. "So they *don't* steal anymore?"

"There have been no confirmed accounts of Ikanni aggression against their neighbors since Dorin Ironhand assumed power," said Van—a noncommittal but strictly factual answer. "All right. Tribe Vaxas next."

"The chieftain of Vaxas is Atariel the Longliver," said Lilim.

"Atariel the Everliving," corrected Van.

"I don't know anything about him."

"*Her*," said Van. "She is startouched, and quite old—her earned name should have given you a hint about that. But otherwise, I don't know much about her either. Little is known about tribe Vaxas in general. For now, I think it's enough that you remember her name, and that she has ruled her tribe for a very long time."

"Tribe Mercura next?" asked Lilim, brightening a little.

Van nodded.

"The chieftain is Galeena Greatmother!" she said excitedly. "She is human, like us, and she is kind and wise. She has ruled tribe Mercura for fifty-five years."

"All of those things are true about Galeena Greatmother," said Van. "However, she is not the chieftain of Mercura."

"What!" Lilim balked at him.

"Galeena Greatmother passed away three years ago. Scaela the Listener was appointed in her place."

"Who is Scaela the Listener!" exclaimed Lilim, mortified.

"A young startouched woman, from what I've heard," said Van. "Though it seems she makes few public appearances. She does not travel from her Seat in the Western Forest, and it is believed she has some illness or affliction that makes contact with others inadvisable. Rumor has it she is cared for only by a few handpicked attendants. She has, however, formally renewed all oaths sworn by her predecessor, including those that place tribe Dolse under special protection."

Lilim nodded along, but her attention seemed to ebb, and her enthusiasm had dwindled. Van stopped there for the day, worried he was setting too quick a pace for a new subject. They spoke instead of inconsequential things until the procession made camp, chatting as friends do and enjoying the fair weather.

Simon was quick to find Van when he returned from the hunt that afternoon, and today, he had the dark girl with him. Van and the foreigner exchanged the hand sign, and Van led them to his tent, drawing suspicious glances from every aspirant they passed along the way. Van studied the dark girl as they walked through camp, remembering Simon's myriad warnings, as well as those of his own tribe's elders. She didn't look dangerous. If she meant him harm, she'd already had every opportunity.

Since she was found almost a year ago, Van had been responsible for her needs as a guest of Seat Dolse. Van felt sure she could have managed on her own, had it not been for the tribe's cold aversion. Farseer Daz chose Van for the job because he trusted his son, and Van in turn chose to set aside conventional wisdom because he wanted to be worthy of that trust. As chores went, it hadn't been demanding—he brought her food and clean clothes once a day, and little else. Sharing a simple conversation with her wasn't asking much more.

The dark girl was only slightly taller than Lilim, though her figure was more mature. Van guessed her adolescence was nearly behind her, as his own was. Her eyes were a more vibrant shade of blue than Simon's—a bright pastel, where his were muted, like cloudy glass. Shabby attire and hair grown wiry from want of being brushed detracted from her other features, which under better circumstances might have been striking.

"One more thing you should know," said Simon, following the direction of Van's gaze. "Dusken are like regular elves in that we both live a lot longer than humans. She might look your age, but she could be as old as I am. Or, for all we know, old enough to be my grandmother."

"Thank you, Simon," said Van, looking away.

The three of them crowded into Van's tent, where he and Simon sat down cross-legged. The dark girl watched them take their places, following suit a moment later so they formed a triangle. The space was markedly more cramped with three occupants, but they had enough room to sit without bumping knees or elbows.

Simon spoke first to Van. "I already explained to her how it works. She told me that you could go first."

"Very well," said Van. "I suppose introductions would be appropriate, since this will be our first time really talking. Tell her my name, and ask for hers, please."

"Practice speaking like I told you," said Simon. "Talk to her, not me. I'll translate word for word."

Van tried again, turning his attention to the dark girl to see if the process came more naturally.

"Since this is our first real conversation, allow me to introduce myself. I am called Van the Scribe. If you would be so kind, what may I call you?"

Simon shifted his spell to her and spoke in a language Van couldn't understand.

The dark girl responded, *"Shale."*

Simon then turned to Van. "Shale. Guess you didn't need me for that one."

Van nodded, trying to keep his attention on Shale. She met his eyes, her expression neutral.

"How old are you?"

Simon repeated his words, then listened to her one-word response. Simon spoke again to Shale, possibly reminding her that their arrangement called for honesty, at which point she repeated the same word. Finally, Simon looked back to Van.

"She says she's fifteen."

Van tilted his head, his eyes narrowed.

Simon shrugged. "That's what she says, kid."

"All right," said Van. "That's two questions. You may tell her it is her turn."

Simon spoke briefly to Shale, who then said a short phrase back—Van guessed five distinct words. Her tone suggested something impulsive, almost teasing, but not categorically dishonest, if such things could be discerned from a few otherwise meaningless syllables.

"Oh boy," muttered Simon, looking uncomfortable. "Maybe we should rethink this. I forgot to tell you, dusken have different sensibilities when it comes to certain things."

"What did she say, Simon?"

His eyes darted. "Some context might be important to—"

"Do it the way you said you would, please."

Simon took a deep breath, closed his eyes, then opened them again.

"Have you ever had sex?"

Van blinked, momentarily disoriented. He finally found himself speaking directly to Shale, nearly forgetting Simon's presence entirely.

"No!" blurted Van.

"Have you ever kissed a girl?"

"No!"

Her head tilted. "Have you ever kissed a boy?"

"No." He gritted his teeth.

"If you could kiss a boy or a girl right now, which would you prefer?"

"That is three questions for you," he snapped. "It is my turn now."

"If you insist."

Van crossed his arms, thinking. "What skills do you take pride in?"

Simon couldn't translate her answer this time, because it wasn't a verbal one. She simply vanished from sight. One moment she'd been sitting there, the next, gone.

"Uh-oh," uttered Simon, speaking for himself again.

"She can turn invisible?" Van studied the empty space.

"I guess so, yeah." Simon's face was taut with anxiety.

Van sighed. "It's all right. I asked her to demonstrate her skills, so I suppose that's what she's doing. I understand."

"You really don't," said Simon.

Van cocked an eyebrow.

"See, I'm running another spell right now, one I can keep up pretty much around the clock," he said. "Lets me see invisible things—call it old sorcerer paranoia. And what you should try to *understand* is that it isn't working on her, which is seriously stressing me out."

Van felt something tug at his earlobe. He looked around and saw nothing.

"She's behind you, isn't she?" asked Simon.

"I believe so."

Van surveyed the tent calmly, panning slowly from left to right. Something soft and warm brushed his mouth, and he stopped. There came a nibble, playful and inviting, followed quickly by a wicked bite that made him flinch back in pain. Shale reappeared sitting in the same position as previously, startling Simon. She licked her lips and smiled.

"You okay, kid?" Simon studied him.

"I'm fine," said Van.

There was a metallic taste in his mouth. Van sucked his lower lip, hoping Simon hadn't noticed the drop of blood. He recomposed himself while Shale spoke a short phrase, prompting Simon to return his attention to Van.

"She says it's—"

"As before, please," Van interrupted.

"It's still your turn."

Van nodded, trying to clear his head.

"Where did you... that is, *how* did you..." Van hesitated, considering his choice of words.

In the end, he decided it was safer to simply reuse the same question he'd asked Simon. It was more open ended and felt less accusatory than what had first come to mind.

"Tell me of your homeland."

Shale giggled. It took Van a moment to realize that Simon must have translated his initial stammering in addition to the question he wanted to ask. He shot Simon a nasty look, but the foreigner only held up his hands, as if to say, *You told me to do it this way!* Shale gave a lengthy response this time, and Van kept his eyes on her as Simon translated.

"I was firstborn to High Priestess Razelle Chivarn, ruler of the nation-city of Eventide. I have a brother, but he was small when I left. Eventide is the greatest nation-city to have risen in the Twilight World in the past five hundred years. It has many vassals, the tiniest and most insignificant of which dwarf the village you call home. The last insurrection against my mother was put down years before I was born, all dissidents rooted out and put to death."

She paused, seemingly thinking over the next part.

"Since that time, the people of Eventide have lived decadently. When I came of age, I realized my mother and her subjects had become soft and complacent with the passage of time, so I took my leave of them. May I have a turn now?"

"Of course," said Van nervously.

"The elf tells me our current travels are related to what you call the 'Journey of Patronage.' Explain this Journey to me, and why my participation was made mandatory."

Van nodded slowly, considering how to answer. She almost certainly knew he had explained this to Simon already, and she could have asked him. But she had chosen not to. She wanted to hear it from Van, in his own words.

"The Journey of Patronage is an ancient rite performed in cooperation and solidarity between the four tribes of Nemia once every nine years. It serves two main purposes. First, it marks a Nemian's coming of age. Anyone who is at least twelve years of age is expected to join the pilgrimage in order to be considered blooded members of their tribe upon their return."

He waited several seconds to allow Simon to catch up.

"Second, the pilgrimage serves as a peaceful means for the tribes to compete to determine Patronage—that is to say, which tribe will serve as the foremost authority in Nemia for the next nine years. Each tribe elects one member of suitable age to represent them as First Ranger, and these individuals are issued challenges by the chieftains of the land. Whichever First Ranger is deemed victorious in the greatest number of challenges wins Patronage for their tribe."

He then listed the names and titles of the First Rangers and Pilgrimage Guides, proudly mentioning that Otep Acrearms had won the game hosted by Farseer Daz, placing tribe Dolse —at least for the time being—in the lead.

Shale considered all this before speaking again.

"How is the status of Patronage enforced?"

"I'm not sure I understand the question," said Van.

"If, at the end of this Journey, the other three tribes are unsatisfied with the result, why do they not rise up against the winner and claim rulership through force?"

"Because it would be senselessly destructive," Van sputtered, surprised at the suggestion, though it did align with what

Simon had warned him to expect of her. "No tribe stands to benefit from pointless bloodshed. Open war could also render the land itself irreversibly ruined, in which case, the victor would have doomed even themselves. Such a thing hasn't occurred since before the founding of the tribes."

"I see," she said dismissively. "And what exactly is expected of me on this Journey? By your own account, there are only four of us who actually matter. Are the rest just here to bear witness to their deeds?"

Van frowned. "As I mentioned, the pilgrimage is a rite of passage for all of us. This applies to you as much as anyone, if not more so. My father, the chieftain of Dolse, risked his life to broker a deal with the other tribes, placing you under our protection. You have been spared from exile and death, provided you undertake the pilgrimage."

Van paused for emphasis, and to allow Simon time to translate.

"We are each charged with seeking a better understanding of our countrymen—the members of the other tribes traveling with us. We share our knowledge, our cultures, and our heritage to strengthen the bonds of friendship between us and further serve the pursuit of lasting peace and security throughout Nemia."

Shale smiled in a way that unsettled Van. "And how am I to do any of that when so many of you find me utterly repulsive?"

"Um," mumbled Van, fighting an urge to swear when Simon repeated the awkward syllable.

"That you sought out Simon and I to have this conversation is, I think, a good start," he finally said.

Shale's smile dropped for a moment. Since she appeared receptive, Van went on.

"I realize it's not ideal that we don't understand your language, and can't communicate with you outside of settings like this one. The best advice I can offer is that you try to speak through your actions. Show us in your conduct that you respect our values, if you want to be accepted. Lend a helping hand when and where you see the need, and the rest should follow."

Van couldn't tell whether she was taking any of it to heart. Her expression had grown distant. If nothing else, Van felt he'd made his best effort to comport himself as his father had prescribed when he saved her life.

Next, Shale asked Van to teach her how to say "please" and "thank you" in his native language. It seemed a good idea—those words would indeed prove useful. Simon took a break from translating as Van guided her pronunciation until she could repeat the phrases adequately. Her Nemian was heavily accented, but discernible.

She peppered him with further questions, and Van didn't interrupt or ask for a turn. What little Shale had told them of herself left him with questions of his own, but he was comfortable letting today's meeting be for her benefit. Her inquiries turned from Nemia to topics that concerned the world at large, and because Van knew nothing of matters beyond his country's shores, he yielded their remaining time to Simon.

Once Simon's spell had nearly run its course, they quickly said their farewells, and Shale told Van that she would seek him out again another day, perhaps after she'd had a chance to put his advice into practice. As she stood and turned to leave, she glanced over her shoulder.

"I apologize if I stole something you were saving for someone else," she said.

And with that, she left him alone with Simon.

"I know why she's here," said Simon after a moment.

"You do?" Van turned to him.

Simon nodded. "If she really is the first child of a High Priestess, then yeah. Their religion calls for all their priestesses to sacrifice their firstborn to that spooky murder god of theirs, the Twilight Prophet. Shale's here because she ran away from home. Because she wanted to live."

For Van, that took time to sink in. "If that's *why* she's here, that still doesn't tell us how she *got* here."

Simon shrugged. "If you're operating under the assumption she's being honest with us, then you can ask her yourself."

Another pause hung between them as Van tried to envision how to approach that conversation.

"Anyway, our time is about up, so..." Simon stood, but hesitated. "Did she actually swipe something when she pulled that stunt earlier? If she did, I can probably convince her to give it back."

"No, Simon," said Van wistfully. "I don't suppose you could."

Shale, as it turned out, intended to act on Van's advice the very next day. While he was sharing midday meal with Lilim, Shale sat down unceremoniously opposite the bonfire. Predictably, most of the other Dolsers took it as their cue to leave.

"What's the dark girl doing here?" whispered Lilim. "She's looking right at you."

"Her name is Shale, and she is a friend," said Van, trying to sound unbothered as he finished his venison.

"You have strange friends, Van the Scribe," mused Lilim.

After Van finished his meal and gave Lilim an affectionate hug goodbye, he went looking for Otep, Shale following close behind him. It was an obvious turn of events, in retrospect, and Van felt frustrated that he hadn't seen it coming.

"What is she doing here?" asked Otep, narrowing his eyes at Shale when they strolled up together.

A large group stood behind Otep today. Orum the Mutable and Wilm of the Horizon were there, along with sixteen others.

"Um," muttered Van. "I believe she wants to hunt."

Otep scowled. "If I allow this, you will take full responsibility for her actions."

Van didn't like the sound of that at all, but he didn't want to see Shale turned away for following his counsel. He agreed.

Van quickly learned the hunt would be another joint effort with tribe Vaxas. He had been looking forward to this chance since the day he'd watched Brynda take down the hornbeast. But now, instead of seizing the opportunity to prove himself a reliable hunter, he was stuck chaperoning Shale.

Further souring his mood was the rain that battered their backs. Van himself was warm and dry under his fine half cloak, but Shale's cheap rags were soaked through in minutes. Van felt a pang of indignity for her that day, trudging along in bitter silence, her long hair hanging in matted clumps.

Eventually, the rangers came upon a stand of trees. It seemed Otep Acrearms was also of a mind to impress—he revealed Orum's abilities as a skinchanger to Brynda. Intrigued, she assembled her archers behind the tree line, hidden from the gazelle Orum would drive their way from the east. At Otep's command, the rangers of Dolse positioned themselves likewise.

Shale watched, then turned to Van.

"*Please*," she said, pointing at his bow.

Van shook his head. Even though he wouldn't be able to use it while babysitting Shale, he remembered what Otep had said to him when he'd lent it to Lilim. He didn't want the First Ranger to see him without a weapon again.

Shale growled, scrunching her eyebrows for a moment, then pointed at his knife. "*Please.*"

Hesitantly, Van handed the knife over. She slipped it partway out of its sheath to inspect the blade, then turned and marched deeper into the woods, seemingly satisfied. With a sigh, Van followed after her.

Shale crouched forward as she trudged through the woods, feeling around in the undergrowth for spoor. Twice, she stood bolt upright and stilled—cocking her head as if to listen and sniffing the air. It was hard to imagine how vastly this ecosystem differed from what she'd known growing up. Living in some sunless cave, the so-called "Twilight World," sounded patently awful to Van. Watching her dig through the mud, though, it was easy to imagine she had the same opinion of the woods.

At length she gave up, and they returned to the others. Van was pleased to see they hadn't yet missed the action.

Shale hunkered in an alcove formed by the entwined roots of two large jackalberries, watching the rangers of Dolse and Vaxas. Van leaned against a sturdy trunk and did the same, listening to the conversations of the archers lying in wait.

Brynda's favorite hunting partners were with her again that day. Van learned they were sisters, Rhys the Catcher and Rhyla the Tamer. When the gazelle finally appeared, Rhys outperformed her older sister, taking three down while Rhyla claimed only two. Brynda Blackblade took no part in the action this time, instead standing back to evaluate her rangers' performance. When the commotion subsided, she decided to make an example of Rhyla the Tamer.

"Take your stance," she ordered.

When Rhyla did as she asked, Brynda walked a slow lap around her, scrutinizing her posture. She made adjustments without comment, pushing Rhyla's elbow up and her hips forward. Van watched Rhyla's expression as the First Ranger placed her hands on her. She tensed. Her breath quickened, and she stole furtive glances at Brynda while she patiently attended her. In that moment, Van felt a pang of sympathy for the young ranger, because it seemed to him she harbored feelings for Brynda that went beyond simple admiration.

"Where is your charge?" barked Otep, startling Van out of his unintended voyeurism.

"My what?" Van glanced behind him.

The alcove under the jackalberries was empty. Shale would have had to pass right in front of him, but it occurred to him that she could pass undetected anywhere she liked at any time. Van swore under his breath and braced himself for Otep's reprimand, but it never came. He was rescued by none other than Shale herself.

She appeared from behind the jackalberries, covered in mud up to her knees and elbows. Stepping lightly, she hopped off the twisted roots to land next to Van and threw two fox carcasses at Otep's feet, putting her hands on her hips and grinning.

Otep and the rangers of Dolse gathered behind him simply stared. Shale carried one fox back to camp, and Van the other, for no member of Otep's party would touch an animal slain by the dark girl.

The rain softened to a drizzle on their march back, and after parting ways with the Vaxals, the hunters of Dolse piled their gazelle near a bonfire to be cleaned by their younger kinsmen. Shale skinned both foxes herself, and clutched at the hides when Van approached offering to take them away.

"She wants them as trophies, then?" mused Otep, observing their nonverbal spat. "Very well. Tell her she may do as she pleases."

"She wouldn't understand me," Van said, frowning.

Otep snorted. "I think she understands you better than you realize."

On his way to Brynda Blackblade's tent, Van rehearsed his plan for the evening's tutoring session. They would start by reviewing synonyms. Galdur Goldeyes was not a quick learner, even with the thesaurus, but Van believed that enough repetition could get through to anyone.

Their last few meetings had made it clear to Van that their lessons were for Galdur's benefit alone. Why the First Ranger of Vaxas would make it her business to elevate the First Ranger of Ikann, he had no idea, but he supposed he could no better explain his choice to elevate Lilim. Whatever was going on between Galdur Goldeyes and Brynda Blackblade, Van trusted it was in keeping with the spirit of the pilgrimage.

Van announced himself in front of the First Ranger's tent, but for the first time, he didn't hear her answer. He waited and tried again.

Still nothing.

To enter without permission would be exceedingly rude. Brynda was of another tribe—and a First Ranger at that.

Then again, didn't he already have permission? And wouldn't she assume only that he was being considerate if he saved her the trouble of getting the space ready?

Van crept inside, finding the tent arranged as usual. He stepped around the table and knelt at Brynda's chest of wooden drawers, retrieving ink and parchment from the first drawer, and quills from the second. As he set them on the table, it occurred to him that knowing what other supplements were on hand could help him in planning future lessons. With that in mind, he checked the lowest drawer as well, but he was quickly interrupted by the sound of approaching footsteps.

Galdur and Brynda entered together, and a moment of dread silence ensued as their eyes fell on Van.

"Please forgive me, First Ranger," Van pleaded to Brynda, his head bowed. "I entered uninvited thinking I might make myself useful by setting the table, but I can tell from your expressions I've overstepped."

Galdur surged forward threateningly and opened his mouth, but Brynda spoke over him.

"There is nothing to forgive, cousin. I asked you to be here. If anything, it is we who owe you an apology, for our tardiness."

The tension dissipated, and the First Rangers took their seats—though Galdur Goldeyes cast venomous glares in Van's direction for the rest of the night.

Van explained the evening's assignment, which focused on varied word choice when writing long texts. As before, he invited his students to use their previous work as a starting point by considering alternatives for words they identified with personally. Brynda completed the exercise with ease, but Galdur Goldeyes grew frustrated, consulting Van's thesaurus several times to help him with his selections.

"What's wrong with reusing the same word to begin with?" complained Galdur.

"Readers find it tiresome," said Van. "Repetitious diction can cause a reader to become bored and inattentive. Worse, it invites the belief that a text's author might simply be lazy. If readers can't trust the author in this way, and if they otherwise find no pleasure in reading a text, they may abandon it, in which case, you would have written it for naught."

Van stood behind them, watching while they worked. Galdur was making fewer spelling errors today, thanks in large part to the thesaurus, but Van winced when he noticed he'd listed "brave" as a synonym for "strong."

When he stepped over to review Brynda's progress, he blinked in surprise. She had used a word he didn't recognize at all.

Coy ~ Shy, Bashful, Coquettish

Van felt put on the spot, and admittedly a little embarrassed. Of course, he could simply choose not to call attention to the gap in his knowledge. But doing so would be a disservice to his students. Besides, Van always enjoyed learning new words, and doing so tonight would give him an excuse to talk to Brynda.

"Brynda Blackblade," said Van. "I must confess, I don't think I've encountered that word before."

"It's somewhat antiquated, so I'm not surprised." She smiled as she met his eyes. "Perhaps I chose it to have a bit of fun at your expense. Or, I suppose you could say I was being *coquettish.*"

Van furrowed his brow, to which Brynda politely chuckled.

"I believe I learned it from my mother," she said, lowering her voice wistfully. "As your assignment requires, it is synonymous with 'coy,' a word I tend to overuse. But it implies something more playful. Specifically, it carries connotations of romantic flirtation."

Van coughed and looked away, his cheeks burning. Galdur narrowed his eyes at him, but Brynda simply fell backward and shook with childlike laughter.

"I'm sorry, cousin," she said, struggling to breathe. "Truly. With that, I believe you may indeed be forgiven for poking your head into my tent. The look on your face!"

Unlike with Galdur, Van sensed no underlying cruelty in Brynda's words. She was enjoying herself, at ease as only someone among friends could be. Van sighed and smiled at her to show he'd taken the joke in the spirit it was meant.

The lesson concluded without further incident. Brynda volunteered herself for cleanup duty, bidding Van and Galdur goodnight. They left the tent together, and Van quickly veered toward his own campsite, eager to get away. But Galdur followed.

"I see the way you look at her, you know," sneered Galdur Goldeyes.

Van balled his fists, keeping his eyes forward.

"Did you hear me, Dolser?"

"I heard you, First Ranger," said Van quietly. "But I have no idea what you're talking about or who you are referring to."

Galdur scoffed. "Playing dumb suits you well enough, though perhaps I'll tell our cousin about your lustful thoughts when next I see her."

Van halted, snapping his head to face him. "I doubt she would believe any such accusations."

Galdur's yellow eyes flashed as he savored Van's thinly veiled distress. "It *is* hard to believe, I'll give you that. Let us make a deal. Swear to me here and now that you'll never again entertain such disgusting intentions, and I'll keep this unpleasantness between us."

Van spoke through clenched teeth. "I harbor no untoward thoughts involving Brynda Blackblade."

Galdur braced his hands on his knees and laughed. "So serious!"

Van stewed in rage and shame while Galdur slowly recovered from his fit of laughter.

"Well, I suppose deep down, Dolsers must realize they should stick to their own kind," said the Ikanni, straightening up with a sigh—but he soon shook with renewed laughter. "Though perhaps even Dolser tramps have standards!"

With those parting words, the First Ranger sauntered away, still cackling with glee. Van watched him go, finally alone, but he was now far too angry to sleep. Angry at Galdur Goldeyes, for certain, but also at himself. He did not have a high opinion of Galdur's intelligence. If even he had noticed Van's feelings for Brynda, it would be foolish to believe Brynda herself hadn't.

It wasn't fair. Van had no intention of ever acting on his feelings. He hadn't anticipated having them to begin with. Instead of returning to his tent, Van wandered the nearby fields. He gazed up at the stars, waiting for his head to clear and exhaustion to call him to bed. Strangely, he thought he heard singing, and his wandering mind again strayed to Brynda.

A little too quickly, he whipped his head around and took a step toward the sound. His foot caught on a rock, and he fell nose first in the dirt. The singing cut off abruptly. A quiet giggle made him look up, still on his hands and knees.

He could only see Shale in the dark because her white hair reflected the moonlight. She whistled, waving him over. Shakily, he stood up, dusted himself off, and walked to where she was.

Shale sat alone on a boulder, its surface smooth and flat. She slid over and patted a spot beside her, staring down at Van expectantly. He accepted the invitation, hoisting himself up and sitting down cross-legged next to her. It wasn't the first time he'd seen her in a place like this. Sometimes, on sleepless nights back home when he took to restless wandering, he'd noticed her—the dark girl—alone in the night, sitting on some solitary stone. He hadn't gone near her those times.

Van didn't realize his nose was bleeding until Shale pressed a square of cloth to his face, staunching the trickle. As disoriented as he was from his fall, and from Galdur's poisonous words still echoing through his head, he didn't resist. She withdrew her hand after a time, seemingly satisfied, and Van watched as she absentmindedly licked a drop of blood off her fingertips.

Once again, Van looked up at the stars, and Shale did the same.

"I don't know how I'm going to keep this up," he said. "And Simon is right, there's nobody I can admit that to."

Shale stretched and lay back, saying nothing.

"I thought I heard you singing," he continued, finding it calming to talk to someone who couldn't understand a word he was saying. "Actually, I thought it was someone else. Or I may have just imagined it. Whatever it was, it sounded nice."

Shale began singing again as they watched the stars together. It wasn't so different from the songs mothers sang to fitful children, on nights when sleep was hard sought. The words were alien, but a quality in them told Van their purpose was to soothe—and because he needed it badly, he allowed himself, just for a while, to be soothed.

Only then, listening to Shale sing, did his thoughts return to what he'd seen in Brynda's tent. He had shut the drawer and retreated to his side of the table before the First Rangers had walked in on him, but he'd first had time to peek inside the old hempen satchel he found in the lowest drawer.

Unmistakably, it had contained the fresh remains of a bird.

10 Nighthawk

"Isn't that the bird all the First Rangers are after?" asked Simon. "The super important one?"

Following his discovery last night, Van's first thought had been to go to Otep. He feared the First Ranger would jump to conclusions, though, and Van didn't yet know if what he had seen was cause for alarm. Ghan Mudcatcher, likewise, might feel obligated to investigate. If the elder accused the First Rangers of Vaxas and Ikann without due cause, it would foster animosity at a tender time, and Van would be to blame.

Simon of the Mists, however, had no stake in the outcome of the pilgrimage, and Van had come to consider him level headed and well informed. Conveniently enough, neither of them had seen Shale that day.

"The Phantom Nighthawk, yes," Van repeated.

"Right," muttered Simon. "Why's it weird for Brynda to have one?"

"Given the belief that the animal died out generations ago, it is weird for anyone to have one," said Van. "Setting that aside, if Brynda Blackblade managed to bring one down, why wouldn't she have claimed credit for the accomplishment publicly?"

Simon thought about it. "Maintain the element of surprise? Play the underdog?"

Van frowned. Whatever small advantage could be gained by keeping the deed secret was insignificant compared to a ranger's pride. A Nemian would understand that. Simon crossed his arms and sighed, evidently noting Van's dissatisfaction with his first answer.

"You only saw it for about a second, right? Are you sure it wasn't ancient—mummified or something?"

Van shook his head. "It was killed days ago, perhaps less. I'm sure of it."

"With your upbringing, I guess you'd know," said Simon. "What about the bag? Any markings on it?"

"Markings?" echoed Van.

"Drawn or painted symbols," said Simon.

Van didn't recall any symbols, but then again, it was the contents of the satchel that had stuck in his mind, not the satchel itself.

"Maybe," said Van. "I'm not sure. Why would it matter?"

"Because the bag could've been fortified with magic," explained Simon. "There are spells that can halt the decay of mortal remains when they're placed inside enchanted vessels. It's used to preserve bodies for viewings prior to burial, that type of thing. A spell like that would work on an animal just as well as a person, except..." He trailed off.

"Except?" Van prodded.

"Except it's a form of necromancy, which is pretty tightly regulated anywhere magic is practiced. For good reason."

"How long could such a spell keep a body from decomposing?" asked Van. "What's the limit?"

"Isn't one," said Simon. "Provided the spell was cast properly, and the vessel isn't opened or destroyed, whatever's inside can be preserved indefinitely."

"But I opened the bag!" Van blurted. "They will know someone tampered with it, and it could only have been me."

"Did you close it again when you put it back?" asked Simon calmly.

"Of course," said Van.

"Then whatever was in there was only in a state of decay for a couple of seconds. Nobody will know the difference."

Van breathed a sigh of relief, but his stomach soon twisted anew. "But if that's what's going on, it would mean Brynda is trying to win Patronage dishonestly."

"What, would that make it harder for you to *admire her gallantry?*" chided Simon. "Come on, kid. If there's as much at stake as you've told me, anybody would cheat."

Van looked away. "If I had been paying closer attention, I could have told you with more certainty about the satchel. Maybe I can get another look at it."

"Maybe we both can," suggested Simon, raising his eyebrows.

Van shook his head. "I couldn't possibly bring it to you, and I can think of no way to get you into Brynda's tent."

"No need for that," said Simon. "There's a spell I can whip together that'll let us see and hear inside her tent from wherever we are, any time."

Van stared, aghast. The trickery one could get up to through spellwork had given him pause before, but this seemed outrageous even by Simon's standards. Still, the foreigner had levied a serious accusation against Brynda Blackblade. Van now felt responsible for uncovering the truth.

"How?" he heard himself say.

"Remote scrying portal," explained Simon. "Another spell that's highly regulated. Totally illegal without a license and a warrant. But we're pretty far from my country's jurisdiction, and I happen to be morally flexible. So, if you really want to get to the bottom of this, I can make it happen."

Van swallowed. "Can we… can we do it now?"

"It'll take some prep work, actually." Simon glanced around. "Do you have something to write with? I'll make you an ingredient list. You'll have to be the one to go and get this stuff. If Ghan or one of the other babysitters caught me asking, they'd probably tell me to take a hike—or put me in time out, or whatever you guys do with troublemakers on the Journey of Patronage."

"And why would they give them to me?" Van crossed his arms. "If their purpose is that obvious, would it not be suspicious, no matter who asked? Ghan Mudcatcher has known me since I was born. He is well aware I have no knowledge whatsoever of magic—he'll see right through me."

Simon thought about it, tapping a finger on his elbow. "Tell Ghan you convinced me to show you a spell. That's basically the truth anyway, right? As long as he thinks it was your idea and not mine, he'll just assume you're 'strengthening your bonds' or whatever, like your dad told us all to do. Scrying magic has plenty of practical and non-creepy applications. Ghan doesn't need to know what we're actually doing with it."

Van was growing more anxious by the moment.

"Aside from the shopping list, there's another little detail you'll need to dirty your hands over."

"Which is?" Van prompted nervously.

"The spell needs a target," said Simon. "Any solid object that's at least the size of, say, a shirt button. I need to enchant it ahead of time—which takes a while—and when I'm done, you'll need to leave it in the spot we want to observe. The scrying portal will connect us to the enchanted object across any physical distance."

"Leave something in Brynda's tent?" Van scrunched his eyebrows. "That... doesn't sound so difficult. I go there every evening."

Simon frowned. "Problem is, we're on the move and traveling light. I could enchant something inconspicuous, like a pebble or a twig, but she wouldn't take it with her when we pack up the next morning. And mixing a new item in with her things probably wouldn't work either, since she'd recognize it as out of place."

The solution was so obvious to Van, it made him feel slightly guilty. "I'll break one of her quills and offer to replace it with my own."

Simon slapped his knee. "Now *that* is what I'm talking about!" He smirked. "Sneaky thinking, kid. I knew you had it in you."

Van grimaced, feeling anything but proud as he fetched the leather case he was given at Stonebasin. "So, the ingredient list?"

Simon dictated, and Van wrote.

2 liters distilled water
1 cup clay powder
1 ounce sodium
1 ounce cadmium
1 ounce cobalt
1 ounce copper

"Got all that?" asked Simon.

"I believe so." Van nodded, studying the list. "However, I should warn you I've never heard of 'cadmium.'"

Simon swore. "Maybe you don't have that here yet." He touched his thumb to his chin, his brow furrowing. "Let's see. What did people use before… Aha! Ask for cinnabar."

Van was familiar with cinnabar. He amended the list.

"All right?" Simon confirmed.

Van reread the list from top to bottom. "Judging by the measurements, should I assume you want all these things in powder form?"

"Yes," said Simon. "Is that a problem?"

Van hummed in thought. "It may be, in the case of copper."

Simon groaned, closing his eyes and pinching the bridge of his nose.

"Malachite. Ask for malachite if you can't get copper. But I'm telling you now, the more substitutions we make, the worse the picture quality will be."

Van attempted a smile. "Malachite should be no trouble. I'm told Ghan has been teaching the younger aspirants to mix dyes, and that mineral is commonly used as a pigment."

"Yeah. I know," said Simon, as if Van had said something stupid and obvious.

The foreigner took a breath and rubbed his eyes.

"So, what else is new? You were supposed to keep me filled in on anything travel relevant."

Van had plenty more on his mind that day, and he'd learned by now how freeing it could be to have someone to confide in that was willing to set propriety temporarily aside. He wanted to tell him everything. Galdur's cruelty as he'd derided him over Brynda. How surreal it had been to find Shale singing in the middle of the night. But Van's time with Simon was limited, and he had promised to use it first and foremost on what was practical.

"Yes," said Van. "In four days, we'll reach the community of Third Stone, where we'll stop to resupply as we did at Stonebasin. Three more days on the road from there, and we will stop again at Farthest Tree. Galdur Goldeyes and his Pilgrimage Guide will decide our route from there, since we'll be entering Ikanni lands."

Simon nodded. "Meaning a week from now, team Ikann takes point. If they say zig, we zig, and if they say zag, we zag. That about right?"

"I... suppose?" said Van, puzzling over the expression.

"That worry you at all?"

"Should it?" Van studied Simon, who wore a guarded look that suggested he was holding something back.

"I guess I still feel like I must have missed something, when it comes to your history with the other tribes." Simon shook his head, his eyes unfocused. "If I knew more about current events in Nemia, I could make some better guesses as to what's got the Inner Circle so riled up."

His eyes returned to Van. "When did things get bad between Dolse and Ikann? Actually, no—how far back does your recorded history go to begin with? When were the tribes formed?"

Van took a breath and recited from memory.

"The tribes of Dolse, Ikann, Mercura, and Vaxas were founded eight hundred years ago. Before then, the land was inhabited by a single people—a unified tribe—but all trace of them is lost. We call them the Meridians, though we don't know what they called themselves. Even their language is gone. We know only that they had their own system of writing, and from that we can infer they spoke a different tongue.

"Their civilization collapsed after a series of natural disasters caused food and other resources to become very scarce very quickly. Factions formed. Feuding ensued as each group sought to secure as much for themselves as they could. There was widespread famine, and war. Only by pledging fealty to the Emissaries did the survivors weather that dark time, and by establishing the system of tribal Patronage, which has ensured peace ever since."

Simon leaned forward. "All right. What about more recently?"

Van summarized the past few decades of tribal Patronage and the various relations between the chieftains of Nemia. The details were still fresh in his mind, but unlike Lilim, Simon was unfazed by the story of Gul the Coming Storm and his abusive edicts.

"That sounds like a bad time for team Dolse, but it doesn't explain the policy shift in Gnosos," he mused, looking pensive. "Not to make light of your history, but it would take something a lot worse to gain that kind of attention. And if those conflicts took place before you were even born..."

Simon trailed off again.

"No, the timeline doesn't add up," he decided. "There's got to be something more recent. For instance, a few years back, there were the Bill Weathers murders in Arbus Arkad. I was reading about those for months. And even in Gnosos, we saw a resurgence of the Idolators of Frenzy—that one shocked a lot of people."

Van shook his head. "I'm sorry, Simon. Murder and such things are rare anywhere in Nemia, and I can think of nothing recent more severe than what took place during the last Cycle of Ikanni Patronage."

Simon fell silent after that, so Van took a turn. "What are the Idolators of Frenzy?"

"I guess you have your own gods here," mused Simon quietly. "One of these days, I'll tell you about the gods the rest of us have to put up with. Suffice to say, Frenzy is one of the really bad ones. God of madness. His followers butcher people, eat them, tear their own eyes out. You name it."

Van shuddered. "Why would anyone worship such a god?"

"Think about it," said Simon. "Nobody who's actually insane chose to be. They were either born damaged, or they suffered some trauma that pushed them over the edge, and now they're just... broken. They can't function as normal members of society. They see things other people can't see, hear voices other people can't hear. Sometimes, those voices tell them to do bad things. Depending on who you ask, someone might say that's Frenzy whispering in their ear.

"Acceptance and understanding, purpose and meaning—those concepts must sound appealing to people who feel perpetually misunderstood. But worship of Frenzy has been illegal for a long time, and everybody whose opinion matters is on the same page about that."

"And what gods do you serve?" asked Van, nervous he might not like the answer.

"None," said Simon.

Van hesitated. "But you spoke as though—"

"Obviously, god-like entities exist," interrupted Simon. "You'd have to be an idiot to believe otherwise, if you've seen what I have. But serve them? No way."

"I suppose that's well reasoned," mused Van, "if the rest are anything like this Frenzy."

"We have some good ones, too," said Simon. "Since the emergence of Arbus Arkad as a world power, the Church of Solaar has become dominant in the West. God of the sun— he's all about high-fives, paying your taxes on time, and helping old ladies across the street. But we can talk about him later."

They were nearing the limit of Simon's spell, so they decided to save a more thorough examination of world religions for another day. Before they parted ways, Van handed his spare quill to Simon, who reminded him to seek out the other spell materials at the first opportunity. Van nodded and promised him he would.

The next morning, Lilim had another surprise in store for Van. It was a pleasant one this time.

"I, um," she mumbled, "I finished what I was working on."

"Oh?" Van scooted closer in the cramped tent, spying the sheet of parchment she'd fished out of her pack.

Lilim, as it turned out, had not been practicing her writing. Drawn on the page instead was a near-perfect reproduction of a scene from *The Bull and the Snail*. The Bull's hoof was caught in a gopher hole while the Snail looked on quizzically from nearby. Not colorized, of course, since Lilim only had black ink, but the image was immediately recognizable.

"You drew this from memory?" Van blurted, observing that he'd never given her the book back after they finished it together.

"I know I didn't get it quite right," she said, "but it was fun to try."

Van tried to keep his voice from cracking. "This is incredible, Lilim."

She smiled shyly.

"Say, would you like to try your hand at an original illustration?" Van suggested, moved by a sudden whim. "Not something copied out of the book, I mean. Maybe..." He cleared his throat. "Maybe a scene from an adventure they haven't had yet."

"Like what?" she asked blankly.

"Well, what might it look like if the Bull and the Snail solved a problem together?"

Lilim frowned, studying her drawing. This, too, was one of her tells, and Van was sure she would become fussy and refuse —but she surprised him yet again. "I'll try."

Van skipped midday meal to ask Ghan Mudcatcher for help with Simon's spell ingredients. Just as the foreigner predicted, the elder grew immediately suspicious.

Van repeated the lie he'd practiced, feeling sick to his stomach as he spoke.

"It's for Simon of the Mists," he explained to his scowling childhood teacher. "As bidden by our chieftain, I have extended a hand in friendship to him, and he has offered to show me what he knows of magic. Providing him with these materials might help me come to know him better."

Van squirmed under the long, judgmental glare that followed, but Ghan eventually agreed to take him to the supply carts. Together they requisitioned the items on his list —clean water and a wooden mixing bowl, salt and powdered clay, malachite, and cinnabar. Unfortunately, the procession had run out of cobalt. Van's next opportunity to procure it would come when the caravan reached Third Stone. There, he could barter for the mineral, if he was lucky.

Van wanted to break the news to Simon right away, but Lilim found Van first.

"I finished it," she announced, sneaking up on him as he weaved between bonfires in search of the foreigner.

"I'm sorry, Lilim, right now I'm—what did you say?"

"I finished it," she repeated with gravitas. "The thing you asked for."

She sat him down, and once she had his full attention, she produced a folded page, handing it to him. When he saw the illustration, he forgot all about Simon and the missing cobalt.

The Bull was wading across a shallow river, the Snail riding on his back. Lilim had even added reeds and other plants that might be found near a riverbed to better capture the scene without the use of color—and she'd done it all faithfully in the style of the original artist. What truly made Van's voice catch in his throat was how close it was to what he'd imagined.

Just like on the night he found her in the alleyway, Van felt that another of life's truths had revealed itself to him. A dream that had only ever been a private fancy was now tangible and within reach. There was order—a deliberate design—where before there was only chaos.

Van handed the drawing back to Lilim and watched her put it away, dimly aware of the tears brimming in his eyes. She yelped in surprise when he pulled her into an embrace a moment later.

"Thank you, Lilim," he said in a shaky voice, still holding her. "I'm so proud of you. I love you so much!"

It was only then that Van noticed Simon and Shale, who'd found seats at the bonfire to wait for him. He released Lilim in time to see Shale cross her arms and narrow her eyes. He told Lilim he had to go, and she nodded, a self-conscious smile on her flushed face.

Shale took the liberty of speaking first when the three of them sat down in Van's tent.

"I'd like to know if I passed your test."

"Test?" Van furrowed his brow.

"When I hunted for your rangers."

Van frowned. He didn't think Simon had made a mistake with her word choice.

"Your question tells me you misunderstood my advice. I apologize for not being more clear. Hunting *with* the rangers of our tribe is considered a privilege, sought for the joy of camaraderie it affords. If you found it a chore, then you have missed the point."

"Of course it's a chore," spat Shale. "Providing food is the work of servants, whether from hunted game or otherwise."

Van couldn't tell if her words sprang from passing irritation or if she was genuinely upset. He was still getting used to speaking to someone through an intermediary. When Simon spoke on Shale's behalf, he always sounded the same, like he was reading aloud from a cookbook. Van tried to listen equally to Shale's tone, so he could feel out the emotions behind her words before Simon spoke them.

"There are no servants on the pilgrimage, so all I can say is that you must change your views if you are to find a way forward," said Van calmly.

"Why should I change my views to suit yours? No one has even bothered to ask me what my views are."

Van sighed. "Try to see the hunt as an opportunity to test your skills, if nothing else. And recognize the value in the company of your kinsmen, should you find yourself in need."

Shale snorted. "I have never needed anyone. And if I wanted to test my skills, I would hunt more dangerous game. Some overproud ranger, maybe."

Van stared at her, finding no response. Shale spoke on.

"The idea seems to bother you," she said with a smirk. "Did you imagine there were no killers in your midst? Some of your rangers are killers, I can tell just by looking. The one called Goldeyes has killed before, I'm certain of it."

Van found his voice. "I'm sure that's not true."

"The green clan's champion as well," Shale went on. "Blackblade. She's claimed more lives than even Goldeyes, I think."

Van shut his eyes and drew a breath. He was in no mood for more accusations against Brynda.

"Are you feeling unwell, *kinsman?*" Shale asked, giggling.

"I am… tired. Perhaps I'm feeling out of sorts."

"Unrequited love can have that effect on a boy."

Van blinked, speaking without taking his eyes off her. "Can Shale read minds? I'm talking to you right now, Simon."

"No," said Simon. "I'd be able to tell. I'm running another spell right now that would detect any—"

"It's fine, I believe you," interrupted Van, "Return to translating when I speak next, please."

Simon's forehead wrinkled. "Although last time, when she turned invisible, I couldn't—"

"Begin translating, please."

Shale was vigorously making the talking sign in Simon's face, annoyed at being left out. Simon sighed, closing his eyes. When he opened them again, Van spoke to Shale.

"I will take a turn now if that is all right with you."

Shale nodded.

"I'd like to know how you reached our lands. By what means did you find your way to Nemia?"

Shale's expression was deadly serious as she responded. "I told the truth to the Queen of Lies."

Van waited for her to elaborate, refusing to be drawn in by such cryptic drivel.

"When my mother beseeched the Twilight Prophet and told Her the time was ripe to collect my head, I spoke to Her as well. I made a bet with Her that between mother and daughter, it was I who would become the more powerful, and ultimately serve Her better. The Prophet listened, and accepted my wager. Rather than decapitate me with Her crystal sword, She sent me here."

Van felt her story in no way answered his question, but he could think of nothing else to ask that might provide clarification.

"I have more questions, if that is all," said Shale.

Van nodded.

"Who is the girl you walk with in the morning, and what is your relationship to her?"

"Lilim the Brave, you mean," Van said, surprised. "She is a dear friend. I have been instructing her in reading and writing, and various other matters, as she was not afforded many opportunities to learn back home."

Her eyes narrowed. "She seems fond of you."

Van shrugged. "We are fond of each other."

"Do you love her?"

"Of course I do," he said without thinking, but then walked back over his words. "Though not in the way I'm concerned you might mean."

"Have you told her you love her?"

"No!" said Van. He stumbled a second time. "Actually, yes. But again, it wasn't meant in the way you seem to be suggesting."

The corner of her mouth twitched in amusement. "Were you careful to explain to her how you meant it?"

"She is a child!" Van sputtered.

"Girls grow up faster than boys do."

"It couldn't have been necessary to explain!"

"You are very insensitive to the feelings of girls, Van the Scribe."

By now, Shale was grinning broadly, while Simon looked bored and disappointed. Van cleared his throat.

"Moving on. I propose we use the rest of our time to teach you more basic vocabulary," said Van. "You may have been on to something when you asked before. Would that suit you?"

Shale nodded, still smiling.

By the end of the hour, he'd taught her twenty or thirty new words along with a few short phrases. Language was a survival skill, too, after all. Before she excused herself, Shale asked him to teach her the Nemian word for "love," and he did, despite a strong suspicion she would later use it to poke fun at him.

"We don't have long," said Simon when Shale was gone. "Status update on the shopping list?"

Van brought Simon up to speed on his efforts, informing him he would procure the final ingredient when they reached Third Stone.

"Fair enough," said the foreigner. "That's only a few days away."

"Why does this spell require all these things?" blurted Van. "I have seen you work magic with nothing but a gesture."

"It's called hedge wizardry," said Simon, his expression forlorn. "Most sorcerers don't touch the stuff."

"Why not?" Van leaned forward. "Is it dangerous?"

"It's an admission of our limits," said Simon. "As a sorcerer, everything I do boils down to a question of comprehension and willpower. See, understanding the physical laws of nature isn't enough to subvert them on a whim. You have to be smarter than them. If you want to throw fire from your fingertips, you have to be able to close your eyes and visualize what fire is *made of.* If you can convince the universe there's fire where there's not, then there is."

Van considered this. "So, the magic used for the remote spying spell—"

"*Scrying.*"

"—isn't something you understand as well as other magic."

"Sure," Simon conceded. "That's a blunt but generous way of putting it. Point is, I need more than just elbow grease for this one. Just like how I trick our brains with the language spell, I'll be tricking these material elements into forming sounds and images. There are sorcerers out there who wouldn't need to bother, but I guess I'm not that much of a badass."

Van nodded, and with that topic closed, Simon changed the subject.

"Seems like you're handling Shale well enough so far."

"How do you mean?" Van cocked his head.

"Well," said Simon, "you haven't asked to call off our meetings or lost your temper with her, even with the creepy cocktail of mean jokes and horror stories she's been feeding you to see if you'll snap."

Van shrugged. "The few things she's told us of herself are amusing distractions, if anything."

Simon studied him. "How is that stuff anything other than pure nightmare fuel for you? Queen of Lies? Crystal decapitation swords?"

"Because it's ridiculous," said Van.

He even chuckled, remembering the look on Shale's face when she'd said it. He was sure Simon would see the humor in it as well, given the foreigner's habit for speaking flippantly of things others found sacred. Instead, he regarded Van sternly, and his tone grew serious.

"As much as Shale freaks me out, it would seriously break my heart to see you turn into an asshole. Don't treat her the way Galdur treats you. Take her more sperskilask."

Van blinked, making the talking sign after a moment. Simon repeated himself, but this time the entire statement came out as perfect gibberish.

Van shook his head, pointing to his mouth and then to his ear, at which point Simon simply sighed and left Van alone in his tent. He skipped yet another meal in order to reach Brynda's tent at the appointed hour. In the short time it took him to walk to the campsite of Vaxas, he sulked from the sting of being likened to Galdur Goldeyes.

Van told himself he would reflect on his interactions with Shale, and reevaluate his approach to the challenge of helping her find a place for herself in Nemia.

He didn't see Shale at all the next day, but on the morning before the procession arrived at Third Stone, she ambushed him on the road. Simon appeared with her in tow halfway through their morning march, catching up to where he walked with Lilim.

"Shale wants to talk," said Simon.

"Now?" Van turned to look at him.

"Apparently."

"Very well." Van faced Shale. "What can I do for you, kinsman?"

Shale didn't say a word.

"Not to you," said Simon, pointing at Lilim. "To her."

Van hesitated, then turned to his young ward.

"Lilim the Brave," he said, "it seems my friend Shale would like to talk to you. This can be made possible through the use of my friend Simon's magic spells. Would you like to talk to Shale?"

"Is it safe?" Lilim asked.

"Simply talking to a person isn't dangerous, I promise. Just remember that she is very different from us, and she may say strange things."

"All right," Lilim said, looking expectantly at Shale.

Van gave Simon a severe look. "If Shale says anything upsetting, please tell me right away."

Nodding, Simon redirected his spell to Shale. She made a brief statement, prompting Simon to switch immediately back to Van.

"She says she'll kill me in my sleep if I tell you what they're saying."

Van sighed. "It would be very inconvenient for me if you were killed in your sleep, Simon."

"So, should I keep going then, or...?" He raised his eyebrows.

Van looked at Lilim. "Lilim the Brave, please tell me if Shale says anything that upsets you."

"I will," the girl promised dutifully.

Van put on an artificial smile. "Thank you, Lilim. Simon, you may do as you wish."

With Simon's help, Shale and Lilim shared a conversation as they all walked along together. It was mostly one-sided. Shale spoke in phrases of varied lengths, while Lilim almost always answered with a simple "Yes" or "No." Van had hoped to puzzle out what they were saying from Lilim's side of the conversation, but her one-word responses made it impossible.

Their talk concluded when Shale bent down to shake Lilim's hand. It could have been a farewell gesture, but it conjured to Van's mind the image of two grown men agreeing to terms. Shale straightened, flashed Van a delinquent smile, and departed without ceremony.

"I guess they're done," said Simon.

"Should I be concerned?" asked Van.

"Are you trying to get me killed?" Simon cocked an eyebrow.

Van looked down at Lilim, who seemed unbothered. "Was Shale mean to you, Lilim?"

"It's private," said the girl, her eyes fixed on the road ahead.

11 Third Stone, Farthest Tree

Van shared the road with both Lilim and Simon on the day the procession reached Third Stone. Since Van would be busy later, Simon spent his spell early, and they talked to pass the time.

Van's sole priority that day was cobalt—the only ingredient they lacked for the spell that he believed would absolve Brynda Blackblade of whatever misdeeds Simon suspected her of. Van had also been excused from holding lessons for Brynda and Galdur until the procession moved on. At least for now, his time was his own again.

When the watchtowers of Third Stone came into view, the other Dolsers quickened their pace, eager for hot baths and warm meals even after so short a time back on the road. Van restrained himself, taking his time to finish an anecdote he'd been sharing with Simon concerning yesterday's hunt. It had been another joint effort between tribes Dolse and Vaxas, and this time, he'd watched Brynda Blackblade's mysterious dagger transform into a javelin, which she'd used to take down a prowling cheetah with an impressive fifty-yard throw.

"You've got it bad, kid," sighed Simon. "Twenty minutes straight, and all you've talked about is Brynda."

"I don't have... Wait, truly?" asked Van, somewhat distracted.

"This is why the rest of the world sends people your age to school. You're supposed to get this stuff out of your system before you go off and try to do something important with your life."

"Shall I show you around the community while we're here?" Van offered, hoping to change the subject. "I realize your spell is almost used, but we could still—"

"Nah, you go ahead," said Simon. "I'm gonna see if Ghan has time to hang out. If he's up for it, this could be, like, our thing."

Van had no idea what that meant, and he didn't bother to ask. Without breaking stride, he bowed to Simon and said goodbye to Lilim, then fell into a jog. He stowed his rucksack under a tree to the side of the road, wanting to be light on his feet when he reached Third Stone's market square. Chances were, it would be busy. For the first time since leaving home, he fished out his coin purse and tied it to his belt.

Most Nemians traded for foodstuffs or services regularly, bartering furs and other trophies for most goods. After Gul the Coming Storm was removed from power, however, a currency was introduced into circulation as part of the effort to repair relations between tribes Dolse and Ikann—the Eastern Plains Farthing.

The coin had a troubled history. Shortly after their distribution, most farthings found their way into the hands of families that were wealthy and kept land. Whether this was thanks to or in spite of the fact that those were the very people who least needed to use farthings to settle debts, Van couldn't say. But it was the reason Van avoided using them whenever possible—they revealed his privileged upbringing.

Van had never in his life needed to spend a farthing, but ever since his eighth birthday, his father had given him two each year as an allowance. Today, he had fourteen to his name. He had set all his coins aside for his pilgrimage year, knowing he would travel far and experience many new things, and that some of those things had a cost.

The road leading past the first watchtower into Third Stone's market was an obstacle course of young mothers who'd brought their children out to greet the aspirants with flower wreaths. Van ducked and dodged through the crowd of wreath-brandishing toddlers as smiling women held the small children up to bar his path. He didn't wish to be delayed, even by such heartfelt gestures, but despite his dogged efforts he was still halted by the long line that had already formed at the apothecary's stall.

It was a full hour before Van finally reached the head of the line, and when he came face to face with the young apothecary, he dispensed with formality, asking after cobalt without preface.

"Cobalt, you say?" The apothecary furrowed his brow. "I'm sorry, kinsman. My supply ran out days ago. A large order from Stonebasin. However..."

"However?" Van prodded, leaning forward and bracing himself against the stall.

"You should look for Logan Longstrider. As captain ranger, he sometimes crosses paths with merchants coming or going from the market," the apothecary explained, concerned by Van's visible distress. "He'll be out ranging now, but he should be back before noontime. Watch the south road."

The apothecary provided the man's description, and Van thanked him fervently before sprinting away in search of a good vantage point from which to watch the road.

Before he found one suitable, he chanced to see Shale walking through the door of the outfitter's longhouse, across the market square. His curiosity was piqued, and because he still felt partly responsible for her, he fought his way back through the crowds and entered after her.

By the time he stepped through the doorway, Shale was at the counter, barking orders at the terrified girl tending the establishment. The proprietor's daughter, most likely.

"Clothing!" said Shale, slapping her palms against the countertop for emphasis, and to ensure she couldn't be ignored.

The girl flinched, but she soon recovered. After glancing over Shale's pitiful attire, a look of understanding crossed her face.

"Wait here, please," she said timidly.

The girl returned a minute later with a leather jerkin that looked about Shale's size. It was plain, discolored in places and worn with age, but still a functional improvement.

Shale narrowed her eyes at the jerkin, growling disapprovingly. Unshouldering her rucksack, she dumped its contents on the counter for the girl to see—half a dozen fox furs and several satchels of fangs and claws in pristine condition. Taken from mourns, if Van wasn't mistaken.

"Clothing," Shale repeated slowly.

The shop girl's eyes widened, and she paused, as though trying to approximate the trophies' value. "Another moment, please."

She disappeared again, this time returning with a wrapped parcel under arm. She led Shale behind the curtain of a changing booth, and after a few minutes, they emerged together.

As she set Shale's old clothes aside, the girl gestured to a mirror. Shale approached it and turned around once, appraising her new outfit.

She wore a knee-length gazelle leather dress, soft and dark with tassels of ermine fur at the shoulders, cinched at the waist by a woven belt with a silver buckle. It fit her much better than her old rags, showing off her figure, which Van hadn't truly noticed until now. Shale finished her new look with a burnished silver bracelet and an anklet of linked chain, at the suggestion of the proprietor's daughter.

As they returned to the counter to negotiate a final price, Van decided Shale would probably be all right on her own. He left the outfitter and soon found a place less crowded to wait while he watched Third Stone's southern approach.

Logan Longstrider returned with his ranging party well past noontime. Van hadn't eaten, fearing he would miss the captain ranger—but now, a new complication presented itself.

Van had assumed that, after a long day on duty, the captain ranger would retire to his home, where he could be approached privately. Logan Longstrider, however, was heading straight for Third Stone's famed bathhouse. The lone structure was perched on a hill beneath a beatific halo of steam that billowed from the natural hot spring there.

Van had been to Third Stone only once before, years ago with his father. Farseer Daz had explained that the bathhouse was the community's premiere attraction, and the reason it was a popular destination for many Dolsers, provided they could afford such indulgences. Van and his father hadn't visited the bathhouse back then, but as an aspirant, Van was old enough now to enter without a chaperon—though with the community so busy today, the entrance fee might be exorbitant.

Committed, Van steeled himself and followed Logan Longstrider up the hill to the bathhouse.

The captain ranger was already headed into the men's bath with a towel by the time Van reached the lobby. He had no choice now but to pay admission if he wanted to speak with him. Van approached the bathhouse greeter cautiously, a kindly looking old woman seated at a table between the men's and women's entrances, where a stack of fresh towels awaited the guests.

Van smiled awkwardly, holding up a single coin. Farthings had been in circulation all Van's life, but he knew Dolsers of older generations still sometimes found the coin vexing.

"How much to go in, please?"

The old woman squinted at the farthing, working her mouth as though she was chewing on something.

"Six farthings," she said at length.

"Six!" blurted Van.

It was almost half his savings. Then again, Logan Longstrider might be his last hope of finding cobalt. Van hurriedly counted out six farthings and handed them over, barely noticing the look of stark surprise on the old woman's face. She opened her mouth as if to say something, but simply closed it again and handed him a towel when she saw how many coins he had in his purse.

Van left his clothes in a basket in the next room, proceeding to the bath with the soft linen towel wrapped around his waist. What awaited was a scene of tranquil beauty unlike anything he had ever seen. The open-air bath was surrounded by blossoming cherry trees, with a natural rise in the rocky basin separating the men's side from the women's. The only other visitor on this side was Logan Longstrider, reclined in the shallow water with his eyes closed and his towel folded atop his head.

Van deduced the steep admission fee had kept most others away, and counted himself lucky to have been able to afford it. He waded into the hot water and settled near the captain ranger, hesitating. The man hadn't noticed him yet, as relaxed as he was. Demanding his attention now seemed rude and intrusive.

A loud splash broke the silence, and a few startled gasps rose from the women's bath, followed by the distinctive trill of Shale's giggle. This did gain the captain ranger's attention. He stirred and looked around in surprise, his eyes falling on Van shortly after they snapped open.

"Hello, lad," he said in a friendly tone. "You must be one of this year's aspirants. Have you come to ask for a blessing of safe travel?"

"Um," said Van. "Rather than a blessing, captain, I was hoping to ask you about cobalt."

"Cobalt, you say?" Logan Longstrider wrinkled his forehead.

Van explained to the captain that it was on the apothecary's advice he had come to find him, recounting what he needed the powdered pigment for. It was the same story he'd given Ghan Mudcatcher, and while it would have been simpler to tell Logan Longstrider he needed cobalt for mixing dyes, Van didn't like the idea of having two lies to keep track of.

"A noble undertaking," Logan Longstrider concurred when Van finished. "I did speak to a merchant selling cobalt today, as it happens."

"You did!" Van leaned forward eagerly.

"But I had no cause to buy any," he said. "His caravan has gone south to sell their cobalt at Stonebasin. However…"

"However?" prodded Van.

"The apothecary's master," said Logan Longstrider. "Jaggra the Jubilant. Third Stone's *former* apothecary, long retired. She may have some cobalt you could coax her into parting ways with."

The man then regaled Van with the convoluted history of Jaggra the Jubilant and her relationship to the community of Third Stone. Her time as apothecary was mentioned almost offhand, quickly giving way to a series of whimsical and nostalgic anecdotes of the fruit pies she baked once a year for the annual crop festival. Following her retirement, she was rarely seen, finding the company of others toilsome. Since then, her vaunted pies had passed from mere notoriety into local legend.

Sitting back in the warm waters, he gave Van directions to her home, which lay almost two full hours north of Third Stone along the road. If he left now, he could still be back in time to get a full night's sleep before morning assembly. He thanked the captain ranger and quickly returned to the bathhouse to find his clothes.

"I am not exaggerating about those pies, lad," Logan Longstrider called after him as he left the fragrant, steaming water. "Ask her about them, if you get half a chance!"

After dressing and pulling his boots back on, Van stepped back into the lobby and caught another glimpse of Shale. She was face down on a high table, a towel covering her from the waist down, as a pair of burly older women massaged her vigorously. Her long hair looked bright and silky, freshly washed and thoroughly brushed for the first time Van could remember.

This time, Shale noticed him staring and regarded him with a sly grin, her cheek pressed to the table. He averted his gaze and continued on his way, feeling just a little more frustrated than a moment ago.

Logan Longstrider was either terrible at giving directions, or he had never visited Jaggra the Jubilant at her home. Closer to three hours passed before Van found her cottage tucked along the road, but the fire of a hearth flickered within. He took it as an encouraging sign.

Van had skipped supper and midday meal both in his pursuit of cobalt. Perhaps that was why his nose was so quick to detect the enticing aroma wafting from the small residence. One of the fabled pies, maybe. He rang the ornate bell that hung outside the door and was surprised when someone called to him from behind the dwelling.

"Come through here!" croaked the voice. "I'm in the kitchen."

Van went around, cutting through the side yard to find a second, smaller door that was propped open to reveal the kitchen. There stood Jaggra the Jubilant, hunched over a clay oven as she carefully removed something from it—the source of the sweet, fruity smell.

"Who are you, then, and what do you want?" The woman scowled at him over the pie in her mitted hands.

Van introduced himself, apologizing for bothering her so late, and once more explained his circumstances.

"Cobalt, you say?" sneered the apothecary. "I've none on hand, and you wouldn't be able to afford it if I did."

"I have farthings!" Van said in desperation.

Jaggra the Jubilant eyed his coin purse as he held it up.

"That's all well and good, but it doesn't change that I'm fresh out. I gave the last of my cobalt to my fool apprentice and told him to fetch a high price for it at market, but the good-for-nothing brought me back only half a sack of grain. You'll find no more cobalt from here to Stonebasin." She glanced him over, marking the way his shoulders sagged. "However..."

Van groaned. "However?"

"I'm guessing you're an aspirant," she said, fanning the pie to cool it. "Which means you're headed north. The supplier at Farthest Tree should have what you seek. Roland the Crooked Spear, a colleague of mine in another life."

"He'll sell me cobalt?" said Van.

"He'll tell you he has none," said Jaggra the Jubilant.

"Um." Van scratched his head.

"I'll write you a note. Show it to him when he tries to turn you away, and he'll let you buy from his reserve. It won't be cheap, mind you. Now, wait right there."

She disappeared into the next room, taking the pie with her. Van's stomach grumbled noisily as he watched it go.

Rather than waiting as he was told, he followed her, partly because he'd spotted something else through the door that was bothering him.

In the living space was a table set for one, complete with knife and fork, and a tall glass of milk. Shale wore another new outfit—leather high boots over cotton breeches and a tan linen shirt with a buttoned collar. Simple, but finely made and well suited to the road. Van briefly wondered how she'd gotten here ahead of him, let alone with enough time left over to have a pie baked to order, but he was decidedly too tired and hungry to care.

"All right, missy, as agreed." Jaggra the Jubilant placed the pie on the table. "Just don't go telling anybody I did this. Not that you could if you wanted to, I suppose."

The older woman left through another door, leaving Van alone with Shale.

He knew that by now, Shale possessed the vocabulary necessary to offer him a piece. But she said nothing when she picked up her fork, maintaining unbroken eye contact as she took her first bite of pie, and he had to look away when a smile began to creep across her face.

Over the next few days, Van made an effort to appreciate the natural beauty of the greater Dolser territories, knowing it would be a long time before he returned to the lands of his tribe.

Day by day, he was acclimating to the demands of the pilgrimage. His hands no longer shook when he drew his bow on the hunt, and he would never forget how proud he felt when he finally took down a gazelle in motion with Otep

Acrearms there to see it. With the right mental acrobatics, he could even survive an evening with Galdur Goldeyes and not lose sleep as a result.

The oasis of his heart was his time spent with Lilim. Their morning lessons were an investment he truly believed in, more rewarding all the time. She'd had no more emotional episodes since they left Stonebasin, and her comprehension was improving by measures.

Their lessons, of course, still required work, planning, and careful thought. Bizarrely, what Van looked forward to most each day was the time during which he could relax and speak his mind—his candid talks with Simon of the Mists.

Shale could disappear for days on end without warning, so Van still had the foreigner to himself on occasion. Simon probed often, sometimes tactlessly, for information about Nemia in his attempt to uncover his own country's veiled agenda. Van didn't mind. He trusted that his interest was well-intentioned, and in any case, Van was just as interested.

"That reminds me," said Simon, on their first day of resumed travel, "what does a Nemian funeral look like?"

"Funeral?" Van tilted his head.

"What do you do with your dead?" the foreigner elaborated. "Some cultures bury them, some burn them…"

"I know the word," said Van. "You just surprised me. In our lands, the deceased are interred in their tribe's ancestral burial ground. It's customary for the family to carry a stone there to mark the place, taken from the village they were born in."

"That sounds normal enough," said Simon.

"An exception is made on the pilgrimage," Van continued, a somber feeling settling over him. "Fallen aspirants are burned in pyres. Ghan Mudcatcher says it's a concession to practicality, given how far from home we might be on the

Journey of Patronage. But some say it's meant as a plea to the Emissaries. If a person passes on before returning home from their pilgrimage, that signifies they were never ours to keep. So, for them, we offer a special prayer to the gods of the land, asking that they take custody of their spirit, and see it safely onward."

"Take custody of their spirit, huh?" Simon's eyes widened dramatically in feigned shock. "Remind me not to die before we get back to Dolsetown."

Hearing the foreigner put it that way gave Van pause. He knew it was meant as a joke, but according to law, people like Simon and Shale didn't belong in Nemia at all—much less were they supposed to die here. Would even the Emissaries grant Farseer Daz's petition, and attend their spirits beyond death? Whatever else the gods were, Van knew they were beings of compassion. He chose to believe that they would.

After leaving Third Stone, the aspirants of Nemia traveled just another three days to reach the border settlement of Farthest Tree. The place where Van would at last find cobalt.

Built as a fort during the reign of Gul, when genuine fear existed that the Stewards of the Plains and Highlands would march in force against their neighbors to the south, Farthest Tree had become a symbol of progress and unity in the peaceful times that followed. By decree of Farseer Daz, the border fort was repurposed, now serving as a place where scholars, artists, and craftsmen could come together in the spirit of collaboration.

Over the years, a sprawling village had grown up around the dour fort, and today more than a thousand men and women of the Eastern Plains called the place home—Dolsers and Ikanni both, with a few atypically adventurous Vaxals thrown in. For Ikanni of Van's father's generation, who now served their tribe as elders, the last Cycle of Ikanni Patronage was a reprehensible departure from the norm, even if younger Ikanni misguidedly thought of it as their tribe's glory days.

"Lilim the Brave, may I come in?" Van knelt outside her tent on the morning they were to arrive.

No answer came.

He tried again, a little louder. "Lilim the Brave, are you awake?"

After several more seconds without response, he entered uninvited. Lilim was curled in her bedroll, glistening with sweat and shivering. Alarmed, Van crawled forward and touched her forehead, confirming she had a high fever. He listened to her breathing, which was labored and gravelly. The air itself was stale, musty, and faintly sweet—the same smell as a sick ward.

Van didn't wait for assembly. He scooped her up and ran.

"Elder Ghan!" he shouted when he spotted the delegates, gathered in conference on the naked tundra between the campsites. "A child is ill!"

Ghan Mudcatcher excused himself and walked to where Van was laying Lilim gently on the ground. She hadn't woken up, but she didn't seem asleep. Her head rolled from side to side as she whimpered, her eyelids fluttering.

Ghan crouched and felt her forehead just as Van had, then pressed his ear to her chest and listened. When he stood up, he turned back to his peers.

"Riverspeaker Gheela," he called. "May I borrow you for a second opinion?"

Tribe Mercura's Pilgrimage Guide approached and stared down at the prone girl.

"The influenza," she said almost immediately "I can tell even without closer inspection. There is fluid in her lungs."

Van opened his mouth to beg them for help, but it proved unnecessary. Gheela held her long staff aloft and then swung it down, stopping when its head nearly touched Lilim where she lay. There was a gust of wind followed by a warm light, and when it subsided, Van could no longer hear the crackle when Lilim inhaled.

"You're a healer," Van said, his voice barely above a whisper. "You've cured her?"

"No," said Gheela. "My magic mends wounds and knits broken bones. Sickness and disease are not my domain. But I have fortified her stamina, to a degree."

Van looked desperately from Gheela to Ghan Mudcatcher.

"The influenza is only sometimes fatal," explained Ghan softly. "With rest, she may recover."

"And medicine?" blurted Van.

"We've none suitable," said Ghan. "And because this is the pilgrimage, the rest she requires would normally be out of the question as well. We are all expected to walk under our own strength."

Horrified, Van shook his head, moving closer to Lilim protectively.

"Calm down, boy," the elder soothed. "None among us seeks any senseless loss of life. Because we will arrive at Farthest Tree this afternoon, there is another way."

The elder gestured for Van to pick Lilim up and follow him. As they ventured to the nearest supply cart, Ghan Mudcatcher explained the choice she would have to make.

For today only, Lilim would be allowed to ride in the ox cart. When they reached Farthest Tree, she could be left behind, in the care of her countrymen. Better than being abandoned in the wilderness, where all she could hope for was a hunting party to chance upon her before she succumbed to exposure or worse. She was lucky, Ghan told him, that her health had chosen today to falter.

"But she would fail the pilgrimage," Van said bleakly.

"As sometimes happens," said Ghan Mudcatcher. "She will be allowed to try again on the next pilgrimage year. And to be frank, she will be better off for it."

Van had never heard of such a thing, but the elder wouldn't lie to him. Lilim didn't wake up even after he nestled her into the back of the cart, her head resting on her rucksack, which he had to double back for, in addition to his own.

The day's march felt gruelingly long, the procession arriving at Farthest Tree a few hours past mealtime. Van spent the time sick with worry for Lilim, trudging alongside her cart to ensure she never left his sight. Simon found him while they were still on the road, and he was quick to recognize something was wrong. Van recounted the situation after he activated his spell.

"So we're leaving her behind?" His voice carried a touch of sympathetic disappointment. "She wouldn't get to finish the pilgrimage."

Van smiled weakly. He appreciated that he didn't have to guide Simon to that realization, or explain its significance.

"I'll let Shale know what's up, if I see her," said Simon. "But kid, if you're right and that really is some strain of flu, you should keep your distance until she's better. I can't have you getting sick."

Simon went his own way, and eventually the silhouette of the old fort loomed into view on the road ahead. It didn't look much like a tree to Van, but it was a welcome sight all the same. He pitched both their tents, but rather than moving Lilim into hers, he left her where she could be found easily, in the shade of a large roadside oak. Still she refused to stir, even as he propped her into a sitting position and folded her hands in her lap.

He was reluctant to leave her side at all, but he didn't want to carry her into the village until he knew where he was going. At the very least, she was surrounded by her kinsmen in case she required attention while he was gone. With Lilim's immediate safety taken care of, Van struck out in search of a healer, again taking his coin purse with him.

Farthest Tree was a small community compared to their previous stops, and the aspirants had been instructed at assembly to avoid walking the streets or loitering in public spaces unless they had a dire need. The visiting tribes outnumbered the locals almost four to one, and the place would be overrun if they didn't practice restraint.

Van, however, did have a dire need, and because he didn't have to fight through crowds this time, he found what he was looking for quickly.

Farthest Tree's house of healing was a place called the Shade of Two Leaves. Inside, Van noted that only a few among the dozens of sickbeds were occupied, but he found no one tending to those convalescing. Retracing his steps, he ended up back outside, where he found an older man working in the garden. After hearing Van's plea, the man informed him he would summon the matron, and told him to wait.

Van sat on the stoop, and as promised, the matron soon appeared from within. She was Ikanni, or so Van guessed from her yellow skirts. He bowed formally and introduced himself as an aspirant of Dolse, once again explaining the situation and begging the matron's help. A bed would be no trouble, but the woman scowled at the mention of medicine.

"Medicine such as you seek is in short supply this far north of Stonebasin," she said. "My own stores are empty, and I haven't the reagents to brew more."

"What would you need, specifically?" urged Van. "I can get it for you. I have farthings."

"Tincture of starlight," said the matron. "Rendered from the fruit you southlings call the sparkleberry."

"I have them," Van blurted. "I can bring them to you!"

"I'm sure you could," she said. "But what you are asking for takes time. My time, as it happens, is valuable and limited. I've a duty to use it for the good of all those in my care."

Van untied his coin purse from his belt and handed it to her without a second thought.

"Please," he said.

She cinched the purse open and eyed its contents—eight Eastern Plains Farthings.

"Bring me the berries, and be quick about it."

Van bowed again and took off at a sprint, returning with Lilim and the sparkleberries they'd foraged together. Resting Lilim on a bed near the door, he turned over the satchel of berries to the Ikanni woman.

As warned, rendering the medicine from the berries was a lengthy process. The matron told Van she would bring the tincture to him at the house of healing an hour past evening meal. He thanked her profusely, promising he would be waiting.

He sat with Lilim for the next few hours, wiping the sweat from her face and neck with a towel he found in a cupboard, which he rinsed periodically in an urn filled with clean, cool water.

When it neared time for evening meal, Lilim at last woke up.

"Oh," she said weakly, looking around. "Where are we?"

"We've made it to Farthest Tree," said Van. "You were running a fever, but you can rest here now. There is medicine on the way."

"That's good," she said, her eyelids drooping. "I don't feel well."

Until that moment, Van had clung to hope that Ghan Mudcatcher and Riverspeaker Gheela were wrong—that Lilim wasn't sick after all, but simply fatigued from the demands of their travels. Nothing that couldn't be remedied with a few extra hours of sleep. But he saw now that his hope had been naive.

Lilim was ghostly pale, her lips cracked and dry. Her eyes were glassy, and she shivered despite the blankets he'd piled on her. Even more frightening, the tips of her fingers were beginning to turn blue. More than anything, he felt terribly sorry for her, knowing how disappointed she would be when he told her what came next.

"Lilim," Van said gently. "Ghan Mudcatcher believes you have the influenza, which I'm sure you know is very serious. We're fortunate to have been passing through Farthest Tree today. Here, you can get the rest and medicine you need without putting your health at further risk."

Lilim listened calmly at first, but then, her eyes widened and she bolted upright when she began to understand what he was suggesting.

"No!" she shrieked. "You can't leave me behind!"

"*Shh*, Lilim." Van glanced around the place nervously. "It's much safer here than on the road, and starting tomorrow you would be expected—"

"I would fail the pilgrimage!" she screamed, recoiling when Van tried to take her hand to console her.

"Not forever." He gestured urgently with his hands that she should keep her voice down. "You would be allowed to try again in just nine years. Imagine how much better prepared —"

"I will not remain a child while you become an adult," she shouted over him. "Take me to my tent!"

Lilim was raving, and Van feared if he tried to cover her mouth, she would bite him. Worried they'd be evicted from the premises if she continued in this state, he had no choice but to do as she asked. He picked her up and carried her back to her tent. She didn't speak to him for the rest of the day, eventually slipping back into an uneasy sleep.

"And where is your girl?" demanded the matron when she returned to the Shade of Two Leaves with Van's medicine.

He had returned to the stoop to wait for her alone.

"She's refused to stay," he said, defeated. "I'll make sure she receives the medicine. Thank you."

The Ikanni woman snorted, handing Van a parcel.

"She sounds like a fool to me, but so be it. See that she drinks every drop. You brought me barely enough to ensure efficacy. There is incense, as well." The matron nodded to the parcel. "Burn it near her when she sleeps, and it will go to work on her lungs."

Van thanked her again before returning once more to Lilim. He roused her briefly before sunset, feeding her the medicine a little at a time to make sure she didn't choke or vomit it back up. When she swallowed the last of it, she lay down wordlessly and slept, rolling over in her bedroll so as not to face him.

Exhausted, Van lit the incense, observing with detachment that he would have to tell Simon they weren't getting any cobalt. He stayed with Lilim in her tent that night, listening fretfully to her ragged breathing as he gradually drifted off.

12 Old Sorcerer Paranoia

"Van the Scribe, why are you in my tent?"

Van woke up to the feeling of being shaken.

"I don't remember inviting you in."

Lilim was perched on him with her hands on his shoulders. She gave another firm shake, frowning in confusion. The color had returned to her face, and her breathing sounded normal. Pressing a hand to her forehead, Van realized with a wave of relief that her fever had broken.

Lilim yelped, freezing when Van threw his arms around her. After a moment, when he began to cry, she returned the embrace and patted his head.

"There, there," she soothed. "It was just a bad dream."

Once Van composed himself, they packed their things and went to assembly together, agreeing to resume their lessons the following morning.

Otep's announcements that day were serious in tone. He commended the aspirants on how far they'd come, but he reminded them that beginning today, they would be challenged in new ways. They were no longer in the lands of Dolse. All were cautioned to remain on guard as they traversed the borderlands, for in truth, no tribe held sway here. They might encounter bandits or worse as they trekked north from Farthest Tree, and if they met with danger, they would be expected to conduct themselves as rangers.

"Regarding today's hunt," Otep said in conclusion, "after many postponements, we are to partner with Galdur Goldeyes and tribe Ikann."

Van swallowed hard. Out of respect for his father's teachings, he had made a sincere effort not to cast judgment on the First Ranger of Ikann. But after everything that had passed between them since Galdur Goldeyes first presented his insulting gift to the chieftain at Seat Dolse, Van's mind was made up.

He hated the man. Galdur Goldeyes was cruel, and simpleminded, and very little else. But Van would not disappoint Otep Acrearms. He would hunt.

Lilim had no recollection whatsoever of the time she was sick, and for that Van was grateful. He would sooner forget it, too. She was quick to piece together what must have happened, though—or most of it—and timidly thanked him for looking after her. She returned to her usual cheerful self as they walked hand in hand that day, remarking casually that the lands of Ikann didn't look so different from their own.

For the most part, Van agreed, though he was conscious of the slight but steady drop in temperature as they ventured ever farther north. Forageable woodlands, too, were becoming more scarce. Most significantly, there was no longer a road to follow. From Farthest Tree, the procession marched in column formation across the naked plains, halting as always at midday to camp.

Van wasn't looking forward to telling Simon that he'd failed to obtain their cobalt, but that conversation would wait until after the hunt. Once he helped Lilim pitch her tent, Van parted ways with her and hurried with bow in hand to meet up with Otep.

He had expected a light turnout, but he was dispirited to see only Wilm of the Horizon and Orum the Mutable with the First Ranger. The four rangers of Dolse nodded warily to each other, offering what little reassurance they could before setting out to find Galdur Goldeyes.

Otep gave Van an affectionate pat on the shoulder as they ambled toward the agreed-upon meeting place.

"I am glad the girl is still with us," he said.

Otep had been there, of course, when he'd brought Lilim to Ghan Mudcatcher and Riverspeaker Gheela. And he'd no doubt seen her up and about again at assembly that morning. Van forced a smile, but he struggled to meet Otep's eyes. His friend's admonition to abandon his oath rang in his ears, even now.

Soon, they joined up with the rangers of Ikann west of camp—seven in total, including Galdur. After the First Rangers exchanged terse greetings, the Ikanni took point with Galdur at the head of the pack. Otep's party followed, giving them a wide berth. Van glimpsed no tracks nor any other sign of an animal's passage, but Galdur marched forward with suspicious purpose.

Van, for his part, was done playing the role of passive observer. Since the day he was relegated to acting as nursemaid for Shale, he had promised himself he would take the initiative on future hunts. He'd hoped to do so on the next joint effort with Brynda and tribe Vaxas. But he didn't mind starting with Galdur Goldeyes—to show the arrogant First Ranger of Ikann he didn't scare him.

Disdainful silence hardly seemed in the spirit of the pilgrimage, after all.

"Well met, cousin!" Van called, breaking off from his group to catch up to the Ikanni. "I'm embarrassed to admit I haven't made the acquaintance of your companions."

The two men walking closest to Galdur Goldeyes were the same rangers who'd handled the sickly horse on the eve of the pilgrimage. They looked almost identical, except that one had the stubble of a beard.

"Hammer and Anvil," Galdur said, eyeing Van as he jogged over smiling. "The twin sons of a blacksmith."

"I might have guessed they were twins," said Van. "Having their given names as well might help in telling them apart."

"Teklan," said Galdur.

"Teklan?" Van asked.

Galdur sighed in irritation. "Their father, whose name was also Teklan, named both of them Teklan. The only way to keep track of which is which is to remember that one is Teklan the Hammer and the other is Teklan the Anvil."

"Interesting," Van said disinterestedly. "Oh! I did want to remind you, since we didn't hold lessons yesterday, to bring the thesaurus I lent you this evening. Not to return it, of course, but for reference. I'd like to review our work on vocabulary again, and I know word choice can be challenging for you."

Galdur clenched his fists and leveled his venomous gaze at Van. Behind him, Hammer and Anvil shared a surreptitious smirk.

There came no explosion of anger, no bitter derision or spiteful retort. Perhaps with the mighty First Ranger of Dolse watching from ten paces away, Galdur Goldeyes might finally be forced to hold his tongue and treat Van with a semblance of respect.

"You're sure this was the way?" Galdur snarled, swinging to face the brothers.

The Teklans composed themselves.

"Very," said Hammer. Or perhaps Anvil.

A few minutes later, the dilapidated forms of man-made structures crested the horizon. The Ikanni quickened their pace, and Van matched it at first. He slowed to a halt and stared, uncomprehending, when he saw the buildings were blackened by flame.

"I'll get the others," called Van, remembering Otep's warning about bandits.

Van regrouped with Otep and his party, shooting them a look that conveyed there was danger ahead. The rangers of Dolse broke into a sprint to catch up to the Ikanni, but by the time they reached the burned encampment—or whatever this place had been—Galdur Goldeyes and his party were already picking it over at their leisure.

"What happened here?" Otep shouted.

"Something terrible, I'm sure," said Galdur as he eyed the remains of a ruined longhouse. "Ah. This way, I think."

Van tried to piece together the scene before him as he wandered amid the debris. This place had been put to the torch, but the flames hadn't finished their work. The area smelled like a doused campfire—wood set ablaze and then extinguished. Whoever had attacked the encampment surely meant to destroy all trace of it, but they hadn't accounted for the rain.

Van stayed close to Otep as he followed Galdur to the ruins of the longhouse. A flag still hung over the empty door frame, half scorched, but recognizable. Painted on it was a simple brown urn, a symbol that marked an establishment as a place of public commerce. A symbol familiar to any Dolser.

At Galdur's command, Hammer and Anvil began pulling up the floorboards.

"What are you looking for, cousin?" muttered Otep Acrearms.

"Food and resources, obviously," said Galdur Goldeyes as he watched his men work. "Southlings have a bit in common with rodents, you see. When they smell a storm coming, they dig a hole."

On the third try, Hammer and Anvil found what they sought. No fewer than a dozen crates of foodstuffs lay hidden beneath the longhouse in a shallow trap-door cellar, as well as stacks of furs and bolts of fine cloth. The brothers hauled all the spoils up, piling them at Galdur's feet.

Prying a crate open, Galdur retrieved an apple and polished it on his tunic. He turned it over in his hand, evidently deciding it passed inspection. He replaced the crate's lid and sat down on it, grinning with sloth satisfaction.

"And that, as they say, is how it's done," said the First Ranger of Ikann, biting into the fruit.

The hunters of Dolse wore grave expressions on their way back to camp, carrying half the found goods. Van tried to remain composed, but inside, he was fuming. The bundle of furs in his arms smelled persistently of wet ash.

"How could such a thing have happened so close to Farthest Tree?" he whispered to Otep through clenched teeth.

"The community's rangers do not patrol the borderlands," the First Ranger consoled. "Had we not been passing through, the place may not have been discovered at all."

"The Ikanni that pillaged it had no trouble *discovering* it," said Van flatly.

"Be careful who you repeat that to, Van the Scribe. Tribe Ikann will say the place was set aflame by bandits, and for all we know, that could be the truth."

"There were Dolsers living there!" hissed Van. "Who else could have attacked the settlement? And in the first place, why would anyone choose to live out here?"

"Most likely, they didn't," said Otep. "When members of our tribe are exiled, they are sent into the desert or across the mountains, but we do not always do the best job of ensuring they stay there. Some exiles defy their fate. They try to build a life for themselves in places such as the one we passed through today, far from the Seats and the reach of law."

"We didn't *pass through*," Van insisted. "Galdur Goldeyes led us right to it, and he knew exactly what he'd find. For all we know, he could have ordered the attack himself."

Otep Acrearms offered no further counsel, and as much as Van hated it, he knew his friend was right. Without proof, they could seek neither justice nor reprisal. Even if Galdur Goldeyes admitted to burning the place down himself, he could simply claim he was defending the sovereignty of Ikann from incursion by tribeless criminals.

Almost immediately after the hunting party returned to camp, Simon and Shale sought out Van, and as he'd still had no time to sort out an alternative arrangement, they once again crowded into his tent.

"That suits you, kinsman," Van said to Shale.

Shale blinked, examining herself. She was wearing the dress she'd bought at Third Stone.

"Hardly befitting a daughter of Eventide's highest house," she said. "But an improvement."

"How have you been faring since we last spoke?" asked Van. "Have you spent time with other members of the tribe?"

"Your kin seem convinced I'm some living portent of doom and have little taste for my company," said Shale. "But it seems the other clans don't know what to make of me at all. To them, I'm something new and… hmm, what word fits? Exotic, perhaps?"

"I see," said Van.

"I've made an impression with some members of the yellow clan."

The hair on the back of Van's neck stood up. "The Ikanni?"

Shale nodded and said "*Yes*" in accented Nemian. "They vastly outnumber you, and their champion Goldeyes is picky about who he hunts with. Many of the yellow clan who imagine themselves *rangers*—" again, she used the Nemian word "—have turned to me as a means of proving themselves to him."

"So you… have been hunting with tribe Ikann?"

"It would be more accurate to say I have been teaching them how to hunt," Shale said. "They were having little success before I stepped in."

"I see," Van said uncomfortably. "And what did you hunt?"

"Crocodiles."

"Those are rather dangerous animals," said Van. "They are not typically hunted as game."

Shale shrugged. "Not by your clan, maybe. But they are by the yellow ones, now that I've shown them how."

Van wrinkling his nose. "I'm surprised they... that is to say, I'm impressed you were able to ingratiate yourself with them."

"It was simple enough," she explained, inspecting her nails. "The language barrier was a nuisance, as always, and I'm sure their instincts told them I was dangerous. But young men have a certain appetite for danger that can be relied upon. Fewer than a dozen went with me last time, but word will spread, and next time there will be more."

Somehow, the idea of Shale spending time unsupervised with a dozen or more young Ikanni men didn't sit well with Van.

"That is two questions, by my count," she said. "May I have a turn?"

"Of course," said Van.

"Something happened on your hunt today." Her expression grew serious. "I could tell from the looks on your faces when you came back. What was it?"

Van hesitated, but out of respect for the rules they'd established, he told her the truth. Shale didn't speak again until he finished.

"So, the yellow clan attacked your people," she bluntly summarized. "How will you retaliate?"

"We won't," said Van. "Otep Acrearms is right. We can't know what really happened, and even if we discovered tribe Ikann was responsible, those people were likely exiles— outcasts no longer under the protection of tribe Dolse."

"But they were still your people," she said. "And in your heart you know Goldeyes played a role in their deaths."

Van shook his head. "You don't understand how hard we've worked for peace. Sowing conflict between the tribes would jeopardize everything we've built. Compared to that, whatever personal beliefs I might have do not matter."

"When the dying begins, those are the only things that should matter," said Shale, crossing her arms.

"And what would you do in my place?" asked Van.

Shale's tone and expression remained matter-of-fact. "Slaughter Goldeyes for all to see, and let it serve as warning to the others. Blood calls for blood. To do nothing shows weakness and invites further offense."

Van thought back to Simon's warning that he should take Shale more seriously, but it now seemed to him that she was the one making light of things inappropriately.

"Obviously that won't happen. Please do not make such jokes."

"Did the elf stutter when he spoke for me? Denounce Goldeyes for his actions and kill him. I assume the yellow clan can't win *Patronage* without their champion. What better chance to remove them from the running?"

Van felt suddenly short of breath. "Speak no more of this, Shale."

"I'll do it for you if you don't have the stomach!" Her tone was becoming heated. "He would never see me coming. I could kill all three of them, if you wanted me to. With the other contestants out of the way, your father would rule Nemia!"

"Stop!" shouted Van. He knew the word didn't need to be translated, and Simon didn't bother to.

Shale stared at him in disbelief. Moments later, her face twisted with anger. She kicked dirt onto Van's bedroll and turned to leave the tent, scrabbling on hands and knees. When she was halfway outside, she pivoted to throw something at Van. The object hit him in the chest and fell into his lap.

"I might have to take back what I said last time," said Simon once she left. "Now, is that what I think it is?"

Van glanced down at the object in his lap. It was a drawstring satchel. He picked it up and opened it so both he and Simon could see its contents—a coarse, glittering powder of deep blue.

"Cobalt," Van said quietly. "But when? How?"

Simon gave him a pointed look. "I told you she paid attention."

"Then, *why?*"

"Well, kid," said Simon, folding his arms, "despite how hard it is to watch the two of you puzzle each other out, I think Shale might actually like you."

Van felt a sudden prick of shame. "What reason have I given her to like me? I must seem as unsympathetic and prejudiced as the rest of my tribe."

"Just now you did, yeah," relented Simon. "But who took care of her for a whole year, after your dad's rangers found her? Who was bringing her food and clean clothes and checking on her every day, when nobody else wanted to?"

Van blinked. "I did those things."

"Uh-huh," said Simon. "I know. I was there. I just wanted you to hear yourself say it."

With that, Simon stood up to leave. His only goodbye was trading Van his freshly enchanted quill back for the cobalt.

As he sat in Brynda Blackblade's tent that evening, Van had never been so nervous. His attention was split between their lesson and his last-minute mental rehearsal of the deception he was about to perform. First, he set Galdur to work on an exercise to tidy his handwriting. All Van needed was for him to make a mistake, and he didn't have to wait long. Spotting an error, he stood up and wordlessly walked around to the First Rangers' side of the table.

Van was generally opposed to dishonesty, and he had no experience with sleight of hand. He remembered being told, though—he wasn't sure by whom—that the best way to conceal an action was to do it quickly and without calling attention to it.

With that in mind, he didn't ask for Galdur's quill when he sat down next to him. He simply took it, and he was so surprised when Galdur made no objection, he struggled to keep his shock from showing on his face.

He redrew the word Galdur had butchered, and just as he was nearly finished, he applied exactly enough pressure to snap the quill's tip.

"Now look what you've done," Galdur hissed.

"Not to worry," said Brynda. "We can share mine."

Van was already halfway back to his seat.

"I'm sorry, First Ranger," he said to Brynda, "but that won't do at all."

He picked up the quill he'd brought and leaned forward, offering it to Galdur.

"It is only right that I take responsibility for what I foolishly broke."

Galdur didn't take it right away, instead casting a sidelong glance at Brynda, like he was waiting for permission. She said nothing, merely watching Van impassively.

At length, Galdur snorted and took Van's quill. "At least this Dolser understands the value of things."

The lesson resumed as normal, though it took time for Van's heart to stop beating quite so fast.

"Are you ready, kid?"

Van sat across from Simon in his tent, the mixing bowl between them filled near to the brim with clear water. Shale, it seemed, was avoiding them, so for today, they were alone. The various material components Simon had requested were arranged within reach. Van's stomach twisted. It hadn't even been a full day since he'd seen Brynda. He felt anything but ready.

"You're certain this is safe?" Van said, swallowing hard. "What if we're found out?"

"I was a military security advisor to the world's most advanced nation for more than half a century," said Simon. "I'm pretty sure I can match wits with your teenage girlfriend."

Drawing a deep breath, Van nodded, and the foreigner set about adding the pigmentation elements to the bowl. The water grew opaque and muddy, but it cleared again when he mixed in the salt. He lifted a hand as if preparing to activate the dormant magic in the bowl, but Van noticed one parcel remained unopened.

"What about that one?" He gestured to the pouch, worried Simon had forgotten something.

"Unnecessary precaution," said Simon without bothering to look at it. "Old sorcerer paranoia, like I told you before."

Van nodded again and waited, chewing on his lip as he watched the bowl.

Peering at Van, Simon offered a last-minute consideration. "She could be getting undressed right now, you know."

"Simon!" shrieked Van, his voice cracking.

"Or she could be picking her nose," the foreigner said indifferently. "Or whatever else people do when they think they're alone."

"Stop the spell! This was a terrible idea, and I don't know how you talked me into it."

"Van—"

"Fine. I'll do it myself." He reached for the bowl.

Simon saw it coming and caught him by the wrists.

"Calm down, kid. Listen to me—honesty now. I'll stop if that's what you really want. And yeah, what we're about to see might be upsetting or uncomfortable. For any number of reasons. But you're an aspirant, right? One with a genuine concern that one of the First Rangers isn't playing by the rules. What do you feel your responsibility is?"

Van clenched his fists, staring into the mixing bowl.

"To learn the truth," he said quietly. "By any means necessary."

"All right," said Simon, easing his grip on Van's wrists and releasing him slowly. "Then let's get this peep show started."

Van opened his mouth to scold Simon again, but his voice caught in his throat. It was too late. The water in the bowl became mirror-like, a reflection of a place far away.

Brynda's tent was vacant.

"That's a little anticlimactic," said Simon.

Van exhaled, only then realizing he'd been holding his breath.

"Where did you say she was keeping the bird?"

Van pointed at the image. "Inside that. The bottom drawer."

Simon frowned.

"Can you, um," Van floundered. "Can you control our perspective in any way?"

"We can move the image anywhere within a few feet of the target."

Anywhere near the quill, Van considered. "Move us into the drawer."

Simon flicked his wrist at the bowl, and the water became as black as ink.

"What happened?" Van stammered.

"I moved us inside a closed drawer with no light source," said the foreigner, moving them back to the center of Brynda's tent. "Seemed easier than explaining to you why that's a dumb idea."

A few minutes passed uneventfully. Van grew restless, tapping on his knee to stem his boredom.

"How long can we keep this up?" he asked.

"Indefinitely." Simon stared patiently into the bowl. "Provided we don't throw out this water, and she doesn't get rid of that quill."

Just as Simon finished speaking, Brynda Blackblade and Galdur Goldeyes walked into the tent together. Van almost jumped when the image moved, and again when the sound of voices rose up out of the bowl—slightly distorted, like an echo in a cave.

"I am simply pointing out, you could have made the attempt for the sake of appearances," Brynda was saying to Galdur.

"And muck around in their filthy pond making a fool of myself?" sneered Galdur. "I think not."

Simon's eyes flicked up. "My other spells won't work across a scrying portal. You'll have to fill me in on what they're saying later."

"Tribe Dolse is emboldened by their victory," chided the murky image of Brynda Blackblade. Her skin and Galdur's were the wrong color, a disorienting purple. "And by their First Ranger as well, I think. Quite a specimen. A stronger showing than I expected from our cousins."

"When we reach Seat Ikann, that brute will learn where he stands," Galdur scoffed. "And tribe Dolse will remember their place."

"I should hope so," Brynda said sweetly. "I can't imagine how embarrassing it would be if you managed to lose at your own game."

"You do your part, witch, and I'll do mine."

"Be quiet, Galdur," said Brynda, her expression suddenly humorless.

"Oh, what's that?" mocked Galdur. "You don't like being called a—?"

"Be silent."

Galdur froze and shut his mouth. Slowly, Brynda swept her gaze around her tent, making a subtle gesture with one hand. Otep had taught it to Van years ago. When used among rangers on the hunt, it meant something akin to, *We are being watched.* Van held his breath again when Brynda's head stopped. The sensation was exactly like the first time he'd seen her, when she was presented at Seat Dolse. Impossibly, she was looking back at him.

In a paroxysm of movement, Simon grabbed the unopened pouch next to him and threw its contents in the bowl. The clay dust immediately clouded the water, and the image vanished.

"Tell me everything they said," Simon ordered. "Be exact."

Van repeated the exchange between Brynda and Galdur, word for word.

"Are you sure that's what he called her?" Simon wore the look of a man who'd come home to discover it had caught fire. "He specifically said 'witch'?"

"It is a very disrespectful thing to call a person," explained Van.

"No. It implies skill with magic," said Simon. "Is Brynda some kind of sorcerer? Have you seen her work with spells?"

"I'm sure the dagger she carries is magical," said Van. "As for Brynda herself, I have no idea what her relationship to magic is."

Simon rubbed his jaw. "All right. We're about out of time, but you're going there next, right?"

"Right," Van heard himself say.

"Can you stick to an alibi?"

Van furrowed his brow. "A *what?*"

"I'm going to tell you what to tell her when she asks about the quill."

Van's blood ran cold. "Why would she ask about the quill? You said this was safe!"

"Do what I say, and it will be."

Van listened intently.

"When she asks about the quill, tell her that I—" Everything Simon said following that was completely unintelligible.

Van made the talking sign, and Simon started over. This time, not a single word came across. Van made the sign again and punctuated it by drawing a finger across his throat.

"*Fuck!*" yelled Simon.

Not an hour later, Van sat in the First Ranger's tent in the Vaxas campsite. The subject of the quill came up even quicker than he could have anticipated.

Brynda politely apologized, explaining offhandedly that she'd broken it. A simple mistake. She and Galdur were now taking turns with her remaining spare, as she'd offered previously.

Van thought hard, his mind turning over Simon's half-finished instruction.

When she asks, tell her that I...

"Think nothing of it, First Ranger," said Van. "To tell you the truth, I'd already gotten used to not having it on hand."

"Oh?" Brynda tilted her head slightly.

"Indeed," said Van. "For a time, I thought I'd misplaced it, but it was brought to light that one of the foreigners had borrowed it without permission. They can be, um... Well, I think the foreigners are still coming to terms with our notions of property ownership. And consent."

"Oh, dear," said Brynda. "Which of the foreigners took it?"

"The male," said Van. "He calls himself Simon of the Mists."

"I see. I heard a rumor that one was talented with magic. Is it true?"

"I believe so, yes," said Van.

"How strange that Farseer Daz would grant them asylum," Brynda mused. "Though, I suppose if we are to honor the chieftain's wish, we should make an effort to know them better." A good-natured smile lit up her face. "I have a funny idea—why don't we invite this Simon of the Mists to our next lesson?"

"Um," stumbled Van.

"Are you on friendly terms with him? Could you arrange it?"

"I can make no promises on his behalf," said Van, "but I would be happy to extend your invitation."

"Thank you, cousin," Brynda said pleasantly. "Please do."

"So you told her I just stole it?" Simon cringed when Van made his report the following day.

Van sighed. "I'm sorry, Simon. I thought perhaps it was what you wanted me to do."

"It was," said Simon. "I just would've come up with a plausible reason to have wanted your quill. Whatever, it's fine. The point is we've transferred suspicion from you to me."

"I'll tell her you declined her invitation."

"Oh, no you won't," said Simon. "Remember what I told you? None of my spells work across scrying portals. But if I can sit down with her, look her in the eye for real, we might actually learn something."

Van shook his head, exasperated. "What could you possibly hope to gain by doing that?"

"For starters, we'll know whether she's a sorcerer," said Simon. "I'll test her for magic, and I'll gauge her familiarity with it. Plus, if my short-range spells pick up any traces of necromancy on her, it's fair to say that tells us everything we need to know about the bird you found."

"Simon, has it occurred to you that if you're right, and she's some dangerous sorcerer, you'd be putting yourself at risk? That it could be a trap?"

"I'm on team Dolse according to your dad, aren't I?"

"Yes," said Van, frowning in confusion.

"So, what would happen if Brynda or somebody else on her team tried to kill one of you guys?"

"That would be tantamount to an act of war," Van responded quietly.

"Grounds for disqualification from the whole Patronage thing, I would hope?"

"Of course," said Van. "Among many other severe consequences."

Simon crossed his arms. "Well, I have a hunch this girl is playing to win, so that means I'm off limits."

Van nodded in reluctant agreement. They would have to wait a day to take Brynda up on her offer, so that Simon's language spell would have time to replenish. In the meantime, they rehearsed what they would tell her in the event they were questioned separately about the history of their relationship. It was in this way, on the year of his pilgrimage, that Van the Scribe of tribe Dolse learned what it meant to have an alibi.

On the night he presented Simon of the Mists to Brynda Blackblade and Galdur Goldeyes, Van could only watch and wonder. He introduced the foreigner, then stepped aside. The next hour was given over to Brynda, who politely but pointedly questioned Simon on his upbringing, his homeland, and—of course—his comprehension of magic.

Owing to the fickle rules of Simon's language spell, Van couldn't understand him when he responded to Brynda. They'd agreed ahead of time to keep to the truth wherever possible, though, so for the most part, Simon would be telling her the same things he'd told Van.

When the topic of magic arose, Simon put on a demonstration of sorts, borrowing Brynda's quill to draw some convoluted diagram at her request. Van studied Brynda's reaction, realizing this must be the test Simon spoke of. Most likely, the diagram was nonsense. If Brynda identified it as such and denounced Simon as a fraud, they'd have their evidence that she was versed in spellwork.

She wore a tired smile as Simon directed her attention to the diagram, and listened patiently to his long-winded fictional explanation of it. If Van didn't know better, he would have said she looked bored. When the time allotted for Simon's language spell ran out, they agreed to stop there for the evening and resume as normal tomorrow.

Brynda seemed unfazed when she said goodnight to Van, and he found himself smiling genuinely back at her, more relieved than he'd felt in days—like a weight had been lifted from his shoulders.

Van had to wait until the following afternoon to talk to Simon again. It marked the fourth day in a row that neither of them had seen Shale.

"No traces of necromancy," declared Simon. "No evidence of any magic, for that matter. Not even basic stuff, like spells to keep her clothes from smelling."

"Then she is cleared of suspicion," Van concluded.

His eyebrows drew together. "What? No. Really powerful sorcerers are capable of masking the presence of their magic entirely. If anything, I was even more worried about her at first. So I tested her, like I told you I would."

"The nonsense thing you scribbled," said Van, nodding along.

"I told her it was a spell for warding off insects, but it was actually category three siege magic. Enough firepower to turn a cornfield to glass—drawn to completion and ready to go with a snap of my fingers. She didn't bat an eyelash."

Van's eyes flew wide. "Why would you do something so dangerous!"

"Because of that right there," Simon said, pointing at him. "Anyone in their right mind who knew what I was doing would have either stopped me or made a run for it."

"So she knows nothing of magic," said Van, exhausted. "Are you satisfied now that she's not some villainous sorcerer who's trying to defraud the Journey of Patronage?"

Simon frowned and crossed his arms. "We still don't know for sure about the bird. And she obviously broke your quill because she figured out somebody was using it to scry on her. I hate to break it to you, kid, but at this point, I have more questions than answers."

Van scarcely heard the various warnings Simon lectured him with after that, none of which amounted to anything more than "be careful around Brynda Blackblade."

Hadn't Simon himself admitted to being inexperienced with the scrying spell they'd used? Wasn't that precisely why Van had run himself ragged looking for cobalt—so Simon could use the crutch he called "hedge wizardry" to defy the boundaries of his own understanding? For all they knew, Van's quill could have started humming and glowing when Simon activated the magic he'd hidden inside it.

Van decided the real lesson in all this was to temper his expectations of the foreigner. Things returned to normal with Brynda the following night, and when Van finished his lesson with her and Galdur, he slept peacefully for the first time in nearly a week.

13 Stewards of the Plains and Highlands

As distracting as Van's ill-conceived misadventure with Simon had been, he was surprised when Otep reminded the aspirants that they would reach their next milestone in a day's time. Seat Ikann was still a full week away, but the community of Sky's Edge lay directly between here and there, and they would be stopping once again to resupply.

From now until the end of the pilgrimage the aspirants of tribe Dolse were visitors in the lands of other tribes, and were thus expected to comport themselves respectfully. Van's peers exchanged nervous glances, knowing they would soon be surrounded and outnumbered by Ikanni—for the first time in most of their lives. But amid Otep's announcements, Van glimpsed an opportunity.

Sky's Edge was home to tribe Ikann's Temple to the Emissaries. Van would offer prayer there, of course, and invite Lilim to join him as she had at Stonebasin. This time, however, he would convince Simon to pay a visit, too.

"Almost time for the next big game already?" said Simon when Van found him that afternoon to convey their immediate travel plans. "Feels like we just left Dolseville."

"Seat Ikann is much closer to Nemia's centerpoint than Seat Dolse," said Van. "Their territories are vast compared to ours, but because of our route, we won't be in them for as long."

And thank the gods of the land for that, he almost added.

"How's the champ feeling?" asked Simon.

"You mean Otep?" Van asked. "Eager to demonstrate his abilities, I'm sure."

"Are you worried whoever's in charge at Seat Ikann will rig things? Won't they at least pick a game Galdur's already good at?"

"That's just it," said Van, turning his palms up. "I'm not sure Galdur Goldeyes is good at anything."

Simon laughed. "All right, so we've got *that* to look forward to. What about Sky's End? Anything worth seeing there?"

"Sky's *Edge*," Van corrected. "And yes, there is. Tribe Ikann's Temple to the Emissaries, which I intend to visit. And Simon, I really think you should come with me this time. You could learn much about the Nemian people there."

Simon frowned, but it seemed to Van that he was considering it.

"Fine," he said. "If you don't think that me being there will cause a scene, I'll check it out. Will I have to get up early?"

Van blinked. "Why would you?"

"Like, for mass or whatever?" said Simon. "What time of day do Nemians go to church?"

"Perhaps we should start over," said Van, trying to parse Simon's words. "You once told me you didn't feel welcome in such places. If I knew more about your own people's attitudes toward the temples of their gods, I might be able to better tell you what to expect from ours. As it stands now, I have no idea what you're talking about."

Simon gave him a concise explanation of prayer and worship as he understood them. As he listened, Van realized it was probably too concise. He prefaced his statements by noting that, in his country, organized religion was not held in vogue. There was almost universal agreement that gods existed, but they rarely, if ever, intervened in the lives of mortals. In Gnosos, therefore, living in service to them was considered a waste of time.

The study of magic in Simon's homeland was divorced from spirituality. But in other countries, temples to the divine were considered authorities on many matters—spellcraft included. Large and well-established churches fostered relationships between people and their gods, though strict rules existed surrounding how frequently these foreign gods required their followers to visit such places, and what they were expected to do there. Simon gave a brief account of morning and evening mass, and of tithing, which to Van sounded outright predatory.

"Obviously, it can change from one god to the next, and there are more gods than you can shake a stick at," said Simon. "Just now, I was talking about the Church of Solaar."

Van was sure Simon would have a better time visiting a Nemian Temple.

"Simon, you should put aside your past experiences and try to keep an open mind. The Temple to the Emissaries is principally a place for quiet meditation. Services are sometimes held, but attendance is never mandatory. The doors are always open for anyone to come and go as they please, regardless of their relationship to the gods.

"We will likely find others there, whenever we choose to go, and yes, some of them might be in prayer. That can take any number of forms. There is no right or wrong way to seek a dialogue with the gods, so long as we treat the Temple and its visitors respectfully."

Van then confessed to Simon that his earliest memory of such a place was when he'd fallen asleep on a pew in the Temple at Stonebasin after he'd brought a book there to read one afternoon. The gods hadn't entered his thoughts at all.

"You should be an evangelist," said Simon, cracking a sarcastic smile. "You make it sound almost palatable."

"Why does Solaar require his followers to give him their wealth?" asked Van, still puzzled over that point.

"It's not like Solaar is personally shaking people down for money," said Simon. "It's the Church, which is operated by run-of-the-mill mortals. They build cathedrals, hospitals, libraries... none of which are cheap. So, belonging to the Church has a membership fee. Who pays for your Temples?"

Van shrugged. "I suppose for us, it's the other way around. People don't belong to the Temple, the Temple belongs to us. Should it come to it, the responsibility to ensure a Temple doesn't fall into disrepair would be the chieftain's. But it has never been a burden for tribe Dolse to maintain the Temple at Stonebasin. If the place is ever in need of renovation, or cleaning, members of the community volunteer freely. When large gatherings are held there, many people bring food and drink to share. I have also heard of our Temple being used as a shelter for displaced families in times of need. The Temple serves the tribe, and the tribe serves the Temple. There has never been a need to make doing so compulsory."

"State religion," supplied Simon. "Most people where I come from would balk at that."

"State religion?" echoed Van, his brow furrowed.

"When a nation officially or financially endorses a specific religious following while denouncing others, like what you just described."

"Is that not typical?"

"The Church of Solaar is a private institution," said Simon. "Admittedly, there's a lot of back scratching between them and the Council of Hierarchs. But officially, Arbus Arkad has no state religion, and there are loads of other prominent doctrines in the West."

Van frowned. "You mentioned before that your people *do* denounce some gods, though. What about—what did you call him—Frenzy?"

"That's not a case of one religion trying to assert dominance over another," said Simon, his face serious. "That's a case of literally every reasonable person in the civilized world coming to a consensus. Endorsing the worship of Frenzy, or any of the Depravities, is basically the same as endorsing wanton murder. Denouncing murder isn't a super controversial position."

"The Depravities?" prodded Van.

"The villains of the story," said Simon, a shadow falling over him. "Karn, Malus, and Frenzy. It's believed they were originally part of the Celestial pantheon, but they stepped out of line, and Solaar cast them down. Some people interpret the scripture more literally, and maintain they were all once a part of the same being—that Solaar cut the bad parts of himself out like tumors. Whatever the case, they're diametrically opposed to Solaar and the rest of the Celestial gods. They embody the worst in people. Our basest instincts, our cruelest and most selfish thoughts. Some write off their whole agenda as payback for whatever Solaar did to them, way back when the planar continuum was first being created and the laws of reality were being written. But it's impossible to say what motivates a god."

Van released a long breath. "I hate to be the one to tell you this, Simon, but your gods all sound awful."

"All right, that's twice now you got me going about the really nasty ones, so I get where you're coming from," Simon conceded. "Let me take a step back. As the unofficial spokesperson for the civilized world here in Nemia, I'll try to give the good guys some representation, too."

Simon closed his eyes in thought. His rigid expression told Van he was trying to take the subject seriously.

"Let's start with Solaar, since we've mentioned him already. If the Celestial pantheon is one big family—and some people think they literally are—then he's the father. He's associated with the sun, justice, and the rule of law. Solaar is seen as a protector, both to the other Celestial gods and to the mortals living on Titan, so long as they're upstanding and moral and all that. Like I said, a lot of public works have been built in his name, which was instrumental to the development of modern Western society.

"Next would be Lunaar, the mother, who's associated with the moon. She's seen usually as a teacher who encourages the pursuit of knowledge, empowering those who seek it, but also sometimes as a keeper of dangerous secrets. Some people think it was her decision that only certain people—like me—are born with natural magical ability."

Simon paused, waiting to see if Van had any questions so far. He didn't.

"Then there's Aurora, my personal favorite. Her biggest church is in Arbus Arkad, in a city called North Kasser. I spent a summer there while studying abroad, trying to pass the

Arcanum Regula exams so I could work for the Gnosian Military Quarter. She's associated with good fortune and bountiful harvests. Some call her Lady Luck, to the point where you might catch gambling addicts praying to her, but that look really doesn't do her justice.

"When I was in North Kasser, they were still dedicating the entire first month of spring to Aurora, and the church would open its grounds to everyone in the city for a few days. The grounds have this huge apple orchard, just acre upon acre of apple trees. When they would open the gates, the whole city would storm the place to pick all the apples."

Simon wore a nostalgic smile smile as he continued.

"That started the tradition of the annual Harvest Festival. People would come together and bake apple pies, or make apple sauce, stewed apples, candied apples—you name it. Nobody ever charged for anything. The church just gave away the whole month's crop. I never visited the church itself, but I have fond memories of wandering the grounds."

"That sounds pleasant," said Van, smiling himself now. "Let me guess, she's the daughter?"

"Good guess," said Simon. "Aurora is depicted most often as the daughter of Solaar and Lunaar. But every once in a while, you'll come across some ancient work that paints her as Solaar's lover, or a mistress."

"It seems problematic that there is confusion on that point," said Van.

"You're not wrong, kid," chuckled Simon, "but these are gods we're talking about. They can be whatever they want, and their relationships are more complicated and vastly more abiding than any you or I will ever have. Maybe Aurora is neither of those things. Maybe somehow she's both. All I know is, I had her to thank for a free meal at a time in my life when money was tight."

Van nodded contemplatively. "And where does Shale's Twilight Prophet fit into all this?"

"Good question," mused Simon. "I can't see her and Solaar getting along, but the entire mythology of the Twilight Prophet exists outside of the Celestial gods and the Depravities. As far as I know, there's no reference to her in any canonical Solaarian texts. If nothing else, let your takeaway be this—there are as many gods as there are people. Maybe more, since the people who came before us had their own gods, too.

"People spend decades studying this stuff and still manage to walk away with an incomplete picture. It doesn't help that the scripture contradicts itself, if you look too hard at it. The whole thing is confusing to the point of being unapproachable. Since gods can't be reasoned with and don't seem to really care what we do, I say spend your time learning something more useful."

Van nodded again, but he felt his attention starting to slip.

"I would have liked to invite Shale to go with us today," he said with a touch of melancholy. "It's been days, and I feel I still owe her an apology. I wish she would stop avoiding us."

"Avoiding *you*, you mean," said Simon pointedly. He shrugged. "I don't know, Van. I think you'll have to take your own advice when it comes to that apology. 'Speak through your actions,' was it?"

Van grimaced. He remembered saying something like that to Shale.

After his evening lesson with Galdur and Brynda, Van took the long way back to his tent, skirting around the campsites of the tribes. It was a beautiful night, warm and cloudless with a light breeze. And as usual, he had too much on his mind.

Any doubts he once harbored about Brynda Blackblade had been short-lived, but he wouldn't put it past Galdur Goldeyes to cheat by any means available to him—at Seat Ikann, and for the remainder of the pilgrimage. But how could he?

The chieftains' games attracted too many onlookers for any contestant to get away with overt foul play. An attempt to award an unfair advantage to Galdur at Seat Ikann would be noticed and denounced at once. What game, then, would the Ikanni choose if they had no choice but to compete fairly?

Van couldn't imagine Otep Acrearms losing in a contest of athleticism. Harder still was to imagine Galdur outperforming Brynda or Sol Starfletcher in any test of intellect.

Despite what he'd told Simon, Van had no idea what Otep was thinking or feeling as of late. They'd hunted together most days since the commencement of the pilgrimage, but it felt like a long while since Van had actually spent time with his friend.

A victory for Otep at Seat Ikann would place him well in the lead over his peers. The idea sent a jolt of excitement through Van. The First Cycle of Dolser Patronage would be an incredible time to be alive. Farseer Daz was no longer a young man—if Otep won Patronage for the tribe, did he intend to make him the next chieftain of Dolse? And if Otep was chieftain, would he still have time to go fishing with Van on sunny afternoons?

Would he still want to?

Something looming in the corner of his vision startled Van out of his bittersweet reverie. He saw figures in the distance, dark against the star-flecked drape of the sky. Too big to be people, and completely stationary. But not the right shape to be trees.

Curious, Van let his feet carry him toward the tall shapes, and when he reached them, he froze. They were stones, each one painted with the likeness of an animal. The oblong monoliths were left here in a circle, standing vertically—save for one that had toppled over, hiding whatever was painted on its face.

A burial ground. Van took a step back, not wanting to insult the spirits of those interred here. A moment later, he turned to leave. These weren't the lands of his people. He had no right to linger in such a place.

After three paces, he stopped and looked back, peering again at the old stone that had fallen. No one was sitting there, of course. But it *was* the sort of place Shale would like. He took a breath and strode through the ring of burial stones, climbing onto the one that had fallen and sitting on its edge, his legs dangling off the side.

"I suppose you might not be there," Van said to the empty air. "And without Simon here, you'd only be able to understand a few words. But I wanted to apologize. I've been dismissive of your views and opinions. You were right— we've done a poor job of trying to understand you. I'd like to try again, if you have any patience left for me."

No response came. Van gazed up at the stars, recalling the words to an old hunting chant. A rhyme Otep had taught him the first time they'd gone out tracking together. The words always sounded lonely to Van, but rangers on the hunt sometimes sang it or hummed its tune to remind each other they had friends close by.

"Whose fields these are I think I know,
Their hearth is cold already though,
They will not mind me stopping here,
To watch their fields at night aglow,
"My tired eyes and restless mind,
Can't but help bleak visions find,
Because I mustn't yield to fear,
I think I too should go in kind,
"The fields are lovely, dark, and vast,
But such moments aren't meant to last,
So turn I now from all that's passed,
So turn I now from all that's passed."

Shale's shoulder touched his, and for a time, they sat quietly together that way.

Lilim happily accepted Van's invitation to visit the Temple to the Emissaries. She walked hand in hand with him all morning, a contented smile on her face. He had once again lent her *The Bull and the Snail,* as she'd mentioned during their last lesson that she wanted to draw more scenes from the book. Simon walked alongside them, ready to activate his language spell when they reached their destination.

The procession reached Sky's Edge well before noon, permitting them most of the day to explore the community at their leisure—which was good news, considering Van would have to ask for directions.

The community was built on a stepped rise, its brightly painted structures visible from leagues away. Foundations of rammed earth supported stone or wooden buildings built three or sometimes four stories tall. Their walls sloped inward to provide the appearance of even greater height, and many had windows of paper stretched over wooden latticework.

"So, this is Ikann," said Simon as the procession reached the main road and began to disperse throughout the urban sprawl. "And not even the Seat. I knew they were the bigger tribe, but you either understated it, or you didn't know the extent of it yourself."

Van nodded, feeling more than a little overwhelmed. He clutched Lilim's hand a little tighter as they shuffled along the busy street. A music troupe stood on a wide stage near the southern approach, singing and drumming to celebrate the arrival of the aspirants. The throngs of travelers flooded forward, drawn toward what appeared to be the community's commercial district as they clambered to trade coin or trophies for designer goods.

"Does all this put things into perspective for you?" nudged Simon.

"How do you mean?" Van took a left arbitrarily at the first fork in the road.

"These were the bad guys not too long ago, right? And if Galdur wins this thing for them, what then?"

"I've told you, the Ikanni are not villains," said Van, echoing his father. "The times you're referring to are in the past, and those responsible are long since gone."

"I hope you're right, kid," muttered the foreigner. "Because if you're wrong, and they win, I would not want your dad's job for the next nine years."

Van glanced at Lilim, and she smiled at him, cheerfully oblivious.

"I've been wondering. Why is it that only one of us can understand you at a time?" Van asked, turning his attention back to Simon. "You, Shale, and I all speak different languages, so it makes sense that it works like that during our three-ways —"

"Phrasing." Simon gave Van a pointed look.

"—but Lilim and I speak the same language. Why can't she understand you right now? And why couldn't I, that time you translated for her and Shale?"

Simon sighed.

"Haven't we been over this? Because I'm not speaking your language right now. There isn't a spell in the world that would let me actually *speak* your language. When I was talking to Lilim I was speaking international common, the language the rest of the world uses. That's what I'm speaking any time I talk to you, to Shale, or to anyone else. By making you the target of the spell, I can trick you into understanding me, but it's always a one-to-one arrangement."

It wasn't a very satisfying answer, but Van had expected as much. He chose to let it go. Finally, he spotted a storefront that wasn't completely overrun. An aged Ikanni man with a long beard sat behind a stall to the side of the road. Van stopped to ask for directions to the Temple, but before they moved on, Simon asked Van if he could help him buy a few things. Van agreed, and they decided he should do the talking, so as not to frighten the elderly shopkeep.

Simon indicated a straw hat and a pair of leather high boots from among the oddments on offer. The bearded man fixed Simon with a suspicious glare before guardedly asking Van what he had to trade.

"Tell him you can use these to start fires," Simon said to Van, producing a few small squares of parchment from a pocket of his floating rucksack.

Van obliged, but the bearded man only grew more suspicious.

"He wants a demonstration," said Van.

Simon blinked. "What, right here?"

Van shrugged.

Sighing, Simon stepped forward with one of the squares. He held it up for the Ikanni to see, and Van noticed only then that the parchment had two symbols drawn on it—one of which he recognized as a component of the extremely dangerous diagram he'd shown Brynda Blackblade. Van put a hand on Lilim's shoulder and pulled her back a pace from the stall.

Holding the square with both hands, Simon tore it down the middle—not completely in half, but just enough so that one of the symbols was divided. He then placed the square on the corner of the man's stall, stepping back to the same distance as Van. He silently counted down on his fingers while the bearded man scrutinized the paper square with a scowl.

When Simon lowered his last finger, the corner of the man's stall burst into flames, sending the Ikanni reeling and singeing his beard. He quickly fetched a rug and beat the fire down before it could cause any damage.

Moments later, they were strolling up the street again with Simon's new purchases, bought for twelve strips of enchanted paper. Because he would have to modify the hat later to accommodate his pointed ears, Simon stowed it for the time being in his pack, bobbing obediently through the air behind him.

"Where did you get the parchment?" asked Van. "The ink?"

"I asked Ghan for it," said Simon. "He let me borrow a brush, too. But it's our girl Shale who I have to thank for the idea—it never occurred to me we could trade for stuff on the road until she showed up in her new cocktail dress."

After another hour, they finally found the Temple to the Emissaries, a building almost indistinguishable from those around it. From the outside, nothing about it seemed special. Van felt a little disappointed. Without the shopkeep's directions, he might never have found it at all.

Predictably, the place was crowded, so they waited outside until a large group finished praying and left. Simon's spell for language had long since run out, but it was no matter. The foreigner could learn much by simply observing, and the Temple itself should require no explanation once inside.

Van sat down on a pew near the back this time, maintaining some distance from the Temple's other visitors, and Lilim sat down beside him. She closed her eyes and prayed again, and seeing her communing with the gods, Van smiled. He looked to his other side, expecting to see Simon, but the foreigner still stood frozen in the door.

Van watched him, perplexed by the shadow of stark horror on his face. He glanced at Van—only for a moment, as if he didn't recognize him—and then fled back out to the street. Concerned, Van snapped his head to whatever he'd been staring at near the front of the Temple. There was nothing there but the altar, and behind it, the statues of the Emissaries.

The gods of the land depicted here were another male and female pair, like those that stood in tribe Dolse's Temple. The female, holding a scepter, even looked a little like Brynda— except, of course, for the broad wings and long tail.

14 Gods of the Land

"Devils, Van. The Ikanni worship *devils*."

"If you are talking about the Emissaries, you should know that all Nemians pray to them," said Van, trying to speak calmly despite the fact that Simon was practically yelling.

A full day had passed since their visit to the Temple at Sky's Edge, and only a day's travel remained between them and Seat Ikann.

"And I would have known weeks ago if I'd listened to you at Stonebasin," Simon's face was even paler than usual, beaded with sweat. "I'm an idiot. A real idiot."

Van wanted to believe Simon was only being sardonic, as was typical of him, but he could tell this was different. This was real distress.

"Simon, does this somehow explain your country's interest in us?"

"It explains literally everything!" shouted Simon. "It explains why they sent me here. It explains Nemia's isolationist policies and the institutionalized xenophobia, the population control—probably even whatever happened here eight hundred years ago. All of it."

"Wait a moment. You said that only something recent could have shifted your people's attitudes toward us," said Van. "We have prayed to the Emissaries for centuries."

"Yeah, but who actually *knows* that?" Simon leaned forward as if moved by a thought. "Foreigners have been granted asylum here before, right?"

"Perhaps one in a decade," said Van, his brow furrowed.

"Is it always your tribe that picks them up?"

"We are the Stewards of the Coast," said Van. "Nemia's southern shores are ours to watch over and protect. As far as I know, there is nowhere else foreigners could come from."

"When was the last one?" prodded Simon. "Before me, before Shale?"

Van thought hard. "My father spoke of a visitor among us when I was very young. The year after my mother died, I think. I have no memory of him—or her. I couldn't have been more than four years old."

"What happened to them?"

"They returned from whence they came."

"How long were they here?"

"I... have no idea," stumbled Van.

"Think. Did they visit the Temple?" pressed Simon. "Did they see those statues?"

"I have no way of knowing that, Simon," sighed Van. "I... seem to recall my father saying they took a respectful interest in our ways, during their time here."

Simon's face was turning red. "Were they a sorcerer?"

Van held out his hands in exasperation. "Simon, I was four years old."

"Why don't you guys do your job and get rid of these people?"

"Historically, we have," said Van. "But since my father became chieftain, he has always called for restraint and open-mindedness in dealing with foreigners."

Simon groaned.

"What is it, Simon?" asked Van in a low voice.

"Your dad messed up."

Van took a breath, choosing his next words carefully. It was time to say what needed to be said, but he feared doing so would irreversibly strain his relationship with Simon. He wasn't looking forward to that.

"Simon, the Emissaries are beings of love and compassion. They aren't anything like Frenzy, or the Depravities, or the Twilight Prophet. They have protected us and blessed us with prosperity for generations."

"Yeah?" snapped Simon. "Is that what they told you? That they love you?"

"Obviously, I have never been personally addressed by the Emissaries," said Van quietly.

Simon looked ready to explode, but instead of losing his temper, he stood up to leave.

"I can't anymore today, kid," he said quietly. "I need time to think."

"Wait," Van pleaded. "Before you go, tell me what this means. If the reaction of your people can be expected to be anything like your own, what does Gnosos intend for Nemia?"

Simon had already turned around and was halfway outside the tent. He didn't turn back, but he did halt for a moment.

"Quarantine enforced by naval blockade," said Simon. "Isolate, and prevent the spread of devil worship. If you had any plans of joining the global community some day, you can kiss those goodbye."

Van didn't ask anything else. He followed Simon out of his tent and watched him trudge off. As reluctant as he was to let Simon simply walk away, he decided to respect his wishes and leave him be.

Lilim found him a short time later, and they shared supper with Wilm of the Horizon and a few other Dolsers at a bonfire. The aspirants of Dolse enjoyed a treat of fresh fruit and savory sausages, purchased by Otep and Ghan Mudcatcher at Sky's Edge, a small reward for their efforts on the pilgrimage thus far. Best of all, there were buttered oatcakes. Van helped himself to two, but even those didn't lift his spirits after how he'd left things with Simon.

Listening to Lilim chatter about her newfound fascination with art gave Van time to clear his head, though only a little. All conversation ceased when Shale strode into the circle of Dolsers, followed by four aspirants Van didn't recognize—all boys close to his age. Their yellow tunics marked them as Ikanni.

After finding a seat, Shale smiled deviously and pointed at Wilm. The Ikanni took a long moment to evaluate him. A few seconds later, she pointed at Van in a way that seemed— at least to him—like a halfhearted afterthought. The boy closest to Shale on the right stood up. He was startouched, though shorter and stouter than Galdur Goldeyes. He turned out his palms as he stepped forward, speaking directly to Van.

"My apologies for the surprise visit, cousin," he said, "but are you acquainted with our friend Shale here?"

"I am," said Van. Irked by the Ikanni's choice of words, he added, "Our tribe took her in by decree of Farseer Daz, my father and chieftain. I have been responsible for her care and well-being since she was found."

"Further apologies, then," said the Ikanni with a quick bow. "If that is true, you know her better than I do. I am Davin the Ordered Stones, and along with several companions of mine, I have been sharing the hunt with your... kinsman? Is it appropriate to call her that?"

"It was Farseer Daz's wish that she be considered a member of tribe Dolse," said Van.

"Is that what he said, specifically?" pressed Davin, his eyes narrowing. "We were all there, of course, but I confess I don't have the best memory. Was the spirit of the chieftain's request not simply that we consider her one of us, should she complete the pilgrimage?"

"Something along those lines, yes," said Van. "Why?"

"Well, it seems to me that Shale was not born to tribe Dolse any more than she was born to tribe Ikann. When she completes the pilgrimage and earns the right to call herself a blooded Nemian, should she not be allowed to pledge fealty to any tribe she likes?"

Van blinked back in shock, then stammered, "That would be unprecedented, I should think."

"That she is here at all is unprecedented," argued Davin with a wry laugh.

Van put his food down and crossed his arms. "Before exploring that notion further, it might be prudent to learn what Shale thinks."

"Such was our purpose in coming here tonight, cousin," said Davin. "I put the question to her myself, but rather than give us a straightforward answer, she wanted to bring us here and… show us something, I suppose."

Van glanced between them. "How could you possibly have communicated an idea that complex to her?"

"She's very perceptive." Davin's gaze grew sharp. "More so than you give her credit for, I'm beginning to think."

"She only speaks a few words of our language," said Van.

"I assume by that, you mean *you* have only taught her a few," said Davin. "We have taught her a few ourselves."

Van looked searchingly at Shale.

"*Early bird catches worm,*" she said, meeting his eyes.

"But you have the right of it," continued Davin. "It would be best if we could talk with her more freely. We wondered if anyone of Dolse could offer a solution to that problem, since she has been among you the longest."

"I have shared conversation with her at length," said Van. "We are fortunate enough to have made the acquaintance of someone versed in the magical arts. A spell of his allows him to comprehend seemingly any spoken language, and to be understood in turn."

"You're speaking of the other foreigner, aren't you?" said Davin, grinning. "A rumor has been flying around that he is some sort of magician. So, it's true."

Van nodded.

"Can you summon him now?" asked Davin. "We could talk to Shale together, and she can explain for herself how she feels about… various things."

"His spell only works for an hour each day, I'm afraid. His services are currently unavailable." Van swallowed, averting his eyes. "They may be unavailable for some time, actually."

"Shale is a ranger of Dolse," said Wilm of the Horizon, speaking up for the first time since the Ikanni arrived. "If there is any confusion on that point, perhaps the one you need to consult is Otep Acrearms. I can indeed summon him now if you like, and I assure you he requires no one to speak for him."

"I meant no offense, cousin," said Davin, taking a step back.

One of the other Ikanni stood up, dusting off his trousers. "We should be getting back, Davin. It grows late."

"Indeed," said Davin, glancing nervously between Wilm and Van. "If you'll excuse us."

The Ikanni all stood, but Davin lingered, seemingly waiting for Shale. She remained seated, not so much as glancing up. She toyed idly with the bowl of food she'd brought with her, refusing to look at anyone. But a smile touched her lips, and for the first time Van could remember, it was an honest smile. She was privately, victimlessly content.

Davin soon gave up, and once the Ikanni were all out of earshot, Van turned to Wilm.

"Thank you, Wilm," he said. "I didn't think... that is to say, I assumed that you—"

"Would have leapt at the chance to be rid of the dark girl?" Wilm supplied. "Yesterday, you'd have been right. But your conduct just now gave me pause, forcing me to consider the wishes of our chieftain."

Van stared, uncomprehending.

"You're rather protective of her." Wilm smiled. "You certainly didn't seem prepared to lose her to tribe Ikann. That is all the testimony I need as to the quality of her character."

Van looked at Shale, and she returned his gaze. But her smile had turned devious again, making him wonder at his own actions. Perhaps after what had passed between him and Simon, the thought of losing anyone else was just too much.

"In any case, I am glad you joined us tonight, Van the Scribe. Your company fosters healthy reflection, it seems," said Wilm of the Horizon. "I don't often see you in camp at this hour."

"That's because I—" Van's eyes widened. He flew to his feet as he realized how much time had passed, spilling what was left in his bowl. "I have to go."

Van was almost half an hour late. When he finally reached Brynda's tent, he saw her favorite rangers stationed outside— Rhys and Rhyla. They crossed their bows over the entrance when he stepped near.

"The First Ranger doesn't wish to be disturbed," growled Rhyla the Tamer.

"Who is it?" came Brynda's voice from within.

"The Dolser boy, Van the Scribe," called Rhys the Catcher, drawing an accusatory glance from her sister.

"Let him in, please," said Brynda.

The rangers withdrew their weapons, and Van offered them a polite but nervous bow before stepping into the tent.

Brynda Blackblade sat alone, and the furniture had all been put away.

"I'm sorry, cousin," she said, sounding tired. "I meant to look for you, but I couldn't find the time. Might we once more postpone our appointments until we've moved on from Seat Ikann? Depending on how things go, it may be several days before we need your services again."

"Oh," said Van. "Of course. I should have known you would want this time to yourself, to prepare for the next game. Please forgive my absentmindedness."

The First Ranger smiled weakly. Van understood he was being asked to leave, but he hesitated. It was one of only two times he'd been actually alone with her. Galdur Goldeyes was always sitting inches away, pinning Van with his poisonous gaze—but not tonight. Curiously, Brynda's hair was wet, and she wasn't wearing her belt or her boots, as though she'd just gotten out of a bath.

"I wish..." Van blushed and stared at the ground. He hadn't meant to say anything aloud. "I wish you luck at Seat Ikann."

"Do you?" she asked, voice ephemeral.

Van's eyes flicked up. Her expression was severe, but otherwise devoid of emotion. She stood up and closed the distance between them, laying her hand on Van's arm.

"You would see me victorious at Seat Ikann? And in the challenges that come after?"

Van tried to say something, but he found no words. Brynda closed her eyes and sighed.

"I'm sorry," she said. "That was unfair."

She wrapped her arms around him and pulled his head down, resting it against her chest. Her skin was damp and smelled of lye.

"I'll need a little help from you when the time comes," she said in a cool whisper. "But I promise it will seem a mere trifle compared to what I've asked already."

The moment lasted only seconds, and Van spent the duration trying to decide what to do with his hands. In the end, his arms remained rigid at his sides. Finally, Brynda released him and stepped back.

"You need to go now, Van the Scribe. After Seat Ikann I'll find you again, and all will be as it was for a little while longer."

Van bowed stiffly and took his leave without a word. As he shambled back to his own tent, he felt far away from himself, his mind lingering on Brynda. Her warmth. Her scent. Her words.

For a little while longer?

After tossing and turning all night, Van spent most of the next day feeling only half awake. He brightened only after he returned from the hunt to find Simon and Shale looking for him. They all exchanged the talking sign, each of them in turn, and retired together to Van's tent.

"I'm relieved to see you." Van attempted a smile at Simon. "I was worried you were upset with me."

"I never said I was upset with you," said Simon, his tone stiff and formal. "I said I needed time to think, and I still do. It's not fair to Shale if I just disappear, though, so for today, I'll translate for the two of you."

"Oh," said Van, his expression falling. "Very well, then. We should start by telling Shale that we'll be arriving at Seat Ikann tomorrow. I haven't had a chance to inform her of our travel plans yet." Van sat up straighter. "Actually, I'm glad you're here together, because I wanted to invite you to watch the First Rangers' challenge with Lilim and me. The preceding ceremonies as well."

"How long are we staying at Seat Ikann?" asked Simon. "Just a day again?"

"At least two full days, I would imagine," said Van. "On the first day, the delegates will be presented to the chieftain, and he will accept their gifts. He will issue his challenge to the First Rangers the following day, most likely, and we will leave when the game is concluded and we have resupplied."

Simon spoke to Shale, summarizing the conversation thus far. When he was finished, she addressed Van.

"What are the rules of the yellow clan's game?"

"We won't know until we reach Seat Ikann," said Van.

"What if the chieftain orders the four champions to slay one another, and declares the last one standing the winner?"

"No!" blurted Van. "The First Rangers would never be asked to simply kill each other. It can't be required in any way for a First Ranger to die as a means of establishing a victor."

Shale murmured something Simon didn't bother to translate, seemingly disappointed.

"Given Rhaggo Bullbreaker's reputation," Van continued, "it is likely to be something athletic in nature."

"Something violent?" Shale said, sounding hopeful.

"Quite possibly." Van nodded.

Her eyes brightened. "Then I accept your invitation."

Van watched Simon and waited, but he had nothing to add. It seemed today's conversation really would just be between himself and Shale.

"You seem to have made quite an impression with the Ikanni," said Van, returning his attention to her. "I apologize if I seemed dismissive before, when you told me you'd spent time among them."

"You're forgiven," said Shale. "You behaved admirably enough when it mattered."

"Then you're aware they were speaking of taking you as a member of tribe Ikann."

Shale nodded.

"How were they able to explain that to you? I realize you're incredibly intelligent, but I would think that would have required... an amount of dialogue."

"The yellow clan are rather transparent in their purpose when they want something," said Shale. "Even more so than your clan, if you can believe it. And, as you said, I made an impression. It was a logical progression of events."

"I see," said Van.

"And the one called Davin tried to kiss me."

"What!" Van blurted. "Davin the Ordered Stones?"

"*Yes*," said Shale, no translation necessary. "Davin with the stones. But I think that was separate. Unrelated to the matter of my joining their clan, I mean. I declined that proposition as well."

"And why did they follow you to our camp?"

"*Mmm*," said Shale. "They found it difficult to accept that I would choose your clan over theirs. When I refused their offer, they wished to compare themselves against your clan's most prominent warriors. Obviously, they would need me to identify those people, so I brought them here."

"You brought them to our camp, and you..." Van trailed off, remembering Shale pointing at him. "You numbered me among the greatest warriors of Dolse."

Shale smiled and shrugged.

"Well," Van sighed. "You did the right thing in rejecting such a ridiculous offer. Their invitation to become a member of tribe Ikann, I mean. The other matter is your own business, I suppose."

"Oh?" Shale raised an eyebrow. "You think it ridiculous? What if I change my mind? What if I want to join whichever clan wins?"

Van frowned. "Defecting from one's home tribe to join another is unheard of."

Shale laughed. "You think your clan is home for me? Nowhere here is my home. Tell me, was it your father's plan to take me prisoner, or to count me among his trophies? Or would he let me choose?"

Van thought about it. "If it was what you truly wanted, I'm sure my father would support your decision, but..." He bit his cheek.

"But?" she prodded.

"But speaking for myself, I hope it's not," said Van. "I would prefer to number you among my kinsmen."

Shale's expression softened. A real smile again, just for a moment.

"Good boy. You pass."

Van didn't know precisely what that meant, but Shale seemed at ease and she'd forgiven him. Like Simon, she was being honest in her own way.

"My turn next, if you don't mind," said Shale.

Van nodded.

"The elf is mad at you today," she observed. "Why?"

Van hesitated. It seemed both rude and extremely awkward to discuss Simon with him present, no less so because he was personally enabling the exchange.

"Simon accompanied me and Lilim to the Temple to the Emissaries at Sky's Edge," he said. "There are statues inside, made in the likeness of the Emissaries. When he saw them, he seemed to recognize them, and he..."

Van's voice faded. Simon could interject at any moment, telling Shale whatever it was he believed about Van's gods.

The thought spurred a chilly pang of loneliness. But as far as Van could tell, Simon had no intention of doing so. He simply translated, and Shale kept her attention on Van, waiting.

"If I understood him correctly, they are known and universally hated by the rest of the world, for reasons he has yet to explain."

Shale burst into laughter.

Van stared blankly. "I'm not sure which part of what I just told you is funny."

"The entire thing is funny!" said Shale, holding her sides. "It's a taste of your own medicine. Now you know how it feels to serve a god others fear and despise."

Van opened his mouth to speak, but then clamped it shut. He wanted to tell her their circumstances were nothing alike, but he couldn't. She was right.

"Wouldn't it be fun to ask the elf which he thinks is worse?" teased Shale. "Your devils or the Twilight Prophet?"

"I understand your point," said Van, "but I don't see the same humor in this that you—"

He started over.

"I never used the word 'devil.'"

Shale laughed again, sighing as she wiped a tear from her eye. "I've known you worship devils almost since I got here. It's probably why She chose this place for me."

"Tell me what you think they are," blurted Van.

Shale raised her eyebrows. "You don't want the elf to explain it?"

"He'll explain it when he's ready," said Van. "For now, tell me what *you* believe. Please."

"Very well." Shale settled into a more comfortable position.

"Devils are the lords of the hell planes, ruling over lesser beings such as demons and diaspora. They wage war on one another in an eternal dispute over territory in a realm that's supposedly infinite, if you can believe anything so pointless. They sometimes scheme to make deals with mortals, bartering trifling services that must seem as miracles to the weak and uneducated in exchange for their very souls."

Van groaned. "He must believe Galdur Goldeyes and Brynda Blackblade are devils too, then. Can you ask him if that is why he is so suspicious of her?"

"He almost certainly doesn't believe those people are devils, any more than you believe they're *Emissaries*," said Shale. "Diaspora are the mortal descendants of devils and terrestrials like us. All those alive today are many generations removed from their devil ancestry, but the physical characteristics of a devil's lineage never fully vanish."

"And what about you?" Van's voice cracked as the cold, lonely feeling crept back over him. "Do you distrust us all as well, now?"

"*Hmm.*" Shale kicked her feet absently. "I don't think I could bring myself to trust a devil. They're frustratingly good at making bad deals. And for better or worse, I have plans for my soul."

Van hung his head.

"But praying to devils because you don't know any better doesn't make you wicked," she continued. "And unless you've done something very complicated and extremely stupid, it doesn't mean you've signed your soul over to one."

An unsettling thought crossed Van's mind. "Perhaps Simon believes such an arrangement has already been made on my behalf."

"Doesn't work that way," said Shale, now rocking back and forth like a bored toddler. "You have to make a pact of your own accord, knowingly and without coercion, face to face with a real devil."

"How would a person even do that?" said Van.

"As I said, it's fairly complicated," said Shale. "Probably impossible now, for anyone without considerable magical talent."

Van stared back at her. "What do you mean, impossible *now?*"

"Something changed a very long time ago. Thousands of years, at least, but maybe much longer. There was a time when things from other planes could come and go freely, and our world was violated time and time again. Something approximating civilization would rise from the ashes, and when it was ripe for the plucking, an army of devils or some other aggrieved cosmic entity would arrive to pillage it all over. Until one day, it stopped. As though a great, unseen curtain was dropped from on high, closing our world to trespass and preventing us likewise from trespassing beyond it."

"What could have done that?" said Van.

"Only the gods themselves, I should think," said Shale. "The first gods, whoever they were. Those that came before the Twilight Prophet and before whatever gods the elf has told you about. They finally took notice that a world was being bullied somewhere in the vastness of their creation, and they deigned to do something about it."

Van rubbed his eyes, feeling a headache coming on. Shale and Simon were from completely different worlds, yet they held the same view of the Emissaries. What knowledge did they share that had driven them to the conclusion they were evil? They couldn't be. There was so much good and so much life in Nemia—and it was all possible thanks to their beneficence.

"I'm sorry," Van said. "This is indeed a lot to think about."

"You're only a child," Shale said. "It's good that you are. Children are the best at putting themselves back together after their view of the world shatters."

"You were lying after all, then," said Van. "About your age."

"Of course I wasn't." Shale crossed her arms. "The elf was clear about the rules, and I don't cheat—but with my escape from Eventide, the trial of my childhood is behind me, while you are still in the middle of yours. You have a better chance of overcoming it than the rest of your clan, in my opinion."

"Thank you for the vote of confidence," Van said weakly.

Having lost his appetite for new information, he remained silent, waiting to see if Shale had further questions. By now, he had lost track of how much time they had left.

"What else might we find to do in the yellow clan's principal city?" Shale asked after a moment.

"I have never been there," said Van. "But once the welcoming ceremonies conclude, and before Rhaggo Bullbreaker poses his challenge to the First Rangers, I imagine we'll have some time to explore the community."

"Then we should," she said, giddy. "It is the throne city of your former oppressors, is it not? There should be no end to the fun we can have. I'll take the lead while we're there if you can't come up with anything."

Van gave her a pointed look. "I must ask that you not seek conflict with the Ikanni during our stay at their Seat," he warned. "There is peace between our tribes now, but that peace could be greatly damaged if a member of tribe Dolse were to attack someone unprovoked."

"Don't worry, *kinsman*," said Shale. "I'll behave."

Van hazarded a glance at their translator. "If we are to go exploring, I will of course invite Simon to join us, to assist with communication and the like," he said. "As well as Lilim. I expect she will be very excited at the opportunity."

Shale's smile faltered for a fraction of a second. "Naturally."

Simon's spell expired a short time later, so Van stepped outside with them. After a quick goodbye, they parted ways for the evening. It wasn't late. Van could have done as he pleased for another few hours, with his tutoring sessions postponed again, but he knew how busy the next few days would be.

Van settled in for bed, hoping to dream about fishing with Otep on a sunny afternoon—or anything, really, that wasn't devils, or Brynda, or the possibility of Galdur Goldeyes somehow winning Patronage for tribe Ikann.

15 Seat Ikann

First came the drum beat. It was a slow, rolling rhythm Van knew well, typically accompanied by a chant exalting the Emissaries. Van took it as a good omen. Chieftain Rhaggo could have ordered the Seat's residents to play traditional Ikanni music as the procession arrived, which would have sent a very different message.

Terraced croplands dotted with farmhouses had dominated the landscape for the better part of an hour when finally, the walls came into view. Beyond the gatehouse with its twin watchtowers, Van could already make out the chieftain's palace, a dark stone colossus against the blue sky. Not far off was the legendary coliseum.

They poured into the northern metropolis through its open gates. As Van passed beneath the fifteen-foot archway, the atmosphere grew unexpectedly dark and quiet as the indomitable walls of Seat Ikann blocked the sun from view and deadened the beat of the drums.

Light and sound exploded back into the world as he emerged onto the street, packed shoulder to shoulder with his bewildered kinsmen. The chanting was audible now—verses of song intermingled with the wordless cheers of countless voices. Flower petals drifted down from above. Glancing up, Van realized that the road leading into the Seat was a sunken lane. Smiling children gazed down at them from street level, throwing fistful after fistful of white and pink petals on the heads of the aspirants.

Eventually, the road drew level with the foundations of the surrounding buildings, and Van beheld a landscape such as he'd never seen—a brick and mortar jungle that stretched as far as the eye could see. The Ikanni cheered their throats raw as the aspirants filed in, and Van spotted armor-clad rangers patrolling the crowds on horseback, keeping order. An order that seemed barely contained, like a pot threatening to boil over.

They jostled forward at a slow pace, and over an hour eked by before they finally reached the place where they would make camp. Van stared in awe when he saw it. A piece of wilderness was preserved here, right in the middle of the bustling community. And it wasn't just some derelict patch of earth such as they'd camped on before. The idyllic meadow was interspersed with black willows and sculpted hedges, complete with a pond at the center and its own drinking well.

For the first time since they'd set out, the aspirants of Nemia made camp as one people. The field alone was bigger than most villages in the lands of Dolse, but not so expansive that the tribes could separate themselves by any boundary of distance as they pitched their tents.

Van hadn't seen Otep or Ghan since they'd arrived, so he supposed the delegates were convening privately somewhere

—perhaps preparing for the presentation of the First Rangers to the chieftain. He scarfed down a light meal of venison and leftover oatcakes and told Lilim to do the same, for it wasn't immediately clear when they'd next eat.

Wilm of the Horizon and Orum the Mutable soon appeared, passing word among the Dolsers that the aspirants were expected at the palace grounds. Van took Lilim's hand, and they followed the flow of the crowds, joined on the way by Simon and Shale. None of them gave the talking sign just yet.

Rhaggo Bullbreaker's palace was a mere ten-minute walk from the campgrounds, built in the shape of a horseshoe with a courtyard at its center. An open balcony protruded at the curve of the horseshoe, the palace's highest point, and upon it stood two rangers of Ikann with glaives, wearing plumed headdresses and gladiatorial armor. Between them sat the chieftain.

Two massive warhammers rested to either side of Rhaggo's golden throne; weapons like Otep's axe, impossible to wield for anyone of normal strength and stature. The giantkin chieftain was massive himself, but looking at him today, it was difficult to imagine him in his prime, swinging those hammers as a challenger in the coliseum.

The chieftain looked soft and sickly pale. Almost corpulent. Rather than stand to greet the aspirants as they assembled in the field below him, he simply raised his goblet in a toast. Van had heard the rumor that the chieftain was infirm. This all but certified it.

"Welcome, children of Nemia," said Rhaggo Bullbreaker.

His voice was guttural, as though he had unchewed food in his mouth, but the words carried inexplicably over the courtyard. Peering more closely, Van noticed something that reminded him of Galdur's magic trinket. An orb of smooth metal, like an oversized marble, hovered in the air near Rhaggo's head. It glowed a dim pink as it caught the chieftain's words and flung them to the far corners of the palace grounds—projecting not light, but sound.

Van made the talking sign, and Simon nodded, starting up his spell.

"Take solace, countrymen, for I won't make you hang on my words any longer than ceremony obligates. You have been long on the road, and tonight, you will avail yourselves of the pleasures to be had here, in the Cornucopia of the Plains. Partake to any extent you desire! My subjects have been commanded to devote themselves absolutely to the delightment of our treasured aspirants."

As Simon translated to Shale, her eyes lit up, and she licked her lips at the mention of "delightment."

"It is my duty to call on each of you to seek a deeper understanding of your peers, and to strengthen the bonds of friendship between yourselves," the chieftain drawled. "But by now, you've either figured that out, or you haven't. Without further delay, I summon the First Rangers of Nemia. Present yourselves to the people of Ikann!"

In similar fashion to the ceremonies at Seat Dolse, each champion was presented in turn by their Pilgrimage Guide and met with a cheer from the gathered aspirants.

Galdur Goldeyes was saved for last, and the roar that erupted through the crowd when he appeared on the balcony put shame to those that had preceded it. Van briefly wondered if the chieftain's magic orb was projecting the scene to the whole of Seat Ikann through some trick of spellwork, like Simon's scrying portal.

Next was the presentation of gifts, beginning with Brynda Blackblade. Once more, she selected a book from the assortment carried by her Guide, Memnon the Still Pool, and presented it to Rhaggo Bullbreaker on bent knee. This volume was a collection of illustrations depicting now-extinct animals, drawn by elders of tribe Vaxas who could attest to witnessing them in life.

Otep Acrearms went next, gifting chieftain Rhaggo the polished jawbone of a lion. It had been fashioned into an article of jewelry to be worn around the neck, inlaid with glittering yellow gemstones.

Sol Starfletcher came forward last, and presented a magnificent leather saddle sized to fit an elephant rather than a horse. Van hadn't seen any elephants since coming to the lands of Ikann, but he knew they were bred farther north for use as draft animals and mounts. Tribe Mercura's gift was a thoughtful one, catering to the chieftain's known love of outdoorsmanship while remaining sensitive to his impaired mobility.

"Your gifts are well received, cousins," said Rhaggo Bullbreaker. "Disperse now, and assemble again at my coliseum tomorrow. There, I will pose my challenge to the First Rangers. Those who wish to bear witness should arrive no later than the touch of the setting sun on the horizon. And to the First Rangers themselves, I will tell you only to come armed for battle!"

Horns blared as the delegates were dismissed from the balcony. Van counted the minutes they spent walking back to camp, calculating how long Simon's spell would hold out and trying to decide what they should do next. For now, he simply followed the crowds away from the palace, keeping tight hold of Lilim's hand for fear of getting separated.

Before they made it out of the courtyard, Van caught sight of Otep Acrearms. He loomed head and shoulders above the crowd, looking around as if searching for something. Or someone.

"Van the Scribe!" called Otep as he spotted Van.

Surprised, Van stopped and waited for the First Ranger to muscle his way through the crowd.

"I hoped I would find you before you wandered off," said Otep. "Rhaggo Bullbreaker has extended an invitation to the First Rangers, one that I can further extend to you."

"What sort of invitation?" asked Van, struggling to shield Lilim from the surge of aspirants hurrying from the courtyard.

"It seems tribe Ikann maintains special accommodations here at the Seat, where the Pilgrimage Guides and First Rangers are permitted lodging during their stay, along with their, ah… entourage."

Van furrowed his brow. "Their *entourage?*"

Otep shrugged. "Up to ten individuals, it was explained. Wilm and Orum will be joining us. With myself and Ghan Mudcatcher, that makes only four. I thought I might invite you and your young friend. Lilith the Brave?"

"Lilim," corrected Van. "May I bring others as well?"

"As I said, the invitation was for up to ten. Who else did you have in mind?"

"Simon of the Mists and Shale."

"Simon of the Mists and *who?*" Otep tilted his head, frowning.

Van gestured with his free hand to his companions, the foreigner and the foreboding stranger most of the tribe knew only as "the dark girl." Otep groaned.

"Very well," sighed the First Ranger. "Meet me where the courtyard joins the road. One of the chieftain's rangers will show us the way. I will fetch Ghan Mudcatcher and the others."

Simon had already translated the exchange for Shale, so Van didn't need to repeat Otep's offer.

"And just when I was growing accustomed to sleeping on the ground," she said with a smirk.

They ambled over to the road and waited. When Otep rejoined them, he had Ghan Mudcatcher, Wilm of the Horizon, and Orum the Mutable in tow. They were accompanied also by a ranger of Ikann, who led them through the streets to their new lodgings.

The path, which cut through Seat Ikann, took them farther from the campgrounds, but much closer to the coliseum—as well as various other fixtures, which their guide explained they would find enjoyable and convenient.

They meandered past a number of bustling storefronts, including one Van couldn't immediately identify, the sign above the door reading simply, "Bespoke Rendezvous." The establishment had a suspicious number of young women with painted faces loitering near the door, most of them wearing lightweight dresses parted at the hip, with plunging necklines.

"I guess I know what I'll be doing this evening," said Simon, looking in the same direction as Van. "You and Shale can take Lilim to find some age-appropriate entertainment. Spell's about to give out, anyway."

Van covered Lilim's eyes with his free hand, realizing belatedly the place was a brothel. He'd forgotten about Simon's less noble predilections—though in all honesty, it was difficult to cast judgment on him. Even as they walked by, Van noticed dozens of would-be patrons, boys and girls alike, approaching the Bespoke Rendezvous. Some were aspirants of Dolse his own age. They eagerly handed over trophies and farthings for the privilege of being led inside by the companion of their choice. No voice spoke up in objection, except the one in Van's head. As far as he knew, he was alone in considering such things frivolous and distasteful.

Following a bend in the road that took them blessedly out of sight of the brothel, they halted in front of yet another green field. It was smaller than the campgrounds, but just as well kept. The soft grass was meticulously swept of any roots or rocks one might catch their foot on. Here stood four houses, one for each of Nemia's tribes, and according to their ranger escort, the charming dwellings were inhabited for only a few days every nine years. The Ikanni called the cloistered retreat Ranger's Rest.

Otep's party was led to the first house on the right and given a verbal tour before they reached the door. There were three floors, the lowest of which served as a parlor and common area. The middle floor was for the delegates' companions—eight private rooms—though they'd only need six. On the upper floor were two more, reserved for the First Ranger and his Pilgrimage Guide.

Each house was equipped with its own open air bath, as well as a serving staff that could run errands or perform chores, such as cooking or washing the residents' clothes and gear.

His job finished, the ranger bowed to them and left. Otep tried the door, which opened to reveal the servants they were told to expect, clad in white robes and shawls covering every inch of their skin. They knelt in silence just past the threshold, barring the First Ranger's path.

Otep ventured a step forward, but one of the attendants raised a hand in objection, gesturing wordlessly at his feet. As one, the aspirants of Dolse looked down and regarded their boots, caked with mud and grime from the road.

Shale understood immediately, kicking off her boots and stepping around Otep. The white-robed servants bowed and moved aside. With a giggle, Shale strode into the house's common area, where she skipped in a wide circle, testing the space, before scampering upstairs to choose a room for herself.

Van and the others were allowed in after removing their own muddy footwear. They took their time exploring the ground floor, including the lounge decorated with big downy pillows, and the pantry, stocked in anticipation of their arrival with fresh foodstuffs. Aside from Shale's footsteps pattering from room to room upstairs, the house was quiet.

Wilm of the Horizon was the first to approach the attendants.

"Music?" he proposed, his voice unsure. "Please?"

One of the white-clad figures stood and left the house, returning shortly with a two-stringed fiddle. A pleasant tune soon livened the space—somber, but expertly played, and certainly preferable to the leaden silence.

Shale bounded back down the stairs wearing only a towel. Halfway to the bath, she wheeled around, issuing an order of her own to their attendants.

"*Rucksack!*" she said, pointing at them.

Two of the robed figures exchanged a glance, and after a moment, one of them stood and left. The group from Dolse had all left their packs at the campgrounds. Van felt guilty on Shale's behalf, wondering how long it would take the poor attendant to figure out which rucksack was hers.

While Shale ran outside, squealing with glee, Van wandered over to the pantry and helped himself to a tangerine.

"Are you hungry, Lilim?" he asked, glancing back at her.

"No." She turned slowly, still in awe of the place. "I think I'd like a bath, too. Is that allowed?"

"It would seem nearly anything we can dream up is allowed," said Van, producing his knife to peel the fruit.

Otep and the others agreed to let the girls have the bath first, so after finishing his snack, Van marched upstairs to find a room while he waited for them.

Sliding a door open, his eyes fell on an opulent featherbed pressed against the far wall, and his exhaustion caught up with him. He shuffled to the bed and sat on its edge, sinking into the downy mattress. Fearing he'd fall asleep if he lay down, he commanded himself to keep his eyes open. It was the first moment he'd had to himself all day, and he spent it dwelling on something Simon said to him days ago.

What if Galdur wins?

He'd tried not to think about it at Sky's Edge, and at the time he was distracted enough that he'd had that luxury. But here, alone in a room more lavish than his father's chambers at Seat Dolse—yet so insignificant in the eyes of Van's hosts that it was gifted to him by accident—he had no choice but to face the naked truth.

The hundreds of mounted rangers in their shining armor, the thousands of voices crying Galdur's name as Van stood beneath him in the shadow of the chieftain's palace... If tribe Ikann ever truly rose in force against his people, it wouldn't even be a fight.

"Van the Scribe!"

Lilim's voice rescued him from his daydream, and with some effort, he hauled himself off the bed and crossed the room to the door.

Both girls were waiting for him in the corridor. Lilim was dressed as before, but Van saw that their beleaguered attendant had located Shale's rucksack. She'd changed into her gazelle leather dress, and today, there was a sheathed dagger tucked into its belt. Van had no idea where or when she'd gotten it, but by now her resourcefulness was more of an expectation than a novelty.

"Are we still going exploring?" Lilim asked, bright-eyed and practically vibrating with excitement.

Van looked at Shale, who put her hands on her hips and beamed.

"I suppose we are," said Van.

By the time they made it back downstairs, Simon was already gone, presumably on his way to the Bespoke Rendezvous for a night of dissolute philandering. Leaving the house, Van caught a glimpse of Otep and Ghan Mudcatcher on their way to the bath with towels around their waists, and he stared after them enviously. Having never seen the elder without his robes on, Van was surprised—and a little impressed—at how well toned his scaly upper body was.

Without further delay, the three of them left Ranger's Rest and took to the streets of Seat Ikann, where aspirants were already in the throes of hedonistic abandon.

On the main road, Shale took the lead, walking briskly as she cut through the dense crowds. Residents of the Seat scrambled to get out of her way when they saw her coming, and Van walked with Lilim in her wake. It was, of course, superstitious aversion that cleared their path for them, but

Van liked to pretend those men and women were standing aside out of deference. Shale's confident demeanor and broad smile suggested she was doing the same.

After a few minutes on the main thoroughfare, Shale hooked a sharp turn and led them down a smaller street. Van's ears soon registered the sound of drums and woodwinds—she was following the sound of music. Her hearing was better than theirs. Much better, possibly.

They came to a painted archway across the road, decorated with paper lanterns and streaming ribbons. Booths lined the street to either side, where Ikanni were hosting games and handing out baked fruit or kebab skewers. Van also spotted a stage where a troupe of musicians performed—the source of the jaunty melody they had followed.

"It's a carnival," said Lilim with hushed reverence.

Van wondered if she'd ever been to one. He gave her hand an encouraging squeeze and smiled at her.

Shale guided them to the stage first, where they stood at the rear of a small crowd, listening to the performers. Most of the onlookers were aspirants, and if Van wasn't mistaken, so was the vocalist—a girl in a dress dyed Mercuran blue. She finished her song and bowed to a round of applause before leaving the stage.

"Come forward, aspirants," called the man on the drums. "Share your songs with us!"

A boy hopped forward eagerly, though Van didn't know from which tribe he hailed. After cupping his hand to the drummer's ear and whispering something, he stepped to the front of the stage and waited for the men behind him to begin playing. Another upbeat tune carried over the crowd. The troupe played well, but Van didn't think the new singer had a future career in music.

"Come up, countrymen. Share your songs!" the drummer called again when the boy vacated the stage.

Van assumed they would move on to some other attraction, but instead—to a chorus of gasps—Shale pushed through the gathered aspirants and climbed onto the stage. The performers stiffened, but Shale simply turned her back on them and faced the crowd. Most turned to leave, and those who stayed only tried to shout her off the stage. But over the din, Shale sang out a sharp, clear note that silenced their jeers and rooted their feet to the ground.

It wasn't at all like the last time Van had heard her sing. This was a song of anguish, a voice crying out against an indifferent and unjust cosmos. A defiant celebration of life in the face of abiding indignity. The language of the dusken was alien to Van, but the melody was haunting and beautiful.

Shale sang alone at first, but at the rear of the stage the troupe's flutist—an old man, bald and weathered—closed his eyes and began to tap his foot. When he found the rhythm of Shale's song, he lifted his flute to his lips and matched her, note for note. Following the flutist's lead, the others soon added the lilting voices of their pipes and the tremble of a horn. The drummer, his grimace softening as he listened, was the last to pick up the beat of the music.

When Shale's song ended, the crowd erupted in applause, cheering and whistling. She bowed to them, then turned to clasp arms briefly with the old flutist before slipping gracefully off the stage. Rejoining Van and Lilim, she led them onward through the painted archway. Van took hold of Lilim's hand as they trailed after Shale, wondering if he was caught in a dream.

"So pretty," mumbled Lilim.

"It was," Van said distractedly, almost to himself.

He stumbled, failing to notice that Lilim had actually stopped to point. Close by, a boy was testing his skill at a game stall, tossing a ring and stamping his foot when he missed whatever target he'd been aiming for. Disappointed, the young carnival-goer turned to sulk away. Lilim hadn't been watching the game itself, but rather staring intently at the prizes on display. One was an armlet of polished bone, set with a bright yellow stone.

"Oh." Van glanced at Lilim. "Do you want to try?"

She nodded emphatically. Behind the booth, the game runner was already waving them over.

"Don't be shy, little flower," the Ikanni man called. "Everyone gets a play. Three tries to win!"

"How do you play?" Lilim mumbled shyly as she stepped up, eyes still fixed on the jeweled armlet.

"Simple as could be," said the Ikanni.

He gestured to a table a short distance behind the booth, on which rested a vase and a stack of brass rings. The man toyed idly with one as he explained the game, tossing the ring up and catching it effortlessly.

"Stand right where you are, no closer, and I'll hand you three rings. Throw one around the neck of this vase, and you'll leave with your choice of prize."

Lilim accepted the first ring nervously, turning it over in her hand to test its weight. It looked barely big enough to fit around the target, which stood five paces away. Taking a stance, Lilim threw the ring in an underhand arc, missing the vase entirely.

"Don't fret, little flower," the game runner reassured her, handing her another ring from the stack. "You've got a feel for it now, and two more tries."

Lilim took a breath, then tossed again. Her ring touched the lip of the vase this time, and for a moment, Van thought it might land. But it only circled the target once before slipping off and clattering to the ground.

"This is difficult," complained Lilim, biting her lip.

"Third time's the charm." The Ikanni handed Lilim her last ring.

Before she could throw, Van stepped forward and put a hand on her shoulder.

"Might we have a demonstration first?" he asked the game runner. "I'm not convinced your rings are the right size."

In response, the man took a ring from the stack and fit it around the neck of the vase himself.

"A tight fit, to be sure. But as you can see, it's quite possible."

"Then perhaps my friend would benefit from observing your technique," said Van, still suspicious.

The man smiled and came around to their side of the booth. Van and Lilim stepped aside, watching as he landed his ring—the same size as all the others—neatly around the neck of the vase.

"To be fair, I've had plenty of practice," he said, retrieving his ring and sitting back down on his stool beside the table.

Van still wondered if there was a trick, though he was at a loss for what it was. Lilim glanced up at him, looking frustrated and uncertain, but all he could do was smile and shrug. She made her third throw and missed, sending her last ring flying over the vase, where it disappeared into a shadowed corner.

She sighed in disappointment, and Van took her hand to console her. As he turned to lead her away from the booth, he noticed that Shale wore a criminal smile, her arms crossed.

"Can my other friend try?" asked Van, peering over his shoulder at the game runner.

"Everyone gets a play," the man repeated.

Shale marched forward, practically pushing Van and Lilim out of the way. Suppressing a shudder that did not go unnoticed to Van, the game runner took a ring from the table and handed it to her. She evaluated the object silently, running a finger along its rim. Then, she made her first throw.

The ring ricocheted off the lip of the vase with a hollow *ping*.

"Close," said the Ikanni, clearly impressed. He gave her another ring from the stack. "You've got a feel for it now."

Shale flicked the second ring, almost thoughtlessly, sending it wide of the target. It was like she wasn't even trying. When the game runner approached her with a third and final ring, she refused, pointing an accusatory finger at him.

"What's the matter?" asked the Ikanni, looking to Van for an explanation.

"I think she wants a demonstration," said Van.

"Wasn't she standing right there when I showed the little flower?"

Van only shrugged.

Hesitantly, the man once again stepped around to Shale's side of the booth—but unlike Lilim, she didn't move out of his way. Muttering under his breath, the man shuffled awkwardly to stand on her other side, but Shale interrupted him again.

"*Stop!*" she said, holding her hand out expectantly.

Flustered, the man once more looked at Van. "Now what's wrong?"

Van glanced between them. "I suppose she's changed her mind?"

Shale stamped her foot and glared at the game runner, holding her upturned hand impatiently in his face. Scowling, the Ikanni handed her a ring before retreating to his stool. Shale inspected the new ring, again running her finger along its edge. A grin crept across her face. On the other side of the booth, the game runner glanced suddenly at the ring he still held—the one he hadn't given Shale—as though he didn't recognize it. He glowered at her with a look of confusion and betrayal.

"When did you...?" he stammered.

Shale's third ring landed cleanly around the neck of the vase.

As they wandered back to Ranger's Rest an hour later, Van gazed up at the night sky, finding it more grounding and familiar than the tall buildings that loomed all around him. The stars had winked to life, and he admired them while trailing behind Shale. At his side, Lilim still stared captivated at the jeweled armlet on her wrist.

"Shale is amazing," she sighed, and then quietly added, "I wish I was more like her."

"I'm glad you are the way you are, Lilim the Brave," said Van. "And in any case, I think Nemia might only have room for one Shale."

Upon reaching their guesthouse, Van finally enjoyed a bath. Because everyone else had already taken their turn, he had the whole pool to himself. He headed back inside feeling restored, then helped himself to more fruit from the pantry, taking his spoils up to his room.

As he lay in his soft featherbed that night, his mind drifted to absent reflections. It was hours now, not days, before the second game of the Journey of Patronage. He wished there was some way, however small, that he could support Otep at times like these. But he doubted he would even see his friend again before he pitted himself against whatever challenge Rhaggo Bullbreaker had in store for the First Rangers at the coliseum.

More likely, Van would spend the time leading up to the game being dragged all over Seat Ikann by Shale and Lilim. Though, if he was being honest with himself, he could think of far worse ways to spend a day. Helping Lilim find her confidence and watching Shale find her voice—both literally and figuratively—were already becoming treasured memories. He fell asleep remembering the street carnival, a pleasant meditation to drift off to.

His eyes snapped open in the middle of the night when he heard a door slide closed somewhere in the house. He listened, half awake, but no further sounds broke the silence.

A thought came to him then, and Van stifled a laugh, turning over in bed. It was just like in stories he'd read. A party of adventurers, their friendships still new and untested, find shelter at a roadside tavern near a turning point in their quest. A brief respite before a pivotal moment. Intimate proximity without warning. In those stories, people were always sneaking into each other's rooms, deep in the night when everyone ought to be asleep.

Van's life was not a work of fiction, though, and in any case, the person he might like sneaking into his room was in another house. Still, the Journey of Patronage would make a fine setting for such a story. Depending on how things went, maybe someone would feel motivated to commit Van's pilgrimage to writing one day.

The principal character would have to be someone like Brynda—beautiful and strong, mysterious and clever. And because she'd be the center of attention for all the interesting parts. Van, on the other hand, would make a terrible protagonist. The only interesting thing about him was that he could occasionally be found in the company of the characters that mattered.

Van drifted back to sleep thinking about books he loved, and the fascinating perplexities of storytelling. In its own way this, too, was a pleasant meditation.

16 Journey's Fulcrum

Van found Simon sprawled on the floor the next morning. When he reached the bottom of the steps, he calmly checked his vital signs, wrinkling his nose at the stench of alcohol that clung to him. He then helped the foreigner upstairs and into a bed.

Van breakfasted on fruit and tomato juice, which must have been brought to the house by their attentive servants well before dawn. It was the first time he had slept past sunrise since leaving Seat Dolse, and he was surprised that Lilim wasn't already up and about. She could be allowed to sleep in, too, he decided. Just this once.

Wilm of the Horizon and Orum the Mutable came downstairs within a few minutes of each other. The surreptitious glances they exchanged as they went about their business in the pantry made Van wonder if somebody really had snuck into someone else's room in the middle of the night.

Shale came down next, dressed in tunic and breeches today, and sat on a cushion next to Van. Ghan and Otep appeared to be gone already, preparing for the chieftain's game, so when Wilm and Orum departed after breaking fast, Van found himself alone with Shale. They waited together in the common area for Lilim.

After the better part of an hour passed, Shale gave Van a look. It wasn't a scowl of boredom or annoyance, as he might normally expect from her. Rather, her expression was one of burgeoning concern.

"I'm also getting a bit worried," he said. "I'll go up and check on her."

Shale followed him upstairs. When Van called Lilim's name outside her room, there was no response. He didn't try a second time before throwing the door open, already feeling a familiar pit in his stomach.

The room was empty, her bed neatly made. Van checked every room in turn, on the off chance she'd switched beds for some reason in the night. With each room he opened, his panic mounted. Every room in the house save for Simon's was vacant.

Van wheeled on Shale and put his hands on her shoulders. "Please, help me find her."

They searched for hours, with no luck. Van trusted his keen sense of direction, even in a place as enormous and unfamiliar as Seat Ikann, but he didn't trust Lilim's. If she had wandered off alone and gotten lost, he assumed she'd go to the first place she recognized and stay there.

He and Shale retraced their steps from yesterday, going first to the street carnival, which stood abandoned during the morning hours. When they didn't find her there, they searched every street and side road they'd traveled with her—all the way from the palace grounds to Ranger's Rest. The effort was both time-consuming and futile.

Shale disappeared briefly. It was only when she came back that Van realized it was already past midday. She'd brought bread and cheese to share with him, because he hadn't eaten. He thanked her and took a few bites while they resumed their search, but he couldn't stomach much. He was sick with worry.

After exhausting every possibility he could pursue on his own, and seeing the sun dipping low in the sky, Van steeled himself and began asking after Lilim among the Seat's rangers. This, too, proved a pointless endeavor. Everyone he spoke to could have seen a hundred girls matching Lilim's description since getting out of bed that morning. There were plenty of things that made Lilim special—her looks weren't one of them.

Then, he remembered the armlet.

Recognition crossed the face of the fourth ranger he stopped when he mentioned the accessory, and the Ikanni gave him directions to a shop called the Binding Principle. It was practically across the street from Ranger's Rest.

Once more, Van and Shale set off the way they'd come, finding the place easily enough. The Binding Principle, it turned out, was a bookshop. They found it empty when they stepped inside, except for a matronly woman reading behind a counter near the door.

When Van cleared his throat, she snapped her book shut and glared at him.

"Is there something I can help you find?"

"A girl, actually," said Van.

"I sell books." Said the Ikanni woman. "If you're in need of a girl, there's a place across the street that—"

"No!" said Van. "She is a friend, and she has been missing all day. I was told she was seen here. A twelve-year-old girl with a bone armlet."

"I suppose you mean my new star apprentice," said the woman, her lips twitching with the hint of a smile. "Which makes you the boy who likes books."

"The... what?" Van wrinkled his brow.

"Come with me," the woman said, setting her book on the counter and standing up. "But keep your voice down. She works better when she thinks no one's watching."

The proprietress led Van to a back room, separated from the storefront itself by a drawn curtain. With a finger to her lips, she pulled it aside just enough so Van could see in.

Lilim sat alone in the tiny studio, a brush in her hand as she worked by candlelight hunched over a wide drawing table. The stool was too tall for her, so her legs dangled above the floor. Van couldn't see what illustration she was working on, but she wore a look of dedicated focus such as he'd never seen before. He resisted the urge to call to her, instead stepping back from the curtain.

"She came this morning, interested in bartering that armlet you mentioned for a book cover," said the proprietress as she led Van and Shale back to the counter. "I told her I had no use for it, and put her to work instead."

"I don't understand." Van shook his head.

The Ikanni woman sighed.

"I make book covers. With the Seat overrun by you aspirants, I can scarcely keep up with the orders coming in." She tilted her chin toward the back room. "She wanted to buy a gift, and she had nothing of value to trade, so I entrusted some of the easier jobs to her. At the rate she's going, she'll finish with plenty of time to reach the coliseum before sunset. Wait for her over there, if that's what you're planning to do."

Unsure what else he *could* do, Van retreated to the reading nook she indicated at the far end of the shop. Shale, seeing there was no emergency, sank into an armchair, yawned once, and closed her eyes while Van perused the books on the nearby shelves to pass the time. Nearly all of them had something to do with equestrianism.

Lilim emerged from the studio a short time later, glancing around the shop for the proprietress.

"I've finished the, um..." She fell silent and blushed when her eyes landed on Van and Shale.

"Show me," said the proprietress.

The two of them returned to the studio, and when the proprietress shot Van a glance and cocked an eyebrow, he followed, taking it to mean he was allowed to tag along.

They stepped around the drawing table to inspect Lilim's work while Lilim herself stood meekly aside and waited. A horse was painted on the freshly brushed vellum, shown galloping across the plains. As far as Van knew, Lilim had never worked with any of the tools he saw strewn about—or with color, for that matter. Even so, the depiction rivaled the work of any scribe at Stonebasin. The animal was true to life, painted in a convincing state of natural motion.

The Ikanni woman nodded approvingly, then passed Lilim a wrapped parcel she had carried under arm from the storefront.

"Your talent would be wasted in the south," she told her matter-of-factly. "Come back here after your pilgrimage. There will be a full-time role for you, with a stipend and accommodations."

Lilim bowed to the proprietress, hugging the parcel to her chest. When they went to wake Shale, her eyes snapped open threateningly as Van reached to touch her shoulder, and he quickly snatched his hand back, reminded of the time he mistook a tree snake for a branch when climbing his favorite knob thorn by the fishing pond.

As recognition crossed her face, Shale smiled at Lilim, then stretched and got up. They left the Binding Principle together, returning to Ranger's Rest to fetch Simon. From there, they'd hurry to the coliseum. Van had spent hours rehearsing how he might scold Lilim for disappearing on her own—for the worry she'd caused him and the danger she'd put herself in. Now, he couldn't bring himself to repeat a word of it.

"It was supposed to be a surprise, but you can have this now." Lilim fidgeted nervously, offering him the parcel while they walked.

Van accepted the package in silence, opening it with care. It was, of course, a book cover—sized perfectly to fit over his copy of The Bull and the Snail. Drawn on the cover was the Bull, in full color, trampling a rattlesnake. Van was at a loss for words—and genuinely impressed that she had figured out it was his favorite chapter. Lilim the Brave had grown unexpectedly considerate, and he wondered when he'd blinked and missed it.

"Olana Bookbinder did that one," Lilim mumbled. "She's much better than me."

"Thank you, Lilim," Van said when he found his voice. "Are you considering her offer? It sounded like an incredible opportunity."

She stared at her feet. "What will *you* do after the pilgrimage?"

"I intend to ask Otep Acrearms for a permanent place in his party," said Van. "If he continues to serve the tribe as a ranger, he'll need companions he can rely on."

"Then you'll go back to Seat Dolse," she concluded.

Van opened his mouth to respond, but closed it again, struck by an uneasy feeling. He'd sworn an oath—to himself and to her—that he'd place her needs first. If art was her calling, and being here was the best way to foster her talents, then this was where she needed to be. Would she follow that path on her own, or would he have to return here with her?

Would helping Lilim the Brave find her way in life require Van the Scribe to lose his own?

Seat Ikann's coliseum was a sight to behold. The arena floor alone was large enough to fit the chieftain's palace and its grounds three times over, encircled by tiered seats. The chieftain's tower, which jutted from the northernmost point of the perimeter wall, offered the choicest view of the impending action below.

Rhaggo Bullbreaker's throne was already perched on the tower, having been moved from the palace with the chieftain riding it like a palanquin. Van could just barely make out the Pilgrimage Guides of Nemia gathered around him, joined by a full contingent of the Seat's rangers.

Simon sat between Van and Shale so he could translate as needed. They'd found seats just ten feet above the arena floor, these lowest sections of the stadium reserved for the visiting aspirants.

Wilm and Orum were close by, as were the rest of Van's kinsmen. It was a small comfort given they were surrounded on all sides by thousands of screaming Ikanni. Without a doubt, this was the single largest gathering of people Van had ever seen, with spectators having come from across the vastness of the Eastern Plains to witness the second game of the Journey of Patronage.

Lilim, of course, was right next to him, overstimulated and clinging to his arm.

"Welcome, subjects," said Rhaggo Bullbreaker as the sun touched the horizon.

The chieftain's magic orb once again cast his voice over the crowd, and all the Seat's residents stood and cheered as he raised his goblet.

"And welcome again, aspirants. The time has come to measure the best among you. Bring them forth!"

Deafening applause greeted the competitors, each one entering through a separate gate built into the curved walls. From the east, Brynda Blackblade, her obsidian dagger free in hand. From the west, Sol Starfletcher, wielding his bow and three arrows.

Otep Acrearms marched through the gate directly below Van, shirtless and barefoot, his axe slung over his shoulder. Galdur Goldeyes emerged last, sauntering from the gate at the foot of the chieftain's tower, due north. He wore his scarlet cape and pauldron today, twirling his paired longswords as he strode forward to a thunderous ovation.

Movement above caught Van's eye, and he looked up, startled. Four enormous kites flew over the coliseum, their purpose unclear until that moment. Each kite's sail illuminated to display a moving image, magic of a kind Van hadn't seen since Simon's scrying spell.

The southern kite displayed Otep's face as if from a pace away, clear enough that Van could make out the perspiration beaded on his brow. He could watch all four of them at once, each kite offering a close-up view of one of the challengers.

"Not bad," said Simon, tipping his new hat back to glance up appreciatively.

"As promised, we shall test their mettle in battle today," boomed the chieftain. "Behold the mourn, most hated of predators in these lands."

At his words, the kites shifted their vantage point, centering now on a fifth gate creaking open. A lone animal slinked from the recesses, head close to the ground as if in submission. It was emaciated, having likely been starved to provoke it to extremes of viciousness beyond what was already natural for its kind.

"To slay one is a rite of passage for young hunters, but a simple task for those who imagine themselves true rangers," said Rhaggo Bullbreaker. "I challenge my contestants, therefore, to kill as many as they can!"

Two more gates opened to either side of the starved mourn, a group of the creatures stalking forward from each one. The first mourn, now emboldened by its pack, lifted its head and bared its jagged teeth.

"You are to collect the tails of these beasts as trophies," roared the chieftain. "Whoever brings me the most shall be declared winner. Your time limit..."

He gestured to one of his rangers, who cranked a lever on a massive hourglass, flipping it end over end so that the white sand ran from the globe at the top to the one at the bottom.

"...is thirty minutes. Begin!"

More gates yawned open along the coliseum's inner wall, admitting thirty mourns in total to the arena floor. These were fatal odds for any four hunters, even working together. But the four who fought today were no mere rangers.

Sol Starfletcher was first to act, loosing his blue fletched arrow toward the sky. Once free, the shining azure falcon circled above him, ready to defend its master. The mourns were undaunted by it—at least at first. Three of them charged, gnashing their teeth, but before they'd closed half the distance to their prey, the falcon became a blur of motion, striking downward and slaying them in the space of a second.

The four corners of the arena quickly became embroiled in violent combat, each encounter displayed in vivid detail by the kites overhead. Brynda and Galdur retreated toward each other, standing back to back on the northeast side. Brynda's dagger elongated to become a spear, giving her the reach she needed to keep the mourns at bay as the prowling creatures encroached.

Van paid close attention to Otep, the competitor he was most worried for—not because he lacked the ability to defend himself with lethal force, but because Van knew he had no love for it. Otep Acrearms had reconciled his duties as a ranger with his conviction that all life was sacred only through a solemn vow—that he would only take the life of an animal to protect or provide for his tribe. Rhaggo's game served neither purpose. This was bloodsport, base and vulgar.

Four mourns rushed the First Ranger of Dolse, just as the dying rays of sunset began to falter. He dispatched three of them with a sweep of his axe. The fourth evaded the blow, waiting it out, and once Otep was off balance, it lunged to sink its fangs into his forearm.

Crimson blood flowed when it bit down, but it was not Otep's. The creature's fangs couldn't penetrate the First Ranger's tough skin, and the strength of its jaw served only to shatter its teeth in its mouth and send them ripping through its gums. The mourn squealed pitifully as Otep raised his arm, lifting the beast off its feet. Otep regarded it for a moment as it dangled there, clinging to him, then swung his arm in an arc and broke its back against the ground.

Five minutes into Rhaggo Bullbreaker's contest, day became night, and the sky grew dark. The arena floor remained illuminated by steadily burning braziers along the walls, the flames causing the shadows cast by prowling mourns to jump and jitter.

Most of the mourns soon lay dead, the greater part slain by Sol's arrow. The First Ranger of Mercura walked among the fallen beasts at his leisure, cutting tails off with his knife while his falcon continued to slaughter the creatures. Across the arena, Brynda cut down five with her spear, still in phalanx formation with Galdur, while the First Ranger of Ikann slew only a single mourn that managed to slip past her.

The sand in Rhaggo's hourglass hadn't even half run out, and already the game seemed over. Before Van could breathe a sigh of relief, however, more gates cranked open, admitting another three score mourns to the floor.

This new pack had been watching from their portcullis prisons, Van realized, and they had learned from the first pack's mistakes. The beasts attacked a few at a time, regrouping between skirmishes at the center of the arena where the light of the fires didn't quite reach. They whittled away at the First Rangers' defenses without reprieve, until exhaustion began to take its toll.

Things were looking dire for Otep Acrearms. He held his axe with both hands now, and his knees were shaking. Through trial and error, the mourns had discovered a chink in his armor—the softer flesh on his sides above the hip. Their claws and fangs found purchase there, and the First Ranger of Dolse now bled from lacerations on his flanks.

Brynda Blackblade had it worse, engaging with the pack on the far side of the coliseum almost without assistance. Her dagger had protected her at first, transforming into a whip as Van had seen before. The weapon struck at incredible range, lashing with blinding speed and a killing force spurred by little more than a flick of her wrist. But there were simply too many mourns.

One slipped through her defenses and sank its teeth into Brynda's leg above the knee. Her whip shrank into a dagger again, and she killed the creature with a strike to the neck—but after that, the weapon changed shape no longer. Van watched as she battled on desperately with her inert blade, pressing one hand to her thigh in an attempt to stem the bleeding.

Shale said something, and Simon didn't translate until Van asked him to.

"She says she's faking it," Simon shouted over the roar of the crowd.

Van snapped his eyes back to the phantom image on the kite's sail. Brynda's eyes were unfocused, and her breathing was ragged. Galdur Goldeyes did little to help, pacing behind her unscathed while she fought for her life. Shale was either wrong or making a cruel joke. This battle wasn't even about winning anymore. Van was sure Brynda was fighting to survive.

Blessedly, Sol's falcon shepherded the last mourns together to finish them off. By numbers, he was well in the lead, and a glance at Rhaggo's hourglass told Van the game would be over in another minute.

"I see you're running out of mourns," boomed the voice of the chieftain. "And breath, perhaps, if my eyes don't deceive me. To conclude these festivities, I offer a parting gift."

One final gate was hauled open, and the few remaining mourns fled from it, more terrified of what was coming than of the radiant bird slaughtering their pack.

"My pet's name is Tabitha," said Rhaggo Bullbreaker, savoring the moment. "She is getting on in years, and I would sooner see her leave this world doing what she loved rather than succumb to the undignified ravages of age."

A hornbeast lumbered into the arena, even larger than the one Brynda took down on their first hunt together. Van held his breath as it stomped forward and pawed at the ground with its massive hoof.

The chieftain continued. "To whichever of you can lay my pet to rest, I say the deed is worth the tails of fifty mourns!"

Van felt his face slacken. Everything that had happened thus far was for nothing. Otep was in no condition to fight on, and Brynda looked prepared to faint. Finally, Galdur Goldeyes stepped forward and whistled to gain the hulking predator's attention, waving his cape in the air like a flag. His restraint thus far was finally explained. He had known this was coming.

All four kites switched their focus to the First Ranger of Ikann, providing a view from four angles as the monster called Tabitha turned to face him.

The hornbeast charged, and even as broad as the arena floor was, it would be upon Galdur in seconds. He gave his swords a final twirl before taking a stance.

In that critical moment, something unexpected occurred. A bird landed on Galdur's head and screeched once, flapping its blue wings. Galdur flailed angrily at it, losing his balance as he shooed it away. By then, it was too late. Van thought he spotted a split-second window during which Galdur Goldeyes could have tumbled safely out of the hornbeast's path. Instead, he chose to stand his ground—a fatal miscalculation.

The enormous predator collided with Galdur, its horn goring him through the left eye. The First Ranger's swords fell from his hands, and his body was lifted off the ground to be shaken like a child's doll as Tabitha bucked her massive head triumphantly from side to side.

Shale leaned forward, eyes sparkling, and Lilim covered her face with her hands. A horrified gasp rose from the crowd as the men and women of Ikann bore witness to their champion's fate.

With another shake of her head, Tabitha threw Galdur's body to roll lifeless in the dirt. Since Otep Acrearms was now helping the badly limping Brynda toward an open gate, the hornbeast turned to face the only challenger remaining—Sol Starfletcher.

Within seconds, the creature charged again, building up momentum. Sol's falcon was faster. It returned to its master's quiver, and Sol drew out a new arrow—the one with red fletching. Dropping to a knee, he braced himself before making his shot.

The arrow glowed like a ruby reflecting firelight as it flew. Van blinked against the brilliance of it, and when the light subsided, there were not one, but two great beasts on the arena floor, barreling headlong to meet one another.

The creature Sol's arrow had become was smaller than Tabitha, but jutting from its broad, bone-plated head were three horns instead of one, each sharp and curved. A prehistoric forebear to the present-day tyrant of the plains.

Rhaggo's pet reared up to trample the beast of three horns, but that proved to be a grave mistake. The three-horned beast saw its opening and charged straight ahead, burying its horns in Tabitha's exposed underbelly. The hornbeast groaned, its weight falling forward as a last spiteful act of reprisal. There was a sickening crunch as the three-horned beast's spine snapped.

Both creatures died at the center of the coliseum, one atop the other.

Chaos ensued. Ikanni rangers rushed onto the arena floor to retrieve the body of Galdur Goldeyes, while the thousands of men and women in the stadium rose from their seats, screaming in outrage. Van saw one man turn to smash his fist into his neighbor's face unprovoked, and at that moment, all thought vanished from his mind except for Lilim's safety.

"We need to go," he urged, turning to Simon.

"Where?"

"Ranger's Rest, if we can make it," said Van. "Do you have any spells that could—?"

Simon interrupted him by tracing a pattern in the air. With a *pop*, a bubble of invisible force emanated from the tip of his finger. Van felt it envelope him and Lilim, along with Shale. Wilm and Orum made it inside the bubble as well before Simon turned his hand and closed his fist, pushing everything and everyone outside the magic barrier away and hedging them back.

The luminous kites above flickered and went dark as their small group fled the coliseum. Van didn't dare let go of Lilim's hand, running as fast as he thought she could keep up with. Shale took his other hand and sprinted along with them, laughing with the mirth of a madwoman.

When they reached the street, Van could already see fights breaking out and property being senselessly destroyed as order collapsed throughout Seat Ikann. By the grace of Simon's magic, they made it back to Ranger's Rest and sheltered there until morning.

17 Devil

Ranger's Rest went untouched by the worst of the ensuing riots. Twice, they had to scare off unruly gangs that strayed onto the grounds with looting or vandalism in mind, but after that, they were left alone. Guard duty was assumed by Wilm of the Horizon and Orum the Mutable. Shale took third watch, allowing the others to get a few hours' sleep.

They abandoned their private rooms, opting to sleep together in the common area in case swift escape was necessary. Lilim fell asleep near midnight, her head cradled in Van's lap, but Van remained awake and alert until dawn, when Otep Acrearms finally arrived with an escort of the Seat's rangers. The wounds on his sides were bandaged, and he wore his travel clothes, freshly washed.

"We are summoned to the palace," was all the First Ranger said, but Van didn't miss the way he clenched his fists, nor the haunted look on his face.

Otep and his companions proceeded without delay to the chieftain's palace. It seemed another careless oversight that Van was counted among them, to say nothing of the little girl yawning and rubbing her eyes and the two foreigners. Among the First Ranger's confidantes, only Wilm and Orum resembled anything like an honor guard.

Ghan Mudcatcher was already there when they were let in, standing with elder Memnon of tribe Vaxas. Van felt small and out of place as they waited in the grand vestibule for the other delegates to arrive.

Minutes later, Brynda Blackblade was shown in with her rangers, among them Rhys the Catcher and Rhyla the Tamer. She gave Memnon the Still Pool a curt greeting and then bowed cordially to Otep, wincing as she put weight on her bad leg, which was heavily dressed where the mourn had savaged her. Van was so relieved to see her alive he nearly fell over, his exhaustion overwhelming him as the tautness in his chest relaxed.

Sol Starfletcher and Riverspeaker Gheela arrived with their party last.

"Where is Rhaggo Bullbreaker?" demanded the Patron tribe's Guide as she stormed through the palace doors.

The chieftain's rangers bristled, but the senior captain among them stepped forward and raised his hand.

"You will be met soon," the Ikanni assured her.

Out of the corner of his eye, Van saw Simon stealthily trace the shape that started up his hour of universal language comprehension.

"Chieftain Rhaggo will meet us *now*," said Gheela, thumping her staff on the marble floor. "Tribe Ikann will be held accountable."

"I beg your patience, cousin," the ranger said. "You will be met."

Gheela's eyes flared as she tightened her grip on her staff. For an instant, Van thought she might strike the Ikanni across the cheek with it, but when Sol Starfletcher put a hand on her shoulder, giving her a meaningful look, she stood down.

They were not made to wait long. Another group of Ikanni arrived from somewhere deeper in the palace and approached the delegates, two of them carrying a heavy trunk. Van's eyes widened, and his mouth hung slack when he glimpsed who walked at the fore.

"It is good to see you safe, cousin," said Goldur Goldeyes, bowing stiffly to Riverspeaker Gheela as his subordinates, Hammer and Anvil, dropped the trunk at her feet.

The moment drew out in silence. When Mercura's Pilgrimage Guide failed to find her voice, Galdur straightened his back and spoke on.

"For failing to protect the aspirants of Nemia while they were guests of our Seat, tribe Ikann will pay reparations to our Patron, and to the families of the deceased."

At a gesture from their First Ranger, one of the brothers knelt, lifting the lid of the trunk. It was brimming with silks, gemstones, and farthings of the Eastern Plains.

The mocking tone was gone from his voice, but he didn't sound at all remorseful. He didn't sound sorry, angry, or even bored. Galdur's words were empty—devoid of feeling of any kind. The change might go unnoticed to a casual acquaintance, but to Van, he seemed a different man. The only evidence of the prior night's events was the black leather patch over his left eye, fresh scar tissue visible around it.

"You have my word as First Ranger of Ikann that those responsible for inciting yesterday's violence have been brought to justice, and that order has been restored throughout the Seat," he continued. "At your discretion, we will observe a period of grieving for those lost before we take up our pilgrimage anew. Chieftain Rhaggo wishes you to know our resources are at your disposal."

"We will certainly grieve," Riverspeaker Gheela said finally. "But not here. None among us would stay a minute longer in Seat Ikann. We resume travel at once, and when this place is behind us, we will make camp and pray for the spirits of the dead."

Galdur maintained calm, unblinking eye contact with her until she turned her back on him.

"You should pray, too, Galdur Goldeyes," she said as she strode out of the palace. "You more than anyone."

"How is he alive?" Simon hissed as they made their way to the campgrounds to recover their tents and other belongings.

"I was hoping you could tell me," muttered Van. His initial shock was quickly giving way to fatigue. "Magic of some kind, I would think."

"No way," said the foreigner. "The best healers in the world couldn't fix that. The only thing even theoretically possible..."

Van watched him sidelong. The sorcerer wore the same troubled look Van remembered from their botched attempt to spy on Brynda.

"*Ex mortuis,*" he said. "But it can't be done. The smartest and most powerful sorcerers in the world have been trying for as long as magic's been practiced."

"You're talking about that other magic again," said Van, his tired mind seeking the word. "Necromancy."

"Yeah," said Simon. "But with necromancy, there's always a price, even for something as simple as stopping a bird from rotting. I don't want to think about what it would cost to actually reverse death."

Van didn't want to think about it either. It sounded complicated, and he was too exhausted besides. The procession exited Seat Ikann via the north gate, as was tradition. From there, they hooked east toward the tundra, and beyond that, the domain of Vaxas.

It was announced that twenty people had lost their lives the night before in the Cornucopia of the Plains. Sixteen were aspirants, brutally assaulted in the immediate aftermath of the competition or trampled as they tried to flee the coliseum. A rumor made its way to tribe Dolse, at the rear of the column, that others were chased down and lynched.

Seven Mercurans, three Vaxals, five Dolsers, and even one Ikanni. The youngest was twelve years old.

The procession camped when the shadow of Seat Ikann no longer loomed on the horizon. Ghan Mudcatcher listed the names of the perished and led a prayer for them. After that, Otep Acrearms declared there would be no hunting until further notice. The rangers of Dolse would seek to take no more lives while they grieved so much senseless death.

When the aspirants dispersed, Van pitched his tent near Lilim's beneath the shade of a jackalberry. She brought him bread and cheese to share for midday meal, but he politely declined. He had been awake now for almost thirty hours. He was too tired to be hungry.

"I'm sorry, Lilim, but I don't think I'll be up to the task of holding lessons tomorrow morning," he said, sitting with her while she ate. "Would it be all right if—?"

"You should sleep," she said, her tone and expression sincere. "I'll be fine."

He nodded. "Thank you, Lilim."

Van stumbled to his tent and collapsed before making it to his bedroll.

He woke up the next morning with a sore back and throbbing feet, cursing himself for falling asleep without even taking off his boots. But he at least felt rested. It was light outside, so he left his tent in a hurry, hoping he wasn't late for assembly.

The sight that greeted him when he emerged froze him in his tracks. There next to his tent, in the misty stillness of dawn, Shale and Lilim slept under the jackalberry. Shale was leaning against the tree with Lilim in her lap, her head resting against Shale's breast as she clutched a fold of her tunic like it was a favorite blanket.

A month ago it would have frightened him, finding Lilim alone and defenseless with the dread visitor shamans called "the dark girl." Today, it made him feel differently. Van wondered if he had finally found what he was looking for when he beseeched Otep Acrearms for his help in protecting her, and he was surprised to discover he considered Shale just as worthy of the task as the First Ranger.

He watched them sleep for a moment longer, then leaned down to rouse them. Just as in the bookshop, Shale's eyes snapped open before he could touch either of them. This time, however, her dagger was at his throat. She glared at him briefly, and he remained stone still. At length, she yawned, sheathed her weapon, and began rubbing her eyes. The movement woke Lilim, who slid off Shale's lap, smiling up at Van with her eyes half open.

"Good morning," she said.

"Good morning, Lilim." Van offered a hand and helped her up. "Why, um. May I ask why you were sleeping outside?"

"Shale was keeping watch," she said plainly. "I stayed to keep her company."

"Keeping watch for what?" Van glanced at Shale, who had already brushed the grass off her breeches and turned to leave.

Lilim shrugged, still groggy from sleep, but then she seemed to remember something.

"Oh," she said. "The First Ranger of Vaxas came looking for you after mealtime."

"What!" Van balked.

"Shale told her to go away."

"What!" his voice cracked.

"Not with words, obviously. But she made it clear she wasn't allowed to see you."

Van put his hands on his head and groaned.

Lilim tugged at his sleeve, oblivious to his distress. "We will be late!"

Aside from the extra prayer at assembly, and the postponement of the hunt, the day felt like any other. Van could scarcely accept that all those lives had been snuffed out at once. The grisly events at Seat Ikann were so at odds with rationality, they seemed like an awful dream. But it had *happened.* And though the tragedy already felt strangely remote, Van told himself he would not forget.

Following midday meal, he went looking for Simon, finding him relaxing by a shallow stream with Shale. Evidently, he'd made a few other recent purchases besides his new hat. The two sat across from each other at a small folding table, a deck of cards between them. The rest of the tribe was further downstream where the water ran deeper, seizing the opportunity to wash their clothes.

When Simon glanced up from his cards, Van made the talking sign, and the foreigner promptly scribbled in the air with his finger.

"We'll be done in a minute," he said, returning his attention to the game.

"You don't have to hurry," said Van. "It's a nice day, and there's no one around."

Simon spoke to Shale, and she nodded distractedly, still focused on her cards.

Van's brow furrowed. "I didn't realize you knew how to play."

"We don't," said Simon. "We're just making it up as we go."

Van blinked, his head tilting to one side. "Is that not difficult, if you haven't activated your spell until now?"

"Trust me," said Simon, "it's funnier this way."

Van cleared his throat. "I wanted to apologize for what took place at Seat Ikann."

He gave Simon a moment to translate. Once he had, Shale set her cards aside and looked up, waiting.

"You already know the Ikanni have paid reparations. For most of us, that is enough. We know how atypical what happened there was. But you aren't from our lands, nor were you raised with our values. You have only your recent experiences to judge us by, and I feel it's my duty to help you make sense of them."

Again Van paused. This time, Shale narrowed her eyes and muttered something in response.

"Simon?" prodded Van.

"She said this is a weird way to start an apology."

Van inhaled and continued. "Please take me at my word when I say the events we witnessed are in no way representative of life in Nemia. The conduct we saw at Seat Ikann isn't just unusual, it's unheard of. You saw us at our worst, and I'm sincerely sorry. I promise you we are better than that."

He bowed, keeping his head down while Simon caught Shale up. She replied with two words, maybe three, spoken in a hiss.

"Word for word, please," said Van.

Simon sighed. "The *events* we witnessed…"

Van straightened his back, looking first at Simon, then at Shale.

"What took *place*," she went on. "You can't even bring yourself to say what it is you're apologizing for. Tell me what I'm supposed to forgive. Perhaps then I'll consider it."

Van stiffened.

"The killings," he said with effort. "I am apologizing to you for the killings, and I am asking you to believe that is not who we are."

"And what do you intend to do about the killings?" Shale pressed. "Accept their trunk of useless baubles and bury your head in the dirt?"

"Whether further measures are warranted is for the Patron tribe to decide," Van said quietly.

"And what if they'd killed me?" Shale demanded. "What if they had killed *Lilim?*"

Van shook his head, his chest tightening. Losing anyone he loved in that way would break his heart forever. "What would you have me do?"

"You already know my views on that," she growled.

Van tried to guard his expression, but a hint of horror must have shown through. He could tell from watching Shale that she saw it.

"And now you're mad at me," she said, standing up from the table. "Again. Over something so stupid. I may as well just—"

"Stop," Van said, raising his voice when she turned to leave.

She stopped. Eyes to the ground, her face half hidden behind her hair, she waited. She looked furious. And bitterly alone.

"I'm not mad," he said calmly. "The opposite, actually. I wanted to thank you for looking after Lilim. She told me you gave up sleep to keep her safe. To keep us both safe. It's not easy to put into words how grateful I am for that. Thank you, Shale."

She glanced up at him, her eyes glassy, and for a moment, Van thought she might cry. She rubbed roughly at her eyes, as if she'd had the same idea.

"How unbefitting..." she said quietly. When she heard Simon translate, she shot him a nasty look.

Van smiled awkwardly, hoping to put her at ease. He couldn't quite tell if it worked, but she did sit back down.

"Apology accepted," she muttered. "Provisionally. I'll hear more later about your plan for retribution. Now, whose turn was it?"

"Nice try," said Simon, translating for himself this time. "It was my turn."

Shale clicked her tongue. Seeing Van's confusion, Simon explained.

"One of the rules she came up with," he said. "If you forget whose turn it is, you lose a turn."

Van stood back, watching them play. Starting with Simon, they took turns drawing cards from the deck, then choosing one from their hand to add to a face-up stack in front of them. On Shale's turn, she slapped paired antlers on her pile—a high value card in most games Van knew.

Simon snapped at her, and she growled, picking the card back up and pondering over an alternative selection.

"What happened?" asked Van.

"New rule," he said. "You can only play double antlers on mean snake."

Van stepped around so he could see Shale's hand. She was holding the requisite card, but she chose a different one to play instead.

"That card is called coiled serpent," Van offered to Simon.

"Not to us, it's not," he replied.

Simon put down another card, and on Shale's turn, some unknown rule allowed her to play two. Simon grumbled under his breath, then drew a new card and considered his hand.

"Will you propose another new rule?" Van asked, seeing him hesitate. "Something that slows her down, or strengthens your own position?"

"Can't," grunted Simon, choosing a low-value card to put on his pile. "After you make a new rule, you have to wait a turn to make any more. That was one of my rules. Pretty proud of it."

A few more turns passed, and at some point both players were excused from drawing new cards. They were down to two each—in Shale's case, coiled serpent, with the paired antlers she'd tried to play earlier. Van sat down next to her so he could watch until the end.

Simon put down his second-to-last card, looking her in the eye. "New rule. If you don't have mean snake when you're down to two cards, you lose a turn."

Shale grinned and played the named card. She then spoke quickly and authoritatively before playing the other—paired antlers, enabled per Simon's earlier ruling. Shale threw her arms up and started giggling, while Simon set his last card aside with a sigh.

"She made a new rule," he explained. "If you play mean snake, you don't have to wait a turn to play double antlers."

"So, she won?" Van raised an eyebrow.

"This time," said Simon, stacking the cards to shuffle them.

She's quite good at things like this, Van considered. "Simon, would you ask her about the ring toss game from the street carnival? She'll know what you're talking about."

Simon obliged, and Shale shot Van one of her bored looks. "What about it?"

"I just assumed there was some trick," said Van.

"Of course there was," said Shale.

"But you figured it out so easily, and turned it to your advantage."

"Of course I did."

Van looked at her expectantly. "So, what was it?"

Shale crossed her arms. "It's not fun anymore once it's been explained. Think it through yourself, and I'll give you a hint if you get stuck."

"All right," said Van, consulting his memory. "When we started playing, the game runner demonstrated that all the rings were the same."

Her eyebrow went up.

"Or, they only appeared to be the same," he corrected himself. "So... the only ring that was actually any good was the one he was keeping hold of. What made his ring special?"

"His was made of fabric," she said. "The ones he wanted his victims to use were metal, more liable to bounce off the vase."

"Then how did you get the good ring from him? I never saw him let it go, and he was the one handing the rings to us. We never got to choose them for ourselves."

The ghost of a smile twitched at the corner of her lips.

"Very well, what's my hint?" said Van.

"Which hand was he holding it in?" prompted Shale.

Van thought about it.

"His left. He was left-handed." Van snapped his fingers. "That's why you didn't move when you asked him to demonstrate. He had to step around you and throw right-handed, so he must have switched the rings around, but then..."

"Mmm?" Shale grinned smugly.

"Are you suggesting he simply forgot which was which, and handed you the good one by mistake?"

"Muscle memory," said Shale. "He'd been handing rings to clueless imbeciles with his right hand all day."

Van's lips pulled into a frown. "You're right, that's not a very satisfying answer."

Shale laughed. "It wasn't a certain thing, in any case. He could have easily remembered and saved himself at the last moment. You and Lilim helped with that, distracting him when he should have been paying attention to his hands."

Van smiled. "It was kind of you to give her the prize."

She shrugged, looking away. "My prize was the charlatan's embarrassment. And the girl was enchanted with it, so, why not?"

Van studied her for another moment, then turned to Simon. "How are we doing on time?"

"Fifteen more minutes, maybe," he said.

Van grew somber again. "Can you tell Shale what you told me, about Galdur Goldeyes? I'd like her opinion."

Simon spoke to Shale at length, and Van watched her expression harden. He also heard the foreigner use the term he remembered—*ex mortuis.*

"There is no magic known to the Twilight World that can bring back the dead," said Shale. "And the elf's homeland is the authority on magic here on Titan's surface. So, if he says it's impossible, then it's impossible."

Van's eyebrows drew together. "Then, you believe Galdur simply recovered? Or was healed?"

"That obviously isn't possible either," said Shale.

"So, what do you think happened?"

"Someone has done the impossible," she said flatly. "Or they appear to have."

Van frowned.

"Whatever the case, there is villainy afoot," Shale continued. "Hence, why I took the liberty of standing guard another night."

"Oh," mumbled Van. "I did need to ask you about that, actually. I'm told someone came looking for me?"

"The champion of the green clan," she said, sounding indifferent.

"If Brynda Blackblade asked for me, I'd prefer for you to have woken me. I'm sure whatever she wanted was harmless."

"You were delirious from lack of sleep. Even if I'd woken you, you would have been useless to her." Her gaze sharpened. "And you're wrong about that woman being harmless. I'm not sure how wrong yet, but I suspect very."

"You must have been as tired as I was," said Van. "You could have at least asked Wilm and Orum for help again, if you feared further danger. I think they've come to trust you."

"That doesn't mean I trust them," said Shale. "I don't trust important things to young boys in general, when it can be avoided."

"Why?" asked Van. "They are our kinsmen."

"Because boys are prone to making stupid mistakes," she said. "They fall in love too easily, and usually with the wrong person."

Van winced and averted his eyes, hating how transparent he was.

Shale sighed. "Fret not, Van the Scribe. You'll be able to do her bidding soon. She said she would return."

"I just hope you weren't rude with her," Van said timidly.

"I would say I got my point across," said Shale, and Van decided against pressing further.

The two started another game of cards, and Simon's language spell gave out partway through it. Van stayed to watch anyway, but when he heard Simon refer to the Emissary card as "devil," his mood soured. That was one more cloud hanging over them, and he still wasn't sure what to do about it. With Simon's magic used up for the day, though, it was a problem for another time. He excused himself, wandering back to camp.

Just as Shale predicted, Brynda Blackblade found him later that afternoon while he was washing his gear in the stream. Rhys and Rhyla walked beside her, the three of them moving together at the slow pace set by the First Ranger's limp.

When he spotted them, Van quickly stood and bowed. "First Ranger! I'm told you came looking for me after I'd gone to bed last night. I'm so sorry I wasn't available."

"Think nothing of it, cousin," said Brynda, letting Rhyla support her when they stopped. "It is good to see you well."

Her leg was looking better today, but Van found himself distracted by a new bandage—a small one on her neck. "Did you, um, hurt yourself?"

"It is immaterial." She smiled weakly as she touched her neck. "A misunderstanding with one of the outsiders. I ventured too close while she was standing watch over your tent, and she pressed a bit too hard when she put her knife to my throat in response."

She laughed, then. "Or rather, now that I'm thinking about it, I suppose she pressed just as hard as she meant to."

"Please accept my apologies!" Van said urgently with another low bow. "I will tell her such conduct is unacceptable."

"You shouldn't," said Brynda. "It's a comfort to know you rest your head under the protection of such loyal friends. You'll need them."

"I wouldn't have gone to sleep to begin with if I'd known you needed me," he stammered. "You did say you might need some time after Seat Ikann."

"That is true," she said. "But I believe I also said it would depend on how things went. As it happens, I need your help sooner rather than later, to perform an evaluation."

"Evaluation?" echoed Van.

A shadow fell over her face. "I need to know if I should be concerned about the convalescence of our cousin Galdur."

Van blinked. "I'm sure he was given only the best care at Seat Ikann. And I know next to nothing of healing and medicine, so I'm not sure—"

"Injury to the brain can have unpredictable consequences," Brynda interrupted. "Among other complications, mastery over new skills can be impeded, or entirely undone. You have spent more time with him than anyone on his reading and writing, and I feel a thorough checkup from his tutor would go a long way in determining whether he's suffered any setbacks."

"Oh," said Van, swallowing hard. "Of course. When would you like me to perform this, um... evaluation?"

"Right away, if it's no inconvenience," she said politely.

Van nodded, scrambling to gather his gear. He then followed Brynda and the sisters back to the campsite of Vaxas.

Galdur sat alone in Brynda's tent, watching Van impassively as he sat down across the table from him. Brynda Blackblade stayed behind Van, wanting only to observe. This way, it felt more like an interview than their usual format—or an interrogation—and Van felt a bead of perspiration roll down his neck at the thought.

"It's good to see you well, Galdur Goldeyes," he said to break the silence. "You gave us all quite a scare."

"Goldeye," he said in reply.

Van stared back. "I'm sorry?"

"Gold*eye*," corrected Galdur, indicating the eyepatch. "Because now I have only the one."

Van suppressed a shudder. He cleared his throat, then began the lesson from the same point as their very first, asking Galdur to write his own name.

GALDUR GOLDEYE

His handwriting looked exactly as Van remembered, but at the same time... different. The letters were drawn with more patience, leaving his script tidier and more legible than usual. Van quizzed Galdur on various other subjects he'd introduced to him previously, and the First Ranger completed each exercise to satisfaction. He worked for close to an hour, unhurried and without complaint.

"Thank you, First Ranger," Van said after a while. "I think we will stop there for the day. Brynda Blackblade, might I see you outside?"

Van and Brynda left the tent while Galdur—without being asked—began to clear the table. They walked until they were out of earshot.

"I don't think you have anything to be concerned about," said Van. "His retention seems intact, and he's following directions without any trouble. He is, um…"

He hesitated, not wishing to speak out of turn. He knew he couldn't be as candid with her as with Simon. Then again, Brynda had asked him to be thorough.

"He's more cooperative than before. It's an improvement, if anything."

Judging by her expression, it was clear Brynda still had reservations. But she questioned him no further. After thanking him for his time, she told him it would be appreciated if they could resume their regular lessons starting the following evening.

Agreeing eagerly to her request, Van made his way back to the Dolser campsite, mulling over the past few days' events. He couldn't seem to shake the feeling he had missed something.

Someone appears to have done the impossible.

Hearing Shale put it that way, it sounded no different from the ring toss game at the street carnival. In this case, though, what was the trick?

"This is gonna be a messy one, kid, if we intend to uphold our agreement about honesty."

A week had passed since the events at Seat Ikann, and it had been raining for days. The seasons were finally changing, which meant that for the most part, sunshine and clear skies were things of days gone by. Until the end of the pilgrimage, the weather would be gray and overcast more often than not.

Shale hadn't been seen since yesterday, so when Van returned from the hunt, Simon found him alone. The look on the foreigner's face told him it was time. They'd sat down together in Van's tent, and he'd traced the familiar pattern in the air.

"I would have it no other way," Van consented.

"All right." Simon drew a breath. "Picking up where we left off, then."

For the first time in many weeks, Van detected an undertone that suggested he was testing the waters.

"The entities you refer to as the Emissaries are called devils by most other world cultures. Furthermore, we're all in basic agreement that devils are categorically evil, never to be trusted or bartered with."

Van held Simon's gaze. "My beliefs won't be shaken just from being told what others believe."

"And I wouldn't take that approach with you," said Simon. "If it was as simple as putting it to a vote, we'd already be done. And anyway, I know you're smarter than that. So, we'll reason it out instead. First, I need you to explain the Emissaries to me, as you understand them."

Van inhaled deeply. "The Emissaries are the gods of the land, protecting Nemia from natural disaster and intrusion by foreign aggressors. For as long as peace has existed between the tribes, the Emissaries have blessed us with bountiful harvests and good hunting."

"Good," said Simon, nodding along. "There's a bit to discuss there. Let's start with 'gods of the land.' Does that imply there are other types of gods besides the Emissaries?"

"It could very well be so," said Van. "Our shamans speak of spirits from beyond our world, sometimes. And what you've told me of your own experiences suggests as much besides."

"That's pretty sound reasoning, and it essentially lines up with the views of the world at large," said Simon. "So, if the Emissaries are just one type of god, what then defines a god?"

Van floundered. "I don't know that I could easily put that into words."

"Can't blame you," said Simon. "It's a loaded question. I don't think there even is a definition that could apply to all gods. Do you mind if I propose one that we might both be able to move forward with?"

Van nodded. "Go ahead."

"Gods are intelligent beings that exist in planes of reality separate from our own."

Van silently repeated the words to himself. "I have no objection to that, but it doesn't seem terribly useful."

"It may seem that way now," said Simon. "But at least we're in agreement on a couple of key elements—that extraplanar entities exist, and they're capable of reason. Now, everything else you just told me more or less amounts to, 'they do a bunch of good stuff for us.' Why do you think that is?"

"To reward us for living virtuously," Van said without having to think it over. "Because they love us."

"How do you know that?"

Van furrowed his brow. "The evidence of their deeds is visible across all of Nemia."

"I have a feeling that's true," said Simon, averting his gaze momentarily as if troubled by the thought. "But I'm not challenging the notion *that* they help you. I'm questioning *why* they help you."

Van blinked. "What other reason could there be?"

Simon tapped his finger on his knee. "How about this—I'll grant you that it's possible they're acting out of altruism, but only if you agree it's equally possible they stand to gain something from the arrangement. If nobody knows for sure, either statement could be true. We'll just say their motivations in general are not well understood. Is that fair?"

Van shrugged. "I suppose."

"Okay," said Simon. "We'll put a pin in that for now, because there's another item we need to touch on. Do you believe people have souls?"

"Shale used that word, too," Van mused, thinking back. "I don't know what it means."

"You might use some other term," said Simon. "I've heard you say 'spirit.' Is that something people have?"

"The spirit, yes," said Van. "The essence of oneself before one is formed."

"Good." Simon sounded a little relieved. "That's really good. Before one is formed... So, what do you believe happens to the spirit after death?"

"We are taught that—"

"No," interrupted Simon, holding his hand up. "I'm not arguing theology with a nation. I'm having a conversation with my friend, who is a rational individual. What do you think happens to your soul when you die?"

Van reined in his anxiety and tried again. "After one's life has ended, their spirit journeys to the halls of their ancestors, where they are reunited with their loved ones—everyone who passed on before them. Those who lived righteously are celebrated forever, while those who led cowardly lives serve and tend to the righteous."

"Good," Simon said again. "I can't give you any points for originality, but that will work for our purposes. As it stands, we're now in agreement on three more points—souls exist, our souls go somewhere when we die, and it's within the realm of possibility that extraplanar entities benefit from rendering aid to mortals."

Van repeated the statement to himself, as before. It sounded technically true, but he was starting to feel uneasy.

"Next, do gods have souls?"

Van rubbed his eyes. "I... I don't know. That's not something I have ever considered."

Simon drew a breath. "Okay, I'm going to tell you some things that I believe about devils now. I'm not going to try to convince you these things are true, I just want you to understand where I'm coming from. The same as you've done for me. All right?"

"All right," said Van.

"Devils do *not* have souls. When they die, they don't go anywhere—for them, that's just the end of the road. They are perfectly aware of this fact, however, and they are capable of extending their own lifespans indefinitely, so long as they have a steady supply of *our* souls on which to subsist. Since they know the alternative is oblivion, they'll do anything to get their hands on souls. Devils are, literally, living furnaces fueled by souls."

Van shook his head in disbelief. "You said you weren't trying to convince me of anything, but you speak as though these things are proven facts—that you have witnessed firsthand the fate of the mortal soul."

"For better or worse, I have," said Simon, his jaw tight. "More times than I ever cared to. But we can't have a fair conversation on those grounds, can we? At the end of the day, I believe what I do because of my experiences, and you believe the way you do because of yours. Context is all anybody has. Remember what you told me, about the aspirants who die on the pilgrimage?"

Van began to recite the familiar words. "We ask the Emissaries to take custody of their spirit, and..." His eyes widened. "No. You're not suggesting—*our souls?*"

Simon shrugged. "I don't have all the answers, Van, but it sounds like you're starting to ask the right questions."

He let those words sink in before continuing.

"I'm going to summarize our conversation so far. Before I do that, I want you to appreciate that we just put a fair amount of energy into making sure we both agree that what I'm about to say is true."

Van swallowed, watching him closely.

"Devils have taken an active role in the development of Nemian civilization, and nobody knows why. Furthermore, Nemia is the only place *in the world* where such an arrangement is being carried out at anywhere near the same scale."

Once more, Van repeated the statement back to himself.

"If you wake up tomorrow feeling one hundred percent fine with that, go ahead and let me know."

Van would need time to fully consider everything Simon had told him that day, not because the idea was beyond his comprehension. It wasn't. And not because he thought Simon was misleading him. He didn't. It would take Van time to return to the question of devils because he was given no time to think about it at all before he came face to face with a far more disturbing question—one he thought he'd put to rest.

Having no appetite, Van skipped evening meal, and in so doing arrived early to the First Ranger's tent in the campsite of Vaxas.

Rhys and Rhyla were not standing guard outside the tent today, but from within, Van heard voices raised in argument. Out of habit, he dropped into the low stance hunters relied on to mask their footfalls while tracking. Under any other circumstance, his tip-toeing would never hide him from the keen senses of a First Ranger, but even an amateur might approach unnoticed under the cover of such noise.

As he drew close, it was Galdur's voice he recognized first.

"...still fail to see why I must put myself through this. Must it really be done at the hands of that condescending brat?"

Brynda Blackblade replied sternly, as if speaking to a child throwing a tantrum.

"As I have told you, these are skills you will require as a leader. Regarding the complaints about your teacher, you are in a prison of your own design. It is not my fault you managed to estrange yourself from every literate member of tribe Ikann."

Van crept closer, still undetected. He could now see through the narrow slit in the canvas covering the tent's entrance. Galdur sat slouched across the table from Brynda, his face in his hands, as if he was sick or in pain. His strange diatribe continued with no regard for Brynda's scolding.

"I can scarcely hold a thought some days. I don't sleep, I barely eat. The joy is gone from everything, like a world without color..."

"And what do you want me to do about it?" Brynda's voice was compassionless as she sipped her tea.

Galdur slammed his fist on the table. It was a miracle Van managed not to jump.

"I *want* you to fix the mess you made. Use your powers, witch. Make me feel again."

Brynda closed her eyes, sighed, and stood up.

"There are older and more reliable ways of convincing a person's body it is alive."

She stepped around the table toward Galdur, pulling her tunic over her head and shaking her long hair out. Van backed away as slowly as he could, his hunter's instinct saving him from the mistake of breaking into a dead run. He retreated stealthily from the tent, sprinting only once he was at a safe distance.

By the time he reached his tent, he didn't know whether to scream or cry. He did neither, instead simply lying in his bedroll with his eyes wide open until morning.

18 Construct

Even as dawn approached Van still didn't feel like seeing or speaking to anyone. But he would make an exception for Lilim.

"Sorry!" she said, hurrying to clean up the space when Van stepped into her tent.

Dozens of new illustrations were spread on the ground, some of them copies of scenes from *The Bull and the Snail,* but others original, drawn from her own imagination.

"You've been working quite prodigiously," Van said once she'd cleared a place for him to sit.

"I think this is what I want to do," said Lilim, gathering up her drawings on hands and knees.

The full gravity of her statement wasn't lost on Van.

"Then you should accept the offer extended to you at Seat Ikann," he said.

She looked up in surprise. "I'll do it back home. That's where you'll be."

Van forced a smile and shook his head.

"The best you could hope for in our lands is working at the Scriptorium in Stonebasin, and the proprietress was right. You wouldn't be given the freedom there to explore your potential and express your creativity."

She frowned. "But you won't—"

"You can come back after a year or so," said Van. "Bring your art with you, and everything else you've learned, and share it with our tribe. Think of how impressed everyone will be with you—Lilim the Brave, all grown up."

A flicker of hopefulness flashed in her eyes, but it was replaced quickly by restless fidgeting.

"I'm not that much younger than you, you know," she said. "When we go home, we'll all be blooded members of the tribe."

"That is true," said Van. "We are all still young, and we are all still growing."

"You never talk about Shale like she's a child," mumbled Lilim.

It was a confusing turn for the conversation, and Van knew that when it came to Lilim's mood, confusion could be swiftly followed by things much worse. He proceeded with caution.

"Shale once told me she'd undergone some, um, unpleasant experiences where she grew up. It is possible she's been through more in her life than we have in ours."

Lilim was still pouting, but that was preferable to the gamut of alternatives. Putting the subject aside, Van began their daily lesson, and when it was done, he tied a length of white cloth around his head to cover his mouth and nose.

"What's that for?" Lilim asked. "Are you sick?"

"Between you and I, no," said Van. "But please keep that a secret. I plan to tell most others I'm feeling unwell."

"Why?" She cocked her head.

Van declined to answer, instead reminding her they were expected at assembly. He offered her his hand when they stepped outside together. She took it and didn't ask again.

Otep excused Van from the hunt without question, telling him to look after his health. He thanked the First Ranger, ignoring the guilt that pricked at his conscience, and then set out to indefinitely cancel his other obligation. Thankfully, he spotted Rhys and Rhyla at the Vaxas campsite before he saw Brynda.

He waved to the sisters, and they approached, though when they saw his face covering, they slowed their pace and kept a safe distance.

"Van the Scribe," said Rhyla the Tamer. "You are ill. The influenza?"

"I'm not sure, to be honest," said Van. "But I'd prefer to take no chances. Would you convey my apologies to your First Ranger and let her know I will return only once I'm recovered?"

"Of course," said Rhyla.

She sounded tired, and her eyes looked puffy. Like she'd been crying.

He remembered something then, a private moment he'd once glimpsed that led him to suspect the older sister harbored feelings for the First Ranger akin to his own. He wondered now if he might not have been the only one that chanced to see what was happening in her tent last night.

There was a door open here, and he recognized it as such. An opportunity to make a connection, to share in someone's heartbreak and vulnerability—however embarrassing that might be—and even learn the truth of what was going on between the First Rangers of Vaxas and Ikann. Or even, perhaps, just find friendship.

"Thank you, cousin," was all he said instead, and with that, he bowed and left.

Now free of his responsibilities, Van returned to his tent and crawled back into bed, this time managing a few hours' sleep. Noise outside startled him, and he awoke with a gargled scream. Hearing it, Simon burst into his tent, panic in his eyes.

"Oh, man," said Simon, relaxing when he saw there was no emergency. "I didn't know you were asleep, sorry."

"It's all right," said Van, thankful to have been rescued from the dream he was having. "Did you need something?"

"I just came to see how you were holding up."

Van bristled. Did Simon know?

"Our last conversation was pretty heavy," Simon explained. "Maybe I should have broken some of that to you a little easier."

"Oh." Van released the breath he was holding. "No. I asked you to be straightforward with me, and you were. I just need time to… consider it all."

"Fair enough," said Simon. "I'll let you go back to sleep. You look like you could use it."

"No!" blurted Van, louder than necessary.

Simon froze halfway out of the tent and glanced back, looking concerned again.

"No," Van repeated, calmly this time. "I've slept enough. Is Shale with you?"

"Haven't seen her," said Simon. "You know how she is."

"Is it still raining?"

Simon poked his head outside. "Just a drizzle."

"Then we should go for a walk," said Van. "It would be a shame to waste your spell."

Simon opened his mouth as if to object, but Van was already pulling his boots on. They stepped outside together, and Simon tucked his new hat over his head, squinting apprehensively at the darkened sky. They walked west, and when they passed Lilim's tent, Van had a thought.

"Do you mind if we bring Lilim?"

"Uh." Simon scratched the back of his neck.

"It seems she has become friends with Shale, and I..."

He floundered, suddenly resentful of his own hesitation. He was tired of not saying what he meant, especially when it was something sensible and completely innocent. He had always felt free to express himself with Simon, even more so sometimes than with other Dolsers. And during their last conversation—regardless of how turbulent it might have been—he had admitted they were more than mere acquaintances. Simon had called them friends. Why should it embarrass him to want his friends to be on good terms with one another?

"I would like it if you were her friend, too," Van finished.

Simon blinked. "Yeah, sure. Let's get her."

Van called her name, then peeked inside her tent when she didn't respond. It was empty. At this time of day, Van was usually hunting, so he supposed Lilim would be with Ghan Mudcatcher. He walked toward the center of camp in search of her, Simon quietly trailing behind.

When he spotted the younger aspirants gathered around the elder, Van remembered the strip of cloth in his pocket. Confusion and alarm crept into Simon's expression as he watched him tie it around his head.

"Tell you in a moment," whispered Van.

He called to Lilim, and she looked up. Van noticed too late that she'd been talking with a pair of girls her age, none of them paying as much attention to the elder as would be expected at the Teaching Circle.

"This is Van the Scribe!" Lilim gushed to the girls when he strolled up with Simon. "Van the Scribe, this is Tali the Tall and Milna Swiftswimmer."

"Well met, kinsmen," Van said with a bow. "Lilim the Brave, Simon and I were about to go for a walk, and we thought you might..."

He trailed off, only then realizing he may have intruded on something important. Lilim was learning how to make friends on her own.

"I will go for a walk!" she said, standing up too fast.

She tripped, and Van caught her. Rather than cling to him, she yelped and yanked herself away, blushing as Tali and Milna exchanged scandalous glances.

Ghan Mudcatcher, meanwhile, paused his lecture to approach them.

"If you are going far from camp, I trust you'll look after her," the elder said.

Van started to respond, but then realized Ghan was talking to Simon. Van couldn't understand him when he replied to Ghan, but the elder touched him lightly on the elbow when he finished and thanked him. With that, the three of them set out from camp.

Lilim found Van's hand only once they were out of sight, instantly at ease and seeming like herself again. A moment later, she held her free hand out to Simon, who was walking on her other side. Simon shot a glance at Van, who met his eyes, saying nothing. Awkwardly, and with an amount of poorly veiled discomfiture, Simon took Lilim's hand.

"So, what's with the mask?" asked Simon. "I thought I told you not to get sick."

"I'm fine," said Van, pulling the face covering down so it hung about his neck. "I'm just telling people I'm sick so they'll leave me alone."

"What happened?" asked Simon.

"Nothing significant." Van kept his eyes on the path ahead.

"You can talk to me, you know."

Van was silent for a moment. "I know."

Lilim became chatty after a while, but blessedly, she directed her questions at Simon, asking where he came from, how he'd learned magic, and why he always looked like he was in a hurry to be someplace else. As always, Van could only understand Lilim's side of the conversation while Simon aimed his spell at her.

"Why do you like sexmaking so much?" she asked eventually.

Simon shot Van a hazardous look. "What do I tell her?"

"Tell her the truth," said Van.

"I don't think I know the truth," Simon murmured.

Van just shrugged. "Then, use your best judgment."

Simon sighed, rubbed his eyes, and spoke to her. Lilim interrupted him a few times with a "Why?" or occasionally, the more worrisome "How?" Simon weighed his response each time, sometimes shaking his head and starting over. He sounded more exhausted with each new question, and perhaps even a little sad. When they were finished, Lilim looked at Van like he was wounded in some invisible way.

"What did you say to her, Simon?"

Simon groaned. "Can we not?"

Van turned to Lilim. "What did Simon tell you?"

"It's private," she said, snapping her gaze away.

Some minutes later, they passed a stand of trees, and Lilim started to squirm.

Van squeezed her hand. "Should we head back?"

"It's not that," she said. "I just… I need to make water."

"Ah." Van looked at the trees.

"You're on your own with that one, kid," said Simon, releasing her hand.

Van took Lilim to the nearest tree and waited on the other side while she conducted her business. He stared at the clouds overhead, pregnant with rain, and made a game of trying to predict when the next storm would come to keep his mind from wandering.

Lilim's scream snapped him back to his senses. He jumped around the tree with his knife drawn, terrified that a mourn had snuck up on her.

It wasn't a mourn. The creature—whatever it was—was headless, five feet tall, and stood on two legs. One of its long arms ended in a hand with seven fingers, thin and dexterous. The other, held high, was something like a crab claw, but in place of pincers were lethally sharpened blades, scythe-like, some of them clicking as they twitched forward or back.

Van couldn't move. He watched in frozen, helpless terror as Lilim cowered against the tree, the metal monster looming over her.

"*Ordo septum tribus!*" Simon shouted, leaping around the tree a second later.

The creature went rigid, and after a moment, it fell sideways, hitting the ground with a groan like a barn door coming off its hinges. Van realized he had fallen, too, though he couldn't remember when. His eyes darted from the creature, to Simon, to Lilim as he struggled to control his breathing. A tingling sensation rippled through the tips of his fingers and his toes.

"Is she hurt?" Simon demanded.

Van couldn't answer.

Cursing, Simon went to Lilim, kneeling to check her for injuries.

"She's okay," said Simon, turning to Van. "What about you?"

"What was that?" Van managed.

"Antipersonnel construct, designation Q-three-eleven," said Simon, lifting Lilim in his arms. "In the Military Quarter, we call them quells."

Van stared at the inert creature. "Is it dead?"

"Wasn't alive in the first place," said Simon. "But yeah, I decommissioned it. Get up. We need to get back to camp."

Van's legs had gone numb. It took two tries before he could stand, and when he did, he couldn't stop shaking.

Simon dropped Lilim, but some unseen force caught her, and she floated after him in the air. Van walked beside her—slowly at first, while feeling returned to his extremities. Lilim cradled herself quietly the whole way back to camp, neither crying nor responding to Van's touch. Her eyes were wide and unfocused. But she was alive, and she was unharmed.

Dusk was falling by the time they made it back, and as the Dolser campsite came into view, Van saw cookfires lit, with aspirants meandering between them at an unhurried pace. It was only then that Simon relaxed, and only a little.

"Maybe it was alone, reconnaissance pattern," he mumbled. "Might make sense if its handler was trying to cover ground quickly."

"What does that mean?" pressed Van.

"It means I was wrong," said Simon, a shadow on his face. "It's not a quarantine. It's an invasion."

19 The Boy Who Cried Q311

When they reached Van's tent, Simon sent Lilim floating inside with a flick of his wrist. His spell had since given out, so he simply pointed at Van, then at the tent.

Stay with her. Don't go anywhere.

Simon's expression was grave, but he seemed in control. That at least was a small comfort. Van crawled through the opening and moved Lilim onto his bedroll, covering her to keep her warm. She had closed her eyes at some point, and now seemed to be asleep.

Van wanted desperately to go straight to Ghan and Otep to raise the alarm, but it was clear Simon understood the nature of the threat better than he did, and he trusted Simon's judgment. He stayed with Lilim until morning, listening fretfully to the nocturnal sounds of the tundra outside for hours. As his exhaustion caught up to him and he started to drift off, his last coherent thought was that he wished Shale was there to keep watch again.

When Van awoke, the sun was up, and he no longer sensed Lilim beside him. He sat bolt upright, panicking, but then breathed a sigh of relief when he saw her huddled by the tent's entryway, her knees hugged to her chest.

"Good morning," she said.

Her voice was steady, and she seemed lucid. No visible signs of shock or trauma.

"Good morning, Lilim," said Van.

She drew her knees tighter. "What happened?"

He hesitated. "We were attacked. Simon of the Mists protected us."

"Was it a mourn?"

He stared back at her, trying to keep his worry from showing. "A mourn, yes."

Lilim smiled. "It's good to have friends you can count on."

Since they'd both overslept, they skipped their morning lesson. Van told Lilim to pack her things, and he did likewise, not wanting to be delayed by the chore later. With that out of the way, they went straight to assembly with their rucksacks, but Van paid no attention whatsoever to Otep's announcements. His only concern was getting the First Ranger alone and telling him what he'd seen.

When assembly concluded and the aspirants dispersed to break down their tents, Van told Lilim to find Simon and Shale, and to stay near them. Confusion clouded her expression, but she promised him she would. Better for her to be confused than terrified. Once she left, he took a breath, willing himself to stay calm.

"Otep Acrearms," Van whispered urgently when he was confident they wouldn't be overheard.

"What is it, Van the Scribe?" Otep furrowed his brow, recognizing his distress. "Is something wrong?"

"To be honest, I don't know." Van raked a hand through his hair. "I was attacked by a strange creature near camp yesterday, and I fear more of them may be lurking."

"Strange creature?" Otep stepped closer.

"Like nothing I've ever seen," said Van. "It would be easier to show you. I can take you to where I saw it."

Otep's gaze sharpened. "Did you slay the creature, or were you made to flee from it?"

"I..." Van floundered, still unsure precisely what had happened. "It would be easier to simply show you. Please."

Otep glanced around. The procession would be underway within minutes.

"Where did you see this creature?"

"West of here," said Van. "Almost directly in our path. If there are more, we could all be walking into terrible danger."

"Take me there." Otep shouldered his rucksack. "We must try to be swift."

Van sprinted most of the way to keep up with Otep Acrearms, whose stride was twice as long. The First Ranger could have gotten there quicker alone, but they still reached the trees ahead of the procession. Van hoped that was enough.

Van dropped his pack and readied his bow, nocking an arrow as he approached the spot. Otep Acrearms followed his lead, his sling in hand.

In one fluid motion, Van stepped around the tree, ready to place a shot—but the space was empty. His eyes fell on the damp, bent grass where the *thing* had fallen, and his shoulders slumped. It was gone.

Otep Acrearms hooked around the tree at the same time, ready for action, but he relaxed when he saw there was none to be had.

"It was here," Van stammered, lowering his bow. "It was right here."

Otep surveyed their surroundings, studying each nearby tree, and then the ground. Thanks to the rain, Van's tracks from the day before were still plainly visible in the mud.

"Who were you with when you saw this creature?" asked Otep, studying the tracks.

"Simon of the Mists and Lilim," Van said vacantly.

Otep narrowed his eyes and put his sling away. "Simon of the Mists..."

"He saved Lilim's life," said Van. "Mine too. Simon was first to act when the thing attacked. He slew it with some spell, I think."

Otep's snorted. "Some spell, you say."

"Otep Acrearms, you must believe me," Van pleaded, disheartened by the First Ranger's brazen skepticism.

"I believe you saw something," said Otep. "You wouldn't lie to me. But I suspect you saw only what Simon of the Mists wanted you to see."

Van gaped at him. "What?"

"An illusion," said Otep. "He wished to amuse himself at your expense, or otherwise instill in you a belief that he is more capable than he really is."

"He would never!" shouted Van. "If you trust my word, then you must be prepared to trust his. He is a friend, and an aspirant of Dolse!"

Otep turned away. "We must return. The procession is soon to catch up to us."

Van wilted. "Otep..."

But the First Ranger was already walking back toward the tundra.

"Come," said Otep. "We will remain vigilant. If there is danger lurking, we will face it as rangers."

Clenching his fists, Van looked one last time at the place the so-called quell had collapsed just hours ago. He could do nothing more after that but collect his rucksack and rejoin the procession with Otep.

Simon and Shale were quick to find him that morning, and as instructed, Lilim was with them, her hand in Shale's. Still reluctant to frighten her, he told her to go find Ghan Mudcatcher.

"But you said to stay with Shale and Simon!" she protested.

"I'm sorry, Lilim," he said. "I need to talk to Simon, and you'd likely find it very boring. I'll look for you this evening, and we can share supper."

She scrunched her face in annoyance, but once again, she did as she was told, adjusting the straps on her pack and quickening her pace in search of the elder.

"Spell's already active," said Simon once she had left. "I wanted to let Shale know what happened, and I figured you'd be back soon enough. But now she's pissed off at me."

"Why?" asked Van, meeting Shale's eyes and reading her expression as the three of them walked.

"She thinks it's your fault that thing was in the woods," he realized, thinking aloud.

"In a nutshell, yes." Simon bobbed his head.

"Tell her it isn't true," said Van. "Or rather, tell her I don't believe you had anything to do with it." He studied Simon for a moment. "You didn't, did you?"

"Of course not," said Simon.

Turning to Shale, he spoke briefly to her, but she only rolled her eyes before looking away. Simon sighed, switching the focus of his spell back to Van.

"How close are we to the nearest major city?"

"Three weeks at least to Seat Vaxas," said Van, recalling the past few days' announcements.

"We don't have that kind of time," said Simon, his expression grave. "Talk to Ghan. Get him to turn the procession around and take us back to Seat Ikann."

"That isn't possible, Simon," said Van. "Ghan Mudcatcher doesn't speak for all the tribes. Even if I asked the Patron tribe, they would never reverse the procession."

"Then the three of us will go," said Simon, more desperate now. "We'll just turn around right now—you, me, and Shale."

"The pilgrimage requires us to move forward, not back," explained Van. "The Journey of Patronage comes before all else."

Simon stepped in front of him, halting him in his tracks. Shale bristled and stopped as well.

"Listen to me, Van, and don't interrupt until I'm done," he said.

Van nodded, taken aback by the fiery resolve in Simon's eyes.

"The pilgrimage is canceled," Simon said flatly. "Your whole life and the lives of everyone in Nemia are *canceled*. The only thing that matters right now is convincing the rulers of your country to sound the alarm and prepare for what's coming. Nobody here listens to me, so I'm going to need your help with that."

Van's blood ran cold. "What's coming, exactly?"

"War," said Simon. "One you can't win. Which is why you need to get me in a room with your leaders, stat."

Van swallowed hard. "So, when you say we need to prepare—"

"To surrender," he said, finishing Van's thought. "Unconditionally. If the tribes resist, people will die. *Your* people. Your dad's people."

"Our rangers will protect us," said Van weakly, remembering the quell and wondering if he believed his own words. "They've protected us for centuries."

"How many rangers does your tribe have who can fight as well as Sol?" asked Simon.

"Sol Starfletcher?" Van drew his eyebrows together. "I don't, um. I'm not sure any ranger of Dolse is as accomplished as the First Ranger of Mercura. Why him?"

Simon looked around, realizing that the next group of aspirants was about to overtake them. They started walking again.

"The game at Seat Ikann was the first time I saw the First Rangers in action," said Simon. "They're supposed to be the best, right?"

"Indeed," said Van. "But the ones who came before them still serve their tribes. The First Rangers of the last pilgrimage, nine years ago. Possibly even the predecessors of those four."

"So, that's what, twelve Nemians still alive and fit to fight at the same level as Sol?"

Van opened his mouth, but nothing came out. In truth, he wasn't sure any of them rivaled the abilities of the Starfletcher.

"I suppose," said Van. "But Simon, why Sol Starfletcher?"

"He's the only one of you who looked like he could go toe to toe with quells and walk away alive," said Simon. "And when Gnosos mobilizes, they won't send just a dozen. They'll send thousands."

Van walked on in stunned silence. Simon grew quiet as well, giving him time to think, though it was clear that he had more to say. Ever conscious that their time was limited, Van willed himself to find his voice.

"What does Shale think?" he asked. "Will you translate for just a moment? Does she agree that my people have no hope of defending ourselves against these things from your homeland?"

Simon spoke to Shale, and she responded without giving it much thought.

"As the elf has already mentioned, there is scarcely any contact between the Twilight World and the civilizations of surface-dwelling terrestrials," she said. "But we know something of Gnosos. If my mother and all her vassals pitted themselves against the elf's masters, it would be a long and bloody conflict. I'm not sure which side would ultimately emerge victorious. Your people are laughably primitive compared to the might of Eventide, so yes, on that point I agree with him. If this truly is a preamble to war, Gnosos would casually slaughter any of you that stood against them."

"Then what do you think we should do?" said Van, growing desperate.

"*Hmm.*" Shale stared at the ground, pursing her lips. "I think... that there must be a way out the elf hasn't considered yet."

Van blinked, uncomprehending.

"The Twilight Prophet wouldn't send me here simply to die," she went on. "That would have been a foolish investment on Her part, and She does not make foolish investments. But until a better path reveals itself, I must once again side with the elf. If you wish to save the lives of your people, you should convince them to lay down arms."

Van took a shaky breath, thinking.

"We shouldn't go back to Seat Ikann," he said.

"Why?" Simon turned to him. "I get that some unpleasant stuff happened there, but they're still—"

"I believe they may be complicit in some terrible conspiracy," said Van. "Galdur Goldeyes and Brynda Blackblade both. Perhaps a scheme orchestrated by chieftain Rhaggo to steal Patronage from tribe Mercura."

Simon blinked, staring at him for a moment. He translated the statement to Shale, who joined him in watching Van expectantly. Over the next few minutes, Van made his best attempt to put his fears into words.

It wasn't easy. Van himself still wasn't sure what he believed. All he had were fractured shards of information—overheard conversations, glimpses of private moments, and facts that, on their own, weren't damning in any way. The unlikely friendship—or whatever it was—that existed between the First Rangers of Vaxas and Ikann. The Nighthawk he'd found in Brynda's tent, which to this day no one had claimed credit for bringing down. Galdur's seemingly impossible resurrection.

The last thing Van told them about was the First Rangers' tryst of two evenings ago, and the bizarre things he'd overheard Galdur say that appeared to instigate it. Whatever unrelated personal grief that moment had caused him, he knew it stood also as further evidence the two were working together toward some nefarious end.

When he finished, Van fell silent and waited for one of them to speak, hoping they would offer a perspective that tied it all together.

"The look on your face tells me you're only just now considering Brynda might be bad news," said Simon at length. "I've more or less suspected they were up to no good since you told me about the Nighthawk."

Van rubbed his eyes. "And Shale? Does she agree with you in this as well?"

Simon spoke to Shale.

She sighed. "Stop giving the elf so much credit just for acknowledging the painfully obvious."

Van could only nod.

"One other recent development I should probably tell you about," said Simon, "goes back to our conversation about scrying magic and old sorcerer paranoia."

Van watched him, waiting.

Simon stared straight ahead. "After you took me to church, I decided to renew all my wards," he uttered. "In light of recent events, I'm kicking myself for not having done it sooner."

"Renew your wards?"

"Persistent enchantments," said Simon, "like that spell I told you about, the one that lets me see invisible stuff. Now, I'm running several others that should keep us generally safer going forward. The main thing to know is that we can no longer be targeted with scrying magic. In activating that particular ward, I learned something a little unsettling."

Van cocked his head.

"Someone's been scrying on us since the start of the pilgrimage."

"What!" Van nearly tripped over his feet.

"Yeah," said Simon. "So we should assume any conversations we had between Seat Dolse and Sky's Whatever were overheard."

Van was wide-eyed. "Why did you allow such a spell to lapse to begin with!"

Simon translated the last exchange for Shale, who replied tersely. He turned back to Van.

"Shale's with you on that one," he said with a sigh. "I guess I figured leaving the wards down was the only way Gnosos might still find me. If someone back home tried to scry me and found out I was still alive, maybe they'd contact me somehow and arrange to come collect me."

"You told me you'd given up on the idea of going home," said Van.

"What I said was I spent a long time trying to make up my mind about it," said Simon. "But now, I'm convinced I'll have to find a way back to Megalomemoria, and soon. I have to figure out who's calling the shots in the Military Quarter and tell them they're making a mistake. First, though, I have to talk to *your* leaders and convince them not to resist, and that they'll only make things worse if they try."

"If what you said about your wards and the scrying is true, then Gnosos must already know you're alive," said Van. "Will that make things easier?"

"Oh, they definitely know I'm alive," said Simon. "But I don't think they were the ones scrying on us."

Van stared back in confusion.

"If they went to the trouble of scrying me up—saw where I was and what I've been doing since I disappeared—it wouldn't have been much harder to actually communicate with me. They haven't. So it stands to reason that somebody else was watching us."

"Who?" asked Van.

"Galdur and Brynda." Simon shrugged. "Or whoever they work for."

Van turned his eyes to Shale, wanting to ask for her thoughts, but Simon interrupted him.

"Gnosos knows I'm alive because I decommissioned that quell last night."

Van snapped his gaze back to him. "How would they know, if they weren't using scrying magic?"

"Because I used my emergency shutdown command. Military Quarter clearance, encoded to my voice. It won't work again—they will have invalidated my codes by now. Honestly, we got lucky back there. Whoever's job it was to void my codes when I went missing probably just didn't bother, assumed I was dead."

"I thought you slew it with some spell," said Van, not liking the sound of *it won't work again.*

"Nope," said Simon. "Constructs can't be directly harmed by most magic."

When he turned to catch Shale up on the conversation, Van used the break in the conversation to consider Simon's statements. To say he felt overwhelmed was an understatement. It was like he was drowning.

"Magic or no magic, if we are attacked, we will defend ourselves," said Simon.

Van realized his attention had slipped. "Was that you speaking, or Shale?"

"Shale," said Simon, "but I'll second that. If push comes to shove, we'll figure something out."

Van swallowed, trying to imagine facing off against one of those creatures in physical combat. "When that thing attacked Lilim, I…"

Simon and Shale both watched him with mild concern.

"I froze," muttered Van, ashamed. "I failed to act when it mattered most. If you hadn't been there, Simon, I don't think…"

He closed his eyes, feeling the sudden sting of tears. "I would never have been able to forgive myself."

"It's not your fault," said Simon. "Antipersonnel constructs emit something like a pheromone that excites the brain's panic response. Slows you down, confuses you. It's always worse in children and the elderly."

"I see," Van mumbled, remembering how Lilim had to be carried back to camp.

Simon spoke with Shale again, and a minute later, Van remembered something else.

"I took Otep Acrearms to where we saw it," said Van. "I hoped I might alert the others to the danger, but it was gone, as if it was never there. Are you certain you killed it? Could it still be out there somewhere?"

"You know, you should really stop talking about quells like they're living things," said Simon. "As to why you couldn't find it again, they're self-disassembling. When they become irreparably damaged or stop functioning for any reason, their constituent atoms separate and rapidly decay. Prevents our technology from falling into enemy hands."

"I see," Van said again dumbly.

"And?" said Simon. "You told Otep about the quell, and what did he say?"

"Um." Van averted his eyes.

"On second thought, don't tell me," said Simon. "He didn't believe you. Or if you told him you were with me, he probably thinks I'm responsible."

Van remained mute.

"Okay. If Seat Ikann is out, I'd prefer we head straight for Seat Mercura," said Simon. "Those are the good guys, right? And aren't they basically in charge?"

"Yes. Seat Mercura should be due west of us," said Van, "but it's even farther than Seat Vaxas, and the desert lies between here and there. We'll be going around it, through the Great Swamp to the north."

"How bad is the desert?" Simon rubbed his chin.

"Very," said Van.

Simon clicked his tongue. "Any faster route around it to the south?"

"None," said Van. "The desert extends south until it meets the sea."

"Well, going south may not be smart anyway," said Simon. "If Gnosos is already on the continent, that's where they would have landed."

Van searched his eyes, his stomach clenching. "Simon, do you think my father...?"

"That's what I'm worried about," said Simon. "And why we need to get to Seat Mercura as fast as possible."

"I'll speak to Ghan Mudcatcher," said Van. "And perhaps Riverspeaker Gheela. She may have a way of getting word to the Patron tribe even if we can't get there ourselves as quickly as we'd like."

"Do that," said Simon. "Language spell's about to fail, but we'll be close if you need us. In the meantime, I'll work on a backup plan with Shale."

"Without your spell?" Van stared back at him.

"Shale's pretty smart," said Simon with a smirk. "We don't need the spell to have a useful conversation. Assuming she gets over being mad at me, anyway."

Van chose not to comment on the implication that he wasn't as smart or as useful as Shale, because he couldn't honestly say he disagreed. He watched her, wondering if she had any parting considerations to add.

She met his eyes, but said nothing. As was sometimes the case with Shale, her expression was hard to read. Anger? Disappointment? No... this might simply be pity. Van bowed to her and Simon, then left in the direction Lilim had gone.

Cornering the elder and speaking with him alone proved more difficult than with Otep. Ghan Mudcatcher was surrounded by children, leading them in song as the procession plodded along. Van's prospects did not improve when the procession made camp hours later. The elder was teaching survival skills today, with close to thirty younger aspirants—including Lilim—gathered around him to observe.

Van had no choice but to sit among them and wait, watching as the elder dug a shallow pit. He assumed Ghan was demonstrating how to build traps, but when the elder stood up and stepped back, Van saw his guess was wrong.

"Nature will do most of your work for you." Ghan spoke as he would at the Teaching Circle. "But remember to leave a high point at the center when you dig, and to place your meal bowls exactly there. If you make the mistake of digging at a uniform depth, you'll learn the hard way how I earned the name Mudcatcher."

Ghan Mudcatcher was building a solar still. Given the season, with potable water literally falling from the sky, Van could scarcely think of a more useless skill to teach.

"Cover it, when you are finished, with a square of canvas," Ghan continued. "The material we use for our tents is treated with animal fat, so moisture wicks from it. Weigh it down around the edges with rocks or loose earth to form a seal, and add some weight in the middle as well—but only a bit!" He glanced from one aspirant to the next. "I warn you again. The first time I tried trapping water this way, I was with my father in the tundra during the driest month of the year. When we uncovered my still on the morning of our second day, my father looked inside and said to me, 'Ghan, you've caught no water. All I see is mud!'"

Some of the children giggled, and Ghan Mudcatcher grinned with satisfaction.

His lesson concluded, the small crowd finally began to disperse. Lilim noticed Van as she was brushing the grass off her legs, but for the third time that day, he sent her away. She was fuming this time, instructed once more to find Simon or Shale and stay close to them. Van knew he would owe her an apology later.

"What troubles you, Van the Scribe?" asked Ghan Mudcatcher when they were alone. "To see you in camp at this hour is unusual."

Van grimaced. He would owe Otep an apology, too. Pushing the thought aside, he told Ghan what he'd seen yesterday and everything Simon had said about it since, but he made a snap decision not to bring up Galdur and Brynda. Asking Ghan Mudcatcher to confront a terrible truth was one thing. To confront two simultaneously might be a bridge too far.

"Simon believes it is imperative we get a message to Seat Mercura and enlist the Patron tribe's help in spreading the word. Lives might be lost if we don't convince the chieftains to meet the people from Gnosos peaceably when they arrive."

Van shook his head, realizing he'd skipped some important details. "Sorry—Gnosos is Simon's homeland, a country which—"

"Simon of the Mists has told me of Gnosos," Ghan interrupted.

Van's mouth hung open. "When?"

"Months ago," said the elder. "Before we set out from Seat Dolse."

"Oh," said Van. He had never considered that any of his people might know Simon better than he did.

"If what you say is true, we would indeed do well to alert the Patron tribe," said Ghan Mudcatcher. "It will be for their chieftain, Scaela the Listener, to decide a course of action from there."

"Is there any way to contact them immediately?" asked Van. "By the time the procession reaches Seat Mercura, it may already be too late for… some of us."

He didn't need to spell out for the elder which of the tribes would be first in the invaders' path.

"If there is a way," said Ghan Mudcatcher in a measured tone, "Riverspeaker Gheela will know it."

"Can we go to her?" Van said eagerly. "Now?"

"That may not be wise," said Ghan.

Van blinked in confusion.

"If we beseech tribe Mercura's Pilgrimage Guide now, we will be obligated to report the full truth," he continued. "As it stands, the full truth is that only you have seen one of these creatures. You were in the company of Simon of the Mists when you witnessed it, and all that you know of this so-called 'quell' is what he has told you."

Van shook his head in despair. "You don't trust him either."

"I trust him," said Ghan Mudcatcher. "But others may not. You know this from experience."

"Otep Acrearms has spoken to you already," Van realized.

"Just as he should have," said Ghan Mudcatcher. "Fear not, Van the Scribe. I will render you my assistance. But we would be wise not to act until the existence of these creatures is a fact accepted by those that are not beholden to a foreigner's view of the world."

Van hesitated. He saw Ghan's point. If the chieftain of Mercura were to react as Otep had, all of Nemia would be in terrible danger. The Patron tribe needed to be shown proof that the threat was real and not the fabrication of an outsider. But to delay conferred a danger all its own.

"What, then, are we to do until that happens?" said Van. "We cannot simply wait for another attack, or hold off until we receive news that there have been attacks elsewhere."

"Are you on good terms with Sol Starfletcher?" Ghan Mudcatcher gave him a considered look. "I know you have shared the hunt with him."

"We've spoken once or twice." It was the second time in the last hour that his conversation had unexpectedly turned to the subject of Sol Starfletcher.

"Hunt with him again, if he'll have you," instructed Ghan, "as often as possible. His talents allow him to survey the land more efficiently than any band of rangers. If those things are out there, he will be the first to spot them. Ensure you are at his side when he does, and tell him what you've told me."

Van nodded slowly. Simon would consider this a setback, but the elder was right.

"Thank you, Ghan Mudcatcher," said Van. "I will do as you say."

Van turned to leave, but he glanced back before he'd made it even a pace. Something was still bothering him.

"Please forgive me, but why are the children learning how to build solar stills?"

The elder, too, had to stop and look back. "If there is anything to forgive, it would be your failure to pay attention at assembly."

Van cocked his head.

Ghan sighed. "Otep Acrearms reminded us just this morning that we will be in the desert soon."

"The desert," echoed Van. "Would we not reach Seat Vaxas quicker by going around it?"

"We would."

Van stared. "Then, why would we do something so senselessly dangerous?"

"Because as much as we've learned to fear the desert, we are also *responsible* for it," said Ghan. "Poor farming practices in the surrounding territories can cause the desert to shrink or grow, and both can be harmful to neighboring ecosystems. We walk the desert on the pilgrimage, therefore, to see how she has fared over the past nine years. And we will build stills when we camp because rain clouds rarely form there, due to the unknowable mysteries of the region's weather patterns. Or, according to some, because..."

The elder trailed off and peered at the overcast sky.

"Find Sol Starfletcher, Van the Scribe," he said finally, turning once more to leave. "Be at his side when it matters."

Van stared after Ghan Mudcatcher, feeling pointedly stupid. He tried to focus on the task at hand, even as a new source of anxiety weighed on him. He didn't need to be told what awaited them in the desert. He'd grown up with the stories, and he remembered exactly how the elder's lecture on desert weather patterns ended.

Or, according to some, because the desert is cursed.

20 Catching Water

Van missed his chance to intercept Sol Starfletcher before the rangers of Mercura left camp to hunt. He'd have to settle for his backup plan—finding the First Ranger's tent and waiting there for his return. Simon had already used his understanding spell for the day, so he wouldn't be able to report his progress yet anyway.

Cutting through the campsite of tribe Vaxas would get him there quicker, and he marked his chances low of seeing anyone he'd prefer not to. Most able-bodied Vaxals would be out hunting or foraging.

But apparently, he'd miscounted his odds.

"Van the Scribe," called Brynda.

His head whipped around so fast, he nearly tripped. She was with Rhys and Rhyla, the older sister supporting her again as she hobbled toward him. Her leg had looked almost healed the last time he saw her, but today, it was as heavily dressed as when they'd left Seat Ikann.

"It seems I overexerted myself and managed to reopen the wound," she said casually, noticing the direction of his gaze. "You can imagine the scolding I received."

"First Ranger," Van stammered in greeting. The thought of meeting her eyes turned his stomach, so he stared at his feet instead.

"I'm glad to see you're feeling better."

"I'm sorry?" Van choked.

Despite himself, he glanced up in time to see her touch a finger to her lips and cock an eyebrow. He remembered then that had forgotten his face covering—and with it, all pretense of being sick.

"Oh!" he said. "I'm so sorry, I—"

Brynda giggled. "You don't have to apologize. I hope you didn't think I would be mad just because you took an evening to yourself. You are free to resume our tutoring sessions whenever it conveniences you."

"Yes," he said, bowing to save himself from her eyes. "Thank you, First Ranger."

Rhyla glanced at the sky and held out her hand, palm up. "It threatens to rain again, First Ranger. Elder Memnon advises your leg should be kept dry."

Brynda ignored her. "Rhyla the Tamer fancies herself my keeper. Does that seem fitting, or should I give her a scolding of her own?"

Rhyla's eyes widened, and her face flushed bright red. Rhys snorted and cupped a hand to her mouth, stifling an outburst of laughter.

Van straightened, but he could only stare past Brynda's shoulder. "As you see fit, First Ranger."

From the corner of his eye, he saw her familiar smile falter —just for a second.

"Did you hear that, Rhyla?" the First Ranger crooned, instantly recomposed. "You might be in trouble."

With a polite laugh, Brynda bid Van farewell, and he bowed as the three turned to leave. Rhys the Catcher glanced back over her shoulder, grinning at Van conspiratorially. Then, he was alone. He tried his best to shirk the unclean feeling the encounter had left him with, and continued on his way to the Mercuran campsite.

Once there, a helpful aspirant gave him directions to the First Ranger's tent, a small and modest structure compared to Brynda's. He sat nearby, forcing himself to smile at the friendly Mercurans who greeted him as they passed, but he soon grew restless.

He stood and started pacing, wondering if he should give up for the day. Walking a slow lap around the tent to ease his nerves, he spotted something curious. A hempen sack stuffed with straw and tied with rope, about the size and shape of a wild boar. It was mounted to a simple wooden frame behind Sol Starfletcher's tent. A practice dummy for archery, Van realized, seeing puncture marks.

Van had been carrying his bow and quiver all day, so he walked ten steps from the makeshift target and took aim. Practicing a learned skill was more calming than pacing listlessly, and after whiling away the next twenty minutes taking shots at the dummy, the tightness in his chest loosened.

"Well placed," said a voice from behind. Van had just sunk what could have been his hundredth arrow in the target, dead center.

Van jumped and spun around, then hurriedly bowed to Sol Starfletcher.

"First Ranger!" he said. "I hope I haven't overstepped."

"You've not overstepped, Van the Scribe," said Sol, retrieving Van's arrow and handing it back to him. "At least not yet, I should say. You look like you have something on your mind."

Van nodded, drawing a deep breath as he prepared to repeat everything he'd told Ghan Mudcatcher, including the counsel he'd received in response. To start with, he recounted what he had seen yesterday, describing the "quell" in as much detail as he remembered, including the hand made of scythe blades.

"...while its other hand looked more like a person's, but with too many fingers."

"Seven, if memory serves," Sol Starfletcher supplied.

"Seven, yes, thank you. I—" Van blinked and fell silent. "You've already seen them."

Sol wore a tired smile. "I first noticed them a few days back on the road from Seat Ikann. I wondered when our hunting parties might catch a glimpse of one. They're adept at hiding, and they have been careful to keep their distance. Until now, I suppose, if what you've told me is true."

The First Ranger's tone held little alarm, and that in itself made Van nervous.

"According to Simon of the Mists, they aren't living creatures at all, but tools of war sent by the people that rule his homeland." Van clenched his fists. "They fear us because... of some misunderstanding concerning our worship of the Emissaries, and he believes we must lay down arms and seek peaceful discourse to show them we aren't evil."

"According to Simon of the Mists..." mused Sol Starfletcher.

Van ground his teeth. It was just like with Otep. He couldn't afford to let Sol make the same mistake and dismiss the threat as just some outsider's flight of fancy. In his desperation to make the First Ranger understand, Van did the only thing he could think to—he provided context. He described, from the very beginning, the unlikely history of his friendship with the man tribe Dolse called Simon of the Mists.

"I trust Simon with my life, First Ranger," Van pleaded. "Ghan Mudcatcher trusts him as well. It's precisely why he sent me here—he believes you are our best hope of proving to everyone that this danger is real."

"Your Pilgrimage Guide is wise," said Sol Starfletcher, touching his thumb to his chin. "But even as a First Ranger, I fear my testimony will be worth little more than your own if we are to convince the chieftains of Nemia to treat with foreigners as your friend prescribes. Unless…"

Van swallowed. "Unless?"

"I'm of a mind to bring one of these creatures down," said Sol. "To slay one and present its body to the delegates we travel with may go a long way in lending credibility to your friend's claims."

"Oh," said Van, his shoulders slumping. "We can't. They, um, take themselves apart, I guess, when you kill them."

"That is most inconvenient," said Sol Starfletcher.

Neither of them spoke for a full minute. The diffuse light of day faded as the sun sagged in the sky, hidden behind the dark clouds that loomed above.

"Hunting them was a dim prospect to start with, I suppose," said Sol. "They have proved difficult to track. The things are as swift as they are silent, and more clever than most beasts."

He held out his palm, gazing up at the clouds expectantly.

"It is a bit like trying to catch a drop of rain by closing your fist around it."

Van thought of Ghan Mudcatcher, building his solar still for the children.

"We set a trap, then. We lure one out of hiding, and we capture it."

Sol Starfletcher raised an eyebrow. "You've an idea in mind?"

"None whatsoever," said Van. "But I know who will."

The next few days were some of the most challenging Van had faced since leaving home. But in many ways, they were also the most rewarding.

The day after enlisting Sol Starfletcher's help, Van brought him to the Dolser campsite, where he met Simon of the Mists. Through their conversation, a plan began to take shape. Van felt a swell of pride that he'd made the historic partnership possible—even though, for the most part, he was left out of the discussion.

Simon couldn't afford to repeat everything he said two extra times, so while he deliberated with Sol, Van sat quietly next to Shale. He could keep up somewhat based on Sol's responses, but it was frustrating trying to work out the particulars when he couldn't understand the other half of the conversation.

For Shale, who could understand neither party, he imagined it was worse. In silent annoyance, she cleaned the dirt from under her fingernails with the tip of her dagger, growling occasionally and otherwise ignoring Van's attempts to placate her with a sympathetic smile.

"Setting aside the matter of Galdur Goldeyes and Brynda Blackblade, I agree that the desert may give us our first real chance to attempt what you've proposed," Sol said in reply to a lengthy statement by Simon.

Van leaned forward and cleared his throat. "Forgive me, First Ranger, but it may not be wise to involve Galdur or Brynda in any way."

Simon and Sol both looked at him.

"They, um," started Van. "I believe they are conspiring to steal Patronage from tribe Mercura."

Sol smiled gently. It was the sort of smile saved for infants, when they became excited at having learned something most people took for granted as facts of everyday life.

"You already knew," Van heard himself say.

"I apologize if I gave you the impression I wasn't very perceptive," said Sol.

"No, I..." Van mumbled. "I believe I may just be an idiot."

Simon translated the exchange for Shale, and she cracked a smile for the first time in an hour. With only a few minutes of Simon's spell remaining, Sol Starfletcher stood up and stretched, extending a hand to Simon. The foreigner shook it, and with that, the group parted ways with the First Ranger for the day.

Van turned to Simon, hoping there was still enough time to learn what had been decided.

"Plan is to disable the next quell we come across and show it to the Guides," said Simon. "We'll figure out what to tell Sol's boss once everybody is on the same page regarding the essential facts. First, that I'm not just making all of this up to get attention. And second, that the quells aren't wild animals, but intelligent weapons."

"Sol Starfletcher mentioned the desert," said Van.

"Flat terrain, no cover," Simon summarized. "Plus, I don't think constructs can move as fast across sand."

"Can you really do it?" Van asked. "Capture one of those things?"

"It won't be easy," said Simon. "But if our new friend does his part, then yeah, I think we can pull it off."

"Do I have a role in all this? Does Shale?"

Hearing her name, Shale's eyes flicked up. Simon shot a glance at her and furrowed his brow.

"Shale seems to think she could take down a quell on her own if she had to," said Simon. "I told her if she tried, she'd get herself killed. You can imagine what a fun conversation that was."

Van nodded, wondering when they'd even had time to discuss the matter. Was it that easy for people to communicate without words? Was Van really the only one who needed everything spelled out for him?

"As for you," Simon continued, "your job from here to Seat Mercura is to stick around camp and not get killed by a quell. Think you can manage?"

Van frowned.

Simon sighed. "I'm serious, Van. If the situation changes, I need you where I can find you—to vouch for me when the time comes, if nothing else. And while we're at it, keep me in the loop on anything new from Galdur and Brynda. I don't want any more surprises on that front."

"I don't intend to ever run into them again, if I can help it," Van grumbled.

"Sorry, kid, but that's not an option. You bailing on them would just tip them off."

Van bristled and glowered at him.

"Don't give me that look," said Simon. "Starting now, our only goal is to keep you safe. To keep your dad and everyone else back at Seat Dolse safe."

To keep Lilim safe, Van added silently, deflating at the prospect of subjecting himself to further indignity at the hands of Galdur Goldeye and Brynda Blackblade.

"That's the spirit," said Simon, recognizing his acceptance. "Now, put your poker face on and go teach that freak how to read."

In retrospect, Brynda's promise that everything would return to normal after Seat Ikann made Van's skin crawl. As the procession marched west toward the desert, he reluctantly resumed their nightly sessions. The only change was that the First Ranger of Ikann was reserved and compliant in a way that seemed totally at odds with Van's concept of him. For Van, it was a relief, but over time he grew to understand the nature of Brynda's concern regarding his recovery. If Van cared in the slightest for Galdur's well-being, he might have been concerned himself.

Brynda, too, returned to normal—or the pretense of normalcy she wore like a mask, that Van now felt ashamed he had fallen so in love with. When he let his guard down, he still felt himself drawn in by it. He smiled when she smiled. He laughed when she laughed. Each small seduction was followed quickly by the taste of bile when he remembered the cold, callous look in her eyes as she'd slipped her clothes off.

In these moments, Van turned his head, pretending to cough or rifle around for something he'd forgotten in his pack. He had no idea what a "poker face" was, but Simon's words were obviously meant as a slight against his notorious inability to conceal his own feelings. He didn't trust himself to keep his face from contorting in revulsion, so he could only try to hide it when it did.

Denied his freedom to participate in the hunt, per Simon's mandate, Van found plenty of time to make amends with Lilim for his recent neglect. She didn't speak to him for almost a full day—he was impressed, frankly—but she relapsed in the afternoon, starved for attention. After pitching her tent, she begged him to come look at her new drawings. He was happy to oblige, of course.

She'd used up nearly all the extra parchment she'd received at Stonebasin, and most of the ink as well. Van donated what was left of his own supply, and she beamed, thanking him.

She showed him a drawing she'd done of Simon, wearing his new hat as he strode through the door of an unmarked building Van hoped wasn't supposed to be a brothel. She had also brought to life Shale's untamed beauty, depicting her in the dark dress she'd bought at Third Stone, dagger held out defiantly toward some unseen challenger.

And she had drawn herself hand in hand with Van. She wore a flowing dress such as he'd never seen her in, and he wondered if she even owned such a thing. She looked older in the drawing, and Van a little younger—so that the boy and the girl in the picture appeared about the same age. They kept up with their lessons in the mornings, as always, but the afternoons became dedicated to art.

It rained more often than not, and when Van wasn't with Lilim in her tent, he was usually alone in his. The day before the procession entered the desert was gray and stagnant, with painfully little to do. They did not break camp that morning, as daytime travel would be impossible on the next leg of their journey. Starting now, they would reverse their circadian schedule and travel by night. To facilitate this, they lingered an extra twelve hours on the desert's barren outskirts, waiting for the sun to set.

After assembly, the aspirants were told to go back to sleep if they could, or otherwise rest and prepare to move again at dusk. Simon spent the time allowed by his spell with Sol Starfletcher, rehearsing the meticulous choreography of their plan—whatever it was. Otep Acrearms took his own advice and went to bed, as did most others. Lilim, of all people, confounded him by spending the day with her new friends Milna and Tali.

With nothing to do and no one to talk to, Van felt restless, frustrated, and miserably bored. It was Shale who saved him, barging into his tent unannounced when he tried to lie down for a nap.

"Hunt," she said, brandishing her dagger.

Van looked at her nervously. "Why?"

"Because ranger."

Van hesitated. Simon would be mad if he wandered off. Or was it allowed, as long as he was with Shale? He decided it was a gray area, and that he could be forgiven for taking liberties in interpreting Simon's instructions. He pulled his boots on, picked up his bow, and left camp with her, pleased to see that it had stopped raining.

They ventured to the very edge of the desert, just an hour's trek away. They saw no quells on their hunt—if it could even be called that—nor did they see mourns, or gazelle, or Phantom Nighthawks. Most creatures of the desert were nocturnal. Small, burrowing things, like rodents and reptiles. Stealthy, with scales or hair that blended against the bone-white sand. They didn't see any of those, either.

Shale was paying more attention to Van than to their surroundings, and he started to wonder if she was only babysitting him after all. If she was, he hoped she cared enough to do so of her own volition, and not at the behest of Simon.

They did find one interesting thing on their walk—the skeleton of an old farmhouse, fallen to ruin in decades past. It was likely built when these lands were still as verdant as the Western Forest, but just as Ghan Mudcatcher had explained, the desert had grown until this place, too, was surrendered to the elements and left behind.

Shale broke into a sprint when she spotted a slab of cut limestone, dragged here from some forgotten quarry long buried beneath the sand. The slab lay by the windswept frame of the house, abandoned and without purpose. An eerie monument to the unrealized designs of whoever once lived here.

Hoisting herself onto it without ceremony, Shale sat down and dangled her legs off the side. Van joined her, and for a while, they watched little clouds of sand spiral off the dunes in the near distance, tiny vortexes dancing down the slopes when the wind picked up or changed directions.

There's no curse here, Van thought. *It's beautiful, in its own way.*

He wanted to believe his thought sprang from more than willful optimism, but long-held fears weren't reasoned away so easily. His upbringing and his intuition both screamed at him to go no further—to turn around and flee toward civilization. Toward life.

Van realized he was trembling, and Shale must have realized it, too, because she started to sing. He closed his eyes and listened to her voice, and by the tiniest of measures, his fears ebbed away.

Spirits were low as the procession set out that evening, the last light of day vanishing over the horizon. Those that had slept all day were lethargic, while those that hadn't were bleary-eyed and disoriented, barely awake.

The desert robbed the aspirants of what little morale they had left. Traversing the soft, shifting sand was taxing, sapping their strength far faster than when they had solid ground beneath their feet. Many tripped mid-stride when their attention wandered. As a result, the aspirants kept a slow pace that first night, shambling joylessly across the unfamiliar terrain.

Van walked hand in hand with Lilim, and against all reason, he felt better than he had in days.

When Lilim was in a good mood, seeing the world through her eyes was a precious kind of magic. Every day a new adventure, every challenge conquered a cause for celebration. Though the desert grew intolerably hot by day, it was pleasantly cool by night. And as conventional wisdom predicted, not a cloud dotted the sky. For the first time in a week, they looked up and saw stars.

Lilim craned her neck and pointed at them, her eyes as bright as they were, naming each one she could remember.

Hours later, when the glow of dawn began to warm their backs, they were ordered to stop and pitch their tents. Shade would be their only relief while they slept, so they covered their tents double thick with canvas and furs taken from the supply carts.

Van built his solar still, and then helped Lilim build hers. At her insistence, he read aloud one of her favorite chapters from *The Bull and the Snail,* until she fell asleep several pages in. He watched her for a minute, mumbling in her sleep, then transferred her gently to her bedroll before retreating to his own tent.

The sand was already hot underfoot, and he had to squint against the glare of sunlight reflected off its shimmering surface. He welcomed the darkness of his tent. The air inside was stale and musty—warm, but not sweltering. He fell asleep within minutes, and his dreams offered brief but sorely needed repose.

Once again, Van was awakened by noise. He couldn't tell what it was or where it was coming from until he sat up. Sand was pouring into his tent at one corner, the canvas whipping violently where it had come unfixed. Whatever was happening, he knew only that he had to get away from it.

He rushed outside shirtless and barefoot—and was almost thrown from his feet by the wind.

Reeling, he whipped his head around, trying to get his bearings. His pulse pounded when he discovered he couldn't see his own tent right next to him. The world beyond his outstretched arm was a blur of hissing sand and howling wind. He braced himself, still only half awake, but the wind shifted again and blasted his face with hot sand.

He staggered forward—or in some direction, anyway—and almost lost his balance a second time when his foot became tangled in something. He couldn't see what it was, and he couldn't bend down to free himself without getting toppled by the wind, so he dragged the thing with him as he stumbled through the storm.

Choking on dust and blinded by sand, he finally accepted that this was not just some dream, which likely meant he was about to die. Before acceptance and despair overtook him, though, there came a glimmer of hope. Voices, barely audible over the ravenous hiss of the wind. They were faint, far away, but he would rather die walking than standing still. He moved toward the sound.

After three steps, his foot landed on a surface that wasn't scalding hot and shifting. He squinted, his vision clouded by tears, as he shielded his face with his arms. *Stairs.* There were stone steps leading down into darkness—the impossibility of it as disorienting as the storm itself. Before he could consider the bizarre sight any further, the wind changed once more and swept him forward. He was somersaulted head over heels, down into the dark recesses.

He had just enough time to think of his father, reminding him to watch where he put his feet, before his head struck a step and his vision faded to black.

Brave

Realizing it was a storm, she pulled her spare shirt from her rucksack and tied it around her head, shielding her face from the windblown sand. Another new trick, and one still fresh in her mind. She hoped *he* would remember, too. But for him, it would be a lesson from long ago, and she worried he might forget. If only she had a third shirt she could carry for him, just in case. Or would she have to offer him the shirt off her own back? How bold, but how embarrassing!

As expected, when she crawled out of her tent, she could hardly see a thing. Fortunately, she had carefully memorized the surrounding area before going to bed, so she set out at a scamper. The wind was strong, and she didn't trust herself to keep her footing if she tried to stand, so she crawled on hands and knees. It was all right. She didn't have far to go.

Once she thought she'd gone far enough, she began groping around, moving in an expanding circle rather than a straight line as she searched. But she found nothing—only more churning sand. Had she gotten the direction wrong? It was a mistake she sometimes made, even when she could see where she was going.

Oh, well.

She said a quiet prayer to the Emissaries, thanking them for the short life they'd granted her, and prepared to surrender her spirit to their care. As she prayed, she observed with disappointment that her life would be ending just when it seemed to be getting to the good part. Surely the Emissaries knew that as well as she did. Since leaving home, she'd made so many new friends and learned so much. And he had only just come into her life. What a waste to finally discover these things only to lose them now.

Shame on you, Emissaries.

And then she found it—a rock. Feeling around the rough stone, she found more, some of them large and buried deep in the sand. There was a recession in the terrain. Moving toward it, she felt the ground beneath her hands become solid and cool to the touch. The mouth of a cave, just as she remembered. As she crawled forward, the howl of the wind behind her softened, and she no longer felt the lash of hot sand on her back. This place was still and quiet.

When she was sure it was safe, she untied the shirt from around her head and set it aside, peering into the dark. The cave was shallow, but plenty big enough for her. Thankfully, the wind didn't seem to be blowing in the direction that might cause the entrance to flood with sand, either. She would survive after all. Apologizing to the Emissaries for saying nasty things, she hugged her knees to her chest and settled in to wait out the storm.

It occurred to her that not everyone would be so lucky, and the thought made her a little sad. As more time passed, she also began to feel a little lonesome. She commanded herself not to cry. She would *not* be crying when he found her. The last time she'd cried in front of him, she promised herself she would never do so again. Outside, the wind was already dying down. She wouldn't cry. She would be Brave.

She hadn't yet realized that she was not alone in the cave.

21 Anathema

Pain was the first thing Van registered as his eyes blinked open. Touching his forehead gingerly, he found it slick with blood. His limbs were heavy, reluctant to budge, and his head throbbed. At first, he didn't want to move, for fear of making it worse, but it occurred to him that if it was that bad, he was already dead anyway. Wherever he'd ended up, he was alone here, and he would have to find his way back to the others without help. Wincing, he sat up.

The fact that he even could sit upright was a good sign; his neck wasn't broken. The pain that pounded through his skull worsened, but only slightly. Turning in place, Van looked in the direction he thought he had come from. All he saw was a wall of sand.

The stairs—hadn't there been stairs?—were buried now. He would have to find another way out, but his eyes were still adjusting to the near-total darkness. Rolling onto his knees, he crawled away from the mountain of sand. He didn't want to stand up just yet—he might bash his head again if the cave ceiling was too low.

No... it wasn't a cave. The cold stone beneath his hands was even and smooth to the touch. This place was man-made. Was he underground? Feeling resistance as he dragged himself forward, he realized his foot was still caught on whatever it had gotten tangled in when he escaped his tent.

Van rolled again and reached down. He then discovered his second piece of good news. He had wrapped his foot around the strap of his rucksack and managed to drag it with him all the way here. He freed his foot and groped around inside the pack. His hunting knife was there, along with his flint and, most importantly, his waterskin, still half full.

His vision had already acclimated enough to tell him there was a light source somewhere in this place, however dim. Looking up, he saw it. A jagged line of daylight stood stark against the surrounding gloom. He had fallen much farther than he would have first guessed—the crack was high above him. As it turned out, bumping his head on the ceiling was the least of his concerns. He stood up, shouldering the rucksack and tucking the knife into the waistband of his trousers.

Once upright, Van wobbled like he had gotten out of bed too quickly, but he managed to stay upright. He also discovered that his earlier assessment was wrong. He wasn't alone.

Someone else had fallen down here and lay prone just two paces away. Van knelt and recognized the person as an aspirant—the portly young Dolser Simon had once accused of stealing food off the supply carts. The boy wasn't breathing, and upon pressing a finger to his neck, Van felt no pulse.

It felt wrong to simply leave him here, but Van saw no alternative. He rolled him onto his back, crossed his arms over his lifeless chest, then stood to continue forward. He didn't make it far before he noticed ash drifting through the still air.

"We meet again, fellow traveler."

Van whipped his head back and saw the dead boy smiling at him. His eyes had opened, but this time, Van knew better than to meet that terrible gaze. The pits in the boy's face emitted something harsh and radiant. Not the absence of light, but its opposite, and... what did that mean? *This time?*

"It seems I'm closer to my mark today, though still early," said the thing that had once called itself Anathema. "How long has it been since we spoke, by your reckoning?"

All strength drained from Van's body. He tried to speak, but his voice failed him, so he bent his will toward moving his hand to the hilt of his knife. It was slow going, his every muscle from the neck down stiff and sluggish. On the ground in front of him, the dead boy was already burning away.

"This one crumbles like the last," the thing said, observing its disintegrating form with cold indifference. "Damaged beyond repair before I even got here. Tell me, have you ingratiated yourself with my true vessel yet?"

With the context of their previous encounter inexplicably restored, Van knew there was only one person that statement could refer to.

"I'll warn her," he hissed, laboring furiously for each word.

"You will," it said, almost amicably. "I've seen that, too. It changes nothing. Your role is inevitable, just as I am inevitable."

"What. Are. You?" Van gritted out. His hand reached his knife, but he didn't have the strength to pull it from its sheath.

"That's very rude," said Anathema. "I'd have thought you would feel honored, getting to talk so freely with one of your *Emissaries.*"

So, it was true. Van and every other Nemian born in the last eight hundred years had been tricked. This was what the gods of the land truly were—this was a devil. His despair sapped the last of his strength and he sagged to his knees. Nothing remained of the dead boy now except a laughing head atop a pile of ash.

"Chin up, child," the evil thing said. "Don't you see? This means you're not to die here. Now get up, put your thinking cap on, as they say, and *get back to work.*"

Van's vision blurred, and he fell sideways as his awareness slipped away. He had no way of measuring how long he lay there, motionless, the smell of charred meat stinging his nostrils. But the moment eventually passed. The acrid smell faded, perception returned, and Van sat up again.

Unlike with his experience at Stonebasin, which he only now could recall in full, he still had his memories when he woke. Or—his stomach sank—whatever memories the thing had permitted him to keep. As for the dead boy, there was nothing left to testify he'd been there at all. No clothes, no charred bones. Not one stray flake of ash.

Curiously, it was easier to see than before, and it took him a moment to understand why. The sun had moved. It must be almost directly overhead now, sending more of its rays through the crack in the ceiling.

By his count, only a few hours had passed since the storm. Or alternatively, an entire day could have passed. As an experiment, Van swallowed. His throat was dry, but he wasn't parched. If a full day had come and gone, he would have been desperate with thirst by now. That said, he still needed to hurry.

He had to find Lilim, and he had to warn Shale.

Van's first good look at his surroundings painted a dreary picture. All four walls of the chamber were uniform in height and width, roughly fifty feet from floor to ceiling and thirty from wall to wall. Climbing to freedom was out of the question. There were no handholds, and even if Van could make it to the top, the crack in the ceiling wasn't big enough for him to pass through.

The place was something like a dungeon—the only way out besides the buried stairwell was a door of iron bars built into the opposite wall. Testing it, he found the door predictably locked, but something about it was off. The hole where a key would go was on *his* side of the door. If this was a prison, it should be the other way around. Stranger still, the lock seemed to need four keys to turn instead of just one.

He frowned and stepped back. He would come back to the lock after he investigated the room's other peculiar feature.

At each corner, a statue stood proudly, true to life in both size and detail. The figures were carved from alabaster stone foreign to the dungeon itself. Inspecting each one, Van was startled to discover he recognized them. And because he did, he knew immediately where he was.

This was a ruin of the Meridians. The statues were carved in the likeness of the last leaders of those people, who became the first leaders of Van's own. From left to right were Dolse the Vigilant, Ikann the Bold, Vaxas the Shrewd, and Mercura the Inviolate.

Van stepped first to the smallest of the four, a startouched girl years younger than her peers who would become the founder of Nemia's most secretive tribe. He stared at her image as if caught in a dream, amazed at how closely the adolescent Vaxas resembled Brynda. He knelt to read the dedication on the metal plaque at the statue's base.

He couldn't, of course. It was written in the language of the Meridians, the meaning of its characters lost to time. Eleven symbols were imprinted on the plaque, and curiously, the first six from the right sat upon dials that could be rotated. He touched one, testing it, and found that it moved easily despite how clearly ancient it was.

The dials reminded Van of the ornate lockbox his father had given him for his fifth birthday. Rather than a key that could be lost or stolen, the little treasure box used combination dials. At five years old, Van was inquisitive, but not very forward thinking. He'd asked his father skeptically if such a box was really any safer than one that opened with a key. Any would-be burglar with sufficient motivation, and who had a bit of time on their hands, could simply guess the sequence.

Farseer Daz had chuckled and challenged him to go ahead and try. Even with a small number of dials, he explained, there were countless possible combinations. The chance that he would get the sequence right by random guess was vanishingly slim.

In the end, Van had unlocked his birthday present only with a hint from his father that the puzzle's answer had something to do with his newfound love of books. Armed with this information, it had still taken him a full day to work out the sequence. The treasure box had opened when the dials were set to spell his new earned name, *SCRIBE,* his father's real gift to him that year.

A combination of six symbols, just like the one in front of him now. Four statues. Four puzzles. Four missing keys. The hairs on Van's arms prickled. Maybe this place wasn't a prison at all. Maybe it was some kind of test.

Van rotated the first dial and counted the symbols on its face—twenty-seven in total, exactly as many letters as there were in the modern Nemian alphabet. He checked each of the other dials, confirming that they were the same. Six dials with twenty-seven settings each meant the number of possible combinations was...

He fell into a sitting position, defeated. He would die of old age before he solved this puzzle. And it was only one of four.

Van wallowed in self pity for an embarrassing duration before he was struck by a realization. Just like on his fifth birthday, he had a hint. In fact, he had as many hints as there were puzzles.

He stood up and rushed to the next statue—Ikann the Bold —and knelt to count the symbols on the plaque. The number was different here. Four rotating dials to the right of five fixed symbols. Van saw a ray of hope.

Dolse the Vigilant was next. Four fixed symbols, followed by eight dials. Van frowned. One fewer than he was expecting. He made a mental note of the discrepancy and moved on.

Last was Mercura the Inviolate, the biggest of the statues because the Patron tribe's founder was giantkin. Seven fixed symbols, eight rotating dials. One off again.

Van thought for a moment, exploring the possibilities. In both cases, the missing symbol corresponded to the same trailing vowel. Did the Meridians not possess such a concept in their reckoning of written language? Was that the only difference, or would there be others he couldn't account for?

He looked to the ceiling. The light was already dimming as the sun moved out of position. Even if he was right, and he had most of the solution, he couldn't work in the dark.

Lowering his head, Van refocused on the dials and spun them into place as fast as he could, his heart hammering in his chest.

Twenty minutes later, Van was out of the cell and sprinting down a corridor. He left all four keys behind, as a favor to whatever hapless passerby ended up trapped down here in another eight hundred years.

The ruins were far larger than Van could have expected. The ceiling had collapsed in places, admitting daylight, but for purposes of escape, the gaps were still out of reach. And when the sun set fully, he would be blind.

He skidded to a halt at a rotunda. Here, the ceiling was almost completely caved in, and for the first time Van saw a path where he might climb up and out. Immense stone shelves were grouped near the center of the room, rising nearly to the ceiling. If he clambered to the top of one, he could probably jump the gap to the surface.

Van wandered to the nearest one, stepping on the first shelf and leaning into it to test its stability—and he spotted something resting there, right next to his foothold. A large, dust-covered book. Even in a race against time with his life on the line, he couldn't imagine not taking a closer look, just for a moment.

He turned the cover, noting that the book's pages were made of something like sheet metal, the letters pressed into them rather than written with ink. He recognized most of the symbols from the room with the statues.

Owing to its unusual design, the volume was extraordinarily heavy. Van wondered why anyone would bother to make a book with such impractical materials, but he supposed that if it had been made from parchment, it would have long since deteriorated.

He turned a few more pages, fascinated, but he froze when he heard a sound. Something was moving around down here.

Quietly, he unshouldered his rucksack and set it on the shelf. And because Van the Scribe would never leave a book forgotten in a place like this, he placed the text in his pack and closed it before drawing his knife and edging toward the shuffling, scraping noise.

A second corridor adjoined the rotunda, this one even more dilapidated than the one Van had come through. When he stepped into it, he saw someone crawling along on their elbows just a few paces away.

"You," said Galdur Goldeye, stopping to stare up at Van. "Of course it would be you."

The First Ranger of Ikann rolled onto his side and pushed himself up to sit against the wall. He was damp with sweat, his breath coming ragged.

Van stammered, "How did you…?"

"I fell." Galdur tipped his chin up toward a section of destroyed ceiling. "From there."

Van sheathed his knife and stooped down, examining him.

"Your ankle is broken," said Van.

"How observant of you," grumbled Galdur.

"And your breathing suggests other injuries," Van continued. "Your ribs, possibly. You shouldn't be moving."

Galdur's face was tight. "The alternative seemed worse."

Van glanced back toward the tall shelves. "I'm going to take you over there."

He looped his arms under Galdur's and shuffled backward, dragging him. The First Ranger hissed as he slid across the floor, either in pain or in protest, but Van ignored it. When they reached the center of the rotunda, he leaned Galdur against the shelf.

"I think I can climb up from here," said Van. "Once I'm out, I'll..."

He hesitated, staring into Galdur's yellow eye.

"I'll send help," he managed.

Van propped his foot on the lowest shelf and reached for his rucksack, but almost at once, he realized it would be too heavy. With the ancient book inside, he couldn't climb the shelf—much less make the leap of faith that awaited him at the top.

He left his pack next to Galdur, focusing instead on the climb. The shelf was ancient, and he still wasn't certain it wouldn't collapse under his weight when he was partway up. If it did, or if his footing failed him when he made his jump for freedom, that would mean falling fifty feet or more. He would almost certainly break his legs and die trapped here with Galdur. Or, if he was lucky, he supposed he might fall on his head and die instantly instead.

To his relief, Van made it to the top of the shelf without incident, steeling himself as he stood on trembling legs to contemplate the final jump. Just a few feet more, and he was free. He took a breath and commanded himself not to look down—though he had a nagging fear that if he did, he might see Galdur peering into his rucksack.

Safely above ground, Van took several shuddering breaths. He didn't trust himself to stand up right away, so he knelt on hands and knees, digging his fingers into the hot sand. The afternoon sun beat down on his exposed back, dazzlingly bright, but he welcomed it after the cold darkness of the buried ruins.

When he finally stood, he ventured one step forward and became instantly disoriented. There was nothing but windswept dunes in every direction, as far as the eye could see. The hole he'd crawled from was practically invisible from up here, and he was right next to it. Even if he could figure out which direction the procession was in, it would be impossible to lead anyone back here without a landmark.

Van wavered, feeling lost and trapped all over again, confined this time not by bars, but by the indomitable vastness of the desert. The survive-or-die panic that had kept him going for hours was fading, and fatigue began to set in, ushered along by the suffocating heat. He reached for his waterskin only to remember he'd left it in his rucksack. Inhaling a sharp breath, he fell to his knees.

For the next few minutes, he contemplated whether he preferred to die in the sun, thirsty and alone, or down in the darkness with a little water to drink, in the company of the man he hated most in this world.

He gazed up at the cloudless sky as sweat clung to his skin, and something up there caught his eye. A bird. He wondered feverishly if it was a Phantom Nighthawk. How funny that would be, if the last thing he saw before he perished of thirst or exposure was the creature of myth said to impart good fortune. But no, it wasn't a Nighthawk. This was a bird he recognized, with feathers a deeper blue than the boundless sky through which it soared.

Summoning his strength, Van lifted his arms and waved. Sol's falcon dropped lower, circling Van twice and then flapping off north at a slow pace, steadily regaining altitude.

He assumed it meant for him to follow, but that wouldn't do. Galdur was still trapped below, and more importantly, so was the ancient book.

Van stumbled to his feet, waving with one hand and pointing urgently with the other toward the hole. The falcon doubled back, circling once more and then giving its wings a wobble in acknowledgment. It soared north again—this time at a much greater speed. Van collapsed to his knees to wait, hoping the procession wasn't too far away.

The sun was setting by the time the wavering figures appeared on the horizon, but it was still far too hot to be exposed, shirtless in the open desert. He counted twenty figures scrambling toward him across the dunes, all shimmering silhouettes. When he was sure they weren't hallucinations, he tried to stand and wave. He toppled sideways instead, nauseous and inexplicably cold—a symptom he distantly remembered was a bad sign for someone in his circumstances.

The rescue party broke into a sprint when they saw him. Otep Acrearms and Sol Starfletcher were at the fore, with Simon and Shale close behind. Van tried to stand a second time. He made it to his feet, but only for a moment. Shale caught him when he fell, holding him upright while Otep and Simon checked him over. A waterskin was pressed to his lips, and he drank deeply while Otep shouted questions at him. Delirious, he could only point at the hole in the ground.

Sol Starfletcher and several Mercuran rangers sprang into action. Luckily, they had a large bundle of rope that they used to fashion something like a cradle, which they lowered into the buried structure for Galdur. They pulled him up a few minutes later along with Van's rucksack.

Amidst the commotion, more from the procession arrived, Riverspeaker Gheela and Ghan Mudcatcher among them. The Ikanni Pilgrimage Guide, Kekrin, waddled forward and began fussing over Galdur, grimacing as he saw the extent of his injuries. At some point, the ancient book was discovered, immediately drawing the attention of the delegates.

"Who is responsible for recovering this?" asked Riverspeaker Gheela, running her fingers reverently over one of the strange metal pages.

"I am," said Van and Galdur in near perfect unison, but Van's voice sounded quiet even to himself, and his head was swimming.

Someone threw a cool, damp cloth over his head and shoulders, providing a measure of relief from the sun. After that, the world became a blur. He drifted in and out of consciousness, vaguely aware he was being carried.

He slept for a time, and when he woke, he was someplace cramped and dark. He bolted upright, terrified he was trapped underground again. Shale stopped him by putting her hand on his chest and pushing him back onto his bedroll. He saw worry in her expression, so he didn't protest.

They weren't underground. It was only his tent—or at least, someone's tent. The one he'd brought from home had probably been lost in the storm. Shale watched him for a moment. When she saw that he was lucid, she poked her head outside and whistled.

"How you feeling, kid?" Simon asked as he stepped inside.

"My head," choked Van.

"Hard to tell if that's the heat stroke or the concussion," said Simon. "But on both counts, I think you're out of the woods. Here."

Van took the offered waterskin, and once again, he drank deeply.

"Simon," he croaked between gulps, "I need you to—"

He coughed, choking on water.

"Slow down." Simon snatched the waterskin out of his hand before he could spill it. "We're safe."

"You were right," Van rasped, his chest tightening. "About devils. About everything."

"I said slow down. What happened out there?"

Van told them everything he could remember, focusing on his encounter in the ruins with the thing called Anathema.

"Tell her, Simon. It's important," he said urgently. "It wants Shale."

Hesitantly, Simon spoke to Shale.

"Thank you for the warning," she said, folding her arms over her chest. "I would surely have promised myself to the first devil that asked, had you not cautioned me against it."

Van stared at her. "Is she… is she being sarcastic?"

"It doesn't really add up," said Simon, ignoring his question. "Devils take souls, not bodies."

"It spoke as though it had seen the future." Van felt a hollow sense of helplessness, his head still throbbing. "What if it's planning to trick her somehow, like my people have been tricked all this time?"

"There can't be a trick," said Simon. "What Shale told you before was right. When you make a deal with a devil, you have to be fully informed about what you're agreeing to, and you have to agree of your own free will."

Van shook his head. His whole body was trembling, and his thoughts were all jumbled. "I don't—wait. Lilim. Where is Lilim? Has she been found?"

Simon looked at Shale, and out of the corner of his eye, Van saw her nod. She had that look of worry on her face again. Far more worry there than there should be.

"Yeah, they found her," said Simon, standing up and holding out his hand. "Come on."

As they trudged through the Dolser campsite, Van looked around. A few of the supply carts had been recovered intact, still loaded with provisions by the looks of them. The oxen that had drawn them all the way from Seat Dolse, though, were gone.

It was night, but the procession was halted. Simon explained that because so many people were still missing, the Guides hadn't called for them to resume travel yet. Hundreds of tents stretched before them, but that wasn't right either. There should have been close to a thousand.

Simon took Van to Ghan Mudcatcher, who was organizing a first-aid effort at a makeshift infirmary, hastily built from several tents lashed together. There were dozens of aspirants here from all of Nemia's tribes, some injured and others tending the wounded. But he didn't see Lilim.

"Van the Scribe," the elder greeted wearily. "It is good to see you well."

Van's sense of duty told him he should offer to stay and help. *How many did we lose?* he might have asked, but all he managed was, "Where is Lilim the Brave?"

"Follow me," said Ghan Mudcatcher.

He led Van back toward one of the supply carts, leaving Simon to take over for him at the infirmary.

"She was found close to camp. One of the first," Ghan said gently. "She took shelter in a cave, and it spared her a grisly fate, but she chose her hiding place too well. It was shared by another."

When they reached the cart, Ghan Mudcatcher untied the canvas tarp that covered it, pulling it aside so Van could see. He then allowed a moment of respectful silence.

"The welt on her ankle marks the sting of the desert scorpion," Ghan said. "It would have been quick, in a girl so small. Perhaps even peaceful."

The cart wasn't piled with food or goods, but with bodies. Their mouths and nostrils were bloody, caked with sand. Broken limbs and twisted necks. The wind must have picked these people up and thrown them.

Lying atop the mound of dead—unmarred by any such brutal trauma and looking so serene with her eyes closed and her hands crossed over her chest, she could be only asleep— was Lilim the Brave.

22 Quagmire

Many more were found in the days that followed. Some were alive, but most had perished. Pyres were built for the fallen, their bodies committed to the flames as was tradition. Some were never found at all and were left behind, buried beneath the sand. More than four thousand aspirants had set out from Seat Dolse, barely over a month ago. Now, they numbered fewer than three hundred. For those still living, the pilgrimage became funereal in nature, a bitter act of solidarity to those lost in the storm.

Wilm of the Horizon and Orum the Mutable were dead. Rhys the Catcher and Rhyla the Tamer of tribe Vaxas were dead. Hammer and Anvil, Galdur's favorite and most obedient subordinates, were missing and presumed dead—along with hundreds upon hundreds of others. Prayers to the Emissaries were offered daily, beseeching the gods of the land to see their spirits safely onward, but listing the names of the departed would have taken far more time than was practical.

The Pilgrimage Guides of Nemia chose to lead the procession back east, risking the desert's wrath no further. A rumor spread among the survivors that Riverspeaker Gheela was to blame for the tragedy. Her talent with magic was said to grant foreknowledge of things such as severe shifts in weather. Thus, it was openly speculated that they'd been led into danger deliberately—a plot perpetrated by tribe Mercura to eliminate challengers and maintain their status as Patron.

Others claimed Gheela's powers had failed her because an evil spirit had taken up residence in the land, heralding the beginning of a dark age for the tribes.

Perhaps in part to diffuse the rumors and atone for her perceived failure, Riverspeaker Gheela made a concession on behalf of tribe Mercura. For recovering the ancient text from the Meridian ruins, Galdur Goldeye and tribe Ikann, by extension, would be rewarded. His accomplishment would be considered equal in value to victory in one of the games of the pilgrimage. By the reckoning of those who didn't know better, this created a three-way tie between the First Rangers of Dolse, Mercura, and Ikann.

Simon urged Van to speak out against the decision, knowing it was he and not Galdur who had found the priceless artifact, but Van didn't bother. In fact, after the desert, Van didn't bother with much of anything. He didn't hunt with Otep, nor did he seek the company of his friends. He abandoned his obligation to tutor the First Rangers, though he heard in passing that Brynda Blackblade was alive. And despite the fact that he still woke up an hour before dawn out of habit, he stopped going to assembly. Instead, he spent that time by himself. Not praying—never again praying—but often meditating over past mistakes.

All had lost loved ones, so it was understandable that for a time, Van's behavior was mistaken for common grief. But after a few days, those close to him noticed he had stopped eating. Otep Acrearms was the first to approach him, thrusting a bowl of food in his face one evening.

"You must eat, Van the Scribe," said Otep. "I understand that you are grieving, and I share in your sorrow. The only way we will survive our grief is to climb out from it together. When you are ready, I am here. You can talk to me always. But until then, you must keep up your strength."

Van took the food and ate a few bites to placate his friend, but the First Ranger's words meant little. Van couldn't share in anyone's grief, because he was not grieving. He was broken.

To the extent that it was possible to do so, Van had also stopped sleeping. Being awake was miserable, a constant reminder of how fundamentally ruined the world was, but he preferred it to the dreams. Whenever he slept, he was adrift, his defenseless mind carried away not by some tranquil river, but by a roaring flood.

In his dreams, he saw Galdur and Brynda in bed together, damp skin grinding roughly on damp skin. He saw Lilim cowering in a windswept cave, afraid and alone, as silent death crept toward her from the shadows. He saw Rhaggo Bullbreaker drinking his father's blood from his golden goblet, and he saw ash falling from the sky over Seat Dolse.

Simon was next to seek Van out. To his credit, he seemed at least to have sensed that Van was experiencing something other than mere grief. Instead of sharing hollow platitudes, he made an appeal to his pragmatism.

"I know you feel like giving up, but there are still people here who care about you. They're worried." He sighed. *"I'm* worried. I won't lie and tell you the worst has passed, because

I'm pretty sure there's still more horror ahead than behind. But I need your head back in the game for whatever's coming. One way or another, it'll be up to us to save lives, and I can't do that on my own. Nobody listens to me." His eyes fixed on Van. "I need your help."

Van smiled weakly and promised he'd make time for him tomorrow. In reality, he had no intention of doing so, because he no longer cared.

Shale gave him his space for almost a week before she finally lost her patience for his mood.

"Hunt," she demanded, barging into his tent unannounced on the sixth night following the desert storm. It was late, but he hadn't been asleep.

"No, thank you." He turned over in his bedroll.

She kicked him in the small of the back, hard enough to leave a bruise.

"Why!" he growled through clenched teeth, shrinking away from her.

"Because ranger," she said.

"I don't want to," mumbled Van. "Just leave me alone."

She kicked him again, in the leg this time. His anger flaring, he pounced up, taking a step toward her with his fists clenched. She looked him in the eye, put her hands on her hips, and stuck her chin out, as if daring him to take a swing at her. He didn't. With a grunt, she pushed him out of the tent, and kept shoving him until he began walking on his own.

Van's bow was long gone, and he hadn't bothered to pick up his knife. He wondered, with fleeting interest, what the chances were of them being attacked by mourns or quells. It was a warm night, but not hot, and it hadn't rained since yesterday. On so pleasant an evening, he could almost forget the myriad unseen forces conspiring to destroy them, any given one of which was laughably insurmountable.

To pass the time, he made bets with himself as to which of their enemies would reveal themselves first to usher in the fall of civilization as they knew it. Galdur and Brynda? Strangely, whatever those two had in store for Nemia was now probably the least of their concerns. More likely it would be between the rulers of Simon's homeland with their army of sentient weapons, or the devil that called itself Anathema. One or both would appear before them, probably soon, and that would be that. No more pointless marching. No more dreams.

They wandered far from camp that night, Shale in the lead and Van shambling after her. He made no attempt at conversation, hoping she would get bored and turn back. She started humming a tune he recognized—one he had taught her, he supposed. She added a few words here and there, where she could remember them.

"To watch their fields at night aglow..."

Van declined to contribute the missing verses. His feet ached, and his whole body felt weaker than lack of sleep alone could account for.

"I'm tired," he said abruptly, turning on his heel. "I'm going back."

Shale stepped around to his front and pushed him to the ground before he could make it two paces. He landed on his rump, and pain shot up from his lower back where she'd kicked him earlier. Sitting there for a moment, he took a breath, and stood back up—only to be pushed into the mud again.

"Very well," he muttered, staying down this time. "I'll just sleep here."

She fell on him, dropping her weight onto his stomach and knocking the wind from his lungs. Pinning his arms with her knees, she grabbed him by the collar and cranked her fist back.

"Why!" he screamed. "Why do you even care!"

He waited for her to deliver the blow, but it never came. Instead of striking him, she unclenched her fist and dug her hand into her belt pouch. She pulled out a crumpled sheet of yellowing parchment, frayed at the edges, and held it in his face. A line drawing of a snail riding on the back of a bull as it crossed a shallow river.

"She loved you! Live for her!"

Van's breathing slowed as he looked at Lilim's drawing. He strained to free his arms so he could take it in his shaking hands, and Shale shifted her weight to let him. Memories of Lilim swam in his mind, the cherished and the troubled both. All of her struggles and achievements. All her hopes and doubts. All her uncertainties—and all her love. His face felt hot, and his eyes were burning.

Grief. Finally, grief.

Van wept with a force that shook his body, and Shale stayed with him while he cried. She slid off of him and pulled his head into her lap, stroking his hair with a touch as gentle as a mother's.

"So turn I now from all that's passed..."

Gathering his courage, Van met with Shale and Simon the next day. Once they were all seated, and Simon had activated his spell, Van bowed his head low and rested his hands on his knees.

"I'm sorry for behaving so childishly. Please forgive me."

"Seeing as how you've been through more in the last few weeks than some people deal with in a lifetime," said Simon, "I guess you get a pass. It's good to have you back, kid."

Shale nodded in agreement. Van glanced between them, grateful for their company. As he picked up the meal bowl he'd brought with him, he spoke between mouthfuls of venison and fresh berries—the first substantial thing he'd eaten in days.

Simon began by catching Van up on what he'd missed over the past several days, reporting that no more quells had been spotted since they'd recruited Sol Starfletcher to their cause.

"Where does that leave us in terms of your plan?" asked Van.

"Pretty much the same place as before," said Simon. "The shot-callers around here won't believe anything I tell them unless we catch one. So for now, totally screwed." He cleared his throat. "There are a couple of new problems, though."

Van smiled feebly. "Of course there are."

"Shale's been scouting ahead of us most nights," Simon continued, "and she doesn't like the looks of where the procession's headed. Some kind of bog."

"The Great Swamp of Vaxas," Van supplied.

"Sure," said Simon.

"What is her concern, specifically?"

Simon muttered a few words to Shale, and her eyes met Van's.

"The air is lethally toxic," she said. "Undetectable to most, and there would be no symptoms following exposure, but to go there would be fatal within days."

"That seems, um." Van hesitated, cocking his head slightly. "How could you tell?"

"There are similar places in the Twilight World," she explained. "The similarities, in fact, are uncanny. Distressingly so."

Van shook his head. "The people of tribe Vaxas have lived there for generations."

"You don't believe me?" Shale raised an eyebrow testily.

"I believe you," Van said quickly. "I'll ask Ghan Mudcatcher about the Great Swamp. He's one of the few among us who has traveled these lands before."

Shale folded her arms and grumbled something unintelligible. Simon made no attempt to translate.

"So, that's one problem." Van returned his attention to Simon. "There are others?"

"The storm that hit us," said Simon. "It wasn't natural. A spell called it—and before you ask me how I could tell, remember what I do for a living and how long I've been doing it."

Van set his bowl aside, his stomach sinking. "You don't think... the rumors that have been spreading about Riverspeaker Gheela?"

"I don't want to believe that your Patron tribe would commit an atrocity like that," said Simon.

"Then, the sorcerers from your homeland?"

"They'd be capable," said Simon. "But they have no reason to do it. There are easier ways to just kill us all, if that's what they wanted."

"Then, who?" whispered Van, fully aware that whoever they were discussing would stand accused of Lilim's murder.

"I'm not sure yet," said Simon. "But I can start working on some theories if you tell me again what it was you saw when you were trapped underground. Be thorough this time."

Van thought he'd been thorough the first time, but he had also been delirious from exposure. Recalling each detail, he told the story again. Simon let him speak and translated for Shale in near real-time, interjecting questions at a few key points.

"…and once I was out of the room, I continued straight until —"

"Wait," interrupted Simon. "How long did that take you? With the dials and the keys?"

Van's brow furrowed. "It was difficult to measure time down there, but around half an hour, probably."

Simon translated for Shale, and her eyes widened a little. She flashed Van a sly smile before Simon continued his interrogation.

"So, based purely on how many settings the dials had, you figured out the entire thing was just a substitution cipher?"

Van blinked at him. "A what?"

"And you cracked it in under thirty minutes," Simon mused. "That would have earned you a scholarship where I'm from."

"I don't know what that means," said Van.

"It means we just figured out what your superpower is," Simon said. "Now, go back to the part where the dead kid was talking to you."

For the third time, Van described his experiences with the entity called Anathema, including his first encounter with it, in Stonebasin. He spoke slowly and paused at regular intervals so Simon could keep Shale abreast of the conversation.

"I'll be honest," said Simon, "this would be simpler if we could conclude you were just hallucinating. Stress, nervous break—something along those lines."

Van sighed, exasperated, but he forced himself to consider it. "Do you think that's possible?"

"Hypothetically, sure," said Simon. "But in this case, no."

He translated the last exchange to Shale, and Van waited for him to elaborate.

"The name of the first kid, the one you saw at Stonebasin," continued Simon.

"Vauna Featherfriend."

"Yeah." He nodded. "I heard that name from Ghan, the day we stopped at Third Stone. He said a kid by that name went missing. I don't think he heard it from you, and I don't think you heard it from him, because according to your story, you were talking to this kid *before* he supposedly disappeared."

"And when Otep told us about Vauna later, I couldn't remember him," said Van. "So, for you to have heard about him from Ghan Mudcatcher..." He sucked in a breath. "Does that prove I didn't simply imagine what happened to him?"

Simon's eyes darted. "There's one other possibility."

"What possibility?" asked Van.

"You won't like it."

Van set his jaw. "Does it involve magic?"

"Yep," said Simon.

Van groaned. "Just tell me."

"The memories themselves could be fake."

Van shook his head and frowned. "How is that even—?"

Before the words left his mouth, he gave up. By now, he knew better than to ask how anything was possible.

"It works like this," said Simon. "If a sorcerer gets their hands on you, and they know the right spells, they can edit your recollection of events. There are limits, of course. Long-term memory is harder to manipulate than short-term, for instance, and only a few minutes of artificial memory can be inserted into most minds without causing serious damage." Simon shrugged. "All I'm saying is, it's possible someone got you alone and fed you some fabricated memories, then edited themselves out of your short-term recollection so you wouldn't realize it had happened."

Van heaved a breath. "Simon, if I can't even trust my own memories…"

"I know," said Simon. "It's a rabbit hole. Madness that way lies, et cetera. Lucky for you, you're friends with me."

Van scrunched his eyebrows. "Meaning what?"

"Meaning I can figure out if anyone's been messing with your memories."

Van sat back. "How?"

"Same way I figured out someone was messing with the weather," said Simon. *"For a living, remember?"*

"All right," said Van. "What do I need to do?"

"For starters, ask Ghan why we're heading into a swamp that Shale thinks will kill us," said Simon. "Then, sit tight for a few days. We're supposed to be stopping at some village—in the death swamp I guess. If I can find what I need there for the spell, I'll give your memories a checkup."

Van shook his head. "I thought our next destination was Seat Vaxas."

"That's because you stopped going to the morning pow-wows," said Simon. "Seriously, our deal was for you to tell me this stuff, not the other way around."

"You're right," said Van, looking at the ground. "I'm sorry."

Simon put a hand on his shoulder, giving it a gentle shake. "It's okay. I'm messing with you. Get some rest, and we'll reconvene tomorrow."

"Yes," said Van, popping the last berry from his bowl into his mouth and stifling a yawn. "Before you go, did Shale need anything?"

Simon looked at Shale, but she only smiled and shrugged.

"Nah," said Simon. "I think she got what she was looking for."

23 Hemlock

The next day, Van woke an hour before sunrise. He dressed for the road, then carefully folded Lilim's drawing, tucking it into the inner breast pocket of his tunic. With a deep breath, he broke his tent down and went to assembly.

The procession would soon leave the borderlands and enter the Great Swamp. Two days hence, they would reach the Vaxal community of Hemlock, where Riverspeaker Gheela would meet with the elders of Vaxas. She hoped to send a message ahead to Seat Mercura, alerting chieftain Scaela to the tragedy that had befallen them in the desert.

From Hemlock, it was four days more to Seat Vaxas itself.

Van wished he could ask the Mercuran Pilgrimage Guide to include Simon's warning about Gnosos in whatever message she was sending to her chieftain. But until they proved that threat actually existed, the people Van trusted most all seemed to agree it could do more harm than good.

Van shared the morning hike with Ghan Mudcatcher, and when he was confident the younger aspirants weren't paying attention, he asked the elder about a rumor he heard regarding the Great Swamp.

"How could you know this?" said Ghan Mudcatcher in a measured tone, narrowing his eyes at him.

"Then it's true?" Van asked, not bothering to hide his shock.

"Indeed." The elder nodded slowly. "As we breathe the air of the Great Swamp, its toxins will take root in our lungs, and from there spread to the rest of our bodies. It is a slow process, only harmful if left untreated for weeks. When we reach Seat Vaxas, you will be given medicine that will shield you from its effects, as I was in my youth."

"Why was this never explained to us?" asked Van.

"It is considered a secret of tribe Vaxas," said Ghan Mudcatcher. "Out of respect for our cousins, it is kept only by the elders of the tribes."

Van frowned. "We'd have found out anyway, if we are to be given medicine at their Seat."

"It would have been mixed into your food, and you'd have been none the wiser," retorted Ghan Mudcatcher. "Now, I don't suppose you're going to tell me what loose-lipped fool spoke to you of this?"

Van hesitated. If it had been Simon, he might have told Ghan. But Van had no idea if the elder shared the same rapport with Shale. In lieu of answering, he thanked Ghan, muttered some excuse about having to be elsewhere, and fell out of step with him.

The procession made camp at midday, and for the first time since the desert, Van joined Otep's hunting party, both because he wanted to feel useful for a change, and because Simon hadn't technically made him promise not to in recent days. As Van jogged up to the group, the First Ranger brightened, smiling and clapping him affectionately on the back. They were joined by only three other Dolsers.

"I apologize for my prolonged absence," said Van as they walked away from camp.

Otep shook his head. "Put it out of your mind. It is good to have you back with us. We will be relying on your skills now more than ever."

Judging by the way the other Dolsers held their weapons—with an amateur's familiarity—Van wondered if Otep's words might actually be true. Without Orum's abilities as a skinchanger and Wilm's expertise as a marksman, they would have their work cut out for them. Van didn't even possess a bow anymore, so he could do little besides act as an extra pair of eyes for spotting tracks.

Despite the frequent rains, the borderlands on the desert's outskirts remained stubbornly arid. They spotted no signs of plant or animal life as they scoured the land northeast of camp. Their only glimmer of hope appeared after an hour, when Van called Otep to show him the hoofprints of gazelle.

"A solitary animal rather than a herd, I think," said Otep, stooping to examine the spoor.

Following the tracks, they soon found the animal in question—alone, as Otep predicted. It lay dead on the ground, stretched in a drying pool of its own blood.

"Is it safe to eat?" ventured one of the less experienced hunters.

"Some would consider it less than honorable to consume the body of an animal killed by another predator," said Otep, crouching for a closer look. "But there are more practical reasons to avoid doing so. These are not our lands, and we do not know what creature may have killed this one."

"It might have been poisonous," deduced one of the other newcomers.

"Any venom in the meat would be neutralized through cooking it," said Otep. "Instead, we will abstain because we cannot know the predator wasn't rabid."

"It wasn't," said Van, studying the wound that had slain the gazelle.

Multiple lacerations marred its flank—deep, clean cuts—seven in number.

"You know what did this?" asked Otep.

Van locked eyes with him. "I do."

Otep held his gaze for a moment, then furrowed his brow.

"You believe it was the thing Simon of the Mists showed you."

"Simon didn't *show* me anything," muttered Van, struggling to rein in his frustration. "I saw it with my own eyes."

Otep stood and turned away from the dead animal. "We will remain vigilant. If there is danger afoot, we will face it, in whatever form it takes."

They didn't find any danger—or anything else, for that matter. After another hour of fruitless scavenging, Otep called off the hunt, and the party returned to camp. There was a silver lining in having so few mouths to feed these days—the success of their hunts hardly mattered any longer.

Van took a share of venison from a supply cart—drawn by volunteer aspirants today, since the oxen were gone—and quickly found Simon.

"Shale isn't with you?" he asked when they sat down in his tent.

"Out on patrol, as far as I know," Simon said through a mouth full of fruit. "You talk to Ghan?"

Van nodded. "Shale was right. The swamp is toxic."

Simon stared at him, waiting for him to elaborate. Van recounted his conversation with the elder, highlighting the fact that he had avoided naming Shale as his source, in case Simon repeated their talk to her later.

Simon wore a troubled look. "That tugs at an old thread a little bit."

"Old thread?" echoed Van.

Simon met his gaze. "Your country's leaders keeping secrets from you."

Van looked at his feet. "Simon, do you think they know? About devils? About what the Emissaries are?"

"Someone must have known, at some point," said Simon. "The founders, maybe. But that was what, a thousand years ago?"

"Nearly," said Van.

"That's a long time." Simon stroked his chin. "Even by my standards. Maybe people lost sight of the truth. Or maybe somebody buried it. I'd be surprised if Ghan or your dad were knowingly furthering the agenda of a devil."

"So, the founders made a deal with devils, and they convinced their followers to worship them as gods?" Van thought aloud. "Why would they do such a thing? Why would anyone, ever?"

Simon shrugged. "Shale had an interesting way of putting it, when you asked her. 'Trifling services that seem as miracles,' I think it was." He rested his palms on his knees. "Here's a classic scenario: you've been diagnosed with an incurable illness. You know you're going to die, but you have unfinished business you'll regret not taking care of. A devil finds you, tells you it can cure you. Claims it can give you your life back with plenty of time to cross off everything on your bucket list—all in exchange for the perfectly reasonable price of your soul. Some people think that's a fair trade, so they agree."

"Can a devil really do that?" said Van. "Heal the dying?"

"A mortal soul is a powerful thing," said Simon. "Devils use that power to extend their own lifespans, like I told you before. But when a devil eats your soul, it also consumes your memories, your knowledge, any ability with magic you might have. So sure, in some cases a devil could probably take part of your soul and use it to cure whatever disease you're dying of."

Van balled his hands into fists. "If anything we are taught of the founders is true, it would have been very uncharacteristic of them to have entered into such a selfish arrangement."

"Maybe they didn't do it out of selfishness," said Simon. "Maybe it was the opposite. Remember what you told me, about how the Emissaries first showed up in your people's history?"

" 'By beseeching the Emissaries and pledging fealty to them, the land was healed and the conflict was ended,' " Van quoted from scripture, his voice low.

"Classic scenario number two: a group of people faced with unavoidable catastrophe make a deal with a devil to prevent it. The scale of their problem is much larger, so the devil needs more than just one soul to hold up their end of the bargain. The ones who strike the deal offer up their own souls first, like a down payment, with the promise of more to come as they rally more people to their cause. That's how you end up with a cult. And at least in Gnosos, they're snuffed out pretty quickly any time they pop up."

"Cults," mused Van, remembering something else Simon had told him. "Like the Idolators of Frenzy."

"Yeah, good memory," said Simon, sounding genuinely impressed. "But if that's what's really happening in Nemia, it would be the largest and longest running cult in history. The term probably wouldn't even apply anymore, since the word itself implies a misguided minority."

"That's what your people intend for us, though, because that's what they believe we are," said Van. "So they'll snuff us out."

Simon grimaced. "That was a bad choice of words," he said. "When dealing with cults, the prescribed approach is usually rehabilitation. A lot of people that get roped up in cults are just... desperate. You get some really bad advice at a really vulnerable time, that doesn't make you a sinner. Those people can be reintegrated into society."

"Even people who have promised their soul to a devil?" said Van quietly.

"Hey, that doesn't apply to you," Simon responded immediately. "We've been over that."

"How many of us does it apply to?"

Simon looked away. "Kid, I don't know everything. I just know we have to talk to the chieftain of your Patron tribe and make them understand the position they're in."

Van didn't push the subject further, but if the best they could hope for was "rehabilitation," he wondered how likely it was that the tribes of Nemia—ancient and proud—would subject themselves to such a thing at the hands of outsiders.

"We found a gazelle on the hunt today," Van inserted, changing the subject without truly changing it. "I'm certain it was killed by a quell."

Simon crossed his arms in thought. "That might make sense. They'd have no reason to kill animals, but they can get confused sometimes, if they wander too far from their handler. Maybe that's good news. It would mean the sorcerers themselves are still farther south."

"Have you spoken to Sol Starfletcher today?"

Simon shook his head. "If he'd spotted any quells, he'd have come looking for me. I don't think we're likely to run into any until we get clear of that swamp. They might not look it, but quells are pretty heavy. If the ground is too soft or muddy, they sink right in. Closest thing they have to a weakness. They'll avoid that kind of terrain if they can."

"I'm not sure if I should be relieved or disappointed," muttered Van.

"Little of both, I guess." Simon put a hand over his mouth to stifle a yawn. "We're about a week from Seat Vaxas, is that right?"

"I think so," said Van. "Though, it depends how long we stay in the community of Hemlock. We arrive there the day after tomorrow."

"There's going to be another game, right?" said Simon. " 'The pilgrimage comes before all else,' and so on?"

"I suppose," said Van.

Truthfully, he hadn't given much thought to the games of the pilgrimage in some time. In the face of everything that had happened, they seemed far less important than he'd once believed.

"Any predictions?" Simon raised his eyebrows. "Should we expect anything like what happened at Seat Ikann?"

Van blew out a long breath. "At this point, Simon, your guess is as good as mine." This time, he was the one who suppressed a yawn.

"We're both tired," said Simon, stretching and standing up. "Shale's out there keeping watch, so you might as well get some sleep if you can."

"Yes," said Van, glancing at his bedroll. "I think I will."

When Simon left, he lay down and closed his eyes, listening to the rumble of distant thunder. The dreams awaited him again, but today, he recognized them as only dreams.

He was roused from a deep sleep by someone calling his name. The voice was feminine. Shale, perhaps, looking to drag him along on another "hunt." He sat up, rubbed his eyes, and pulled the tent's entrance open.

Before him stood Brynda Blackblade, and today, Shale wasn't there to send her away. Van stood up slowly, hoping the movement might conceal the change in his expression.

"It's good to see you well, Van the Scribe," she said, almost shyly. "I know I must be intruding, but I hadn't seen you in some time, and I wanted to offer my condolences."

"Condolences," said Van—a hollow, nervous echo.

"I understand you lost someone close to you," she said.

Her smile was meticulously constructed, sad and gentle. It told him she understood his hurt and shared in it. That she wanted nothing more than to ease his pain, and that only she knew how. A private, personal smile made just for him, with lapidary precision.

"Yes," said Van simply.

Brynda nodded. "She is with the Emissaries now."

Van bit the inside of his cheek hard enough that he tasted blood. It was all he could think to do to stop his face from contorting, but still, Brynda seemed to notice a change in him.

"I'm sorry," she said demurely, stepping quickly back. "It's untoward of me to speak of her like this. I never had the chance to know her."

"Thank you for your sympathies, First Ranger," Van forced out. "It means more than you know."

She hesitated, like she wanted to come closer, but was afraid to.

"I'd prefer it if you called me Brynda," she said. "I haven't felt like a First Ranger for even a minute since leaving home."

Van nodded, saying nothing. She did step closer, then.

"This might also be untoward, but should you ever need someone to talk to, I'd like it if you talked to me. Without Galdur, I mean. Just us."

"I see," said Van.

She searched his face for a moment longer. Then, perhaps finally seeing the depth of his aversion, she gave a shallow bow and excused herself. When she was several paces away, she glanced over her shoulder at him. If Van didn't know better, he would have sworn she was holding back tears.

"I can see I've been a poor friend to you, Van the Scribe. But I think it's important for those of us that are still here to remind each other that we are alive."

Van watched her go, then shuffled back into his tent. No longer trusting sleep, he lay on his back and simply waited for time to pass.

They crossed into the Great Swamp of Vaxas late the next morning. Its boundary was marked by a line of twisted trees, overgrown with vines and lichen. Far in the distance, Van could see the Mountains at Land's End, a sheer wall of igneous rock that stretched from horizon to horizon. Across those mountains lay the lifeless wastes no tribe claimed as their own, where exiles were sent to die.

The ground softened under foot as they entered the swamp, quickly turning into ankle-deep mud—the kind of soft, spongy earth that clung to one's boots and threatened to throw them off balance.

Memnon the Still Pool led the way, threading a path along the winding, narrow trail through the swamp. The footpath was all but invisible, overgrown with sedge grass indistinguishable from the reeds that grew in the bog, and barely wide enough for five to walk abreast. With a single misstep, they might lose the path altogether. The unfortunate and inattentive among them would then sink immediately up to their knees. Van briefly wondered if they would have to abandon the supply carts, but miraculously, none were lost as they trudged onward.

More species of mushroom grew in the Great Swamp than Van had seen in the whole of his life. Some were as tall as trees, and others glowed faintly in the scattered light that penetrated the canopy. Occasionally, things unseen disturbed the bog's surface, sending ripples across the still water. Van suspected that whatever was moving down there was bigger than the common toads he'd seen thus far along the trail.

Many aspirants wrinkled their noses at the persistent odor of organic decomposition, but in Van's opinion, it wasn't so different from how the fishing pond at Seat Dolse might smell on a warm day. Certainly, nothing about it suggested the presence of fatal toxins. He wondered how Shale had known.

Around midday, word was passed down the column that Kekrin the Nose, the Ikanni Pilgrimage Guide, had tripped and fallen into the bog, vanishing completely below the water's surface. Though immediate action was taken to rescue him, he was never seen again. Tribe Ikann, now under the sole leadership of Galdur Goldeye, waived their right to halt the procession and honor his service. For most, the event served only as a sobering reminder that, despite so much recent death, there was no guarantee they were out of danger.

The procession made camp on a section of the trail that was relatively broad and dry. Before retiring to plan the next day's travel with his First Ranger, elder Memnon advised the aspirants not to clean their gear in the swamp's waters, nor to drink from it—not that any of them would have dared.

For his own aspirants, Ghan Mudcatcher demonstrated the technique of tapping tree trunks to obtain water that was safe to drink, and pleasantly sweet. Brynda Blackblade reappeared after a time and invited her Dolser cousins to forage with her, promising to show them which mushrooms were edible, and of those, which tasted best. Otep Acrearms accepted her offer, leaving camp to learn whichever of the Great Swamp's secrets she might share. Van abstained and found other ways to pass the time.

Among other things, the Great Swamp was home to an abundance of insects. Though Van was unsure how many were of the biting or stinging variety, he quickly formulated a plan to keep them at bay. One of the trees close to his tent resembled the eucalyptus common near Seat Dolse, so he gathered wood scrapings from the trunk and burned them in his meal bowl, relying on the smoke as a deterrent.

Shale seemed curious what he was doing, so he showed her his method and explained his reasoning, despite Simon not being on hand to translate. They sat together in his tent, watching the incense burn. Once she grasped its purpose, she made him go with her to collect wood scrapings of her own.

Van talked absently while they worked, mostly of inconsequential things. He had no idea how much she understood, but she watched and listened, nodding or shrugging when it seemed appropriate. He made a mental note to teach her more Nemian when Simon was available, and when they didn't otherwise have more important matters to discuss.

Some of the things he wanted to tell her, he wished she did understand. And some of them, he preferred Simon wasn't listening in on.

Eventually, Van returned to his own tent and bedded down for the evening. Like most nights since the desert, he knew the dreams were waiting for him. Perhaps the dreams were just a part of life now. He would learn to live with them, too.

They resumed travel at first light, reaching the community of Hemlock in a little under four hours. It was a small settlement, but because there were so few aspirants remaining, they could be comfortably accommodated. The headman here was called Owen the Sprawling Roots, a shaman and old acquaintance of elder Memnon. He was aggrieved to learn of the tragic events in the desert. Facing the gathered aspirants, he made a public vow to see them safely from Hemlock to Seat Vaxas. Headman Owen's ability with magic allowed him to commune with animal spirits, a talent elder Memnon and Riverspeaker Gheela would use to convey the procession's circumstances to Seat Mercura, still many leagues away in the Western Forest.

While the delegates conferred in private, the aspirants were invited to explore the community at their leisure. Shale and Simon set off together, presumably to barter for whatever was needed to perform Simon's memory-authentication spell. Having no idea how long that would take, Van accepted the headman's offer and looked around on his own.

Hemlock's dwellings and public houses were built from light wooden frames, propped at an elevation that suggested the area was prone to flooding. Narrow walkways, also built on stilts, connected the various buildings to form a grid—like the web of some giant spider. The walkways converged in places, creating open terraces where people gathered to trade or prepare meals.

Not yet hungry himself, Van sought refuge away from the crowds. After zigzagging along the wooden walkways for a time, he found a quiet corner of Hemlock that was host to a number of small workshops, the nearest of which bore a plaque painted with the image of a quill.

Testing the door and finding it unlocked, Van let himself in. Sure enough, it was a bookshop.

The aged proprietor was slumped, snoring, at a round desk near the center of the shop, so Van tried to move quietly across the creaky old floor. He would be happy with anything to read at all, but he still found himself hoping Vaxal literature was a little more diverse than Ikanni writing. The lowest shelves were reserved for picture books and children's stories, so Van started with those. Picking one with an interesting cover, he sat on the ground with his back to the shelf to page through it.

It was a story about a little girl who could talk to dead people. The spirits of the deceased went out of their way to visit her, and she alone could see them. She could even hold full conversations with these wandering spirits, and they all had useful things they couldn't wait to tell her. In each short chapter, some problem would arise in the girl's community, baffling her young playmates and the adults in her life. She would then receive advice as to how to solve it from a friendly ghost.

Van enjoyed the artwork—except for the fact that the little girl looked like a prepubescent Brynda—but he had no idea what lesson a reader was supposed to take away from the story. The girl always solved the problem single-handedly, took all the credit by claiming the knowledge of the dead as her own, and was showered with praise by the clueless, unquestioning masses.

Also detracting from the narrative were the inconsistencies riddled throughout. All of the spirits that visited the girl seemed to remember her from their own lives, even though it was established they'd died long ago, while the principal character couldn't be older than ten.

Van was scowling at the book's last page when he heard footsteps approach. Looking up, he saw Simon and Shale standing over him. When they made the talking sign, he put a finger to his lips and indicated the sleeping proprietor. They waited at the door while he returned the book to its shelf and crept his way back across the noisy floor.

"I'm sorry," said Van, once they were outside. "If I had known you would need me so soon, I would have stayed someplace easier to find."

"It wasn't exactly hard to figure out where you were," said Simon. "Hanging out alone in a bookstore is pretty on-brand for you."

"Predictable," Shale agreed, her Nemian sounding better every day.

"Should I ask what that is?" Van gestured to a hempen bag floating through the air after Simon.

"We did some shopping," said Simon, not glancing at the bag. "I found everything I need for the spell. And Shale got you a present."

Van looked at Shale, but she didn't seem to notice.

"Nothing too expensive, I hope?" said Van.

Simon shrugged. "She's been collecting pelts for weeks. As for me, as long as I have paper and a brush, I can essentially print money. Cost isn't the issue. The real problem is that a lot of modern medicines haven't been invented here yet. So just like last time, we'll be improvising a little."

Van followed, curious, as they led him to the door of a small house. To his surprise, they walked right in after a quick courtesy knock. Simon addressed the resident curtly—a young mother cradling a sleeping baby—who stood up and hurried outside, leaving the three of them alone in her home.

"Simon?" Van cast him a sidelong glance.

"We came by earlier and told her we wanted to borrow the place for a while," said Simon. "Don't worry, we paid her."

"You explained all this to her without your language spell?" marveled Van.

"*I* explained it," said Shale. As he translated, Simon directed the floating sack to the middle of the room, where it settled on the floor. "I've grasped enough of your language to negotiate a simple transaction."

While Simon emptied the sack and began sorting through its contents, Shale busied herself rearranging the furniture. She dragged a barrel half full of drinking water from one corner and a wooden stool from another, pulling them toward the center of the room next to a table.

"*Sit,*" she told Van, pointing to the stool.

When he sat down, Shale picked up a folded leather case from the pile of goods Simon had dumped on the floor, unfolding it on the table. Inside the case, which was the sort craftsmen used to store tools for precision work, was a pair of scissors, a straight razor, an ivory comb, and a hand mirror.

It was the mirror Shale chose first, holding it for Van so he could see his reflection—which he was startled to discover he barely recognized. His hair was overgrown and matted, and the shadow of stubble on his upper lip and along his jawline had thickened, looking mangy and unclean. His eyes strayed to the razor again. So, this was Shale's present.

"I need two things from you before I get started," said Simon, standing up and stepping over to him with a glass vial in one hand and a stoppered gourd in the other. "Thing number one—a few drops of blood."

"Truly?" said Van.

"Truly," said Simon.

Looking at the vial, Van took a breath. He drew his hunting knife from its sheath, and before he could lose his nerve, ran the blade's edge along his palm. Squeezing his hand into a fist, he held it over the vial while Simon kept the glass still, waiting while several drops of blood dripped into it. Shale watched with childlike fascination, and when Simon withdrew the vial, she took Van's hand to tightly wrap a band of clean linen around it.

"Thing number two?" Van winced as he flexed his bandaged hand.

Simon unstoppered the gourd and handed it to him. "Drink this."

Van took it and sniffed at its contents, his face twisting as the stench of alcohol burned his nostrils.

"Simon, I don't—"

"You just gave your blood to a sorcerer," said Simon. "Are you really going to draw the line here?"

Van sighed, shut his eyes, and put the gourd to his lips. Daring a sip, he found the liquor much stronger than any mead or wine he'd ever sampled at home. The taste was overpowering, and strangely earthy, calling to mind the mushrooms that seemed to grow everywhere in the Great Swamp. Shale put her hand on the gourd and tipped it back, forcing him to swallow a mouthful. He coughed once as he pulled it away, handing it back to Simon with his eyes watering.

"All right," said Simon. "I'll need ten minutes or so. Shale will keep you company while I get everything ready."

With that, he vanished into the house's pantry, leaving Van alone with Shale.

She stepped around the table and unwrapped another parcel, revealing a stiff bristle brush and soapstone—the expensive sort, rendered from lye and animal fat. She wetted the brush in the water barrel she'd dragged over and scrubbed at the soapstone with it, working up a foamy lather.

She hummed while she massaged it onto his face, and as awkward as Van felt, he kept still and didn't protest. He had only ever shaved his face a handful of times, and was scarcely used to performing the task himself. He tensed when Shale picked up the razor, but quickly relaxed when he saw how easily she handled it. Terrifyingly, he sneezed just when she was getting to the tricky part. Seeing his nose wrinkle, she withdrew the razor before she could nick his throat.

He mumbled an apology, and she slapped him softly on the back of his head before returning to her task. Van found it easier to sit still after that if he simply shut his eyes.

When Shale finished with the razor, she patted his cheeks and neck dry with a towel, then set it aside and reached for the scissors. She completed the next step of her restoration effort as swiftly and confidently as she had the first, walking in several slow circles around Van—teasing his hair straight with the comb and performing exploratory operations with the scissors.

Each time she circled him, she paused, bending down to measure his hair's length by twisting the locks together between her thumb and forefinger, comparing the left side to the right. He couldn't help but open his eyes again when he noticed he could feel her breath, caught off guard by the closeness of her face. Too focused on her hands, she didn't react to his staring, if she even noticed at all.

Eventually, she stepped away and propped her hands on her hips with a satisfied smile. Van opened his mouth to say something, but a wave of dizziness swept over him then. Ghostly lights danced at the corners of his vision, and the floor beneath him seemed to shift.

"Looking good, kid," said Simon, reemerging from the pantry. "How are we feeling?"

"Strange," said Van, working his mouth around the word.

"Good," said Simon.

Van watched Simon's wavering image transfer a syrupy liquid from a mixing bowl he was carrying into the water barrel that still stood close by. A pale glow emanated from within the barrel, reflecting on Shale's face as she stared expectantly into the water. The gentle gleam reminded Van of the moonlight playing off the ocean's waves at night.

"Pretty..." mumbled Van. Or perhaps he only thought it. He pursed his lips to keep himself from speaking again until spoken to.

"We're running out of time for the language spell," said Simon. "I'll just talk you through this for now, and we'll go over the results tomorrow."

Van nodded, his head lolling.

"First, we need a baseline. A memory we all know is real that you don't have any particularly strong feelings about. Think back to the first time we talked to Shale together."

Van felt his cheeks warming. A smirk spread across Shale's face as she peered into the barrel, the light within changing, and Simon raised his eyebrows.

"Oh," said Simon. "I didn't... Sorry, that one won't work. Just think about the first time you and I talked, I guess."

Van refocused and tried to calm his breathing. It was just like when they'd spied on Brynda, he realized, except this time, Shale and Simon were peering into his own head. He couldn't see into the barrel for himself, too dizzy to stand up, but he still felt blindsided and terribly self-conscious. In fairness, though, it was more or less what he had expected.

"All right, good," said Simon. "Next, think about the thing that talked to you when you were trapped underground. Anathema, right? You've met it twice. Think about both times, if you can remember it all clearly."

Van did as he was told, feeling that same powerlessness wash over him anew as he recalled the devil's words. *Your role is inevitable, just as I am inevitable.* His friends' expressions grew serious as they watched the glowing barrel.

"Last, one more real memory," said Simon. "Something good this time. And remember, it should be something one of us was there for, so we know it actually happened."

Naturally, Van wanted to think of Lilim, but she was no longer there to attest to the authenticity of the time they'd shared. Instead, he closed his eyes and turned his thoughts to the time he'd spent with Lilim and Shale together. As he recalled exploring the streets of Seat Ikann and their brief, private adventure at the carnival that night, he discovered all over again how precious a memory it was. He cracked an eye open to gauge the expressions of his friends.

Gazing into the light, Simon's grimace had softened. "Yeah, that's the stuff."

Shale watched silently for a little while, too, but then something about Van seemed to gain her attention, and she rushed to his side. She was holding him. That was when he realized he was on the floor, though he had no idea how he'd gotten there. Simon stooped to examine him, pushing his eyelids apart one at a time, as if to check his pupils.

"What they gave me must have been too strong," Van heard a distant voice say. "You'll sleep off the worst of it. Do you think you can manage some water before we get you to bed?"

But it was too late. Van's vision blurred, and his senses deadened. He closed his eyes again and this time found himself drifting into a fitful sleep.

24 A Priori

The dream began the same way it always did. The procession was camped in their thousands, an endless sea of tents blanketing the fields south of Farthest Tree. Van had gone to bed after helping Lilim drink the tonic he'd bought from the matron at the Shade of Two Leaves, and lighting the medicinal incense. Now, Lilim was shaking him awake, asking why he was there in her tent. He sat up with a start and held onto her as tight as he could, as tight as if his own life depended on it...

There, there. It was just a bad dream.

And then he smelled it, so foul it made his eyes water, like spoiled meat thrown on an open flame. He held Lilim at arm's length, searching for her eyes. But she had no eyes. Just empty pits in her skull too painful to look at, as dark as the sun was bright.

Your role is inevitable, just as I am inevitable.

Van gasped, waking up all over again. The softness of the light creeping into the tent told him it was early morning. He'd slept for close to twelve hours—assuming he wasn't still asleep now.

His whole body was sore as if from rigorous exercise when he sat up, and a dull pain hammered behind his eyes. Something moved beside him.

Shale.

She sat up a moment after he did, eyes still misty with sleep, and pressed a hand to his forehead. Apparently satisfied, she crawled to the entrance of the tent and called for Simon.

Van shivered, recalling the last time he'd woken up like this. Next, Ghan Mudcatcher would take him to the battered oxcart to show him the bodies.

"Feeling better?" asked Simon, stepping into the tent.

"Thirsty," Van rasped.

"Figured you would be."

Simon threw him a waterskin. Drinking from it, Van concluded he really was awake, not trapped in another nightmare. The water was molasses-sweet, drawn from the trees of the Great Swamp.

Simon crossed his arms, sighing. "Good news first, or bad news?"

"Good, please," said Van, wiping his mouth with the back of his hand.

"Your memories are real."

Shale, meanwhile, was rummaging for something in the dim light of the tent. Finding the hand mirror, she held it up for Van. Today's Van the Scribe was a marked improvement over the haggard and unkempt one from the day before. The stubble was gone, not a blemish left by the razor, as there might have been had he done the job himself. His dark, naturally coarse hair was still longer than he liked it, trimmed only to a half-inch, but the cut was clean and even.

"Thank you," he said quietly, unable to shake the feeling that he was looking at a stranger.

"*Welcome,*" said Shale, setting the mirror aside and offering a wrapped bundle next.

"That's from both of us," Simon explained as Van accepted the parcel, carefully unwrapping it in his lap.

Inside was a brand new tunic, chestnut brown, and a matching pair of cotton breeches. What arrested his attention, though, was the immaculate bow carved of dark yew wood and the fine leather quiver.

It was stocked with ten arrows fletched with eagle feathers. Five had bodkin heads, suitable for smaller game, and five bore heavier broadhead tips. An archer could tell them apart by touch because of the cut of their fletching.

"This is..." Van fumbled for words. "Thank you. Truly."

He set the bundle beside him and returned his attention to Simon. "And the bad news?"

"The same as the good news—your memories are real," Simon repeated in a dreary tone. "Which means we need to figure out who or what Anathema is."

"A devil, surely," said Van. "It even said as much, that it was one of the Emissaries. What else could it be?"

"I know, I saw for myself. Here's a hot take—maybe don't believe everything it told you," said Simon, "Or *anything* it told you, for that matter."

Van held his gaze. "Simon, I realize it has taken time for me to accept all the things you've told me, but I believe you. About devils. About everything. *I believe you.* Are you now telling me that you were wrong?"

"No," said Simon. "The statues at the temple were definitely depictions of devils. It explains too much about your culture. What I'm saying right now is that Anathema might be something different. Something new."

"All right," Van said slowly. "Tell me your theory, then."

"My best guess at present," said Simon, "is that it's a mortal sorcerer."

"A mortal sorcerer," said Van, disbelieving. "In other words, someone like you."

Simon nodded uncomfortably.

"Someone from your homeland?"

"A Gnosian could probably do all the things you saw," said Simon, choosing his words carefully. "But just like with the storm in the desert, they wouldn't have a reason to. The Gnosian military has an army of constructs, and all the time in the world to do things by the book."

"Then, a Nemian?" Van's stomach twisted. "Why? Why do such a thing, and then claim to be a god?"

"For a sorcerer, it's one of the oldest tricks there is," said Simon. "You show up someplace where the locals have a primitive understanding of magic, scare the shit out of everybody, and then tell them to fall in line or be struck down. Easy way to start a cult."

Van swallowed. The last time they'd spoken of cults had also been in the context of devils.

"The body-snatching angle is admittedly weird," said Simon. "Those kinds of spells exist, at least in theory, but I don't know why anyone would do it. Steal someone's body just to—what, melt it? Turn it to dust? After saying a bunch of pointless creepy stuff to some kid who isn't even in a position to do anything for them?"

Van bristled at being referred to as "some kid who isn't in a position to do anything," but he didn't object, since it was an accurate if slightly offensive appraisal. Shale was making the talking sign at Simon, frustrated at being left out of the conversation, so he took a moment to catch her up.

"I disagree with the elf about the body snatching," she said. "I think it makes perfect sense."

"How so?" said Van.

"People have envied each other's bodies since the beginning of time," she said matter-of-factly. "Clearly, whoever spoke to you has an inferior or otherwise compromised body, so he's shopping for a new one."

"But the bodies it takes just fall apart." Van shuddered, remembering.

"Those were experiments, were they not?" said Shale. "Trials and errors. A prelude to the main event."

Van stared at her. "The main event being…"

Shale produced the hand mirror again, inspecting her reflection with a pleased smile. "Whatever else this Anathema is, I must admit he has an eye for quality."

"Why 'he?' " asked Van, reluctant to dwell on what she was suggesting. "I still don't think it's a person."

"Whatever spoke to you certainly has a man's arrogance," she said dismissively.

"Speculation isn't helpful right now," Simon interjected, speaking for himself this time. "We don't need to know what it is or why it's doing all this. We need to know *how* it's doing it." As always, he had to repeat his statement to each of them.

Van nodded, thinking aloud. "If it could take any body it wanted at any time of its choosing, it would have already taken Shale."

"Exactly," said Simon. "So, what are the rules? Why the kid in the temple at Stonebasin, and why the other one in the desert?"

A contemplative silence fell over the tent as they each considered the question.

"The first child, at your village of Stonebasin," began Shale, "he wasn't a participant in the pilgrimage, was he?"

"No," said Van. "He was too young. Is that significant?"

Shale frowned and crossed her arms. "It somewhat quashes a theory I was developing."

"I'd like to hear it anyway," said Van.

She kicked her legs absently. Van still wasn't sure if that meant she was bored, distracted, or merely irritated with his inability to keep pace.

"If your initial conclusion was correct, and Anathema is a devil, it would make more sense if all the bodies taken thus far belonged to participants," she said.

"Why?" asked Van.

When she spoke again, Simon didn't translate right away. He gave her a look, as you might give someone who'd just said something insensitive or inappropriate in polite company.

"What did she say?" Van prompted.

Simon took a breath. "Because your Journey of Patronage is obviously a contrivance invented by devils for the purpose of harvesting souls."

Van blinked. Simon had suggested something similar once, but this was different. Shale wasn't tip-toeing around the subject. She was throwing it in his face.

"So, the reason Anathema hasn't taken you is because it really can't?" said Van, trying to be useful despite the shock of her bluntness.

"Because I'm not one of you," she said, nodding along. "However, as I said, that theory is imperfect. The child at Stonebasin should have been safe as well, and he wasn't."

"But you *are* an aspirant," said Van. "My father made it so. Would this not place you in jeopardy, too, according to your theory?"

"My theory is—or rather was—that only Nemians on the pilgrimage are prey for devils, though I hadn't figured out the trick yet." Her gaze sharpened. "Devils are clearly the masterminds behind your *Journey of Patronage,* and they clearly want you to die as a matter of course while attempting it. You may have forced me to come along, but that doesn't make me one of you. At least, not in any sense that seems to matter to Anathema. But considering your first encounter with him didn't involve another participant, I've obviously overlooked something. In view of the basic facts, the elf's guess seems more likely. Although..."

"Although?" pressed Van when she trailed off.

She stopped kicking her legs and sat up straight.

"I think your intuition that he is something other than a mere mortal should be taken seriously," she said. "The elf's magic may have let us peruse your memories, but you remain the only one who has stood in Anathema's presence. If he was a devil, I think you would feel it was so. You would simply recognize it—so, for lack of any better advice, I say trust in your intuition."

Van let out a breath. Being encouraged to trust himself for once was enormously refreshing.

"Speculation," grumbled Simon. "Unhelpful. I'll do some brainstorming on my end, and we can talk about this more later. In the meantime, if either of you come up with theories about how Anathema's picking its targets, don't keep them to yourself."

Van nodded, wondering if he should ask Ghan Mudcatcher for his thoughts again. The elder was no shaman, but he knew far more about spellcraft than Van did. But how was he supposed to have that conversation without explaining the truth behind the question? How do you tell a person the gods they've served and prayed to all their life are actually soul-eating monsters?

"Simon, I know you told me not to trust what Anathema said, but I need to know—is there some magic that would allow a person to witness the future? It spoke as though it had seen events yet to come. Was that truly just a boast meant to frighten me?"

Simon tapped his knee, thinking. "In total honesty, I don't know. There are only theories."

"Could you provide an overview of those theories?"

"People spend decades studying this stuff, Van, and even then—"

"Please," Van interrupted. "I know nothing of magic beyond what you've taught me. Just tell me if it's possible."

Simon inhaled deeply. "In the West, religious groups sometimes use words like 'clairvoyant' or 'oracle' to describe people born with supernatural magical abilities. Powers bestowed on them by gods, according to the Church. Well, *imposed* on them might be more accurate. Talking about it like it's a gift, or some noble calling, is a little... never mind. The point is, sometimes these people claim they've been granted visions of the far future or distant past."

"Were you not born with such magical abilities?" said Van. "You once told me such powers were common in your homeland."

"A lot of Gnosians are born latent sorcerers, yes," said Simon. "That's different. People like me don't draw power from anything other than ourselves. For us, it's all logic and force of will. Your shamans are usually called 'druids' in the West, meaning they draw power from things like plants and animals—natural sources of life. But the Church's 'oracles' are tangled up in the occult. They draw power from things outside the terrestrial plane completely."

"Things like devils?" said Van.

"Sure, maybe," said Simon. "But devils can't see the future. A power like that would have to come from something like an actual god. And according to the Church of Solaar, gods only touch the minds of flesh-and-blood mortals."

"How often does that happen?"

"Impossible to say." Simon shook his head. "There must be thousands of people in the world right now trying to convince somebody they've seen the future. Most are garden-variety con artists. Every once in a while, though, someone makes a prediction that comes true."

"So, it's not unheard of," said Van.

"That's what the Church maintains," said Simon. "But from a statistical standpoint, it's only a matter of throwing darts at a board."

Van cocked his head.

"Think of it this way. Powers or no powers, if a thousand people make a thousand predictions about what's going to happen tomorrow, or a week from now, odds are at least one of them will nail it," said Simon.

Van frowned. "In that case, why not use magic to authenticate that person's memories as you did with me? You would know right away if they'd actually had a vision or if they were making it up."

"Two reasons," said Simon. "First, the obvious. There aren't enough sorcerers, let alone the time and resources, to go around sifting through everybody's memories constantly. And even if that wasn't a problem, not everyone would consent to the spell, given how invasive it is."

Van nodded. He trusted Simon, but he would never subject himself to the same procedure at the hands of a stranger.

"Second," said Simon, "the insanity problem."

"Insanity problem?" repeated Van.

"Once in a while, the Church comes forward with someone they think is the real deal, and they ask a sorcerer to go ahead and validate their memories," said Simon. "In nearly a hundred percent of documented cases, the individual in question turns out to be insane. The memories of the insane can't be validated—everything in their head registers simultaneously as real and not real, because their concept of reality doesn't match ours."

"*Nearly* all cases," said Van. "Meaning there are cases in which you've examined the memories of a person claiming to have seen the future, and found them not to be insane or lying."

"Ninety-nine percent are bullshit," said Simon. "The remaining one percent are inconclusive. Most of the time, the visions are related to events that won't happen for hundreds of years, so nobody knows if they mean anything. There's also the possibility that the sorcerer performing the memory audit messed up the spell."

Van sighed. "You're right. That wasn't terribly useful."

"Tried to tell you," said Simon, throwing up his hands.

No one spoke for a moment.

"I, um." Van cleared his throat. "How long was I asleep? I'm sure it was still early when I collapsed, but I feel as though I haven't slept at all."

Simon translated this to Shale, and she immediately perked up. She spoke a few words with an uncharacteristically furtive tone, and Simon rolled his eyes before repeating them to Van.

"Oh my, you don't remember?"

Van blinked. "Don't remember what?"

She looked away. "I'd rather not say in front of the elf."

"Oh, no," stammered Van. "Did I do something? I'm sorry!"

"To be so daring and then simply forget..." she mumbled, as if to herself.

"What did I do!" Van blurted.

"You are very insensitive to the feelings of girls, Van the Scribe."

Van opened his mouth to beg forgiveness, his mind racing over what unspeakable and untoward thing he could have done, but Shale's composure broke before he could get a word out. She doubled over laughing, holding her ribs and blinking away tears.

"Okay," said Simon, sighing as he got stiffly to his feet. "I think we'll call it there. Get something to eat. You skipped dinner, and you've been losing too much weight. Drink plenty of water, too."

Simon departed, leaving Van alone with Shale while she composed herself. Her laughter subsided, and she lay on her side, smiling up at him, her eyes wet with tears.

"Funny boy," she said at length. With that, she stood up and left.

Putting on fresh clothes felt almost healing. Van stuffed the old tunic and trousers he'd worn since the desert—foul smelling and caked with grime—into his rucksack and promptly forgot about them. Then, shouldering his new bow, he went for a walk to clear his head.

His conversations with Simon left him with too much on his mind lately, and talking with Shale was beginning to have other effects on him that made it difficult to sit still. He wasn't ready for those feelings yet. That part of him was still too recently hurt.

As he strolled along the stilted walkways of Hemlock, he noticed the aspirants who'd survived the storm mingling more freely than they had before. Vaxals talking with Mercurans, Ikanni with Vaxals, and even Dolsers sharing conversation with Ikanni. As much as the desert had taken from them, their loss had also brought them together. Today, they were one people, the divisions between them forgotten in the face of something greater. Even the incendiary rumors about Riverspeaker Gheela seemed a thing of the past.

Van found a quiet place from which he could see the trunk of a large willow. He gripped his bow and assumed a square stance, testing the strength of its draw. Nocking one of the bodkin-point arrows, he aimed and made a shot, cleanly sinking the arrow into the willow's bark. He didn't quite hit the tree at dead center, despite his target being only forty yards away and completely stationary. He scowled, frustrated at how out of practice he was already.

"You've replaced your bow."

Van startled at Sol Starfletcher's voice, turning around and bowing awkwardly. The First Ranger offered a smile that seemed slightly forced.

"It is good to see you making time for your marksmanship again."

"My friends gave me…" Van faltered as he looked at the bow in his hand. "They gave me a bit of a talking to, actually."

"I am glad to hear that," said Sol. "I think you needed it, if we are being honest."

Van nodded, trying to return the First Ranger's smile. He found his eyes drawn to the quiver on Sol's back.

"You still have it," he couldn't help saying. "Your arrow of red fletching, the one that broke at Seat Ikann."

"Wood, steel, and feathers," affirmed Sol Starfletcher. "But the spirit of the noble beast within is gone."

"I'm sorry," mumbled Van, unsure whether it was the appropriate response.

"Another such spirit might be entreated and bound to an arrow one day," Sol mused. "Though, most likely, it will be a weapon for another Starfletcher to wield. It took me years to strike an accord with my arrows, and I think three will prove to be my limit."

"Was, um," Van cleared his throat. "Was Riverspeaker Gheela able to send a message ahead to Seat Mercura?"

Sol nodded. "With help from headman Owen."

"I know we haven't captured one yet, but I wonder if we should have mentioned the quells," said Van.

"I considered it," Sol Starfletcher replied. "But headman Owen's magic requires messages be kept short, and the message my Guide sent was too important to abbreviate."

"Kept short? Why?" Van asked, studying him.

"Because, despite a popular belief to the contrary, the horned owl is not a very intelligent bird."

Van furrowed his brow.

"Headman Owen made a pact with an animal spirit to hear my Guide's message," Sol explained. "The owl is on its way to Seat Mercura now, to pass it on. An owl's memory leaves much to be desired, so we try not to ask too much of them."

"An animal spirit," Van muttered, remembering the headman's brief address as he welcomed them to Hemlock. "Like the ones in your arrows?"

"Similar, perhaps," said Sol. "Though, the spirits in these arrows might take offense at being compared to a common owl."

"My apologies," said Van, not certain whether he was apologizing to Sol or to his arrows.

"It might interest you to know that Riverspeaker Gheela's message included a warning to our chieftain—that she suspects Galdur Goldeyes of conspiring to violate the laws of the pilgrimage."

"Truly?" Van lowered his voice, glancing around.

Sol Starfletcher nodded. "I shared my suspicions with her, and she confessed that she has harbored similar misgivings since the... implausible recovery of Ikann's First Ranger. We also agree that Brynda Blackblade is likely involved, though we left that detail out, since we are sending our message only with the help of a Vaxal shaman. Our chieftain is wise. She will likely draw the same conclusion herself."

"Thank you for telling me." Before Van could say anything more, a bell rang in the near distance. "I think that means midday meal is ready. Would you care to join me?"

"Another time, Van the Scribe," said Sol Starfletcher. "Vaxal cuisine does not agree with me. I was actually heading out to explore the environs, and to scout the path from here to Seat Vaxas before we travel tomorrow."

"That sounds prudent, First Ranger," said Van. "Be safe."

"You as well," said Sol Starfletcher, stepping off the wooden walkway and trudging off into the sodden undergrowth.

In pensive silence, Van made his way to the cookfires, where he waited his turn for a bowl of hot stew. As he was looking around for a place to sit while he ate, he spotted Ghan Mudcatcher, who was staring at him intently. Van meandered over to him and took the spot next to the elder.

"You gave me quite a scare just now, Van the Scribe," said Ghan Mudcatcher after a moment, stirring his stew.

Van turned to him, curious. "Scare?"

"I thought some ill fate had befallen my chieftain, and he was visiting me in spirit form."

"Oh," said Van, suddenly self-conscious.

Ghan took an exploratory nibble of stew, but recoiled from his spoon and hissed at it. Still too hot, Van presumed. "You must think your father has lived forever. The same as any son, I suppose. But I was there when our chieftain was born screaming into the world, when I was a young man myself."

Van watched him, unsure what to say.

"You look so like he did at fifteen. Pugnacious and stubborn. Handsome and charismatic. In those days, we didn't call him Farseer. He was Daz the... well, you can ask him yourself once we're home."

Van smiled, but his lip was trembling, and he had to look away. The elder patted his knee.

"You've come far, boy. Your father will be proud. Just a little farther now, and these hardships will be behind us."

Van decided against burdening his childhood teacher with notions of body-snatching devils and evil sorcery. Instead, he spoke of his fondness for his friends, showing the elder the sleek hunting bow they'd given him. For a long while, they reminisced about days gone by, and by the time they remembered their stew, it had gone cold.

25 Seat Vaxas

"So." Simon's voice lilted. "You and *Shale.*"

Seat Vaxas was still two days away, and their march through the Great Swamp grew more challenging by the hour. Van's boots sank into the mud with each step, the effort made worse by the weight of his rucksack.

As usual, Simon's pack bobbed through the air behind him, and Van glanced at it enviously. Somehow, he knew better than to ask if his friend could extend him the same magical charity.

"I don't want to talk about it," said Van.

"Why not?" Simon slogged through the mud beside him. "If you can't talk to your friends about girls, who can you talk to?"

He was clearly offering Van a diversion, and he did appreciate the thought. But for him, the topic of romance was anything but relaxing.

"I made a serious error in judgment by allowing myself to develop feelings for Brynda Blackblade," he said, eyes on the treacherous ground ahead of him. "There is too much at stake to become distracted with such things again."

"Come on. Don't let what happened with her leave you jaded," said Simon. "You're too young to pull off that look, and you know it isn't fair to compare Shale to Brynda."

Van glanced at him warily. "You warned me yourself that dusken are pathological liars. Naturally cruel and manipulative, remember?"

"And you convinced me I should form my own opinions," said Simon. "And I have. Shale is… well, out of your league, for starters. But if she's interested, why not?"

Van gave no reply.

"Fine, fine. I'll drop it. For now. I've been meaning to ask, though, did you notice anything off about her while we were at Hemlock?"

Van's brow furrowed. "What do you mean by 'off?' "

"Not sure yet," said Simon. "The way people treated her there made me wonder if they'd seen dusken before."

"I didn't notice," said Van, feeling disappointed in himself as he admitted it.

Simon's expression remained serious. "And it was Shale who noticed the swamp was poisonous. Something about it reminding her of home, right?"

"I wish I could simply ask her," said Van.

Neither of them had seen Shale since the day before. She was keeping her own company again, which she still did from time to time without explanation or excuse.

"Me too," said Simon. "I have a feeling she'd tell you things she wouldn't tell me."

Van bobbed his head thoughtfully, wondering if it was true.

"You might be able to score some more over-the-clothes action, too, if you play your cards right."

Van scowled at him.

"Sorry," said Simon, raising his hands in surrender. "You're right, I promised. Seriously, though, how are you the only prude in this country?"

They continued their march in silence after that. Van didn't see Shale until the following evening when he found her with Simon, in the middle of their bizarre card game.

Apparently, the game had evolved since the last time he'd watched, countless new rules having been introduced by both players over the course of the pilgrimage. In its current state, it no longer resembled any game Van knew.

Simon had been sparing with his language spell since they left the desert, saving it for emergencies whenever possible. So, Van watched them play without any one of them able to understand the others.

Shale was quick to maneuver coiled serpent onto her pile of cards, and before Simon could establish a rule that stopped her, she threw paired antlers down on top of it and held her arms up victoriously.

"Double antlers on mean snake!" she shouted, giggling like a lunatic. *"I win!"*

Van offered polite applause, and Shale stood up to take a bow while Simon gathered up the cards, grumbling under his breath.

The day before reaching the heart of the swamp, Van also found time to talk to Otep Acrearms. He spotted the First Ranger sitting alone in camp, looking despondent during the afternoon hours when Van assumed he should be out foraging with the Vaxals. Surprised, he approached and sat next to him.

"Otep Acrearms," he said searchingly. "How's it going?"

Otep stared at him, confused. Van quickly realized he'd used a Simon-ism and tried again.

"Are you not joining the Vaxal hunting party today?"

Otep sighed. "My appetite for Brynda Blackblade's company has soured somewhat."

Van leaned toward him. "What happened?"

"Something she said…" mumbled Otep distractedly. "We are to test ourselves in another of the pilgrimage's games when we reach Seat Vaxas, as I'm sure you're aware, and it has been weighing on my mind. I asked if she had any hints as to the nature of her chieftain's challenge, telling her that I was in a mood to earn another victory for tribe Dolse. Mere banter, of course, but she seemed to take it humorlessly."

"What did she say?" said Van.

"She said only, 'the game of Atariel the Everliving cannot be won.' "

Van furrowed his brow, and Otep shrugged.

"It left me unsettled," said Otep. "Perhaps I am reading too far into things. Regardless, I decided to spend the day in camp rather than with her."

"I can understand that," said Van. "I also have… very little appetite for her company."

Otep cast him a glance. "That surprises me to hear."

"Why?" asked Van, startled.

"I have seen you coming and going from the campsite of our Vaxal cousins," said Otep. "Or rather, I used to. Early on in our journey, during our first hunts with her, you seemed to hold a high opinion of Brynda Blackblade. I wondered what had changed, but you did not appear to want my counsel. So out of respect, I have tried to let you keep your own."

Van was lost for words. It did feel like it had been a long time since he'd had an earnest conversation with his friend, but it wasn't as though he was avoiding him. Not consciously, at least. Thinking about it, Van decided to tell Otep the truth —or what little of it wouldn't terrify him.

"I… think I may have been in love with her, actually. She was so fascinating and mysterious at first. But after the desert, everything else began to seem insignificant. I distanced myself from everyone, Brynda Blackblade included." Van locked eyes with Otep. "I'm sorry if I've treated you coldly in recent days, Otep Acrearms. I am always grateful for your counsel."

"If anything, I should be the one apologizing, Van the Scribe," said Otep. "That you've chosen the company of the foreigner and the dark girl over my own tells me I've been a poor friend."

Van blinked, surprised again. While he had made no effort to keep his time spent with them a secret, he didn't think anyone was paying much attention. Before he could mount a defense of Shale and Simon, Otep spoke on.

"I am deeply sorry for what happened to Lilim the Brave." His voice wavered. "I am sorry I was not there for her."

Van lowered his gaze. It was a hard thing to hear from Otep, the person who'd warned Van not to get involved with her. Who, before they'd even left Seat Dolse, had casually predicted she would be among the first to die. And who had refused Van when he'd begged him to help look after her—to give her better odds, however slight, that she might cheat her fate and live.

Even now, that memory was as clear in his mind as if it had happened yesterday. And while he could choose to tell Otep how angry he still was—how angry he would be for the rest of his life—those words would come from a place of bitterness. Van found no bitterness in himself for Otep

Acrearms. Rather than driving them apart, he chose words he hoped might bring them closer together, though they came with difficulty.

"She was so full of love," was all he could manage.

"As were you for her," said Otep. "I see only now how much you needed her."

Van had missed Otep's friendship, unencumbered by titles and accolades. It was good to be reminded that connection still existed. But he knew tears were coming, and he sensed his hurt was still something that needed to be felt alone.

He thanked Otep for his company and wished him luck in the next game, not knowing if they would have a chance to talk again before then. With a bow, he bid his friend goodbye and retreated to the solitude of his tent.

Was that how it had really been between Van the Scribe and Lilim the Brave? Was he the one who'd needed her, and not the other way around? Lifting her up had been his source of direction, a goal that was visibly, measurably meaningful. Knowing he mattered to Lilim was how he knew he mattered at all, and now that she was gone, the feeling had vanished with her.

In what way did he matter to Shale and Simon? They, who battled devils and matched wits with gods? Van lay awake that night feeling small and lost—lonelier, he thought, than he had ever been.

At the heart of the Great Swamp, there was a lake. Its still waters were black as pitch, dotted with lily pads where dragonflies or speckled dart frogs stopped to rest. Few among the aspirants had ever seen a body of water so vast, and even Van might have mistaken it for the sea if he didn't know where he stood.

Walkways of mossy stone stretched across the dark expanse, an architectural feat reminiscent of Hemlock, but on a far grander scale. The paths' intersections formed wide plazas, where ziggurats jutted toward the gray sky. The tallest among them stood directly ahead—the chieftain's palace—nestled in the shadow of the Mountains at Land's End.

Drowning out all other sound was the rush of water in the distance, carrying from the mist-shrouded falls that flanked the palace on either side.

The Seat's denizens watched the procession march up the centermost path, but unlike the residents at Seat Ikann, they didn't cheer, nor did they chant or throw flowers in celebration. They merely observed them in their silent masses, like witnesses at a sentencing.

When the surviving aspirants reached the first plaza and began to spread out, Van saw the throne of Atariel the Everliving. A tall-backed chair of knotted wood with white flowers blooming along the twisted branches near the top. The old woman who sat there looked more like some aspirant's misplaced grandmother than a chieftain of Nemia. A knowing smile graced her weathered face, half-hidden behind a shock of white hair.

Her expression held no warmth. It was the smile of someone having a private laugh at another's expense. Twenty Vaxal rangers waited in formation behind her, all dressed in ceremonial masks and carrying spears. They fanned out to encircle the travel-weary visitors.

Memnon the Still Pool knelt, prompting the aspirants of Vaxas to do likewise. The tribes of Dolse, Ikann, and Mercura then knelt in turn before the chieftain's throne, until the Seat's rangers and Brynda Blackblade were the only figures left standing.

Brynda walked alone through the crowd of lowered heads, drawing her obsidian dagger as she strode to the woman on the throne. Van glanced up, sensing the wrongness of the moment, and others began to do likewise. The First Ranger's dagger stretched and twisted to become something new—a scythe—and at a gesture from her chieftain, the old woman obediently vacated the throne.

Atariel the Everliving sat and faced the aspirants of Nemia then, black scythe in hand, watching them with cold indifference. Waiting for them to understand.

"What is the meaning of this?" demanded Riverspeaker Gheela, flying to her feet.

"Don't be facetious, Mercuran," said the chieftain of Vaxas. "My *meaning* should be clear enough."

Still kneeling, Simon activated his spell and began quietly translating to Shale. Her hand was on the hilt of her dagger, and she looked coiled, ready to spring.

"You have walked among us falsely," Riverspeaker Gheela hissed, pointing her staff. "This is an unforgivable violation of our laws, and a flagrant act of defamation against your own people. You will stand before your Patron to face judgment."

"I will indeed stand before Scaela," said Atariel. "But at a time and place of my choosing. As to the judgment of the Patron, I'll face that as well." She narrowed her eyes. "Though I have my own predictions as to who will hold that title when the time comes to decide my fate."

Van looked around in a panic. Close by, Otep Acrearms stared back at Atariel the Everliving, face set and countenance grim. None aside from Gheela had yet stood, keenly aware they were surrounded.

Who else knew? Elder Memnon, certainly. What about Galdur Goldeye? Van found the Ikanni First Ranger's face in the crowd, marking the smug grin that stretched across it. Of course he'd known. Riverspeaker Gheela voiced Van's next thought for him.

"Who else is complicit?" she snapped. "Were the aspirants of your tribe aware of this farce?"

"Obviously not," said Atariel, crossing her legs and leaning on her scythe. "They are as innocent and oblivious as the rest of you."

"They will be permitted to continue on to Seat Mercura, then," Gheela declared.

"To be used against me as hostages?" said Atariel. "No, I think not."

Gheela's ursine nostrils flared. "You will submit to the authority of—!"

"I submit to *nothing!*" roared Atariel, her voice sending ripples across the dark water of the lake. Riverspeaker Gheela flinched and stumbled back, nearly dropping her staff.

Finally, Sol Starfletcher stood and rushed to her side, bow drawn and blue-feathered arrow nocked. As one, the veteran rangers of Seat Vaxas leveled their spears at him.

"Stand down, boy," said Atariel, staying her rangers with a raised hand. "I could kill you with a word. Even if you bested me now, who would then save you from the poison you've been breathing for days? You would die choking before you reached your Seat to tattle on me. Ask your Guide. She'll tell you it's true."

All eyes looked to Gheela, whose bravado faltered. Slowly, Sol Starfletcher lowered his bow.

"*I* am the only authority here," continued the chieftain, standing from her throne. Her scythe rippled in her hand, like a liquid surface disturbed by a falling stone. "I declare Scaela the Listener an enemy of Nemia, and until she is removed, tribe Vaxas no longer recognizes Mercura's Patronage. Rangers, see our guests to their lodgings, and make sure they are fed."

She turned on her heel and marched toward the large ziggurat that towered between the waterfalls, its cascading steps standing silent vigil in the shadow of the mountains. Van peered over his shoulder at her retreating figure as he and the other aspirants were shepherded from the plaza at spearpoint, hating her, and hating himself for failing to recognize her for what she was.

He didn't realize he was clenching his fists until Shale took his hand. Her touch steadied him, leading his mind away from the abyss of hopelessness and back toward reason. But it did nothing for the hate.

"Simon," Van whispered. "Ask Shale if she still thinks she could do it."

It took Simon a moment to understand, but once he did, he looked at Van like he was a dangerous and unpredictable stranger.

"No, kid. We can't be the ones to start that ugliness. There are bigger things at play here."

When they reached another junction, they were separated from the aspirants of Vaxas. Those that remained were led to one of the smaller nearby ziggurats, whose entrances were heavily guarded. The chambers in the upper reaches of the pyramid structure weren't large enough to accommodate them all, so they were further divided into several smaller rooms.

Van stuck close to Shale and Simon to make sure they were kept together. Otep and Ghan Mudcatcher were also among their group, along with about half of the remaining Dolsers.

Four Vaxal rangers assumed positions at the sole entrance, two inside the room and two just beyond the threshold, but otherwise, the Seat's "guests" were left to their own devices.

Almost at once, Otep Acrearms stormed up to the guards, towering over them as he demanded to be allowed to see the other aspirants of his tribe. Surprisingly, they allowed it without challenge. None from their group had even had their weapons confiscated, Van observed, though the guards insisted Otep be escorted.

"The chieftain wishes it to be understood that you are not prisoners," explained the masked Vaxal as Otep loomed over him. "She asks only that you refrain from venturing outside for the time being."

"Then we are prisoners indeed," Otep summarized, but he questioned them no further. Escape from captivity was a secondary priority, Van realized. For Otep, making sure the aspirants of his tribe were safe and accounted for came first.

Van glanced around, examining their confines. To the left stood two rows of bunks, blankets folded on each modest bed. To the right, a long table set with food. Most of the aspirants flocked to Ghan Mudcatcher moments after Otep left, seeking solace in the elder's leadership. Ghan could do little to mollify them, but he confirmed that the chieftain's warning about the swamp's poisonous vapors was no bluff. He encouraged everyone to eat and drink, trusting that their hosts would still provide the medicine that would save their lives, despite what other villainy they had planned.

Simon had been whispering with Shale since they were herded into the ziggurat. Van watched and waited for them to finish, hoping he would have enough time left to tell Van what they were planning.

Finally, Simon turned to Van. "I was asking if she could use her trick to sneak past the guards and have a look around for us," Simon explained. "She said it wouldn't work. Didn't want to tell me why."

"That's discouraging," said Van, releasing a long breath. "I would have thought turning invisible would solve some part of this problem."

"I don't think Shale turns invisible," mused Simon, rotating in place as he evaluated the room floor to ceiling.

Van frowned. "What are you—?"

"Go put our bags on the beds near that window," Simon interrupted, eyes fixed on a narrow opening situated high along the wall. "Claim three next to each other. I know there's supposed to be medicine in the food, but don't eat anything until I look at it."

Van sighed and nodded. Others were already claiming bunks for themselves, so he hurried to move their rucksacks to the ones Simon had indicated. Because the bags were too heavy to carry all at once, he made three trips.

Once he'd delivered the last of their bags, he scrutinized the window. It looked big enough to squeeze through, and there were no bars. But how to reach it? Theoretically, Otep Acrearms could simply lift one of them up when the guards weren't looking. And then what? It would be a long drop on the other side, though perhaps Simon could ease the fall with magic.

"Is the food safe?" asked Van when he returned from his chore.

Shale ignored him, picking at a morsel of meat stuck between her teeth. Simon's mouth was full, and his spell seemed to have lapsed. So, by way of answering, he showed Van his fist and hooked his thumb up toward the ceiling. Van distantly remembered the gesture meant "all's well," or something to that effect. He stepped around Simon with his meal bowl in hand.

Van's eyes fell on a greasy platter that had been piled with kebabs moments ago, and he scowled at Shale. She shrugged and licked her lips. Shaking his head, Van helped himself instead to some sort of mushroom porridge.

By now, many of the Dolsers were resigned to their circumstances, huddled anxiously on their bunks with their food while they waited for the First Ranger to return. Unsure what else to do, Van did the same.

Otep Acrearms strode back into the room not long after Van finished his porridge. The aspirants crowded around him, eager for news—and to hear his plan, if he had one.

Otep drew a deep breath. "I have found where Sol Starfletcher and the Mercurans are being held. I was allowed to come and go freely, as any of us are, at any time—so long as we remain inside the ziggurat."

Because the Vaxals weren't overtly mistreating them, the First Rangers of Dolse and Mercura had agreed not to attempt escape until they understood more fully what their captors had in store for them. This was the heart of Seat Vaxas, after all, and they were greatly outnumbered. As much as he hated it, Van saw reason in their restraint. Even working together, it was unlikely that Sol and Otep could guarantee every aspirant's safety through a show of force.

Van didn't bother trying to convey the decision to Simon. Otep's resignation, and the fallen expressions of those looking to him for guidance, surely told all. Simon sighed, sitting cross legged on his bunk while he dealt a game of cards for himself and Shale, who moved to sit across from him without further invitation.

Van watched them play for a time, but he was too restless to sit still for long. Eventually, he decided to test the limits of his supposed freedom. When he stood and started for the door, Shale abandoned her game and jumped up to join him. Van glared at Simon, wondering if this was another of his ideas, but the sorcerer was already reclined on his mattress, his face covered with his hat.

Shale still wore her dagger, but Van left his knife and bow behind—in part to communicate to her that he wasn't looking for a fight, but also because he didn't think being armed would make a difference.

Van glanced at the guards as he left the chamber, wondering if he would be stopped or followed. He wasn't, though more Vaxal rangers stood guard in the corridor that cut through the ziggurat's upper reaches. Wherever they went, he and Shale were watched. It was the structure's cavernous lower reaches Van intended to investigate—hoping to ease his nerves through activity, mainly, but also because what he'd glimpsed down there had left him legitimately curious.

Visible over the balcony-like parapet of the outer corridor was a *village*—farther down than where they were led in, which meant beneath the surface of the lake itself. A mammoth cave, accessible by stone stairways that wound along the wall of the ziggurat, lay hidden down here. Stepping off the stairs and into the surreal landscape, Van saw all the basic fixtures he would expect of any community throughout the Eastern Plains. Homes, workshops, gathering places— even gardens and trees.

Van craned his head back and glimpsed dim natural light. The highest point of the ziggurat above them was left open to the sky, admitting fresh water to the subterranean village with every rainfall and permitting enough daylight that select plant species could grow.

With Shale beside him, Van walked the streets of the underground community almost in a trance. Residents of the Seat lived and worked here. Rangers patrolled among them, always watching—but aside from the constant surveillance, Van and Shale were not disturbed.

When Van tired of walking, he found an old stone bench and slumped on it. He watched an elderly Vaxal in threadbare overalls tend his garden while a pair of toddlers chased each other around his tiny cottage.

Considering how many ziggurats Van had seen spread across the lake, Van supposed Seat Vaxas was as expansive and populous as Seat Ikann—or it had been at one time. Hundreds of years ago, there might not have been a lake at all. The surface walkways could just be the tops of sunken buildings. The Seat would have been extraordinary in ancient times, with its pyramids of sparkling stone towering over bustling street markets, before whatever happened here that transformed the land into a twisted morass.

"I shouldn't have suggested trying to kill her," Van said to Shale, who sat quietly beside him. "My anger got the better of me. I'm sorry. I know you've spoken offhandedly about killing in the past. Advocated for it, even. But I'm starting to think you've never killed anybody, either, and I would never want you to do such a thing for my sake."

Shale was kicking her feet, rocking back and forth on the bench. It was hard to tell how much she understood, but he knew she learned quickly, and she often surprised him.

"Simon says you don't turn invisible," he went on. "But I'm sure I saw you do it. Or rather, I *didn't* see you, which I imagine was the point. I don't suppose you'd tell me what he meant?"

She glanced in his direction, probably recognizing his tone as inquiry, but she remained silent. The top button of her collar had come undone, and Van tried not to stare.

"He also asked me if I thought you'd been acting strangely since we came to the Great Swamp. Something about the people here treating you differently, like they had seen dusken before." He turned to face her. "I think he's worried about you, not that he would ever say so."

No response.

Van sighed. "I worry about you too, sometimes. I don't think you'd hide anything from us—at least, not anything crucial for us to know. You're entitled to your privacy, if it's a personal matter. I just mean that... I worry you get lonely. Simon also seems to think that, um..."

Van coughed into his hand, feeling supremely awkward.

"That you might be interested in me. Those were his words, I believe. He may have just been making fun of me, now that I think about it. He does that sometimes. You both do. And I don't mind, really. I know you care, and of course I trust you. I suppose what I'm saying is that it's hard to imagine what he suggested was true. After all, you could find someone so much more worthy for, um. That."

Shale stopped swinging her legs and watched him.

"If it was true, I would be flattered, but I don't think I could... I mean, anyone would be honored, obviously, to... to have you consider them for—"

"*Honest,*" she said, pointing at him. "*Loyal. Patient. Humble.*"

He blinked, suddenly embarrassed. "Thank you."

She held his gaze for a moment, then roughly pushed him off the bench.

"Too humble!" she said, standing to lean over him, her hands on her hips. The pose made the situation with the undone button slightly precarious. *"Sometimes brave better. Brave like she was."*

Van's rear end hurt where it had hit the cobbled stone, but it was a dim and distant feeling compared to how her words struck him. *Brave like she was.* It was like a splash of freezing water on a hot day. As the moment stretched on, all he could think to do was smile. Shale sighed and offered him a hand, helping him to his feet before spinning around and strolling off the way they'd come, humming quietly with her arms tucked behind her back.

Van followed her back to the upper reaches, still smiling to himself, thinking back on something she had said to him once —about how easy it could be to fall in love.

When they returned to their room, they found Simon sound asleep. Otep and Ghan were conferring privately in a far corner, but Van could tell at a glance nothing new had been decided.

He sat down on his bunk, too anxious to sleep at this early hour. Shale likewise returned to her own bed, just to the right of Van's. Along the way, she stealthily plucked Simon's deck of cards from his rucksack.

Van watched as she sat down and began thumbing through the cards, pausing to crimp a corner whenever she encountered paired antlers or coiled serpent.

"I thought you said you didn't cheat," said Van, a little disappointed.

"Elf started it," she replied, not looking up.

Van cleared his throat. "Teach me to play?"

Shale narrowed her eyes at him, seemingly thinking it over. At length, she jumped off her bunk and sat down across from Van on his, handing him the deck.

"Deal."

"How many?" he asked.

She stared at him, raising an eyebrow in question.

"How many cards? What number for each player?"

"Seven," she said.

Van dealt the cards in the fashion he was used to from his father's favorite game, Hunter's Quarry. When both players had seven, Shale took the deck and separated it into three stacks, placing these between them.

"Who goes first?" asked Van.

Shale answered by placing a card face up in front of her. Sleeping elephant. Van did the same, playing one of his own sleeping elephants to start his pile.

On Shale's turn, she drew a card from the middle packet and played another. Oaken mask. Assuming he should draw as well, Van experimentally took a card from the packet on the right, noticing its corner was creased. Predictably, it was one of the deck's three coiled serpents.

Van began placing the newly drawn card on his pile, because his opening hand included paired antlers, which he remembered was important. But Shale raised a hand in protest.

"Not allowed," she said, pointing at his coiled serpent.

He paused. "Why not?"

She gestured to the last card she'd played. *"Attack mode."*

The game went poorly for Van after that. Shale extorted various pre-existing rules he knew nothing about, emptying her hand quickly, and any time he began to catch up, she proposed new rules to hamper him.

She laughed when she beat him, and hearing her laugh curbed Van's worries. They played a few more rounds, and now that Van understood his feelings a little better, he forgave himself for stealing another glance at Shale's undone button while she was focused on her cards. The sunlight streaming through the window above them eventually dimmed. Having given up on the prospect of escape for the day, they reached an unspoken agreement that they should try to sleep, and turned in.

Hours later, Van awoke in the dead of night, his eyes gradually adjusting to the darkness. For the first time in so long, it wasn't a nightmare that had woken him, but a simple, everyday need. He quietly pulled his boots on and stood up.

Shale sat up so quickly, Van wondered if she had been asleep at all. She looked prepared to follow him again.

"No," he whispered, holding up his hands. "I, um. I'm just going to find someplace to relieve myself. You don't have to come."

She narrowed her eyes at him.

He cleared his throat. "I need to make water."

Still nothing.

"Privy," he tried.

At that, understanding finally crossed her face. She yawned, lay back down, and rolled over.

Van tiptoed to the door, trying not to wake the other aspirants, sleeping fretfully in their prison that was not a prison. When he explained himself to the rangers on guard, one of the Vaxals nodded and escorted him to the facilities.

After conducting his business and emerging from the privy, he was startled to see three more rangers waiting for him with the first.

"You are Van the Scribe," said one of them.

"I am." Van swallowed nervously.

"You will come with us."

Van's pulse quickened. He glanced at their spears, suddenly wishing he hadn't told Shale to stay behind.

The rangers led him away from the ziggurat, back across the stone walkways that spanned the lake. When they reached the first plaza, they told him only to wait before leaving him alone. And so, with an uncomfortable sense of exposure, he did.

The grim shadows of the ziggurats made him feel small and out of place, so he turned his back on them, gazing out over the water instead. The surface of the lake was as still as a mirror, reflecting the glow of fireflies drifting in the gloom, like embers cast from a bonfire.

"Still so beautiful, even after all this time."

Van almost jumped into the water. When he turned to face her, he saw that she had dispensed with her ranger's getup. Tonight, Atariel the Everliving wore a chaste emerald dress with a silver torc around her neck—attire more befitting the chieftain of Vaxas—yet she still looked as young and attractive as the day he first laid eyes on her.

Van knew it could only be a glamor, some mendacious twist of spellwork. Her black scythe, too, was nowhere to be seen, but that didn't mean she didn't have it with her, in some inconspicuous form.

"What do you want?" he said, letting a swell of anger mask the tremble in his voice.

"Only to talk with you." She glided forward to stand next to him by the water.

"I don't want anything to do with you," he spat—and she *winced,* as if she was the one afraid of him.

"I know," she said quietly. "You won't see me again, if it's any consolation. I took the wrong approach with you, and I've realized it far too late. I should have told you the truth from the start."

"That you're a liar and a traitor, you mean?"

"Yes," she admitted, closing her eyes and laughing nervously. "And things much worse besides."

She crossed her arms, holding herself as silence descended on them.

"What do you want?" Van repeated, unclenching his fists.

She drew a stabilizing breath. "A favor."

"Why would I ever do anything for you?" he demanded.

"May I finish?"

Van glared at her and waited.

"It is customary that First Rangers on the pilgrimage present gifts to the chieftains of Nemia as they travel the land. Seeing as I won't be going with you to Seat Mercura, I need you to pass my gift along to Scaela the Listener."

"Why not have your minion Galdur do it?" said Van.

"Because I don't trust him," she said.

"Clearly you do," Van said bitterly. "You've gone to great lengths to position him to win Patronage for tribe Ikann, undermining our laws at every opportunity. I've seen the Nighthawk. I know you've given it to him. I'm going to expose him and stop you."

She let her arms fall to her sides. "I trust Galdur Goldeye to do only what is in his own best interests. My gift to Mercura's chieftain cannot be entrusted to a man as selfish and arrogant as he."

She produced a leather pouch no bigger than Van's coin purse, and he eyed it suspiciously.

"What is it?"

"A weapon," she said simply.

"A *weapon*," Van scoffed. "I could show it to Simon. He would tell me what it is, if you won't."

"You could," she said. "Your Gnosian friend would tell you it's dangerous and urge you to let him destroy it."

Van bristled. When had she learned that word? Did Simon tell her the name of his homeland the one time he'd spoken to her?

"You would give me a dangerous weapon, to be used against the chieftain of Mercura," said Van, shaking his head incredulously. "This can only be another joke at my expense. Did you really imagine I would agree to this?"

"A dangerous weapon, yes," she said, her eyes downcast. "But not to be used against Scaela. I'll deal with her as I've dealt with other adversaries. No, this weapon will rescue us from a far greater threat."

"What threat?" asked Van.

Finally, she met his eyes. "The one that calls itself Anathema."

26 Motive and Intent

Van's eyes bulged. "You know about…?"

"For a long time, yes," said Atariel the Everliving. "And I'll tell you what I can, if it isn't too late for there to be honesty between us."

"What is Anathema?" Van blurted.

"A cosmic entity of great power," she said, "currently at war with the old lords of the hell planes, and about to win. Beyond that, all I know is that it means us harm, and that it seeks to secure passage for itself here by obtaining a mortal vessel."

"It's not a—?" he slammed his mouth shut before he could say it.

"What, a devil?" she said. "If it is, it would be the most powerful such creature in existence. That it needs a mortal body to inhabit in order to cross between planes suggests otherwise, though. If anyone has actually glimpsed its true nature and lived, it's you."

Van's heart was hammering in his chest, but he was more terrified than ever that it was somehow still a trick. For all he knew, she could simply be reading his mind—he'd learned from Simon that such outrageous things were possible. How could he be sure?

He thought of Shale, holding her as clear in his mind as he could.

Whatever else this Anathema is, I must admit he has an eye for quality.

Van spoke cautiously. "What do you mean, mortal vessel?"

"I wasn't shown that part," said Atariel. "Only that it would be someone close to you, and that you alone could convince them to stand against Anathema. You may not have even met them yet. Whoever they are, they will be of a singularly unique lineage if they are to make a viable host for such an entity."

"You speak as though you've seen the future," he said.

"A prophecy," she said, holding his gaze. "Passed down by the chieftains of Vaxas since the founding of the tribes. You are named in it, Van the Scribe."

Van's stomach dropped. *Your role is inevitable.*

"Then you've already failed. Anathema's seen it, too. It already knows everything."

"Not everything." She indicated the leather pouch. "Not about this."

"Tell me what it is, then," said Van.

"I can't," she said flatly.

Van scoffed, letting his bitterness show.

"Anathema devours conscious thought," she went on. "There isn't time to train you to resist that kind of psychic intrusion. To tell you now would jeopardize all, so you can't know until the last moment. When the time comes, it should require no explanation."

Van narrowed his eyes at her. "You want me to secretly carry a dangerous weapon into the presence of Mercura's chieftain, the rightful Patron of Nemia and your stated enemy, and I can't know what it is or even speak of it to my friends?"

"That is what I am asking of you, yes."

"Then tell me the truth," he said, exasperated. "Why do you oppose Scaela the Listener? Why go to such lengths to steal Patronage from the Mercurans?"

"Because she is an enemy of our people," answered Atariel. "The oldest enemy. You'll see for yourself when you get there. But you have my word that you won't need to dirty your hands in that conflict. The threat of Scaela is mine to face. Yours is Anathema. Only if we both succeed will there be a future for Nemia."

"And Gnosos?" he demanded.

She cocked her head. "What of Gnosos?"

Did she really not know? Was she not trespassing in his mind after all but actually, finally telling the truth? Van faltered.

"I don't even know what you look like," he said. "You certainly can't look like *that,* if even the Vaxals didn't recognize you."

Of all her lies, he wondered at himself for choosing that one to be the most hurt by.

"Keenly observed," she said, smiling weakly. "But if this is to be our last goodbye, I wanted you to remember me as you met me."

"I never met the real you," Van muttered. "If I remember you at all, it will be as a villain and an impostor."

"About almost everything that has happened between us, you would be right to think that," she said, offering the pouch. "Just not about this."

Van reached out hesitantly, but before he took it he asked her one last question.

"Why me?"

She seemed to consider it.

"Because you are the Snail. And you have a story to finish."

The chieftain permitted the aspirants of Nemia to leave Seat Vaxas the following morning. Now representing only three tribes, the procession numbered just two hundred and thirty-seven. During the day's march, however, one of them stepped off the path and vanished into the bog. So when they made camp on the evening that marked the fifty-eighth day of their pilgrimage, they numbered two hundred and thirty-six.

The mud of the Great Swamp finally gave way to solid ground, and they traveled southwest toward the Nym, the mighty river that divided the Eastern Plains from the Western Forest. The Journey of Patronage dictated that they cross at the Bridge of the Emissaries, still many leagues to the south. The river could be crossed by ferry, if the group were willing to trade ceremony for haste, but the size of the procession—even in its diminished state—made doing so impractical. And the seasonal rains made it dangerous besides.

Four days after Atariel the Everliving's treachery was revealed, the most perilous part of their journey was behind them. No more desert curses. No more hungry bogs. In the Western Forest, they wouldn't even have mourns or hornbeasts to contend with. The aspirants would be safe in the lands of Mercura, and thanks to the message Riverspeaker Gheela had sent ahead from Hemlock, the Patron tribe's rangers would be ready and waiting to receive them. As Van marched alongside the other members of his tribe, the chatter he overheard echoed a singular conviction: the Patron's justice would be brought swiftly against the duplicitous chieftain of Vaxas, and the divisions she'd sown would begin to heal.

Before turning south toward the Bridge of the Emissaries, Riverspeaker Gheela announced they would make a detour to the nearby hub of agriculture known as Homestead. Not a planned stop, but necessary, given that Homestead's annual yield accounted for the better part of all produce in the region. Control of those crops would be strategically vital in any open conflict between Mercura and Vaxas—should it come to that.

Van could only assume Gheela intended to gauge the loyalties of Homestead's population. The community was home to Vaxals and Mercurans alike, and it would be valuable to determine who they might side with if they learned of the brewing conflict. Or, for that matter, if they knew of it already, and had already taken sides.

In the few days before they reached the farmlands, Van spent as much time with Shale and Simon as he could.

"I don't think it bears mentioning," said Van on their first morning out of the Great Swamp, "but the Nighthawk was almost certainly given to Galdur Goldeye, and that places tribe Ikann in the lead to win Patronage. Nobody knows but us."

"Sol knows," said Simon. "I mentioned it to him when we were first going over our plan to catch a quell."

Van swung to face him. "Did he tell Riverspeaker Gheela?"

"Don't know," said Simon. "You'd have to ask him."

"What should we do?" said Van. "If Ikann wins Patronage, Bryn—Atariel will use their authority to denounce tribe Mercura. Wouldn't that spell poorly for the other tribes?"

Simon rolled his eyes. "They're your country's rules, Van. You tell me."

It wasn't the first time they'd rehashed these points. Simon's only concern these days was Gnosos, which was understandable. Van was worried about the quells, too. But he was also worried about everything else, and he missed having someone to talk to about it.

Shale, for her part, didn't seem worried about anything at all, though she did enjoy rubbing Van's face in the fact that she was right in her predictions about relations between the tribes.

"I warned you this would happen," she chided every time the events at Seat Vaxas were brought up. "The blue clan was too greedy, and now the green clan is fed up. Goldeyes and the rest of the yellow ones probably don't even care that they're being used as puppets. The only part of this that's even remotely surprising is that you didn't see it coming."

Frustrated, Van turned to Ghan Mudcatcher for a sympathetic ear, but his next conversation with the elder likewise took an unexpected turn.

"I would ask for your advice about something, Van the Scribe," said Ghan as they shared evening meal at a bonfire.

"My advice?" Van snapped his head to face him, caught off guard by the role reversal.

"It concerns the dark girl. Shale, I should say."

"I had no idea you knew her name," said Van.

"Because you are terrible at paying attention to things," scolded Ghan Mudcatcher. "I came to know her in the days after the desert, when you were keeping to yourself and oblivious to the world around you."

"Oh," said Van, wondering if he should apologize.

"She leads hunting efforts, sometimes, for those whose skills Otep Acrearms deems lacking. I joined her on one such excursion, out of curiosity, and found myself impressed with her technique—not just as a hunter, but as a mentor to the novices."

"I see," said Van, not yet sure where his advice came in.

"She could be more than a ranger," continued Ghan Mudcatcher. "She could be a warrior of Dolse. Loath as I am to admit it, we may need fierce fighters in the days to come. My question regards how best to motivate her."

"Motivate her," Van echoed.

"That she is willing to share her skills is encouraging, but she seems to find no joy in the pursuit. She merely tolerates it. I wondered if you had any ideas as to how we might convince her to take a more active role in the tribe's affairs, and to find fulfillment in the undertaking."

Van hesitated. "Have you spoken of this to Otep?"

"I have not." Ghan stared at his meal bowl. "Our First Ranger has very, ah… traditional views regarding foreigners."

Van nodded in agreement.

"She doesn't have an earned name, does she?" The elder brightened at an idea forming. "Perhaps we could give her one as a gesture of good faith, as we did for Simon of the Mists?"

Van thought about it. "I'm not sure she would like that very much."

"Oh," said Ghan, deflating. "Truly? Then perhaps to start with, I should simply make an effort to know her better."

"The lack of a common language is something of a hurdle," said Van.

"Indeed." Ghan Mudcatcher nodded slowly. "She learns quickly, though. With help from Simon of the Mists, I have been teaching her ours."

"Oh," said Van. "That explains some of her, um, recent leaps in vocabulary and comprehension."

"You have spent more time with her than I." Ghan Mudcatcher fixed his eyes on Van. "What drives her? What are her goals, after the pilgrimage?"

"I'll give it some thought," said Van. "If I have any ideas, I'll share them with you."

Ghan Mudcatcher smiled, then patted his knee and stood to leave. Alone again, Van stared into the bonfire, feeling like an idiot. In truth, he had no idea what motivated Shale, or what she wanted in life. When he did think about her—which, in recent times, was not infrequent—his thoughts were seldom productive, and seldom noble. Disappointed in himself, he resolved to do better.

Betting on Shale to mysteriously vanish again sooner or later, Van waited for a chance to broach the subject with Simon in private.

"I know that look." Simon narrowed his eyes at him when that opportunity came, two days later. "You have something weird you want to ask me."

"It's about Shale, actually," Van said, averting his eyes.

"Oh?" Simon's voice piqued with interest.

"I wondered if you had any idea what motivates her."

"Motivates her to do what, exactly?" pressed Simon with a grin.

"Please get your mind out of the gutter, Simon," said Van, borrowing a phrase he'd learned from the foreigner himself. "I'm asking if you have a sense for what inspires her or spurs her to action in general. What does she want out of life? What are her aspirations?"

Simon sighed. "It's a real bummer how serious you are sometimes. Anyway, why ask me and not her?"

Van frowned at him.

"All right, point taken," said Simon. "She'd probably make fun of you. But that's just how she is, right? If you really want to get to know Shale, you might have to stomach some of that."

Van nodded, brooding.

"Any other news?"

Van shook his head. "Nothing significant. We'll reach Homestead tomorrow, I believe. From there, it's ten days to the Bridge of the Emissaries."

"Tell me more about this bridge." Simon paused to take a knee and re-lace one of his boots. "The river, too, while you're at it. It sounded like a big deal, but we kind of glossed over it last time."

"The Bridge of the Emissaries spans the river Nym," Van said in review. "The watercourse marks the boundary between our lands and the Western Forest, enabling trade between communities in the north and south. In the right season, it can also be fished. The Bridge itself is a spectacular sight, or so I've heard. It was built over a century ago, a cooperative effort between the Vaxals and Mercurans. There is no other point along the Nym where a person can walk from bank to bank."

"Must be some river," said Simon.

"Two full leagues across in some places," said Van. "But its narrowest point is less than a tenth of that, which is where we'll cross."

"I still have no idea how long a 'league' is," said Simon. "Can you give it to me in anything sensible? Miles? Meters? Feet?"

"It would be a somewhat ridiculous number, in feet."

"Take a stab at it anyway," said Simon.

Van drew his eyebrows together in thought. "At the point where we'll cross, perhaps a little over two thousand?"

Simon's eyebrows lifted. "Your Nym might be bigger than the Chapa in Obek. Most people think that's the biggest river in the world." He stared at Van. "How'd you build a bridge over that?"

Van shrugged, a smile pulling at his lips. He knew nothing of bridge building, but it amused him to see his friend impressed with Nemian ingenuity, for a change.

"Could I have another turn?" said Van, changing the subject.

"Sure."

"I wanted to ask you about magic again," said Van. "The types of things it can and can't do, categorically."

Simon waited while Van considered how to word his question.

"I know it's possible to read a person's mind," he began. "Like what you did back in Hemlock, when you looked at my memories. But I had to give you my blood, and it seemed as though you had to prepare in other ways as well."

"Is there a question in there somewhere?" Simon raised an eyebrow.

"Are there other circumstances in which my thoughts could be read? Without my knowledge, or permission?"

Simon took a breath. "First, remember our conversation about hedge wizardry. Material supplements—*intermediaries,* to use the textbook term—are a crutch that let you tap into magic more complicated than your natural talent allows. A latent phrenomancer might not need them. So categorically, yes, a powerful enough sorcerer could read your mind without you knowing."

Van grimaced.

"But that's not something you have to worry about," said Simon. "I put my wards back up, remember? As long as you're hanging out with me, nobody can scry you or peep inside your head."

"What about when I'm not with you?" muttered Van.

"The effect lasts about forty-eight hours," said Simon. "If we lost track of each other for a few days, then it might be a problem, but we haven't had that issue."

Van relaxed a little, thinking back to his various encounters with Anathema. "And you reestablished your wards immediately after I took you to the Temple at Sky's Edge."

"Right," said Simon.

That was well before Van's second meeting with Anathema, and prior to that, Van had no memory of the creature in his mind at all. By Simon's logic, Atariel couldn't have pried the information from his mind.

"You've still got that look," said Simon. "Going to tell me what's really on your mind?"

"No." Van pushed the leather pouch deeper into his back pocket. "Nothing, I mean. Thank you."

Simon eyed him skeptically, but he didn't press the subject.

That night, Shale didn't return to camp, which gave Van more time to think—and to join Sol Starfletcher on another evening hunt. Rather than chancing upon each other as before, this time, Sol sought Van out.

"First Ranger!" Van said when he noticed him approaching. "Is there danger?"

"Nothing impending," said Sol, smiling reassuringly. Or trying to.

"Then, how can I be of service?"

"Just as before," said Sol. "I need a good luck charm."

Van nodded, eager to have anything to do. He ducked into his tent, fetching his bow, and together they walked west.

Sol Starfletcher was unusually talkative that night. Van found it strange for the stoic Mercuran, until he considered that the desert had probably changed the First Ranger's life as much as it had his own. Just like Van, Sol would have lost friends, comrades, confidantes. Perhaps even some intimate companion Van never had the chance to meet. It was entirely possible that all Sol wanted from him that evening was his company—anyone's company—so Van lent him a sympathetic ear. Even in doing so, he realized he was woolgathering.

"...as such, I thought to ask for your perspective on the matter," Sol Starfletcher was saying.

Van shook himself from his thoughts. "Sorry, my perspective?"

The First Ranger patiently started over. "Regarding Atariel the Everliving. I hunted with her only once or twice, when she was masquerading as Brynda Blackblade. I confess, she had me fooled for a few days."

"A few days," Van repeated slowly. He'd been strung along for over a month. Even now, with her deception laid bare... He sensed his mind wandering again and forced himself not to think about it.

"She has served as the chieftain of Vaxas for many years," continued Sol Starfletcher. "Never once did she strike me as a fool. There must be a reason she chose this year's pilgrimage to stage her rebellion. You knew her better than I—or at least, the person she pretended to be. I wondered if you had any ideas that might explain her motives."

"Well, to start with, she picked the year of the pilgrimage because she's arranged for Ikann to win Patronage," said Van.

"If tribe Ikann as the new Patron denounces tribe Mercura, it would be *your* tribe starting a rebellion if you stood against Vaxas."

Even to his own ears, it sounded brazenly insensitive, like something Shale or Simon would say. But it was true, and Van wanted to know whether the full gravity of the situation had dawned on anyone but him. As it stood today, the best outcome they could hope for was a tie between Sol and Galdur Goldeye—and even then, only if Sol won at Seat Mercura.

"Yes, that much occurred to me," said Sol Starfletcher with a pensive expression. "But my tribe was Patron during the last pilgrimage year. And the one before that. Moreover, relations between Vaxals and Mercurans have been good for as long as can be remembered. So, why now? What has changed?"

"Perhaps it isn't tribe Mercura that Bryn—" Van caught himself. "That Atariel the Everliving takes issue with. Perhaps it's something more personal."

Sol eyed him with a glimmer of genuine interest.

"Your chieftain, for instance," Van continued. "Scaela the Listener succeeded Galeena Greatmother only recently, did she not?"

"I hadn't considered that," mused the First Ranger. "However, our new chieftain has vowed to uphold all oaths sworn by her predecessor, and our treatment of our neighbors has not worsened under her leadership. A personal vendetta would be curious indeed. Chieftain Scaela has never even met Atariel the Everliving, so far as I know. And as I suggested before, Atariel is no short-sighted fool. It is hard to imagine she would endanger her people over a private grudge. Nevertheless..."

Van waited as Sol's eyes shifted in thought.

"Nevertheless, it is something I hadn't considered," he concluded, somewhat noncommittally. He offered a weak smile. "Thank you for sharing your thoughts with me, Van the Scribe."

"I wish I knew more of Scaela the Listener," Van said cautiously. "In our tribe, it is the council of elders that nominates a new chieftain and ratifies their station. Is it the same with tribe Mercura?"

"In our case, it was Galeena Greatmother herself that wished Scaela the Listener to succeed her when she passed on," said Sol Starfletcher. "As far as our elders were concerned, that was all the testimony needed as to her worthiness."

Van nodded. "My father always said Galeena Greatmother was the wisest person he'd ever met. I wish I could have—"

A haunting shriek pierced the night air, cutting his sentiment short. One shrill note, almost musical, such as Van had never heard before. Except in imitation, years ago at the Teaching Circle.

Sol Starfletcher drew his arrow of blue fletching and broke into a dead sprint. It was all Van could do to keep up, fumbling for his quiver as he scrambled after him. The call sounded again, closer this time, and when Van looked up, he saw it—a silhouette gliding low against the starlit sky.

The First Ranger of Mercura planted his feet, skidding to a stop and loosing his arrow, which became another bird in pursuit of the first. Sol's falcon caught the Nighthawk easily, and the two avian predators grappled midair, locked together as they spiraled toward the ground.

The Phantom Nighthawk's tragic call echoed once more before the radiant blue falcon tore its throat out with its beak.

Seconds later, Van was there beside Sol, standing over the place where the blue falcon had smashed into the tundra— merely an arrow now, at rest beside a cleanly slain bird.

Sol returned the arrow to his quiver and picked up the Nighthawk by its talons, rotating it to admire the pristine pinion feathers. He smiled again, this time with confidence.

"In case it was in question, I do not intend to surrender Patronage without a fight."

27 Verdan'ias

Sol Starfletcher presented his trophy to the aspirants of Nemia the next morning, and the announcement was met with applause at a joint assembly of the tribes.

All but the Ikanni were cheered by the news, taking up their daily march almost with a spring in their step soon after. They would skip midday meal, keeping up a brisk pace until they reached Homestead in the early evening. Few complained, knowing that a hot meal would likely be waiting for them there—baths and real beds, too, if they were lucky.

Van shared the road with Shale and Simon, regaling them with his firsthand account of Sol Starfletcher's impressive feat. He was the only witness, after all, and at least for the day that made him something of a celebrity.

"Patronage will now be decided entirely by chieftain Scaela's game at Seat Mercura." Van's words tumbled out with nervous excitement, concluding his lengthy monologue.

"Good news for the home team," said Simon. "But wait a minute, wasn't the rule that we would count their feathers or something?"

"Their pinion feathers, yes," said Van. "And?"

Simon rubbed his chin. "What if Galdur's bird has more feathers?"

Van gave him a pointed look. "Two birds of the same species can't have a different number of primary flight feathers, Simon."

He threw his hands up. "Wow, sorry for asking. When would I ever have needed to learn that?"

"Perhaps we should still try to expose Galdur, though," Van thought aloud, ignoring his outburst. "If we can recover the enchanted bag and show it to the elders of Mercura, it would prove he cheated, and tribe Ikann would be disqualified. Could we do the scrying spell again? Would it be easier without..." He swallowed. "Without *her* here?"

Simon sighed. "Maybe. But is that really how you'd want to solve the problem?"

Van peered at him. "What do you mean?"

"At the end of the day, whatever's going on between Vaxas and Mercura is a political issue. Probably an important one. Do you really want me, an outsider, picking a side in that? Sure, I could step in and play the all-powerful sorcerer card, but then where does that leave your country, if they have to come out and admit they can't do these things for themselves?"

Van furrowed his brow. "Weren't you the one who suggested it to begin with?"

"Yeah, curiosity got the better of me. In retrospect, I shouldn't have meddled," said Simon. "And for better or worse, I have other things to worry about right now. Gnosos.

Anathema. Having two full-time jobs is stretching me pretty thin, sorcerer or not. So if you want to take matters into your own hands over this whole Patronage thing… well, you might really have to do just that—take them into your own hands. Whatever you decide, just be smart, and be careful."

Van struggled to hide his frustration. "Won't you already be involving yourself in our politics when you approach chieftain Scaela about the quells? Why stop there?"

"That's not a political issue," said Simon. "It's a moral one. If Nemia forces Gnosos into a fight, the only outcome will be an egregious loss of life. All I'm worried about right now is preventing a massacre."

"You're an aspirant of Dolse," Van muttered under his breath. "You have the right to worry about anything you want."

Simon either didn't hear, or he'd pretended not to, instead taking the next few minutes to translate the conversation to Shale. Surprisingly, she offered no rejoinder today. Her only contribution was a disinterested murmur.

"May I speak to Shale?" Van asked.

Simon closed his eyes, exhaled, and then opened them again —a tell that he was stepping out of the discussion and switching to word-for-word translation.

"I wanted to ask you something," began Van. "It may be personal, so if you'd rather not answer, you don't have to."

"A personal question from Van the Scribe," said Shale, eyes downcast. "How exciting."

"What do you plan to do after the pilgrimage?" he asked. "Will you come back to Seat Dolse with us? You could make a life for yourself there, if that's what you wanted. Ghan Mudcatcher believes you could become famous among our rangers."

She rolled her eyes. "If there is still a Seat Dolse to return to after this ridiculous pilgrimage, and if your people aren't ruled by lunatics by then, I suppose I would consider it."

Van bit his lip. She sounded so annoyed. Why? Perhaps because he was still tiptoeing around the real question. Shale would never skirt around a difficult issue for anyone, and she probably found it belittling when others tried to for her. Van sucked in a breath and tried again.

"What would you choose for yourself, though? Setting aside everyone else's feelings, how do you want to live your life?"

"Two months," she sighed.

Van blinked. "I'm sorry?"

"You should be," she said. "It was two months ago that you first spoke to me. That is how long it's taken you to ask me that."

Her words stung, and Van stared at the ground in shame. He hadn't anticipated being so angry with himself.

"You're right," he said with effort. "I'm sorry. I've been terribly impertinent. I do want to know what kind of future you hope for, though."

"How should I know!" she snapped. "I've spent my entire life convinced I wasn't to have a future at all. I was born to die, my mother's proof of fealty to the Twilight Prophet. I thought that was all life had in store for me, right up until I rested my chin on the executioner's block. So excuse me if I haven't had time to daydream of becoming a ranger, or any other stupid thing!"

Facing forward again, she quickened her pace and stormed away, leaving Van alone with Simon.

"I didn't expect her to be so upset with me," muttered Van.

Simon gave him a funny look. "You actually have kind of a hard time with people, don't you?"

Van blinked at him, lost.

"She's not mad," explained Simon. "Not at you, anyway. The thing is, Van, not everybody has their whole life figured out at your age, the way you seem to think you do. For a lot of us, thinking about the future can be pretty terrifying, and I have a feeling Shale would eat dirt before she admitted she was scared of anything."

Van frowned. Scared? *Shale?*

He groaned in frustration. "How am I supposed to know that's how she's feeling if she won't tell me?"

"By spending less time thinking about how *you're* feeling," said Simon.

Neither of them spoke after that, and Simon's spell lapsed in silence a short time later.

After skipping a meal and spending half the day fantasizing about supper, at first the aspirants didn't know what to make of what they found when they reached the outlying villages of Homestead.

A great number of tents and shanties dotted the landscape between plots of wheat and barley, built hastily and without forethought. The people coming and going from them looked haggard and road-wary, some of them even more so than the bewildered aspirants.

The shanty-dwellers, evidently, were just as curious about the newcomers. A number of them, mostly children, wandered into their path to form crowds, drawn to the reassuring presence of the First Rangers and Pilgrimage Guides. The procession was called to a halt amid the chaos, at which point Ghan Mudcatcher and Otep Acrearms struck out to track down the local headman.

While the aspirants loitered uncertainly in the grassy lanes between fields, even Van attracted his share of attention. His heart nearly jumped into his throat when he turned and saw a ghost.

"Lilim?" he croaked.

The little girl, ambling curiously toward him, stopped and cocked her head. "No, I'm Chiana."

"Oh," said Van. "Please excuse me."

Now that he was really looking, he saw that her eyes were green, not brown. And she was taller. And her nose was more upturned. And in fact, nearly everything about her was different.

"What, um," he stammered. "What are you doing here, if I may ask?"

"I came with Grandma," she said shyly.

"Came from where?"

She fidgeted with her fingers. "Three Rivers."

Van recognized the name, though he had never been there. Three Rivers was many leagues to the south, where the Nym split as it joined with the sea.

"That's quite far," said Van. "Why did your grandma want to come here?"

"Because Papa told us to run," she said, her voice matter-of-fact. "That's what he said to do, when the metal men came."

Van's stomach dropped, but he forced himself to stay and listen to her story in its entirety. He thanked her politely when she was finished, trying to keep his panic from showing, and when Chiana strolled off to find her grandma, he broke into a run.

He didn't have to look far before he found Simon with Shale, surrounded by another group of children who were all gawking and laughing. Apparently, the funny-looking foreigners with their pointy ears and uncanny complexions were a source of great amusement. Shale narrowed her eyes at the children venomously, recoiling from their grasping little hands.

"Simon!" Van gasped, bracing his hands on his knees to catch his breath. "It's the quells. Villages in the south have been attacked!"

Simon made the talking sign and shook his head. Of course. The spell had already been used up, in accordance with the inconvenient laws of magic that, to this day, no one had bothered to explain. Van groaned and turned away, this time searching for Sol Starfletcher.

Finding the First Ranger of Mercura was even easier—he was at the center of the largest gathering of displaced southerners. It was clear from the way they looked at him that they had learned who he was—the champion of the Patron tribe, here to save them and restore peace. Van hesitated, seeing in Sol Starfletcher a poorly concealed mix of pity and exhaustion as he offered the refugees blessings and words of comfort. He did not envy Sol in that moment, and he decided against becoming one more needy voice vying for his attention.

With nowhere else to turn, Van resigned himself to waiting for Ghan and Otep. Hours passed before they finally returned, and they brought grim tidings with them.

"There is fighting in the south," Otep Acrearms announced to the aspirants of Dolse. "We will camp here only long enough to provision ourselves for the next leg of our journey, and then continue on to the Bridge of the Emissaries. We resume our march the day after tomorrow. As we travel south, we will gauge how far the conflict has spread, and if we do encounter danger, we will intervene only if it is necessary to save lives. Our priority is reaching Seat Mercura to share what we have learned with the Patron tribe and help them marshal their forces."

"Is it the Vaxals?" asked a nervous youth in the crowd.

"The timing of this news is indeed suspect," answered Otep. "Atariel the Everliving has had long to plan her treachery. It may well be that she placed agents in the southern villages, with instructions to begin sowing discord and thus hamper our passage."

No, Van thought helplessly. *It's not her—it's Gnosos. We have to listen to Simon!*

But until he could present proof of his friend's claims to Otep and the other delegates, convincing them of anything would now be more difficult than ever.

As daylight faded, the aspirants of the tribes pitched their tents among the refugee camps. Kindly farmers brought them fresh bread and goat cheese for evening meal, and even with Homestead providing asylum to thousands of displaced southerners, there was plenty to go around—at least for the time being.

After mealtime, Otep Acrearms led a group of aspirants to the nearby villages, where they would help local rangers and medicine men organize a distribution effort for the travel-worn southerners. Van made sure he was among the volunteers. While most were tasked with carrying foodstuffs and fresh water to the camps, a few would take count of the injured and provide first aid.

Van was relieved to learn that "injured" generally meant a sprained ankle or some other minor hurt sustained on the road. Remembering the brutally slaughtered gazelle he'd found while hunting with Otep, he wondered if any among these refugees had even seen a quell. It was hard to imagine the unarmed elderly and children surviving a close encounter with the metal monsters from Gnosos.

Van noticed there were few young men and women among the southerners as he moved from camp to camp delivering blankets and changing bandages. From what he could piece together, most that were of fighting age had stayed behind to secure escape for their families.

The group from Three Rivers had traveled the farthest, having abandoned their homes to flee north three weeks ago. It was in their camp that Van heard the closest thing he would get to an eyewitness account, from an old woman whose son had led a group of men with pitchforks into the woods in pursuit of the encroaching fiends.

Her testimony carried a glimmer of hope. If the quells were hiding in the woods, maybe they were still quietly observing rather than attacking openly. If so, it might not be too late for those who'd remained in the south.

The woman also had a scolding to impart on her grandchildren that suggested she had her own ideas as to who or what was to blame for their troubles. Watching and listening as he unpacked a load of goods to leave with them, Van grew increasingly uneasy.

"You shouldn't have laughed at them," the old woman reprimanded a little boy and girl, referring to the outsiders who'd arrived with the procession.

"But their eyes and ears are so big!" said the little boy, cupping his hands to his head and flapping his fingers for comic effect.

The boy's sister promptly burst into laughter, but the old woman lunged forward and struck the boy across the cheek, silencing them both.

"No more foolishness!" she said. "The pale one might be harmless enough, but the female is a darkling from the underworld. She'll hit you with a curse if she catches you laughing at her—steal the breath out of your lungs and knock you stone dead!"

"She wouldn't really, would she?" whimpered the boy, his eyes watering as he held his stung cheek.

"Sure as you can bet," said the woman. "Those things lurking around back home are her servants, mark my words. She's come here ahead of them to have a look around, and before you know it we'll be leaving this place behind, too."

It was almost midnight when Van finally trudged back to his own tent, feet sore from the day's long march and hours of volunteer labor. The latter had been insightful, though. And in any case, he preferred lending a helping hand over languid fretting.

Curiously, Simon was waiting for him when he returned to their campsite, and for a little while longer he was denied his bedroll.

"What's wrong?" Van asked when he was close enough to speak without raising his voice.

Simon pointed at a tent some distance apart from the others. Shale's, Van thought.

"Is she all right?"

Simon gesticulated impatiently, again indicating the tent. Without further argument, Van went to Shale's tent and knelt outside, listening. When he recognized the sound of muffled sobbing, he looked up at Simon, concerned.

"Was she hurt? Injured?" he whispered, hoping Simon would recognize one of the words even without his spell.

Simon shook his head, scowling.

"Then I'm sure she would prefer to be left alone," said Van.

He moved to stand up, but Simon shoved him gently back toward Shale's tent, fixing him with a stern glare. Something in his expression reminded Van of his days as a student of the Teaching Circle. He was sure Ghan Mudcatcher used to give him that same look when he suspected Van of neglecting his studies.

Van took a breath and called to her. "Shale, are you all right?"

The barely audible crying fell silent, and no reply came. Van looked helplessly at Simon again, but he only crossed his arms and began tapping his foot.

"May I come in?" Van called.

Nothing.

Van drew a breath. "Right. I'm coming in."

Shale sat up in her bedroll when Van crawled into the tent, eyes flashing angrily. But the venom behind her gaze receded quickly. She seemed withdrawn, pulling her knees to her chest and backing away from him. As expected, her eyes were red and puffy.

Van shuffled closer and sat down cross-legged, leaving her as much room as he could in the cramped space. He cleared his throat awkwardly, unsure what to say. Really, he was just glad she wasn't hurt.

"I didn't mean to be so pushy this morning," he said with a hint of uncertainty. "I only wanted to know more about you. There's nothing wrong with being unsure about the future. And really, there's no hurry to commit to anything. As clever as you are, I'm sure you'll have the chance to explore many possibilities. I only asked you about it because..."

She watched him guardedly.

"Because I'd like to help you," he said. "If you want me to, I mean."

Shale had untensed, but to Van, she still looked joyless. Worn down. Nothing at all like her usual self. Van doubted whether his words alone could have done that to her, no matter how self-centered and insensitive they'd been.

"You might also have overheard the way people here are talking about you," he continued quietly. "That would make me feel lonely, too. They're only afraid. People can be surprisingly ignorant when they're confused and frightened, saying things they don't mean. Anyone who has actually gotten to know you can see how dependable you are, and how hard you work. Lilim trusted you. She admired you, too, I think. You should have seen the drawing she did..."

He hesitated, wondering if bringing up Lilim would only make her feel lonelier. It was hard to tell if he was helping at all, rambling on like this, and she probably couldn't understand half of what he was saying. He stared at the ground for a moment. Then, he had an idea.

"Would you teach me how to say 'I'm sorry' in your language?"

She stiffened and cocked her head, perhaps realizing the conversation had taken a turn.

Teaching Shale how to speak Nemian was practical and obvious. Learning her language, on the other hand, served no purpose whatsoever—except to demonstrate to Shale that he was thinking more about her than himself.

"I'm sorry," he said slowly, then pointed at her. "But in your language. Please?"

"Verdan'ias," she said with an unfamiliar, almost wistful look in her eyes.

"Verdanyas," attempted Van.

She giggled. *"Verdan'ias."*

Van put his hands on his knees and bowed his head. "Verdan'ias."

He looked up again after what felt like the appropriate amount of time. Meeting her eyes, he was pleased to see her expression had become teasing and mischievous. She was herself again. Fleetingly, he wondered if she'd tricked him into saying something silly instead of what he'd meant to, but if it had cheered her up, he didn't mind.

"It's good to see you smile," he said, smiling back at her. "It's also quite late, so I will let you sleep."

Van shuffled around to leave, but he didn't make it far.

"Stay."

He froze, looking over his shoulder at her. "Um."

Shale slid over on her bedroll, spreading her small blanket on the ground and gesturing to it. Nervous, Van crawled on top of it and lay down. Her face was inches from his, and her expression became unreadable once more.

"Don't look," she whispered.

Heat flushing to his face, he rolled over. Shale scooted closer and wrapped her arms around him, pressing her forehead to his back. Every few seconds, he felt her shudder, as though she had hiccups, or was trying not to sneeze. He understood after a moment that she was crying again.

It was the first night of good sleep Van could remember since the desert, rejuvenating and blessedly dreamless. The tent was empty when he woke up, and he realized with a start that it was already midday. Stepping outside, Van was greeted by a gray afternoon that threatened more rain. He looked for Shale and Simon, but finding neither of them, he gave up and strolled toward the closest farmhouse in search of Otep.

The First Ranger gratefully put him to work again. This time, he was assisting with the effort to inventory the supplies the procession would take with them.

Their caravan would be well provisioned, the local headman piling them with enough fresh produce to keep them fed until Seat Mercura, even if the hunting was bad. The best news, though, was that they would have strong, healthy oxen to draw their carts again. No longer would the aspirants themselves have to pull them in shifts.

At midday meal, to thank the aspirants for their help with the refugees, a group of local farmers brought them pan-seared lamb chops and barley porridge.

Van helped himself to a bowl of porridge and two oatcakes, fresh-baked and distributed freely. But while he was a guest at Homestead, he declined any meat he was offered. As a hunter, he had his qualms about consuming farm-raised livestock, despite Ghan Mudcatcher's assurances that there was nothing ignoble or unsustainable about the practice.

The rest of the aspirants needed no convincing, eating their fill and then some. The lamb chops also proved useful in coaxing Shale and Simon back to camp from wherever they'd been. Van waved when he saw them, and they joined him once they had their food.

Simon cast his language spell only when they'd moved away from the crowds, and Van used the first several minutes to apprise his friends of everything he'd learned since reaching the farmlands. Surprisingly, Simon and Shale had already pieced most of it together themselves.

"Which is why, starting today, we're taking an extra precaution," said Simon. "I'm taking Shale south along the road to survey the area, and I want you to come with us."

Van stared at him, curious. "How far are we going?"

"As far as we can before my spell wears off," he said. "When it does, we'll turn around and head back. That'll be our routine every night from here to Seat Mercura."

"Are we looking for quells?"

"We're looking for anything out of place," said Simon. "Which is why we need you. We're not from here, so you'll tell us if anything seems off."

Van furrowed his brow. "Sol Starfletcher would be better suited to that task. I'm as much a stranger to this part of Nemia as you are."

"Sol's busy," said Simon. "He'll have eyes in the sky keeping track of us, though. Come on. Time's wasting."

Van nodded. "I'll get my bow."

Simon sighed. "A bow's not going to make a difference if—"

"I'm getting my bow," Van repeated, returning to his tent.

They followed the trade road south from Homestead. To the east, the barren tundra offered little by way of scenery, but the sun setting over the reed fields to the west was a pleasant enough view. Though the crossing point was still days away, they were already just a few leagues from the floodplains of the Nym.

Scrutinizing the landscape, Van didn't see anything he would call out of place. Shale entertained herself while they walked, practicing some trick with her dagger. She first concealed it by reversing her grip on its hilt, then revealed it an instant later in her other hand. Even right beside her, Van completely lost track of the weapon during the transfer.

Simon halted them around the time Van expected his language spell to lapse. He turned around once, scanning the environs. They had come to a stop near a curve in the road, where it meandered around the base of a hill.

"Is everything all right?" asked Van.

"You tell me," said Simon.

Van shrugged. "I see nothing."

"And is that normal?"

Van paused and reevaluated their surroundings, paying closer attention this time. The tundra. The reed fields. The bend in the road. Directly ahead, the hill, where there stood a meager copse of trees. Had it been this quiet on the road yesterday? Hadn't there been crickets chirping, and birdsong? He faced Simon again.

"Let me borrow your knife," said Simon, reading his expression.

Van unfastened it from his belt and handed it over. Taking a knee, Simon used Van's hunting knife to draw a symbol on the dirt road.

"What's that for?" pressed Van, worried he might not explain otherwise.

"It's an alarm," said Simon, standing up and stepping back. "If a construct comes within a mile of here, we'll know."

He waved his hand at the glyph. The intricate symbol vanished from sight, the dirt of the road smoothing itself back over so as to appear undisturbed. Seconds later, the glyph returned, hovering a few inches off the ground this time and glowing bright red, as though it was drawn with lines of fire. At the same time, a copy of it appeared in miniature, floating next to Simon's shoulder. The small one was whistling obnoxiously.

"Is it supposed to do that?" Van winced at the shrill sound.

"That's exactly what it's supposed to do," growled Simon, his expression dire. "Stay behind me."

Van was about to point out that "behind" was a relative term, useless without a point of reference, but movement caught his eye before he could speak.

Two humanoid shapes emerged from the trees on the slope ahead of them. Even from afar, Van recognized their clawed hands, disproportionately large for their stunted bodies. They moved toward the road, closing distance with unnatural speed by digging their bladed arms into the ground and flinging themselves—a rolling, bounding motion, like a frog's leap.

They're faster than gazelle, Van realized with mounting horror as he fumbled for his bow.

Remembering what Simon had told him about their "pheromones," he fought for calm and focused on keeping his body moving. He managed to take two full steps back and nock an arrow before the sensation hit. The panic, the stiffness that gripped his limbs, it was artificial. As long as he knew that, he could resist it.

Shale, meanwhile, leapt into action without a moment's hesitation, charging the quells with her dagger in hand.

One quell skidded to a halt to meet her, swinging wide with its scythe-like claws. Its upper body rotated completely as it slid along the ground, like a nut twisting on a bolt. The extra torque added lethal momentum, but Shale saw it coming. She tumbled under it, striking along its flank where the liver and kidneys would be on any creature of flesh and blood. Sparks flew as her blade glanced off the quell's metal skin, not so much as leaving a mark.

The other construct rolled to the side and barreled past Shale without losing speed, leaving her for its counterpart to deal with. Van took aim at the metal fiend, just twenty yards away now, and placed a shot. He hit his mark dead center with one of his broadhead arrows—which snapped in half, failing even to distract it.

If Van had been alone, he would have died before he could reach for his quiver a second time. Luckily, he wasn't. Simon stepped in next to him, and for the first time, Van saw his friend harness the magic that had elevated him to the highest echelons of the Gnosian military.

While the oncoming quell was still mid-bound, Simon shifted his weight to his back foot, raised a hand, and snapped his fingers. An area of solid ground beneath the quell transformed instantly into a pit of mud, and when the construct landed, it sank like a stack of bricks.

Van had another arrow nocked, but he had no viable target. Terrified, he glanced up the hill, where Shale was still locked in harrowing melee with the first quell.

Its unnatural agility allowed it to attack relentlessly, every blow delivered with enough force to tear a man in half. Somehow, Shale was even faster. She danced past the cascade of scythe blades, maneuvering around her foe and inflicting exploratory cuts as she searched for some chink in its armor— but finding none.

"Come on," Simon yelled to Van.

Van chased after him as he sprinted up the hill toward Shale, but they both stopped and wheeled to face the road again when a sickening crunch sounded behind them. The other quell, covered in mud, had dug itself free, having tunneled through the earth with its bladed hand like a giant mole. It jumped, and this time, it would land claws first on Simon in a single bound.

Simon snapped his fingers again. A wall of stone—ten feet high and three times as wide—erupted from the ground, and Van heard a sound like a sledgehammer striking rock as the construct collided with the barrier on the other side.

When they swung back around to pursue Shale again, Van's stomach dropped. Her fight with the first quell had taken a horrifying turn. After dodging another brutal volley of attacks, the construct surprised her by lashing out with its other arm. Thin fingers elongated, snaking out to catch her around the neck. She snarled as she was lifted off her feet, kicking at the quell and sawing futilely at its wrist with her dagger. The quell held its other arm high to deliver the killing blow, blades clicking as they ratcheted back.

Van stopped and took aim, hoping to buy her even a second more. Before he could loose his arrow, something happened he couldn't explain. The quell released Shale and stepped away, then stood there as if confused, its upper body questing from side to side in futile search. Shale was backing away from it, holding her bruised throat with one hand, when Simon shouted something that gained her attention. In response, she threw him her dagger.

Simon almost lost his balance catching it, but once he had it in hand, a flash of light engulfed the blade. It was no longer a dagger, but a spear. Simon threw it back to Shale.

Catching it nimbly, she leapt at the quell. Her enemy seemed to remember where she was at the last moment, reorienting itself to face her, but it was too late. She drove the spear home center mass. This time, the weapon struck true. The quell froze, impaled, then sagged to the ground. Still gripping the spear, Shale collapsed on top of it, panting as she straddled the inert construct.

Seconds later, the other quell rounded Simon's wall of stone, and he snapped his fingers once more. A maze of new obstacles and hazards sprang up to slow its advance, but never fully halt it. Just when Van thought the game was played out, a bolt of lightning arced down from the sky and struck the quell square on its head, or rather, the smooth crevice between its arms where a head should be. Van fell back, half blinded by the flash, his ears ringing from the boom of thunder that followed. He couldn't puzzle out what had happened until he spotted the bright blue falcon sauntering away from the slain construct.

Simon's chest heaved with every breath, his eyes fixed on the quell with his thumb and middle finger pinched together. Meanwhile, Van staggered to his feet and ran to Shale. The quell she'd grappled with had already melted away to nothing, and for some reason, so too had her spear. She was on hands and knees, gulping for air, and only when Van knelt to check her for injury did he see how close it had come—and how many times. There were cuts all along her arms, and a single gash on her cheek. Most were shallow grazes, barely breaking the skin, but any one of them would have lost her a limb had she been a fraction of a second slower.

Her eyes were unfocused, darting back and forth in shock. She didn't seem to notice his presence at all until he put his hands on her shoulders. Tensing, she looked at him startled, then threw her arms around him and buried her face in his neck.

"Verdan'ias," she said, shivering.

It seemed to Van a strange time to be apologizing.

"I know," he said, holding her steady. "I love you, too."

28 Blood and Black Fletching

"Hold still," Simon murmured, crouching next to them.

He pressed two fingers to Van's temple, and when he withdrew them, a luminous gold thread followed. He pulled a length of it out of Van's head, then took it in both hands and tore it like a ribbon of parchment. The strange thread flickered and vanished.

"What are those?" Van watched as Simon repeated the process with Shale, who was still shaking in his arms.

"Tracers the quells left on you," he replied. "Would've identified you as priority targets to any other constructs in the vicinity."

Next, Simon drew a fresh alarm glyph in the sand. When the new one didn't start glowing or whistling, his shoulders finally relaxed. Van took it as a sign that the danger had passed and helped Shale to her feet.

They followed the blue falcon back to camp, meeting up with Sol Starfletcher on the road part way. Simon's spell had lapsed, so Van took the liberty of explaining what had happened—not that it warranted much explanation, considering what they were carrying with them.

The dead—or rather, "decommissioned" construct—was impossibly heavy. Only by virtue of Simon's magic were they able to convey it to camp. Van was curious why the one slain by Sol's falcon hadn't simply crumbled away like the others, and he said as much to the First Ranger.

"You will have to ask Simon of the Mists," said Sol Starfletcher as they drew closer to camp. "It had something to do with striking several of the creature's vital areas simultaneously, though I'm afraid the rest was lost on me. We have been rehearsing the technique for some time."

Van kept Shale's arm around him until the tents came into view. She wasn't badly hurt, and almost certainly could have walked under her own strength, but having her close was a comfort. For her part, she didn't object.

They attracted some attention as they marched through camp. A scattering of aspirants spotted Simon puppeting the inert construct along with his levitation spell, and a crowd began to form.

Sol Starfletcher was quick to fetch Riverspeaker Gheela, and when she arrived, her first priority was to prevent a panic. She ordered the quell brought to her tent, where it could be kept out of sight until she made sense of what it was.

Van waited patiently while Sol related the basic facts to his Pilgrimage Guide, who listened with a stern gravity. When he finished, she called an emergency conference of the delegates. Sol insisted that the foreign sorcerer would be integral to the discussion—if not the focus of it—so Simon was allowed to stay. Van and Shale, however, were told to disperse until morning with the rest of the crowd.

"But we were there!" Van protested as Sol Starfletcher led them out of the tent. "Shale was nearly killed, and as for Simon, he can't even speak for himself!"

"The situation is delicate, Van the Scribe," Sol said gently. "Allow me to take the lead for now. The loyalties of your companions will not be cast into doubt, you have my word."

Van turned to Shale, hoping for a fiery rebuttal, but she had no more fire left in her that day. All she could manage was a sigh and a weary shake of her head before she turned on her heel and stalked away.

Wondering if she wanted him to keep her company again, Van followed for a few paces, but she turned and gave him a look that said this time, it really was best if she was left alone.

Frustrated, Van paced the perimeter of the campgrounds until late into the night, watching the tundra for signs of movement. He could only imagine how confused and anxious Simon must be, unable to understand the delegates as they studied the metal monster from his homeland, arguing over his trustworthiness with only Sol Starfletcher there to vouch for him.

When morning came, Van was among the first to arrive at assembly. All tribes gathered as one to hear Riverspeaker Gheela recount everything that had been learned and decided at Homestead.

"The elders here claim no foreknowledge of Atariel the Everliving's plot," she declared. "They have denounced her crimes in the name of ongoing peace and have pledged Homestead's rangers to tribe Mercura, the rightful Patron, should we require them to bring the chieftain of Vaxas to heel."

Many of the aspirants cheered—though Galdur Goldeye continued to brood in silence. A surge of fresh anger coursed through Van as he watched the First Ranger glower at the Mercurans from his place in the crowd. In that moment, he vowed once again to reveal tribe Ikann's sinister ambitions, and soon.

Gheela stepped aside, then, to allow Sol Starfletcher to come forward with Simon. The fallen quell floated into view from behind them, and gasps rippled through the crowd as the construct settled to the ground for all to see.

"The creature before you is responsible for the violence in the south that drove our countrymen from their homes," said the First Ranger of Mercura. "Others like it have invaded our lands, more dangerous than any pack of mourns or rampaging hornbeast."

He gestured to Simon, who stepped up awkwardly. He still hadn't activated his spell, Van realized.

"It was only with the help of Simon of the Mists that I brought this one down. In doing so, we have grasped their true nature. These things are called 'quells,' and they are not of Nemia. They were sent here, from a land across the sea, and their only purpose is to kill."

The crowd was incensed. Cries of "Death to outsiders!" reached Van's ears, and one particularly spirited aspirant even threw a stone.

"Hear me, friends!" Sol shouted, raising his voice over the clamor. "I tell you again, it was Simon of the Mists himself who alerted me to this danger. He has earned my trust, and it is no overstatement that his cooperation has already saved lives. That, I think, should earn him your trust as well."

The hostility began to subside, the crowd quieting. Sol watched them for a moment, measuring their tempers, then gave Simon a nod. As if sensing his time had come to make a good impression, Simon of the Mists forced a regrettably artificial smile and faced the crowd. He threw up his arms, the first two fingers of each hand extended, and took a bow.

"It means peace!" Simon explained to Van later, once the procession was marching south from Homestead.

"Oh," said Van. "That seems… in poor taste, somehow."

They walked near the head of the procession, where they could gain the attention of the Guides and First Rangers swiftly if needed. Ahead of them, Sol's falcon soared in a slow, curving pattern, scouting the way.

It was no longer necessary to hunt, given how few of them were left and how well supplied they were from their stopover at Homestead. It was decided, therefore, that until they reached the Western Forest, they would redouble their pace, marching until well past midday with only a few short breaks. In this way, they would reach the Bridge of the Emissaries in less than a week.

Van would be covering even more ground because of Simon's plan to place an alarm ahead of the procession's path each night—one more hour south to set the spell, and another hour back to camp. By now, Van was as well acclimated to hiking as he supposed he would ever be, but just thinking about their new routine was enough to make his feet hurt. He had long suspected that exercise and athleticism were not highly valued in Simon's country, and he wondered fleetingly how he managed to keep up.

"Sol Starfletcher mentioned I should ask you about the quell," said Van, fumbling with the sheet of canvas that covered his head and back from the rain.

Like so many things, Van's half cloak had been lost in the desert. He missed it on days like these, when the seasonal rains beat down on them for hours.

"What about it?" said Simon, only nominally more dry under his hat.

"Why didn't it fall apart and disappear like the others? The one that was killed—um, decommissioned—by Sol's arrow."

"The only reliable way to disable one is to destroy all their primary sensory apparatuses while causing minimal damage to the chassis," he said. "If a construct can't see, hear, or feel, then it can't self-diagnose. It won't initiate the disassembly process because it doesn't know it's been damaged. Has to be done in a quarter-second or less."

"Oh," said Van. It made about as much sense as he'd expected. "And what about Shale's dagger? You did something to it, but then it fell apart, too."

Van had lent Shale his hunting knife after her fight with the quell. For use in combat, it was far inferior to the blade she'd lost, but Van preferred her armed with something.

"It's like I told you before. For sorcerers, magic is a private conversation with reality. All I'm doing when I cast a spell is lying to the universe about what the laws of physics are. When I spelled Shale's dagger, I needed it to be tough enough to punch through a construct's exoskeleton, so I had to tell a pretty big lie."

Van walked closer to him. "What sort of lie?"

"Quells are made of adamantine steel," said Simon. "Almost as hard as diamond. So, I had to give her something even harder."

"I can't think of anything harder than a diamond," said Van.

"Neither could I," said Simon. "I just made something up."

Van blinked at him. "Does that... does that work?"

"Not for very long," said Simon. "Things that aren't supposed to exist tend to stop existing pretty quickly, laws of nature and all that. Hence, why it fell apart after a few seconds. That wasn't the tricky part, though."

"It wasn't?"

Simon cast him a sidelong glance. "How strong do you think you'd have to be to push a diamond through solid adamantine?"

"I hadn't considered that," said Van, stealing a glance at Shale. "Extraordinarily strong, I suppose."

"Shale's a tough cookie, but I don't think even she could pull that off, so I cheated with the sharpness, too. The tip of that spear was closer to a cloud of gas than a physical object. Hydrogen chloride, nitrogen oxide—a few other special herbs and seasonings. My home brew recipe for scrambling the elemental structure of adamantine."

"In other words, another made-up substance," Van supplied.

"I like to think I'm pretty impressive when I roll up my sleeves," said Simon with a smirk. "But my real talent has always been old-school tetramancy."

"Tetramancy?"

"Tetra, as in *four*," said Simon, holding up four fingers. "Earth, fire, air, and water. People used to call it storm magic, a long time ago."

"I've heard Ghan Mudcatcher call it that," said Van. "Thank you, Simon. I'm glad you're willing to explain these things to me."

"Why wouldn't I be?"

Van gave him a look.

"Okay, fair enough," said Simon. "If there was a time when I seemed less than eager to teach you this stuff, I'm sorry. Old sorcerer paranoia—you know the drill. Handing out state secrets to people you don't trust is dangerous. But I have for a while now. Trusted you, I mean. That said, the more you know, the safer you are."

Shale hadn't spoken a word to them all day. She walked quietly beside them, keeping Simon between herself and Van. Simon took a few minutes to relay the conversation to her so she wasn't left out.

"Mmm," was her only distracted reply.

Simon switched his spell back to Van and raised an eyebrow. "What's up with Shale?"

Van shrugged.

Simon lowered his voice. "Something happen between you two?"

"Of course not," Van said immediately.

"Hey. What did we say about honesty?" Simon protested with a scowl.

"My apologies," mumbled Van. "You're right. Something happened, and it is private."

"Wow," said Simon. "Teen angst, on top of everything else. And here I thought we were friends."

They hiked for several more hours after the language spell lapsed. When the procession finally made camp by the reed fields, it was nearly time for evening meal. Before Van ate, he went ahead with Shale and Simon to set up the alarm.

After walking in stiff silence for the better part of the day, and with no hunting to look forward to, Van was left feeling foggy-headed. He'd grown to appreciate the aches that followed disciplined exercise, but this was becoming drudgery. He was exhausted in all the wrong ways. As thankful as he was for the company of his friends, his relationship with Simon was best enjoyed for only an hour each day.

Shale, on the other hand, was increasingly capable of holding a conversation without Simon's help. Their relationship, too, was changing. Since their encounter with the quells, she had gone to great lengths to avoid being alone with Van. So, yet again, he was left to his own devices.

It was in these moments, when he felt he truly had no one to talk to, that Van missed Lilim the most. He strolled through camp as the sun dipped low, looking for something to take his mind off things. The rain subsided, and patches of sky became visible through the clouds, deepening from blue to orange as evening approached.

By chance, Van found Otep Acrearms with Ghan Mudcatcher at a bonfire. They were alone, and if he didn't know better, he might have thought they were arguing.

Ghan glanced up at Van, who bowed apologetically, prepared to excuse himself. Before he could, the elder waved him over.

"Come and sit, Van the Scribe," called Ghan Mudcatcher while standing to leave. "The First Ranger, I think, would prefer your company over mine just now."

Hesitantly, Van stepped over to them, bowing again to Ghan Mudcatcher before accepting his seat. His childhood teacher surprised him by returning the gesture. From an elder, a bow was a sign of respect reserved for blooded members of the tribe. Van stared after him, bemused as he walked away.

"I suppose you've come to tell me what a fool I have been," muttered Otep.

Caught off guard, Van pivoted to face him. "What?"

"I should not have dismissed you, when you warned me of those creatures," said Otep. "I drove you away. You went to the foreigners, and they have proven themselves more worthy of your trust. I struggle to imagine how disappointed in me you must be. How disappointed you have been for some time, I suppose."

Van didn't know what to say. He hadn't come to gloat or demand an apology. Really, he was just bored and lonely.

"I don't blame you, Otep Acrearms," said Van after a moment. "For any of it. You have always acted in the best interest of the tribe. Is that not what it means to be First Ranger?"

Otep chuckled bitterly. It was strange to see him like this, beaten down and angry with himself. Van knew exactly what he must be feeling. He had been wrestling with the very same feelings himself since the desert. Otep Acrearms was awakening to the reality that the world was far bigger—and far less forgiving—than anyone had prepared him for.

Otep sighed. "I will strive to re-earn your trust, Van the Scribe. You may have to be patient with me, though, because I have no idea how."

"I do," blurted Van on a sudden impulse, remembering Simon's advice about taking matters into his own hands.

Otep searched his expression, waiting. Van took a breath, steeled himself, and told his friend everything he knew about Galdur Goldeye. He felt it necessary to first recount his unlikely role as Galdur's literacy tutor before getting to the important part—the Phantom Nighthawk, still unaccounted for and almost certainly entrusted to the Ikanni as part of Atariel the Everliving's greater scheme.

"Then her design truly was to usurp Patronage," Otep mused. "Not for herself, but for tribe Ikann."

"He could still win," Van emphasized. "There is only the game left at Seat Mercura to break the tie, unless we expose him now."

"By finding this enchanted satchel," Otep supplied. "Though, to hear you tell it, even Simon of the Mists was not certain of its magical properties."

"If we can find it and show it to Simon, he'll know right away," said Van. "Whatever he concludes will be confirmed by the shamans of Mercura."

Van watched Otep and waited. His face was set in silent deliberation. Van understood his hesitation, being asked to place his trust in a foreigner's hunch.

"I would be a fool indeed to ignore you again," said Otep, his tone hard with resolve. "I think it is time I paid Galdur Goldeyes a visit."

Van had expected that confrontation would be Otep's first response. Still, his stomach twisted with anxiety as he followed his friend to the tent of Ikann's First Ranger.

"We should find Sol Starfletcher," whispered Van as they wove through camp.

Otep shook his head. "The Starfletcher has already shouldered more than his share of burdens on this pilgrimage. It is time I demonstrated myself reliable enough to deal with minor nuisances on my own."

"He'll be armed," Van warned. "Will you not at least bring a weapon?"

"I am weapon enough for that coward," said Otep flatly.

Van swallowed, hoping it was true. Come to think of it, he had never actually seen Galdur fight. Even during the game at Seat Ikann, the First Ranger's plan had been to bide his time and wait for an easy victory, the strategy of a man who knew he was otherwise outmatched. Otep Acrearms, on the other hand, was a living wall of muscle, towering head and shoulders over any opponent. It was hard to imagine him losing, armed or otherwise.

"You should go now, Van the Scribe," said Otep as the tents of the Ikanni came into view. "Galdur Goldeyes would be an idiot in my opinion to let this matter come to blows, but if you are right and he eschews dialogue in favor of violence, I would have you elsewhere."

"Otep, I—"

"Your presence would only hamper me," Otep insisted, coming to a stop and facing him. "Laying a villain low is one thing. Doing so while ensuring your safety would be another. Please."

Van nodded, standing dumbly in place.

Otep put a hand on his shoulder. "I will find you when it is done."

When Otep turned and marched toward Galdur's tent, Van stood rooted to the ground. He was no longer the boy who'd set out from Seat Dolse. Whatever was about to happen, he would at least bear witness. Van waited for Otep to gain some distance, then followed after him stealthily, relying on the numerous Ikanni milling about to mask his presence.

Ahead of him, Otep reached Galdur's tent, and after announcing himself, he went inside. Van followed seconds later, slipping around the tent to crouch behind it, hidden in the shadows. All of Galdur's favorite henchmen were dead, so there was no one keeping watch that might spot Van brazenly eavesdropping and send him away. All he had to do was keep still and listen.

Inside the tent, a heated conversation unfolded in hushed tones. Van couldn't make out the words, but he didn't think Galdur was fool enough to lay a hand on Otep here at camp.

Sure enough, they emerged together just minutes later. From his place of hiding, Van watched them turn to face the reed fields.

"I hid it there," said Galdur, pointing. "We will retrieve it, and I will turn it over to Riverspeaker Gheela. You have convinced me to confess my deeds."

"Lead on, Galdur Goldeyes," said Otep with obvious skepticism.

"As you wish," said Galdur, bowing submissively. "But please, let it be Goldeye, because now I have only the one."

Van prepared to follow them, but seeing Galdur's swords sheathed at his hips, he hesitated. If he hurried, he could still run for help. He could find Sol Starfletcher, or if not him, Shale and Simon. But would doing so be a dishonor to Otep?

Van's initial goal in confiding in Otep—almost more so than bringing Galdur to justice—had been to restore his friend's confidence. To give him newfound direction, a way to right a wrong and mend his battered pride. Because Van knew too well the hopelessness of moving forward without direction...

Judging by the splash of color he glimpsed through the clouds, Van marked that the light of day would fail soon. Otep and Galdur waded into the field of reeds. It could only be a ploy—Otep must know it as well as Van did. There was no chance in his mind that the First Ranger of Ikann would simply surrender.

His heart pounding, Van sucked in his breath and followed them, crouching low to remain hidden in the tall grass.

On any other day, the sight before him would have been hauntingly beautiful. The setting sun played off the yellow grass, turning the reeds a warm gold against the brushstroke of the horizon. The ever-shifting wind whipped them wave-like in gentle swirls. The two men trekked through the reeds for close to twenty minutes, Van shuffling after them unseen. The grass came up to Galdur's waist, but for Otep, only to the knee.

"This is far enough, I think," said Otep Acrearms at length, halting abruptly.

Galdur turned to face him, his expression a mockery of surprise.

"It is perfectly obvious that you brought me here only to do away with me," Otep said, clenching his massive fists. "You are free to make the attempt."

Van saw the flicker of a smile at the edge of Galdur's mouth, and in a flash, his swords were in his hands.

"If you insist," he said. "Come then, brute. Come and die."

Otep answered the challenge, crossing the distance between them in a stride and throwing a haymaker. His mighty fist came down with enough force to shatter bone, and Galdur barely managed to dodge the strike. Galdur's expression told Van he was well aware the fight would be over in a single blow.

Giving no quarter, Otep lunged forward again and swung with both arms—a cross jab to the face followed by a savage hook aimed at the ribs. Galdur slipped between the strikes and maneuvered behind Otep, taking a stance. But he was forced to duck immediately as Otep threw a backhand sweep that would have taken Galdur's head off his shoulders.

They squared off anew. Otep threw another punch with his full weight behind it, and missed again. Van could have sworn he saw Galdur smirk as he dodged the next jab and hook combination. When the next backhand came, he was prepared for it. He stepped under Otep's fist, clipping him along the side with one of his swords, and at once dispelled the myth that the First Ranger of Dolse had skin that could turn a blade.

The spray of blood flecked the grass scarlet, and Van barely managed to cover his mouth to stifle a scream.

Otep glanced at his wound with indifference. The gash was superficial. He resumed his offensive, feinting this time with an extra jab. Van thought the surprise attack might throw Galdur off balance. It didn't. Their first exchange had revealed Otep's technique to him, and he had taken his measure. He moved past Otep's guard like a dancer doing a pirouette and slashed him twice more, once on the arm and again across the shoulder. Shallow cuts, like the first.

The battle continued in that manner for an agonizing duration—Otep always on the attack, and Galdur always ready with a reply, inflicting minimal but measurable damage. Otep's only weapon was his legendary strength, and he had been completely disarmed of it.

Galdur was too fast, and worse, he was a better fighter. He had crossed swords in mortal combat before, probably many times. It was more than just experience. He exulted in it.

Van shrank into himself, watching in horror as the difference in skill and agility between the two men was laid bare. Galdur used his next opening to test the limits of that difference, sliding both swords along Otep's abdomen as he danced past another failed assault. Otep roared and doubled over, clutching his side as blood streamed between his fingers.

"So, this is the First Ranger of Dolse," taunted Galdur, twirling his swords as he circled his opponent. "So proud, and so lost. Can't fish your way out of this one, can you?"

Otep took the bait, lunging at Galdur—but he was growing desperate, his movements slow and clumsy. Galdur clipped him on the forehead this time, drawing a crimson line that wept blood into Otep's eyes.

Otep Acrearms threw one last punch, staggering blind at his opponent. Galdur dodged effortlessly, stepping in and using his twin swords like a gruesome pair of scissors to saw into Otep's midsection. Otep swayed for a moment, clutching ineffectually at the gaping hole in his belly. Then, the First Ranger of Dolse—strongest man born in a generation and protector of the small—fell slain, his body vanishing into the reeds.

Van's mind went blank as he watched his friend die. He didn't have his bow, and his hunting knife was gone. It hardly mattered. Even armed, he wouldn't have stood a chance. He didn't care. With his vision blurred by tears of unthinking rage, Van readied himself to rush Galdur head on. Were it not for the hand that fell on his shoulder, he would have died, too, as a pointless gesture of solidarity to his murdered friend.

"Stand down, Van the Scribe," said Sol Starfletcher. "I will take it from here."

Galdur's sadistic grin slipped when he saw the First Ranger of Mercura step forward, but only for an instant.

"Impeccable timing, cousin," sneered Galdur. "I was just wondering how I would bury this beast on my own. Did you happen to bring a shovel?"

Sol unshouldered his bow wordlessly.

Galdur sighed, his expression falling. "Must we? Very well. Two for the price of one it shall be."

Crossing his twin blades in front of him, Galdur watched Sol draw his arrow and take aim. Surely, even a swordsman of Galdur's caliber wasn't faster than the azure falcon—a living lightning strike. Then again, did he really need to be? If he preempted Sol's line of attack as perfectly as he had Otep's, he might cut the bird out of the air just by positioning his swords along its path. Sol Starfletcher would be disarmed, too, leaving him with only...

Van looked again. Sol hadn't drawn his blue arrow. He'd drawn the black one.

Galdur tensed as Sol let the arrow fly, but he had barely pulled his bow to half draw. The arrow stuttered a single yard before arcing down into the reeds, well short of its target. The moment stretched on, both men standing as rigid as statues—Galdur with his swords crossed, and Sol with his bow held level across his knees, somber as a eulogist.

When his new opponent failed to make a move, Galdur pivoted to the offensive. He rushed Sol Starfletcher with his swords held low, concealed in the grass. Before they could clash, he yelped and hopped backward, sucking air through his teeth like he'd stepped barefoot on a sharp stone. Sol watched him without reaction as he shook his head and recomposed himself.

With renewed ferocity, Galdur lunged again. The first sword slashed in a low, wide arc—a feint. Sol recognized the trickery and jumped away, bringing his bow up to block the second strike, an overhead swing that carried the full momentum of Galdur's charge.

Van winced at the deafening clang. The sharp steel should have cut through the carved wood like a knife through butter. Instead, it was as though Galdur had smashed his sword against an anvil. He clenched his teeth and reeled back, fighting to keep his weapon from rattling out of his hand.

Sol retook his passive stance, waiting. Galdur's next attack garnered the same reply, but this time, he knew better than to try to sunder the bow. His attacks were quick and light, no longer delivered with lethal intent, but aimed at breaking posture. When he thought he had Sol off balance, Galdur spun his swords around and brought them down together. Sol Starfletcher simply held his bow up like a shield, adeptly blocking the assault.

Galdur stepped back, seemingly recalculating his strategy, and smiled. He came forward once more, blades spinning. At the last moment, he reversed his grip and drove them toward Sol's ribs from either side. Van bit down on his lip, thinking for one horrible instant that it was over. Sol's bow could catch the broad side of a sword, but it couldn't block a straight thrust.

Sol switched his grip as well. Clutching his bow at one end with both hands, he jumped clear of Galdur's drive. Wielded like a club, the bow had the greater reach. As he danced away, he walloped Galdur hard on the ear.

Galdur staggered, spinning as he tried to recover. As before, Sol simply lowered his bow and waited. Galdur took a shuddering breath, crossing his swords to advance again, but his hands were shaking. Had the knock to his head really been so severe?

Their next exchange was one-sided, heavily in Sol's favor. Galdur moved sluggishly, swaying like a drunk, and Sol sent him stumbling away with a blow to the chin that made him spit blood.

"What did you...?" Galdur groaned, suddenly unable to even lift his arms.

His swords clattered to the ground. As he teetered in place, his expression flashed with anger and confusion. Then, his yellow eye closed, and he collapsed, disappearing in a flutter of golden reeds. In the silence that followed, Van finally stood up.

As the last light of day guttered out, a black snake slithered out of the tall grass and up Sol's torso. It coiled around his arm, moving to his outstretched hand and returning to its former state—a simple arrow with black fletching.

Sol placed it wordlessly in his quiver, watching the wind sweep over the darkened reeds for a long moment before he turned his back on them and returned to Van.

"We must go," said the First Ranger of Mercura. "It is done."

29 Bridge of the Emissaries

"We can't just leave him," choked Van, stumbling through the reed fields as he trailed after Sol.

"He will not be left," said the First Ranger. "Otep Acrearms will be given a proper ceremony, you have my word. In order to do that, however, we must first alert the others and summon help."

As they trekked back to camp, a single coherent thought asserted itself in Van's mind over the horror of watching his oldest friend die. Tribe Mercura had won. With all of his peers now dead or disqualified, Sol Starfletcher had secured Patronage for his tribe.

To avoid widespread panic, Sol quietly invited Riverspeaker Gheela and Ghan Mudcatcher to his tent, where he recounted the evening's tragic events. This time, Van was allowed to stay, providing his testimony as the only other witness. It was decided that a public announcement would be saved for morning.

Ghan Mudcatcher dropped his head into his hands and wept when he learned of Otep's fate. When their meeting concluded, Van walked his childhood teacher back to his tent and stayed with him, comforting him in his grief, but he wasn't yet ready to grieve himself. Truth be told, he didn't think he had much grief left in him.

The elder was inconsolable. After perhaps an hour, he lay back in his bedroll, exhausted, and drifted restlessly in and out of sleep.

"It was my fault," Van confessed, his tone devoid of emotion. "I told him about Galdur, and that's why he confronted him. That's why he's gone."

"It is not your fault, child," muttered Ghan Mudcatcher, his eyelids fluttering. "It is mine. So many lives... their spirits... May the Emissaries..."

Van watched the old man toss and turn, haunted by a memory of something Simon said. An old thread, he liked to call it.

They're keeping secrets from you.

"What haven't you told me?" whispered Van.

No answer came. The elder was elsewhere, perhaps lost in a nightmare, if his troubled expression was any indication. Van finally knew what it looked like from the outside.

He shuffled out of the tent, intending to go back for Otep without delay, but he didn't make it far. The First Ranger of Mercura stood watch over the sleeping campsite, spotting Van easily with the help of his circling falcon. He reminded Van gently that stumbling through the reeds in the dark would make him an easy target should the quells attack. Sol politely urged him to get some rest, assuring him they would search for Otep at first light.

Van retreated to his tent with a fresh pang of bitterness and nothing to do but dwell on Otep's death. He alone had set his friend on the path that had gotten him killed, and for what? Pride? Pride was a sickness of the mind, as contagious as it was fatal. Honor? Honor was the perennial grift of the wicked, their oldest and most dependable instrument of predation.

Sleepless, Van was the first to arrive for morning assembly, where the news was met with shock and disbelief by all the tribes. Sol Starfletcher urged the aspirants to understand that Galdur had acted alone, but still the Dolsers stared at the Ikanni with looks of open betrayal. Van watched numbly as the good will so hard earned between the tribes of the Eastern Plains was undone in an instant.

Volunteers were recruited to hurriedly search the reed fields for the bodies before the procession resumed travel. Van was among them. Concerned and confused, Simon followed after him with Shale.

"What the hell happened?" asked Simon.

A strangely appropriate turn of phrase, Van thought distantly.

"It is as you heard," he said. "Otep Acrearms confronted Galdur Goldeye, and was killed. Sol Starfletcher then arrived and killed Galdur Goldeye."

"Did you tell Otep about the Nighthawk?"

"Of course I did," said Van, his tone low. "How else could he have learned?"

Simon shook his head while Shale moved close, staring at Van intently.

"Don't worry," said Van. "I'm fine."

"Bullshit," growled Simon.

"I won't bury my head in the sand or wallow in self-pity like before," said Van. "I promise. Help me look for him, if you want."

The aspirants searched for hours, Sol Starfletcher and his blue falcon leading the way. But the reed fields were expansive and virtually featureless. There were no landmarks to guide them back to the scene of the ill-fated battle. To make matters worse, it had rained again during the night.

Van recounted the events of the previous night while Simon's spell held. Simon asked few questions, while Shale was principally interested in Sol's arrow of black fletching— the dread viper whose poison had slain Galdur. She was worried about Van, too, though—her concern echoing Simon's. Van was grateful, hoping that, if nothing else, it meant she was done avoiding him. As one might expect, Shale's condolences were a touch macabre.

"You couldn't have saved him," she said, taking Van's hand and squeezing it, the way he used to for Lilim. "It was always going to end that way between Acrearms and Goldeyes."

The statement was so fatalistic, it caught Van off guard— especially considering who Shale was and everything she had been through.

Wasn't she only alive because she had taken her destiny into her own hands and changed her fate? How was Van supposed to reconcile that with the notion that Otep was gone just because he was fated to die? It was easier to imagine she didn't mean it, that she was only trying to ease Van's conscience by absolving him of blame.

"You say that as though nothing anyone chooses even matters," said Van.

"Of course it matters," she said, faintly annoyed—the way she sounded when he'd missed the point. "The choices we make are the only things that matter. But it is a mistake to believe you can make others' choices for them. Acrearms made his choice long ago. It was the wrong one."

They found no bodies in the reed fields. No blood or bent grass. No trace at all, in fact, to suggest anyone had even been there. Sol Starfletcher called off the search near midday.

"You gave your word," Van fumed when he caught up to the First Ranger, who was now leading the volunteers back to camp.

"And it pains me that I must take it back," said Sol. "But you know better than anyone that time is of the essence, Van the Scribe. We must gather our belongings and press on to Seat Mercura. The safety of the living is a poor trade for the honor of the dead."

"What if Galdur survived?" Van demanded. "What if he simply got up and walked away? He has done it before."

"At Seat Ikann, you mean," said Sol Starfletcher. "Yes, we all saw it. Galdur Goldeyes should not have lived. But with the immediate attention of the most talented healers in the Eastern Plains, and with Atariel the Everliving herself at his sickbed, who knows what might have happened? When Galdur Goldeyes fell last night, he fell alone. And there is no living thing that survives the venom of my arrow."

Van wasn't convinced. He would have searched for Otep all day, and the next, if needed—his friend was owed that. They should have at least stayed long enough to find conclusive evidence of Galdur's wrongdoing. But as usual, the decision wasn't his.

The aspirants broke their fast before starting south along the trade road. They hiked through scattered rain showers until nightfall, setting an ambitious pace again the following morning.

With the reed fields behind them, and the eastern bank of the Nym itself in view, they were now just days away from the Bridge of the Emissaries. Van searched for Shale and Simon after pitching his tent that evening, hoping for an hour of inconsequential conversation to distract him, but his friends were nowhere to be found.

Shale was off on her own somewhere, and Simon was with Ghan Mudcatcher, who had grown reclusive and despondent after Otep's passing. Briefly, Van considered looking for Sol Starfletcher to pass the time, but he was still angry with him for breaking his promise.

His mind wandered as he strolled aimlessly through camp, until he found himself outside the tent of Riverspeaker Gheela. With nothing else to do, he announced himself on a whim, entering when the Mercuran Pilgrimage Guide replied with a curt "Come."

"Van the Scribe," she said, not looking up from the book she was studying, left open on a low table. "How can I help you?"

"Good evening, Riverspeaker." Van cleared his throat. "I'm sorry to bother you. I was only…"

He trailed off when he recognized the book in front of her by its peculiar sheet-metal pages. It was the first time he'd seen it since that terrible day.

"The relic from the desert ruins…" he breathed.

"Indeed." She nodded. "Please, sit. What did you need?"

"Nothing," said Van, accepting the invitation and peering eagerly at the relic. "Have you deciphered it?"

"Regrettably, I am not sure it's possible to," she said quietly, running her fingertips over a page. "The Meridians did not speak our tongue. Only a few samples of their writing are known to exist at all."

"That's wrong," Van blurted. "Their language was the same. It's just their alphabet that's different."

Gheela looked at him. "How could you know that?"

"Because I would be dead if it wasn't so."

Van went on to describe his harrowing ordeal in the underground ruins. Though he omitted all mention of Anathema, he told her in detail about the room with the statues—and the puzzle with the keys. He also mentioned that it was he, not Galdur Goldeye, who had found the relic afterward.

"I'm sorry the credit for your discovery was awarded to that man," she said, her expression ponderous. "If only you'd had the time and tools to copy the engravings from the plaques you saw down there..."

True enough, he had given Lilim all his remaining ink and parchment by then. Van did not, however, think it particularly mattered.

"May I borrow a quill?" he asked. "And some parchment?"

She supplied the materials and watched without comment as he wrote from memory. He scrawled each word twice—once using the letters of the modern Nemian alphabet, and a second time using their Meridian counterparts. Eight words in total, comprising twenty unique characters—a map of more than two thirds of the complete alphabet.

DOLS IKANN VAXAS MERCURA VIGILANT BOLD SHREWD INVIOLAT

"If the word ends with a silent vowel, you drop it. See?" Van pointed with the quill. "That's the only difference. Or rather, the only difference I am aware of."

Gheela picked up the parchment, carefully studying the symbols. When she handed it back to Van, her brow was furrowed in thought. "But you saw these symbols only once, nearly a month ago now."

Van stared back at her. "Yes?"

"You have eidetic memory?"

"I... what?" Van said, frowning.

She rotated the relic to face Van, then pushed it toward him.

"Translate this part." She motioned to the first line of characters on the first page.

Van studied the text briefly and scribbled down a translation, underlining an empty space for the only symbol he didn't know. From context, it was obvious enough which letter it was. He handed the parchment back to Gheela when he was finished.

THEGODSO_THELANDARNOWHER

"The gods of the land... are nowhere," she read.

"There doesn't seem to be any indication as to where one word ends and the next begins, so it could actually be read two ways," Van suggested.

She studied the parchment again, rereading the jumble of words. "I see."

The tent fell silent as Gheela carefully put away the quill and parchment. She set the relic aside as well, leaning forward and staring curiously at Van.

"When we reach Seat Mercura, I'd like to ask chieftain Scaela if we might borrow you for a time."

"Borrow?" said Van.

"You appear to have a gift, Van the Scribe. Before you return to the lands of Dolse, I would bring you before the elders of Mercura and task you with translating the relic in its entirety. If you find the arrangement amenable, of course."

Somehow, Van felt he had little choice in the matter. It was all too familiar, like Brynda Blackblade asking him to mentor Galdur, and he wondered if his "gift" would once more become his curse.

"You honor me, Riverspeaker. It would be my pleasure to make myself useful for as long as the elders of your tribe require." He bid her good night, standing to leave with a polite bow. Once outside, he continued his lonely walk through the campsite, turbulent emotions at play within him.

If Van was even half right about the relic, translating it could be the catalyst of irreversible change for the people of Nemia. He would have to proceed with caution until he knew who among them was ready to accept the truth, and who was still slave to the lie—if not the architects of it. Van had no reservations about serving the truth. If he was to become its herald, then so be it. But he would just as soon not martyr himself for it.

Though Gheela had asked him to translate just the first line, he had privately translated the second for himself.

The gods of the land are now here.

Beware the Emissaries.

When they stopped to rest the following afternoon, Van shared midday meal with Shale and Simon—spiced pears and oatcakes from Homestead. Shale took a double helping of fruit, but she turned up her nose at the oatcakes. Van was slightly forlorn to learn she didn't like his favorite snack, but he quietly decided never to mention it.

"How is Ghan Mudcatcher?" Van asked Simon while they ate.

"He'll be all right," said Simon. "Everyone's just been through a lot."

Van nodded, brushing crumbs off his lap.

"Speaking of which," said Simon. "How are you holding up?"

"I'm fine," said Van.

Simon fixed him in a glare, but Van changed the subject before he could press further.

"Before you accuse me of neglecting to share our travel plans, remember that we'll reach the Bridge of the Emissaries tomorrow. Once across, we will be in the Western Forest, and Riverspeaker Gheela will likely arrange for us to travel the rest of the way to Seat Mercura under the escort of the Patron tribe's rangers."

"The elf tells me you speak highly of this bridge," Shale chimed in. "Why is it significant?"

"Supposedly, it is impressive from an engineering standpoint, considering the width of the Nym," said Van. "And as aspirants on the pilgrimage, some of us may wish to stop and ask for the river spirit's blessing before we cross."

"Hold up, *river spirit?*" interrupted Simon. "Why am I just now hearing about a river spirit?"

Van shrugged. "I didn't think you would find it interesting. According to folk legend, the spirit of the Nym brings good fortune to travelers and presides over the changing of the seasons."

Van marked the incredulous look in Simon's eye and furrowed his brow, feeling obligated to continue.

"No one has ever seen anything actually living in the river, aside from common fish. Even Ghan Mudcatcher believes the river spirit to be a mere fairy tale."

Simon shook his head. "I don't know. Sounds too much like religious mumbo jumbo to me. I don't need to remind you what we found out the last time we went down that rabbit hole."

"We're crossing the river, Simon," said Van, exasperated. "As countless others before us have done without incident. There is no other way to reach Seat Mercura this time of year."

Simon crossed his arms. "If there's a monster in the river, you're buying me a drink."

Van sighed. "Whatever you want."

Simon caught Shale up on the conversation, and she giggled, setting her eyes on Van. "If the elf is done with you for today, I need you for an errand."

"What kind of errand?" asked Van.

She slipped Van's knife out of its sheath, which was still tied to her belt, and regarded it judgmentally.

"As sweet as it was of you to lend this to me, your blade leaves much to be desired. I'm sure there are still a few among us carrying more serviceable weapons. I intend to seek them out and barter for one."

"You haven't needed my help in that regard for some time," said Van. "Why now?"

"It's true, communication isn't the obstacle it once was," said Shale, flashing her scheming smile. "But I'll take you with me all the same. You can be a second pair of eyes in making sure everyone involved is treated fairly."

Van mumbled his agreement, and they left Simon to eavesdrop on unsuspecting aspirants for the remainder of his spell.

They went to Shale's tent first, where she retrieved a pair of fox furs and no fewer than ten rabbit pelts. Splitting the load with Van, she marched directly toward the campsite of Ikann at a pace that suggested she knew precisely what she was looking for.

Walking through the sparse field of tents, Van glanced around at the Ikanni, huddled in solemn groups near low-burning bonfires. These were a leaderless people now, having lost both their Pilgrimage Guide and their First Ranger, the latter posthumously denounced as a murderer and a coward. They'd set out from Seat Dolse with confidence. Today, they were adrift—branded by the permanent stain left on their tribe's reputation by Galdur Goldeye. As he shuffled through their camp, Van found he actually pitied them.

Shale strode up to a bonfire and announced herself to the gathered Ikanni by throwing her share of the pelts on the ground. Van deflated when he recognized one of the aspirants here.

"Shale," said Davin the Ordered Stones, standing up and offering a quick bow. "It has been some time. Oh, and Van the, ah..."

"Scribe," Shale supplied impatiently, then pointed to the sheath at Davin's hip. *"Dagger."*

Davin eyed her for a moment, then glanced at the heap of pelts. Hesitantly, he slipped his dagger from its sheath—a fine ten-inch blade with a wedge tip and crossguard.

"You're asking for this?"

Shale propped her hands on her hips and waited, but Davin only smiled and shook his head.

"I'm sorry, cousin. My price is higher," he said, stowing the blade.

Shale let out a low growl and made a grasping motion at Van. He handed her one of the fox furs, which she threw atop the others before crossing her arms and narrowing her eyes at Davin.

"You misunderstand me," crooned Davin with a smirk. "I have no need for furs and pelts. My blade is yours for nothing but a kiss."

The rest of the Ikanni went wide-eyed while Shale turned to Van for clarification—or... for some other reason? Thinking about it, Van found it hard to believe she needed such a thing explained to her. Was she asking *permission?* Somehow, that sounded even less like Shale.

"He, um," muttered Van as she stared at him expectantly. "He wants you to kiss him."

She cocked her head and frowned. Van touched a finger to his lips, then pointed at Shale, and finally gestured to Davin. Shale raised an eyebrow. Seemingly in thought, she looked at Davin, then at his dagger, and finally sidelong at Van. Van shrugged.

"Dagger first," grumbled Shale.

Davin obliged, untying the sheathed blade from his belt and tossing it to her. She caught it, drawing it halfway to inspect the blade's edge. Satisfied, she resheathed it and tucked it away. Without fuss or fanfare, she strode forward, grabbed Davin by the collar, and pulled his face down to meet hers. She smashed their lips together, holding the pose for all of three seconds.

In an act of youthful exuberance and extremely poor judgment, Davin let his hand creep up behind Shale. He grabbed her by the rear, pressing her closer. She broke away the moment she felt it and struck him backhand across the face, dropping him to his knees.

He laughed, touching his jaw tenderly. "Apologies, cousin. Your lips were so sweet, I couldn't help myself!"

What happened next went unnoticed by everyone but Van —she was too fast. In the blink of an eye, the dagger was out of its sheath again, free in her hand, and Van finally understood why he was there. He stepped forward and placed a hand on Shale's shoulder. She whipped her head to face him, her expression clouded by shame and rage.

Wordlessly, Van held her gaze. They hadn't needed words for some time, he realized, to say anything that truly mattered. He let his eyes speak for him, telling her what he needed to in the private, unspoken language they had come to share.

Shale shot Davin a final, disgusted glance as he picked himself up off the ground, then wiped her mouth with the back of her hand and spat at his feet. With that, she stormed away. Gathering up the pelts and fox furs, Van bowed curtly to the Ikanni before following after her.

Shale slowed her pace just enough to let him catch up. Once he was beside her, she moved closer, so their shoulders touched.

"Jealous?" she said apologetically.

"Why would I be?" he said.

She gave him a searching look. *"Promise?"*

He only smiled at her in response. They took their time strolling back to their own campsite together with Shale's new dagger—which hadn't cost them a thing.

The sound of rushing water grew louder as the procession moved steadily closer to the Nym. They trekked alongside the mighty river for hours, just a stone's throw from its frothing current, before the Bridge of the Emissaries finally appeared ahead of them where the road forked. Even Simon's eyes bulged at the sight.

Built of smooth, gray sandstone in eighteen spans, the profile of the ancient bridge resembled the curve of an archer's longbow. As they drew closer, Van realized the stone was glistening, slick from recent rainfall. This prompted a polite reminder from the remaining two Pilgrimage Guides that the aspirants should watch their step when it came time to cross.

As predicted, many of them first stopped along the riverbank to beseech the resident spirit's blessing. Gheela demonstrated the customary prayer of safe travel for those that had never visited these lands, but Van only watched from a distance with Shale and Simon.

Sol Starfletcher, meanwhile, appeared preoccupied with something at the foot of the bridge. For lack of anything better to do while the procession was halted in prayer, Van ambled over to investigate. As bitter as he still was, he couldn't avoid the First Ranger forever.

"Is something the matter, Starfletcher?" Van called as he approached.

Sol stepped aside so Van could see what had caught his attention—the remains of a large bird, its decaying flesh washed almost completely away by the rain. An owl, if Van had to guess. As understanding dawned on him, he whipped his head to Sol Starfletcher with burgeoning alarm.

"It would seem the message we sent from Hemlock did not reach the Western Forest," confirmed the First Ranger.

"Was this deliberate?" Van whispered, casting a nervous glance back toward the praying aspirants.

"It is easy to imagine so, with as much villainy afoot these days as we have grown used to," said Sol Starfletcher. "But there were few to begin with who knew of our message, and fewer still with the means and motivation to prevent its delivery."

"What, then?" sputtered Van. "It just… died?"

"Many things could have happened," mused Sol, turning his back on the feathered remains. "As I told you before, they are not the smartest of animals. But just because I remain open to other theories does not mean I don't share your suspicions. We will keep our eyes open as we venture into the forest."

With that, he jogged over to Riverspeaker Gheela, presumably to share his findings. The unsettling news was not immediately made public, but Van assumed Simon would want to know right away. Van hurried back to his friends, giving them the talking sign. Once Simon cast his spell, he relayed what he'd seen.

Simon was quick to echo Van's concern that foul play was involved, but he had no more explanation to offer than Sol. Shale remained silent as Simon translated to her, growing pensive as she stared distractedly over the bridge.

Some minutes later, the aspirants of Nemia finally started across the Bridge of the Emissaries. Many stopped a second time as they passed the midpoint, gazing out over the parapets at the swiftly running waters of the Nym. Most would never see such a vista again, so the Pilgrimage Guides leading the formation didn't hurry them.

"You say something?" Simon said to Van. They were waiting toward the rear of the column for those ahead of them to tire of the view and move on.

Van drew his eyebrows together. "No?"

Simon gave him a funny look as they shuffled forward, only to be halted again when the next group stopped to admire the view. The crossing was slow going, and when it was Van's turn to stand and gape, he'd already had his fill of the bridge. He pushed forward, wanting only to reach the lands of Mercura on the far bank.

"What?" said Simon.

"I didn't say anything, Simon." Van gave him a puzzled look.

Moments later, Van nearly slipped on the wet stone when a scream ripped through the air behind him. Wheeling around, he saw several younger aspirants looking down at the river, their hands clapped to their mouths in shock. Following the direction of their gaze, Van saw nothing out of place. Just the raging currents.

"What happened?" he called out, shouldering his way back through the crowd.

"Someone jumped," croaked a girl, her voice shrill and trembling. "Someone climbed up and stepped off, right here."

She pointed at the low parapet, but of course, there was nothing to see. Another scream came from the other side of the bridge, and Van swung around in time to see two young aspirants disappear over the edge. Even more alarming was what lay past them, emerging from river—a thing come to life from the pages of storybooks. The immense black tentacle swayed whiplike just long enough for Van to glimpse it before withdrawing beneath the rushing water.

Panic broke out. Shouts, strangled screams, and cries filled the air. Van didn't know if they were because of the tentacle, or because more people were jumping. Some aspirants slipped and fell, only to be trampled by the surge of the crowd as everyone still on the bridge scrambled to get off of it.

"It's a cephaloform," he heard Simon shout. "Get off the bridge!"

"What do we do!" Van shouted back, unable to see him or Shale.

"Don't listen to it!" yelled Simon.

Another tentacle surfaced, much closer this time, and Van was struck by how massive the thing really was. The black appendage crashed down over the full width of the bridge and swept ten aspirants off their feet, sending them screaming into the river. Van braced himself and pushed toward Simon's voice, hoping not to be toppled by the fleeing aspirants or another monstrous tentacle. He was still closer to the south-facing parapet than he would have liked, and as he staggered toward safety, two more aspirants mounted the low wall and stepped off in front of him. Most terrifying of all was how calm they looked when they jumped—as if they were *relieved.*

Why? Why were they jumping? Van stopped to look, wanting to understand. That was when he heard it. A voice called to him, serene and familiar. A voice he knew and trusted intuitively, even as contradictions fought to assert themselves in the back of his mind. Someone had told him not to listen, but why? The soothing voice promised peace eternal, and it couldn't be lying, because it knew what peace looked like. The voice promised rest—dreamless rest. It promised to reunite him with his loved ones, taken unfairly before their time. He would be with Otep and Lilim again. He would be with *his father.*

Shale flung her arms around his waist and pulled him off the parapet. They fell flat on the bridge together, and Simon's magic rescued them from being trampled. The same spell he'd used at Seat Ikann summoned an invisible globe of force that stopped anyone nearby from coming within five feet. Van's friends carried him to the western bank, not trusting him to move on his own for fear he might try to kill himself again.

The aspirants didn't stop running until they were almost a full league from the Nym. Many collapsed in exhaustion, some of them cradling themselves and weeping. Van was among the former, struggling to catch his breath. Shale and Simon dropped to their knees beside him, relieved to see that he was lucid and uninjured.

"You okay, kid?" asked Simon, panting.

Van could only stare blankly at him. "I think my father is dead."

30 Ex Mortuis

The lands of Mercura were like an oil painting brought to life, the landscape dominated by the colossal majesty of the giant sequoias. As wondrous as they were, the famed trees of the Western Forest made Van feel uncomfortably small. A hundred feet in circumference at the forest floor and three hundred feet tall, they dwarfed all other plant and animal life throughout the verdant ecosystem.

Only glimpses of sunlight peeked through the canopy most days as they traveled west along the road. Thanks to the tight-knit canopy, however, they enjoyed a measure of relief from the rain. Simon voiced his appreciation by reminiscing about a tree species called "redwoods" in a land across the sea that grew even taller than the sequoias, but because of how implausible and unimaginative his anecdote sounded, Van assumed he was making it up.

It would be weeks before they reached Seat Mercura, at the heart of the forest. In the days that followed, they crossed paths with a number of traveling merchants, some of whom brought news from the Eastern Plains.

The aspirants learned that Farseer Daz was dead. The metal monsters known as quells were spreading like wildfire across eastern Nemia, and tribe Dolse—or what remained of it—was rapidly losing control. No pledge of relief had come from Rhaggo Bullbreaker, and as far as anyone knew, the bulk of tribe Ikann's fighting force was sheltering behind the strong walls of their Seat.

Van had known since the day they crossed the Nym. That that news didn't surprise him was explained by what the river spirit had whispered into his mind, and that it didn't bring him to tears was explained by the fact that he had come to accept tragedy as commonplace.

"I'm sorry about your dad," said Simon on the day everyone else found out. "We're going to stop this. I promise."

As an inspirational speech, it fell somewhat flat. Van heard the tremble in his voice. He saw how angry with himself Simon was, but despite it all, Van knew he was trying his best. He would try his best, too, if only to show his friend he was appreciated, and that he wasn't alone.

"How do you suppose the cephalo-thing knew?" asked Van.

"Cephaloform," Simon corrected, watching him warily. "Deep ocean dwellers. One must have swam up your Nym and gotten stuck. They can read minds, communicate telepathically, and they hunt by infecting their prey with psychic compulsions. Some people think they can... well, like with your dad, I guess."

"So? What do you want to drink?" asked Van.

"Huh?"

"You were right about the river spirit," Van said matter-of-factly. "You told me I would owe you a drink. What kind do you want?"

Simon's gaze softened. "Van…"

"Yes?"

He had to look away to find his voice. "You know, when we lost Lilim, it sort of seemed like you just gave up on life. I wasn't sure we were going to get you back. A lot of awful stuff has happened since then, and I'm worried something even worse is going on with you now."

Walking at Van's other side, Shale squeezed his hand, as if sensing his conversation with Simon turning serious. Van gave her a smile, tired but affectionate.

"I'll be all right," he said. Simon didn't press further that day.

Eight days after their ordeal at the Bridge of the Emissaries, they stopped at Greatmother's Cradle, a community significant to tribe Mercura because of the talented medicine men and botanists who lived there. The place was renowned for its innovative greenhouse, an enormous structure with a ceiling of vaulted glass, where the community's elders bred and tended to more than a hundred species of exotic plants for their myriad restorative purposes. Only a hundred and ninety-eight of Nemia's aspirants had made it there to see it.

The news of chieftain Daz was hardest on Ghan Mudcatcher. Coming too soon on the heels of losing Otep Acrearms, it drove the elder deep into a morbid depression. Out of concern, Van accompanied him on an errand in the village while the procession was camped.

"What are we looking for?" asked Van, trying his best to sound cheerful.

"Yarn, beads, and crow feathers," Ghan said somberly.

Van knew what those things were used to make, but he also knew that Ghan Mudcatcher enjoyed explaining things.

"What for?" asked Van.

"To fashion bracelets of remembrance," said the elder. "I have lost my chieftain and my First Ranger both, so I will wear two. Beads of turquoise for Otep Acrearms, and cedar wood for Farseer Daz. If you like, I will help you choose some of your own."

Van stared at the ground in thought. He would be buried alive under remembrance bracelets if he made an honest effort to honor all the dead, but perhaps he would wear one for Lilim.

Upon reaching the village market, they bought beads from a gemstone dealer. Ghan Mudcatcher paid the man with cowrie shells, a currency accepted throughout the Western Forest. Van chose carnelians for his bracelet, then followed the elder back to the cabin the local headman had loaned him. Along the way, Ghan made one more stop, at the apothecary, where he bought no fewer than three gourds of moon's milk. Van hoped his teacher didn't intend all of it for personal use, but he made no comment. Reminding an elder to look after his health would be disrespectful coming from an unblooded aspirant.

Later that afternoon, after Ghan lay down for a much needed nap, Van returned to the village wearing his bracelet of carnelians and crow feathers. Something there had caught his eye earlier, and now that he was alone, he intended to investigate.

On the outskirts of Greatmother's Cradle stood an almshouse—a two-story building with a log frame and a stone foundation. It was big enough, Van estimated, for two hundred beds or more. What Van found strange were the dozens of additional beds that had been arranged in rows outside, beneath canvas sheets propped up on poles to shield them from the rain.

Nearly all these beds were occupied, mostly by feverish elderly, while young men and women tended to them. There were far too many infirm here for a community so small, and Van intended to find out why.

Borrowing the strategy he'd devised at Homestead, Van wordlessly joined the volunteer care workers in tending to the sick. No one at the understaffed infirmary questioned his willingness to lend a hand, and for a time, he made conversation with the few lucid patients he could find.

"Papa?" croaked a woman old enough to be Van's grandmother as he sponged perspiration from her face and neck with a damp towel. "Papa, is that you?"

"No, ma'am. My name is Van."

"I picked flowers today, Papa," she said, smiling. "The pretty blue ones you like, out behind the house. I made you a wreath, see?"

She held her hands out for Van, which of course were empty, but he thanked her all the same. Soon afterward, a girl too young to be an aspirant appeared with a bowl of soup, and she helped the old woman sit up to swallow a few spoonfuls.

"What's wrong with them?" Van asked.

"The phage," replied the girl plainly. Then, glancing up, she seemed to notice him for the first time. "Oh, you're one of the pilgrims! I'm so sorry."

"It's no trouble," said Van. "What's the phage?"

"The lake sickness," she explained. "They've probably had it for years, since before the grownups told everyone to stop drinking the well water. It makes them forget. Sometimes it happens fast, but it can be slow, too. The last thing they forget is how to breathe."

"It's not catching, is it?" uttered Van nervously.

The girl shook her head. "Only if you drink the lake water, or from the wells farther south."

Van spent the rest of the day collecting shards of information until he could piece together the whole story. He had to talk to several more care workers before he could knit the truth together, weeding out the inconsistent bits of superstitious mysticism. Some ascribed the illness to vengeful spirits. Others claimed it was karmic reprisal visited on those who had lived too long in sin. But most at least agreed on the timeline and the illness' impact on local populations.

What the Mercurans called "the phage" first appeared five years ago, cropping up in communities to the south near Lake Nymera. Fortunately, the elders of the tribe were quick to recognize it. Signs were posted warning travelers not to drink from the lake, and all wells in the area were sealed. Spread of the phage was halted, but to this day, no one knew for certain how many denizens of the Western Forest had imbibed the tainted water.

Van was shocked to learn that Galeena Greatmother herself had succumbed to the lake sickness following her last visit to the region. The afflicted all experienced rapid cognitive decline followed by eventual respiratory failure.

When he left the almshouse, Van went searching for Simon, wondering if his knowledge of magic—or the broader world in general—might offer perspective on such an affliction. While cutting through the village, however, Van was diverted yet again.

A crowd had formed around a hooded figure, and when Van stopped to listen to him speak, the voice that carried over the small gathering turned his stomach with its familiar arrogance.

"What you have heard is false!" shouted the cloaked man. "But I swear an oath, here and now, to bring the truth to light. To root out the authors of these disgraceful lies, that they might be brought to justice!"

Van staggered, disbelieving. As he backpedaled, he nearly collided with Sol Starfletcher, who strode onto the scene with Riverspeaker Gheela. The delegates would have recognized the speaker's voice just as easily as Van had. The crowd parted for them, and upon noticing their arrival, Galdur Goldeye threw back his hood. He jumped off the stall he'd mounted, his arms flung wide in greeting.

"Cousin!" crooned Galdur, his tone honey-sweet. "You have no idea how glad I am to—"

Sol silenced him by grabbing his collar and shoving him back a step.

"*How?*" he hissed through clenched teeth.

Galdur feigned surprise, making no effort to defend himself. The Ikanni in the crowd bristled, poised to defend their twice-resurrected champion. Seeing that they were on the brink of violence, Sol was forced to release him.

"What did you do?" Sol lowered his voice. "What did you do with the body of Otep Acrearms?"

"Did something happen to the First Ranger of Dolse?" Galdur smoothed his tunic where Sol had wrinkled it. "What terrible news. I had so much respect for that man."

"Your wicked deeds are known to all, Galdur Goldeyes," said Riverspeaker Gheela. "This is a shameful farce."

"Shameful? Farce?" said Galdur with mock indignation. "Please explain, cousin. It seems I missed something important while I was delayed. And let it be Goldeye, if you don't mind, for now I have only the—"

"You murdered the First Ranger of Dolse in cold blood," Gheela snapped, eyes flaring. "And you attempted to kill my own First Ranger!"

Galdur turned in place to let the crowd see him, raising his voice in defiance. "A serious claim, Riverspeaker! And who, pray tell, brings such accusations against me?"

"Sol Starfletcher himself witnessed your villainy," proclaimed Gheela, brandishing her staff.

Galdur's rebuttal was immediate. "How convenient. For the Starfletcher to be the only First Ranger left standing, why, I imagine tribe Mercura would win Patronage without having to lift a finger." He spun to address the crowd again. "Hear me, friends! These are the fabrications of a coward. Nothing more than a ploy by the Mercurans to steal another nine years of Patronage from us."

As the Ikanni cheered, Van shouldered his way toward the delegates, prepared to defend Sol's testimony—but the First Ranger of Mercura cast him a grave look that warned him to stay silent.

"If it's to be the Starfletcher's word against mine, I would have us revisit this matter at Seat Mercura, where the dispute can be judged fairly," declared Galdur, whose suggestion went unchallenged. "Until that time comes, I will fulfill my duty as First Ranger. I will protect the aspirants of Ikann and pit my skills against those of my peers to win Patronage for my tribe!"

Again, the Ikanni cried out in celebration. Though they were few in number compared to the Mercurans in the crowd, their combined voice—reunified and restored to purpose under Galdur—was oppressive.

Following Sol Starfletcher as he stalked away in disgust, Van caught up to him. "Why?"

"Because that man is not above killing for the sake of mere convenience," said Sol. "I shouldn't need to remind you of that. And because I do not want your death on my conscience, this will remain between he and I."

Van opened his mouth to protest, but it was clear Sol was in no mood for discussion. He left with Riverspeaker Gheela, presumably to prepare a statement as they scrambled to make sense of yet another bizarre and frightening turn of fortunes.

"Yeah, it's really him," mumbled Simon as he reentered Van's tent. "Same guy we left Seat Dolse with. It's not an illusion, and there isn't a whiff of necromancy on him, just like last time."

Simon's spell was already nearing its limit. Van and Shale had stayed behind while he went to the village to see the events still unfolding there for himself. He didn't believe Van's rushed account, but he seemed now to have accepted the truth.

Van considered calling into question Simon's ability to see past illusions. He had obviously failed to do so in the case of Brynda Blackblade, and with Shale, too, if her talent to vanish from sight on a whim could be lumped into that category. In the end, he decided against it, forfeiting the remainder of the hour to Shale so she could debate with Simon privately.

For the Ikanni, Galdur's return was cause for celebration. For most others, it was another ill omen. After a few days, though—for all of them equally—things returned to something akin to normal. The day they left Greatmother's Cradle marked three months since the beginning of their pilgrimage. A detachment of Mercuran rangers conscripted by Riverspeaker Gheela accompanied them from the community, and the half month of travel from there to Seat Mercura was devoid of any new horrors.

It was on that last long leg of his pilgrimage that Van finally carved out time for grief and mindfulness. With patience, and through self-forgiveness, he learned he could find peace in his grief. On some days, he could even find happiness.

Before reaching the Seat, they passed through one more community—a place the Mercurans called Sunbeam. Evidently, a number of influential playwrights had been born here over the years, earning Sunbeam its reputation as a hub of art and culture. The community's history still attracted today's most prestigious theatrical talents, and when Shale learned there would be a show on the evening of their stopover, she insisted Van take her to see it.

Van was pleasantly surprised to discover the play was an adaptation of a story he knew. As such, he was able to follow the plot despite the clumsy acting. The performers used various out-of-date flourishes of speech—a stylistic staple of modern theater Van found tedious—so he asked Simon to translate for Shale while they watched.

The story followed a pair of ill-fated lovers from different tribes whose families were embroiled in an old and bitter rivalry. They vowed to die in each other's arms if they couldn't share a life together, then spent most of their time on stage bemoaning the unfairness of their circumstances. In the play's final act, there was a sword fight, and predictably, both characters perished.

Van was impressed with the swordplay, though it led him to suspect the performers had been cast more for their acrobatic talent than their acting prowess. Shale, meanwhile, giggled without restraint at the choreography, pointing as her eyes teared up. Her expression changed only at the end of the final act, when the lovers died together, run through by their own swords. Shale grew quiet as they professed their love eternal in their last moments, her lips parting slightly as her breath caught in her throat.

Van had long since given up on the play, but watching Shale, he found that all he wanted in the world was another day just like that one. He craved it fiercely, and he was prepared to fight for it, if that was what it took. Yet even in that moment, his resolve was curbed by a sense that, when they at last reached Seat Mercura, his budding suspicion would be confirmed. That the world—whatever he might want from it—was ending.

31 Seat Mercura

There were no embattled walls at the heart of the forest, nor some deadly swamp to warn trespassers away. If the Patron tribe's Seat was protected by any physical barrier, they had passed it weeks ago, when they crossed the Nym. Seat Mercura's palisades were the Mountains at Land's End. Its castle moat was the sea itself. Neither gate nor signpost marked their arrival—rather, it was as though they had been here all along. Seat Mercura was the Western Forest itself.

Rangers met the procession and guided the aspirants to their accommodations, a placid meadow where dozens of log cabins hugged a shallow pond. Four such hamlets awaited them, one for each of Nemia's tribes. Today, the visiting aspirants represented only three—and they no longer numbered thousands, but a mere few hundred. Most of the picturesque cottages would stand eerily vacant during their stay. By the same token, though, the choicest of lodgings would be in no short supply—those cabins closest to the water or the road.

Even the smallest dwelling could sleep eight, but Van, Shale, and Simon claimed one just to themselves. Considering everything that had gone wrong since they were last hosted by a chieftain of Nemia, Van hadn't the slightest idea whether Scaela the Listener intended to observe the usual formalities. Neither, apparently, did anybody else.

The aspirants dispersed trance-like throughout the community, each coming to terms in their own way and at their own pace with the fact that it was finally over—they had lived, when so many others hadn't. Surviving, as it turned out, was no easy thing to make peace with, their gratitude and relief laced with a strange sense of guilt.

Simon was determined to speak to the chieftain without delay, but Van was as much a foreigner here as he was—he had no clue where to find Scaela the Listener, or Mercura's council of elders. Sol Starfletcher had promised he'd seek them out once he had arranged an audience with his tribe's leaders. Until then, they could do little but explore and catch their breath after the day's march. Van observed with newfound detachment that a few more hours wouldn't make much difference, given how long it had been already since they last heard news from the Eastern Plains.

Leaving his rucksack in their cabin, Van strolled absently around the pond, yanking off his boots and lying in the grass as a cool breeze swept off the water. A short rest might be just the thing to sharpen his senses for whatever was next, and it was a comfort when a few minutes later, Shale stretched out to join him. It was his first moment alone with her since Homestead, but before he had a chance to consider how to make the most of it, they were interrupted—much sooner than expected—by Sol Starfletcher.

"Van the Scribe," said the First Ranger, standing over him. "Your presence is requested."

Van sat up. "Just me?"

"My chieftain wishes to speak to Simon of the Mists later," said Sol. "For the time being, I am ordered to summon you, as well as your, ah… partner?"

The statement was punctuated by a surreptitious glance at Shale, breathing rhythmically with her eyes closed and her fingers intertwined behind her head. Van was certain she was awake and listening.

"I'm not going anywhere without Simon," said Van.

Sol hesitated. "Chieftain Scaela was insistent, I'm afraid."

"Then I'm not going." Van lay back down, satisfied to see the twitch of a smirk at the corner of Shale's mouth.

Sol looked over his shoulder at the two armed rangers accompanying him, who seemed on edge. If Van didn't know better, he might suspect they were prepared to drag him before their chieftain under threat of force. Perhaps moved by the same thought, Sol Starfletcher spoke more for their benefit than for Van's.

"Very well. Let us find Simon of the Mists, and we will go together."

Luckily, locating Simon took fewer than five seconds. He was just across the pond at their cottage, waiting impatiently for Van's signal. When Van whistled, Simon was out the door, across the green, and glowering restlessly at the Mercurans faster than Van could pull his boots back on.

Simon gave the talking sign as they left the pond, but Van shook his head, wanting to save the spell's full duration for when it mattered most. He also gave Shale a look, noticing her hand had strayed to her dagger. The way the rangers were shepherding them along, bringing up the rear as if driving cattle—or prisoners—was making her nervous. Van preferred she didn't pull her weapon, but he appreciated the sentiment. It was making him nervous, too.

A short walk brought them to their destination, a grotto hidden beneath a hill formed by the conjoined root structures of three ancient sequoias. A rope was tied around each trunk, stretching from one tree to the next in a triangle, with prayer flags hanging from them to mark the location. Scaela the Listener's audience chambers awaited below. When Sol approached with Van and one too many companions, two figures in robes and masks stepped silently across their path to bar their entry.

"Young Van would not take no for an answer," said the First Ranger. "And I will not tolerate anyone laying hands on him."

The figures looked at each other in silence, their wordless deliberation reminding Van a little of the house attendants at Ranger's Rest. The silent strangers seemed to reach an agreement. Granting Sol's concession, they turned to lead the chieftain's guests down the cave-like path behind them. The Seat rangers didn't follow, merely taking up guard outside the entrance without comment.

It was more than just some dank hole in the ground. The path widened as it spiraled down at a shallow angle, illuminated by candles suspended in woven cradles. The cavern itself was equal parts natural formation and man-made edifice, stalactites juxtaposed with intricate reliefs carved from the living stone around them.

At length they were admitted to a central chamber palatial in scale, a tall curtain of trellis vines dividing it across the middle. On Van's side, two more of the chieftain's robed servants stood in wait, and between them, Galdur Goldeye, grinning smugly as he submitted his trophy Nighthawk for inspection.

"Your achievement is recorded, First Ranger of Ikann," wafted a pleasant voice from behind the curtain of vines. "You may leave us. Sol Starfletcher, come forward."

Galdur bowed to the unseen speaker, leaving the Phantom Nighthawk with the robed attendants, its purpose served. The First Rangers traded combative glances as they walked past one another, and before Van could tear his eyes away from Galdur's retreating figure, Simon caught him by the wrist.

"I could understand all of that," he breathed.

Van frowned at him. "You used your spell already?"

"No," he responded simply, perplexed.

"The same with me," said Shale—in her own voice. "Everyone, all at once."

Unbidden, the robed figures silently departed the chamber, leaving Sol, Van, Shale, and Simon alone in the chieftain's presence.

"Is that Van the Scribe whispering with his friends back there?" called the sing-song voice. "You make a strong first impression, boy, though perhaps not a positive one. I asked to speak to you without the Gnosian."

Van drew himself up, crossing the floor to stand beside Sol Starfletcher.

"Simon of the Mists is my kinsman, and I trust him with my life," he said. "He has traveled far and at great risk to speak with you, chieftain. His message is of the highest importance."

"He's going to make this next part pointlessly complicated," replied the voice, as if warning a curious toddler not to touch a hot kettle.

Van shook his head. "I don't understand."

And then, he did. The trellises parted to reveal Scaela the Listener, rising from her simple throne with feline grace. Her sleeveless gown with its plunging neckline revealed ample skin the color of crimson velvet. A plumed crown fit neatly over her horns, and her long tail twitched from side to side as she stretched her wings.

Simon acted before Van could process what he was seeing, snapping his fingers to send a white-hot bolt of lightning arcing toward Scaela. She swatted it away with a lazy wave of her hand.

"Oh, dear," she said. "I won't get a word in edgewise."

Simon was already working on another spell—tracing symbols in the air that danced sparking off the tip of his finger, spinning together to form a complex pattern. The sigil shone bright and buzzed like a hornet's nest. Shale, too, was crouched and ready to spring, her dagger free of its sheath.

With a flick of her wrist, Scaela disarmed them both, along with Van for good measure. All three hit the floor with their arms pinned behind their backs, bound by golden manacles and gagged. Only Sol Starfletcher was left standing, frozen in silent, wide-eyed shock.

"That's better," Scaela sighed. "Who first, then? The Gnosian? Because he has something so important to say?"

She sauntered forward and stooped in front of Simon, pulling the gag from his mouth.

"I'll kill you," he spat. "You think I haven't killed devils before? I will not let—"

"Oh, my!" Scaela said, sliding the gag back into position. "Van the Scribe was right! We couldn't possibly have had a productive conversation without *that* nugget of wisdom."

Scaela bent over Shale next, studying the controlled fury in her expression.

"And this must be the promised companion. I must say, I was not expecting a dusken. We had a bet going and everything."

She reached down, removing her gag, but Shale only glared at her in contempt.

"Interesting," mused Scaela. "*She's* the smart one."

Van's turn came next. He wondered if it would be best to follow Shale's example and hold his tongue, but he was hardly thinking clearly. Questions churned in his mind, demanding answers. *What do you want? Why are you here?* But as the gag came off, the question he chose was...

"How long?"

"Who, me?" said Scaela innocently. "Let's see. I arrived in Nemia shortly before the death of Galeena Greatmother. Three, three and a half... maybe four years? Time passes strangely here."

The invisible weight pinning Van down forced him to crane his neck, until his eyes locked with hers. "Were they wrong?"

"Almost certainly, dear, but about what?"

"That things like you can't come here," said Van.

"Things like me," she sighed, turning her back on him and gliding to her throne. "We have to get permission, these days."

Simon sputtered an angry string of muffled words, still gagged with his head to the ground.

"Will everyone behave now?" Scaela sat down and smoothed her gown.

Van stopped struggling against the restraints, and a moment later, so did Simon. Accepting their submission as a "yes," Scaela waved her hand. The fetters vanished, and the crushing weight was lifted. They stood up.

"Permission, my ass," growled Simon, rubbing his wrists. "You lied to somebody. You cheated."

"You know I couldn't have," replied Scaela.

"No one in their right mind summons a devil," spat Simon. "I can count on one hand the people still alive who are even capable."

"In their right mind, and still alive..." Scaela echoed.

"Galeena Greatmother," Van blurted, the hint leading him straight to the answer. "She forgot what you were, because of the phage, and she..." He turned to Simon." "What *did* she do?"

"The elf doesn't know," said Shale, watching Simon flounder. "You just heard him admit it."

Sol Starfletcher cleared his throat, visibly unsettled. "Chieftain?"

"You're still here?" said Scaela tersely. "Leave us. Go and prepare for the game."

Sol bowed, but he lingered a moment longer. "Chieftain, Galdur Goldeye should be disqualified and imprisoned. His accomplishments are a farce, and he is a murderer besides."

"Is that so? And have you brought any evidence to support that claim?" Scaela's brow twitched in irritation. "To disbar him without verifiable cause, then appoint my own First Ranger the victor unchallenged, I would be playing right into the hands of Vaxas. That woman wants nothing more than for me to reveal myself a tyrant. If only just to spite her, I don't think I will."

Sol grimaced. "Chieftain—"

"Leave," she commanded. "It hardly matters who wins, at this point."

Sol stood rooted in place, stunned. At length, he did as he was ordered and vacated the chamber.

"Now, where were we?" said Scaela, her eyes falling on Van. "Oh, yes. You wanted to know how I was brought here. We had better start at the beginning, or you might get confused and start acting foolishly again."

She leaned forward and swept her arms across the chamber in mock obeisance.

"The Journey of Patronage. What do you make of Nemia's tawdry little pageant?"

"It's your trick for robbing these people of their souls," snapped Shale.

"Just so," said Scaela. "Though, I take issue with your choice of words. Everyone has to be informed and willing, after all. And who among them wouldn't be? Imagine it—at the moment of your death, to come face to face with your loving gods, ready to reward you for living in virtue by making you a part of them forever."

"No," Simon interjected. "Even if somebody out there was stupid enough to agree to that, no one in this country has the comprehension of magical theory even approaching what it would take to contact the hell planes."

"There you go again," Scaela chided. "Magic this, magic that."

Simon shook his head in exasperation. He might have turned violent again, had he believed there was half a chance of winning. Shale, though, seemed to sense there was a game afoot—and begrudgingly, she agreed to play.

Facing Van, Shale asked, "When did it start?"

"The Journey of Patronage?" Van clarified, trying to keep up. "The tradition has existed since the founding of the tribes, eight hundred years ago."

"Your people have been trapped for that long…" she thought aloud. "But perhaps even longer. There was a disaster, yes? The land was dying, and some Nemian made a deal with a devil to heal it."

"Some *four* Nemians," Scaela corrected. "And it took a veritable army of us to fix what they did to this tortured continent."

"And could the founders of your tribes have done what the elf says is impossible?" Shale asked, eyes still on Van. "Contacted the lords of hell, and brokered a trade?"

"They were the best of us," Van offered, feeling less than helpful. It was a meaningless verse from scripture.

"If they could communicate with the hell planes," added Simon. "And that's a pretty big *if*—that's still a far cry from summoning devils into the world."

"Yet, it was done," said Scaela. "By means of the same mechanism Galeena Greatmother employed quite recently. And that woman had an infant's understanding of magic."

Shale spoke in a low voice to Van. "Which one of them was the first absolute ruler?"

"Mercura the Inviolate was the first Patron," said Van.

"What traits did she share with the Greatmother?"

"He," corrected Van. Staring at the ground, he thought it over. "Um, nothing that comes to mind. Mercura was giantkin, born in the mountains. Galeena Greatmother was a human of the Western Forest."

"Is that the answer, then?" Shale turned to Scaela. "The people you claim did this had nothing in common—neither lineage nor mastery over magic. All you have to do to rewrite the laws of reality is become the ruler of Nemia?"

"Not rewrite them, no," said Scaela. "But the laws of reality *will* save you a seat at the table."

"This is a load of crap," snarled Simon.

Scaela ignored him. "There is a place, one that exists outside and between all places, called the Court of Chivalry. As suggested by your Gnosian friend, only a select few terrestrials know of it. The entity that presides over the Court recognizes a handful of you at a time as representatives of your world's interests to the extended planar continuum. One of those individuals, for the last eight hundred years, has been the Patron of Nemia."

"What… interests?" Van rasped, his throat going dry.

"The Court of Chivalry oversees deliberations pertaining to interplanar travel," said Scaela. "It is a stage for negotiation between appointees from different worlds—different *planes*—mediated by a judge of sorts. Its purpose is to ensure planar transposition occurs if, and only if, the representatives of both worlds in question agree on the terms."

"I'm done," said Simon. "There's no way any of this is true. If it was, you wouldn't be telling us. You wouldn't tell anyone."

"It's important that you know," said Scaela. "*And* that you understand. Elsewise, both our worlds are done for."

"Okay, that's it. We're getting out of here," Simon said to Van and Shale, backing toward the chamber's exit with his eyes trained on Scaela. "I'll come up with something. I just need time to think."

"I could simply restrain you again," said Scaela, drumming her fingers on the arm of her throne. "But very well. Go and have yourselves a good little think. The final contest of the First Rangers will be held tomorrow. It should be worth a laugh. Once it wraps up, we'll talk again. I'd prefer to have you well rested and attentive when we go over the *really* scary part."

Before Van turned to leave, he caught her mouthing the word—*Anathema*—eyes bulging for dramatic effect.

When they emerged from the grotto, Sol Starfletcher and the other rangers were nowhere to be seen. Only Scaela's white-robed servants remained, offering Van and his companions no more farewell than they had greeting.

Simon spoke again, but Van could no longer understand him. He gave the talking sign, and Simon swore loudly before activating his spell.

"We get our bags, and we run," he said. "We leave the forest, and we… shit, I just need to…"

"I don't think we can run, Simon," said Van.

Strangely, Van's mind was clearer than it had been in days. What good would it do to panic now? They were so far out of their depth, it was almost freeing.

"What does Shale think?" Van glanced at her. "I'd like to know her vote."

"Since when do we vote?" snapped Simon.

Van furrowed his brow. "Haven't we always?"

Flustered, Simon spoke to Shale, repeating everything for her in the fashion they were used to. Van carefully gauged Shale's expression when she gave her calm reply. He glimpsed resignation there—but perhaps not hopelessness.

"Okay, looks like you win," grumbled Simon. "We stay put. What's the plan then, boss? Find someplace comfortable to wait, make it nice and easy for the devil worshipers when they come around to carve us up for dinner?"

"If Scaela the Listener wanted us dead, wouldn't we be dead already?" said Van. "She wants something from us. If we can find out what, maybe we can… I don't know, bargain with her?"

"Oh, she wants something, all right," snapped Simon. "Our souls. The only thing any devil has ever wanted, or ever will want. This garbage about cosmic judges and courts is just smoke and mirrors."

"If she asks for our souls, all we have to do is say no. You told me as much."

"You aren't getting it," said Simon. "Most of the time, people making devil deals are talking to them across something like a scrying portal. One plane of reality to another, at a safe distance. This devil is actually here. She could lock us up and torture us, use magic to keep us alive until we begged her to let us die. We'd give her our souls—or anything else she asked for—just to make it stop."

Van thought about it. "She hasn't, though. There's something she hasn't told us yet. Until she does, I don't think we have much to gain from scrambling for a plan besides a headache."

Simon gave up on Van for the day, using the remainder of his spell to argue back and forth with Shale. With no consensus between them, they parted ways at the end of the hour. Simon stubbornly confined himself to their cottage while Shale left on her own, headed for Seat Mercura proper. As for Van, he went back to the pond and lay down, right where Sol Starfletcher had found him earlier that afternoon. Staring at the sky, he entertained himself by trying to guess what it all had to do with Anathema—and what might possess a devil to reveal the secrets of the universe to mere mortals.

Raucous celebration overtook Seat Mercura that night, stretching well into the next day. By late morning, thousands of Nemians from communities across the Western Forest had arrived to witness the final game of the Journey of Patronage, an unprecedented head-to-head contest between the two remaining champions.

Van found the festivities tasteless, even setting aside the fact that these people had no idea there was a devil masquerading as their chieftain. As ever, he avoided the crowds, instead meandering to the appointed place once he learned when and where Scaela's challenge would be issued.

The game was to be a foot race, from the plateau of the nearby Mount Falkrist to the field beneath it, where seemingly the entire population of the region was gathered in screaming anticipation.

Owing to Scaela the Listener's yet-unexplained fixation with Van, he was invited to join her personal entourage for the event. Together with Shale and Simon, he followed the chieftain's palanquin as it climbed the long mountain path borne by four stoic attendants, all hidden beneath masks and robes. They would watch the race from the mountain's precipice, which offered a premier view of the First Rangers' winding course.

Galdur Goldeye and Sol Starfletcher marched ahead of them, maintaining a standoffish distance, with Ghan Mudcatcher and Riverspeaker Gheela following a few paces behind. The elder of Dolse had no champion in the running, but he was still a Pilgrimage Guide. It was his privilege and duty to stand as a witness of record for the tribal games, a status that commanded the respect of Nemia's chieftains. Or the smirking pretense of respect, as the case may be.

"Where did you go last night?" Van whispered to Shale, an experiment to discover whether they could communicate unassisted, as they had the last time they were in proximity to Scaela.

"I took the liberty of learning what I could about the Listener," she said, eyeing the veiled palanquin. "As far as anyone knows, she assumed rule of the blue clan only recently, so to start with, I searched for evidence of abuse under her authority. After that, I spent time in the city's archive reading through your histories for any mention of the Court of Chivalry. In both cases, I found none."

Van nodded along at first, but then he did a double take. "Wait a moment, you can read Nemian?"

"Not usually," replied Shale.

"Then, how?"

She reached into her belt pouch and produced a glass bottle with a heavy stopper. Inside it was a tightly rolled strip of parchment.

"What is that?" He peered closer.

"Magic better than the elf's, for understanding," she said, stowing the bottle. "I have three more, if you want one."

"Where did you get them?" sputtered Van.

"From the Listener," she said flatly. "Who else?"

He grabbed her arm. "You went back to her? Alone?"

She narrowed her eyes at him and pulled away. "Wasn't it you who pointed out we'd be dead already if she wanted us to be? You were lazing by the pond, and the elf was sulking. I was being useful."

"You were," Van conceded with a sigh. "Thank you. But please, take me with you next time. You don't have to do this alone."

Her expression softened into a familiar teasing smile. She tucked her hands behind her back and nudged him playfully with her shoulder.

"Are you worried about me, *kinsman?*"

Despite an urge to take her hand, Van decided not to. Showing affection of that kind and having it reciprocated was still too new. He was still learning what it meant, and how it felt—but among other things he knew it made him feel vulnerable. Van wished never to feel that way anywhere near Galdur Goldeye.

They reached the plateau after a strenuous hike—fairly high up the mountain, but not the absolute peak. The chieftain's attendants rested her palanquin perilously close to the ledge. Stealing a glance at Simon, Van couldn't help but wonder if he was thinking about giving it a shove. The First Rangers were allowed a rest before the race, during which time food and drink were provided, since it was already past midday.

Biting into a plum, Galdur strolled toward Scaela's palanquin and peered over the ledge contemplatively.

"Chieftain," he said, chewing. "You said it was a race to the bottom. Are we required to get there by means of the same trail we came up?"

"Use whatever path and method you like," Scaela crooned from behind the palanquin's drape. "If you imagine you can climb down faster than the Starfletcher can run the trail, you may do so."

Galdur laughed joylessly, tossing the pit of his plum off the side of the mountain and watching it fall.

"If I didn't know better, I might say we came here only to satisfy your curiosity concerning a certain rumor."

"What ever do you mean, First Ranger?" Scaela said innocently.

He only scoffed, still standing over the precipice. Minutes later, Sol and Galdur were asked to take their positions. Sol jogged to the top of the trail, where Scaela's attendants stood to mark what was ostensibly the starting line. Meanwhile, Galdur stayed planted where he was beside the palanquin.

"Are you quite sure you want to start from all the way back here, Galdur Goldeye?" asked Scaela.

"Just call the start and enjoy the show," said Galdur, limbering up.

"As you prefer," she said. "Shall I count you down? Three, two… begin."

Galdur turned wordlessly toward the cliff and, without ceremony, stepped off the ledge. The onlookers, some of whom seemed considerably more surprised than others, stared at the place he'd been just seconds before. Moments later, they heard the faint but distinct crunch of bone breaking further down the mountainside, presumably as Galdur crashed into some rocky outcrop hundreds of feet below.

Everyone rushed to the ledge to look down, but there was nothing to see. They were too high up to make out the faces in the crowd gathered at the finish line, and they couldn't see through the treetops and undergrowth at the foot of the mountain.

"I would say it's decided one way or the other," called Scaela from her palanquin. "Feel free to take your time on the way down, Starfletcher."

Sol Starfletcher set off at a jog despite Scaela's flippant suggestion, and the rest of them followed.

"You know something we do not," Sol said tersely without breaking stride.

"The magnitude of that understatement is impressive, First Ranger," replied Scaela.

"About Galdur Goldeye," he said. "You believe there is a chance he is alive down there. If he is, it will be the third time he has shrugged off death. How?"

"It is not my responsibility to explain the mysteries of the cosmos to you," she said, all childish gaiety gone from her voice.

"Yet you'll explain them to him," said Sol, glancing at Van.

"Unlike you, that boy is in a position to do something that actually matters."

"Was he right?" Sol demanded. "Did we come here only to indulge you? Why gamble Patronage over something so petty? We are in Seat Mercura. There are a hundred ways you could have him killed if you merely wanted to know whether he would spring back to life."

"I'm sure I already told you that none of this matters," said Scaela.

Sol lowered his voice. "There are limits to what even a chieftain may say or do before it becomes treason."

"Oh?" chirped Scaela, once more sounding entertained. "You would threaten me, knowing what I am?"

"I am beginning to think precious few of us know what you really are."

With that, Sol quickened his pace and broke away. Riverspeaker Gheela hurried after him, deep concern written on her face. Following her lead, Ghan Mudcatcher hastened his step. Van, Shale, and Simon were alone with Scaela again, not counting her unassuming attendants, stiffly conveying the palanquin without comment or complaint.

"We've a ways to go yet." Scaela drew the palanquin's drape aside and stretched out. "And you've had a chance to sleep on things. Shall we pick up our discussion from where we left off? Any lovely epiphanies since last time?"

Simon shared his first. "You were the one scrying on us. The Listener. It's right there in the name, like you were making fun of us from the start."

"Until you blocked me out, yes," Scaela confirmed. "Knowing you'd soon be playing a high-stakes game on our behalf, we wanted a peek at our cards. Though, since you've brought it up, let's dispense with the silly Nemian honorific going forward."

"Your actual name being?" Simon prompted.

"Look how clever the Gnosian thinks he is!" Scaela laughed. "There is much to be learned from a name. Too much, in some cases. But, as an olive branch, I'll tell you anyway. I am Scaela sub Bethren sum Centus Minaré."

Van cast a questioning glance at Simon.

"They're titles," he said. "Like on a business card. Sub means she works for somebody, a step up from rank and file, but not the top of the food chain. And the Centus Minaré are…"

Simon clamped his mouth shut, unable to finish—either because he didn't know, or because he didn't want to make it true by giving voice to it.

Scaela finished for him, "The Host of Ninety-Nine, accompanied by a prefix establishing my membership thereof."

"The heaviest hitters in Malus, the uppermost hell plane," muttered Simon after a pause.

"You've used that word before," mused Van, "for one of the Depravities."

"Good memory," said Simon. "According to Solaarian canon, the Depravities made the hell planes in their image and named them after themselves."

"May we discuss something useful, now?" asked Scaela.

Simon shot her a glare. "Not before you answer one more question."

She sighed. "Go on, then."

"In the desert, were you the one who hit us with that storm?"

Van stumbled, and Shale caught him by the arm.

"Guilty as charged," said Scaela. "And before you waste more of my time, yes, I provoked the cephaloform hiding in your river, too. In my defense, I was outvoted on both matters by my counterparts. They hoped these events might kill our darling Ms. Chivarn. When they failed to, they ordered me to see to it myself. Since by then it was already too late, I refused. You're welcome."

For once, Van was piecing it together faster than Simon, though only because he knew ahead of time where Scaela's story was going. Somehow, this was all leading back to Anathema.

"Shale?" Simon balked. "Why? I thought for sure you were going to say it was so the Host could get their hands on more souls."

"On any other Patronage year, you'd be right on the money," Scaela said. "This year, however, we won't be the ones collecting souls—or anything else."

"Uh-huh," said Simon. "Before you sideline us again, tell us how you were doing it in the first place."

Shale answered for her. "The Court of Chivalry."

"Just so!" Scaela clapped slowly. "Ms. Chivarn really is the brains of this operation."

"Don't call me that," hissed Shale.

Scaela plowed on, ignoring her.

"The agreement between the Patron of Nemia and the lords of Malus, ratified by the Court of Chivalry, was as follows.

First, the Host of Ninety-Nine would be brought physically to Titan in order to restore the Nemian landmass to habitability. Second, the Host would return willingly to Malus no later than their task was complete—once Nemia could again support ongoing life. Third, no member of the Host would seek to sow influence or effect change during their time here, social or otherwise, beyond the purview of their established objective."

"And what did you get out of the deal?" said Simon.

"The founders promised us their souls, to start with," said Scaela, her eyes brightening. "But as payment, it was woefully inadequate considering the favor they sought. To settle the debt, we put our heads together and came up with the Journey of Patronage. We initially wanted to hold one every other year, but the founders haggled us down to every nine. The soul of any mortal unfortunate enough to die in Nemia during the pilgrimage year is detained—sent to a private oubliette beneath lord Bethren's citadel on Malus. When the year is up, they have a very short, very simple conversation with a member of the Host."

"At which point you ask them for their soul," supplied Simon.

"*Any* mortal, you said," Shale muttered. "Not just the participants..."

"And this Court just abducts souls?" said Simon. "With no warning? Without consent?"

"The Court of Chivalry is the final authority on planar transposition. The last word," said Scaela. "The *only* word. Unlike us, the Court doesn't need informed consent, and it has no scruples. No agenda either, for better or worse. The

Court is logic and motion. Nothing more, nothing less. It carries out whatever the representatives decide—the eternal impartial mediator."

"If that's true, all they would have to do is say no," said Simon. "Your kind still has rules. Somebody dies, pops into a dungeon in hell like you're saying, they immediately know something's wrong. You ask for their soul, they say no, and then they go on their merry way."

"We've already been over this," said Scaela. "You might say no, but nearly every Nemian says yes. We're gods to them. Even as we lick our lips and tell them we're going to gobble them up, their upbringing tells them it's their destiny. Their reward for a life lived in virtue. They're bred for it. It's their *pedigree*."

"What happened to 'sow no influence?' " Simon demanded. "If it's the Court's job to hold you accountable, how do you explain the emergence of a religion built on the institutionalized worship of devils?"

Scaela smiled. "That's the best part. It happened all on its own."

"Bullshit," spat Simon.

"The founders tried to warn their followers, in the early days," she went on. "It was too little, too late. The ignorant masses saw us. They *saw us* work our miracles across the land, sprouting forests out of deserts overnight, breathing the pulse of life back into exsanguinated riverbeds. Of course we seemed as gods. You think anyone would choose the *truth* after that? And once the founders were gone, there was no one left to tell them otherwise. The floodgates were opened. They prayed to us. They built us temples, wrote us hymns. Don't believe me? Ask the boy."

Simon searched Van's face. What must it look like right now? It was difficult to imagine an expression that fully conveyed the shame and failure of an entire people.

"So, what changed?" pressed Shale.

"You'll get your answer this evening, when I take you to visit the Court."

"Visit...?" echoed Van and Simon in unison.

Scaela drew her palanquin's veil closed again, thus ending the conversation. Turning his eyes back to the trail, Van saw they had nearly reached the bottom. The flagpole in the field ahead, which marked the finish line for the First Rangers' race, was swarming with cheering Ikanni.

As expected, Galdur Goldeye was alive and well, dressed in shreds of clothing and covered in blood that could only be his own. Despite his sorry state, he didn't have a scratch on him. The aspirants of his tribe had hoisted him onto their shoulders to parade him in circles around the flag, singing his name, while a much larger gathering of Mercurans looked on in grave uncertainty. It was the beginning of a new Cycle of Ikanni Patronage, which the tribes of Nemia would formally recognize when the First Ranger returned to his Seat in the Eastern Plains.

Once they reached the foot of the mountain, Scaela congratulated him and gave a short address. She vowed to recognize the authority of her new Patron and pledged them her fealty, assuring the crowds that the rule of law would be upheld as fairly and justly as ever under the stewardship of tribe Ikann. Her voice carried the calm confidence looked for in a leader in times of doubt. She hit the right notes with all the expected decorum—here was one chieftain of Nemia turning over rulership of the land to another in the spirit of ongoing peace and humility.

In reality, she was laughing at them. Van felt sicker the longer he listened, and he fled the field before his stomach could turn. His pilgrimage was ending the same way it began —feeling overwhelmed and unprepared, desperate for someplace quiet to escape it all. His mind retreated to the alleyway at Seat Dolse all over again, where he met a girl named Lilim and named her the Brave just to keep her from crying. He promised that girl life. A rich life, full of rewarding experiences. Now, less than a quarter-year later, she was dead.

No. Worse than dead, he realized. Her soul itself had been eaten by a devil. Her spark—or whatever a soul was—had vanished from creation, forever. A wave of grief brought him to his knees with a groan, and as he knelt in the grass, he found he had no more strength to draw upon than the boy who'd hid in the alley that night.

But today's Van the Scribe had friends beside him. Simon took his right arm over his shoulders, and Shale his left. Together, they helped him away.

32 The Court of Chivalry

"This is crazy," Simon said to no one in particular, having activated his spell the moment they stepped into their cottage. "As a ploy to steal our souls, it seems rather convoluted."

He spoke the second, marginally more helpful statement on Shale's behalf. Van already felt disoriented by their usual arrangement, having to once again acclimate to Simon's translating.

"It's not," said Van as Shale helped him to a bed. "It's about Anathema. You just didn't see…"

"Spell it out for me then, since you have it all figured out," said Simon.

Van collapsed onto the mattress, burying his face in a pillow. "I don't. Hopefully, it'll make sense after she takes us to this Court place."

Shale sat next to him and talked with Simon for a while. At first, Simon repeated the conversation to Van, but when he realized Van had no interest in participating, he gave up. Listening to them argue untranslated, Van distracted himself from his darker thoughts by trying to decide which language sounded prettier. Simon's was more guttural, with too many harsh sounds. If Van had to choose, he preferred the language of the dusken. Or perhaps he just preferred the sound of Shale's voice. When the hour was nearing its end, Van stood up and shuffled to the door.

"Where are you going?" snapped Simon.

"To look for Ghan Mudcatcher."

"Why?"

"To clear my head," Van said. "If something happens, have Shale find me."

Outside, Seat Mercura was wholeheartedly embracing Scaela's decree to greet the new Cycle of Patronage with optimism. The festivities roared around him. Overindulgence in drink seemed a common theme, the aspirants partaking of wine and mead for the first time as blooded kin. A few had already emptied their stomachs and then fallen asleep in puddles of their own vomit.

What a poor way to set the pace for the rest of your life, Van thought. In truth, though, a part of him understood the desire to be apart from oneself—to forget, even if just briefly.

Only after scouring the village for hours did Van consider that his childhood teacher, too, might be in the mood for quiet solitude. He returned to the pond, and sure enough, he found Ghan Mudcatcher alone in a cottage not twenty paces from his own.

"Van the Scribe," said Ghan, answering his knock at the door. "Come in and sit. What troubles you?"

The cottage was dark, all the curtains drawn and the windows shut. Van took the liberty of opening them, allowing some fresh air and sunlight into the room—or what was left of it as day turned to night outside.

"Nothing in particular," Van mumbled, taking a moment to appreciate the breeze.

"That couldn't possibly be true," said Ghan with a rueful laugh. "But it is thoughtful of you to look in on me without seeking to dwell on the problems of the hour."

There were candles in a chest of drawers by the door, just as in Van's cabin. He took a few out and fit them onto the holders stored alongside them.

"You asked me to get to know Shale better," Van said, lighting one candle, and then a second off the first. "I think I have, a little."

Ghan favored him with a grin. "I suspect you would have done so even without my asking."

Van attempted a smile, blushing. "What do you think of her?"

"As a romantic pursuit, you mean?" said the elder. "You already know I consider her worthy as a ranger of our tribe."

Van nodded.

Ghan scratched his scaly chin. "Our laws forbid contact with foreigners. Intimate contact doubly so, I should think."

"My father overturned those laws," said Van. "He spared her life at risk to his own. He wanted to give her a chance to find a place for herself here."

"Indeed he did," said Ghan. "And I know now that he made the right choice." His lips twitched with a smile. "I do not think, however, that our chieftain imagined you would want to jump into bed with her."

"I don't care about that," said Van.

It wasn't the most honest of statements, but it was at least true that there were things he cared about more.

"What, then?" prodded Ghan. "You worry she won't make you a good wife someday?"

"The other way around, if anything." Van gazed listlessly at the floor as he sat down on a bed. "I fail to see how I could possibly be a worthy companion to her."

"Worthy of *her?*" Ghan snorted. "You are the son of Farseer Daz and the cleverest boy I know. You wield blade and bow as well as any ranger, and your mind runs as swift as a gazelle. When we return home, beautiful and talented maidens from across Nemia will travel to Seat Dolse to wed you. That girl should count herself lucky if she manages to claim you for herself first."

Van responded with a smile—a real one, this time. Ghan Mudcatcher didn't deal in shallow flattery. When he said something, he meant it. Reality, however, was quick to ruin the moment. His old teacher might not realize it, but there was a question hidden in his counsel. Return home to *what?*

"Did any of it matter?" he murmured. "Anything we've done this year, I mean. And anything we choose to do from here."

The elder's expression grew pensive.

"When I was your age, I wanted to be a ranger," he said. "The same as everybody else, I suppose. But I was terrible at hunting. I was clumsy with a bow and deathly scared of mourns, not to mention hornbeasts and every other predacious thing living in the Eastern Plains. My family was well connected with the chieftain, though. So despite my lack of talent, I could have done anything I pleased."

Van watched him intently. He had known Ghan Mudcatcher his entire life, and he had never heard this story. He wondered if anyone had.

"When I returned from my pilgrimage, my father sat me down and gave me a talk. He told me that some people are born talented, excelling right away at whatever they set their mind to, while others master a skill only through years of dedication. He then told me there was a third category of people, the one to which I belonged, who would always be terrible at most things, and only ever good at a few. After that, he gave me a choice. I could become the most useless ranger in a generation, or I could put my skills to work for the good of the tribe."

Van stared, his words failing him. At length, his teacher put a hand on his shoulder and looked him in the eye.

"Even when we feel destiny itself is conspiring against us, we must have faith that what we choose matters. In moments of doubt, surround yourself with those you love, and move forward with them in hope. After all, what else is there?"

Scaela sent for Van and his friends that evening. This time, her robed attendants came to the cottage themselves, escorting the three of them directly to the grotto under the sequoias, where the trellis vines were already parted. The devil awaited on her throne, a mocking smile on her lips. As soon as he stepped onto the floor, Van spoke loudly, cutting her off before she could baffle them with whatever cosmic revelation she had in store.

"Were you the one who ate the soul of Lilim the Brave?"

Scaela blinked. "Am I really going to have to explain every little part of this?"

Van held her gaze and clenched his fists.

She sighed. "As of this moment, *nobody* has eaten the idiot girl's soul."

"What?" sputtered Van, deflating. "But you said—"

"Shut up and listen. The souls of the dead are held as payment to be evaluated by the representative of Malus *after* the Journey of Patronage. Not before. Not during. As it happens, we're here to discuss an alternative to anybody having their soul eaten at all."

"What alternative?" Van blurted.

"If you speak out of turn again, I'll sew your mouth shut," she said, her gaze sharpening. "We await one other, then we depart for the Court. Be patient."

Van wanted to ask who the "other" was, but he didn't want his mouth sewn shut. He took two full steps back and stood quietly next to Shale and Simon. He didn't have to wait long to find out who they were expecting.

"What are *they* doing here?" Galdur Goldeye scoffed, glaring at them as he entered the chamber. When his eye fell on Scaela, he froze.

"What in—?" he stammered.

"Surprise!" said Scaela, clapping excitedly. "It's your friend the Emissary, here to teach you about being the next Patron of Nemia. Are you ready to see the Court of Chivalry?"

"The what?" said Galdur, groping for his swords.

The audience chamber disappeared. Van's ears popped as he found himself floating in an endless, featureless nothing, devoid of sound, light, and direction. Somehow, he could still see within the void. Everyone from the grotto was there in the nothing with him, positioned relative to one another more or less where they had been, except that Scaela was now standing and Simon was missing entirely.

Motion flickered in Van's periphery. He looked down, or up, or both—possibly neither—in time to see a pattern bloom from a single point in space. Black and white geometry unfolded at a dizzying speed and scale, providing the sensation of falling, though he wasn't sure he was moving at all.

Van considered shutting his eyes to combat the nausea, but then, in a blink, it was over. They were standing on something like a checkerboard, its expanse stretching as far as the eye could see in all directions. Stricken with vertigo, Van fell to the floor.

"You said there was no magic," he groaned, not yet trusting himself to stand.

His voice sounded strange—muted, distant, like he had clapped his hands over his ears.

"Comparing this to mortal magic would be like mistaking the glint of a candle for the sun in the sky," said Scaela, her voice likewise muffled.

"Where is the elf?" said Shale in the same drowned-out tone.

"The sorcerer in your company is Gnosian," an unfamiliar voice answered—calm, epicene, and clear as a bell. "Per the request of another representative, he will not be granted consultation."

Everyone turned to the speaker. At the center of the boundless checkerboard, a desk had appeared. A caped figure sat behind it, clad from head to toe in ornate armor. The plating seemed at a glance more form than function, complete with pauldrons and a visored helmet.

"That's interesting," Scaela said to the thing behind the desk. "Whose rule is that?"

The figure said nothing. Fighting the tremble in his limbs, Van got to his feet. He couldn't tell how far away the armor-clad figure was. With no point of reference anywhere throughout the uncanny landscape, it was difficult to judge size or scale. Intuition, though, told Van that the desk—and the individual behind it—were of extraordinary stature.

"The only time he doesn't answer is when one of you made a rule that he isn't allowed to," Scaela explained, her answer reminding Van in an unsettling way of the card game Shale played with Simon.

"How can you tell it's a 'he?' " asked Van.

"He, she, it," drawled Scaela. "I don't care, and it doesn't matter."

"What is this?" Galdur surprised everyone, including himself, when his voice rang clear.

"You stand in the Court of Chivalry," said the suit of armor. "Conflux of the planes. As Patron of Nemia, you are a recognized representative of Titan, now vested with powers of litigant."

"Powers?" Galdur narrowed his eye.

Van wondered if he recognized even a single other word the thing had spoken.

"It means you're allowed to talk," said Scaela.

Galdur ignored her. "What is Titan?"

"It is the name of the planet you live on," the suit of armor explained patiently.

"I would appreciate it if you allowed me to take the lead, Mr. Goldeye," said Scaela. "The adults in the room have things to discuss."

Galdur hesitated, sizing her up. A god of the land. His Emissary. But the notion of "power" had clearly piqued his interest.

"Am I allowed to speak, or aren't I?" He glanced between Scaela and the resident entity of the Court.

"The floor is yours, Patron," the entity affirmed.

"You call me Patron," said Galdur. "But I won that title for my chieftain, Rhaggo Bullbreaker."

"Incorrect," it shot back. "As the contestant victorious in Nemia's Journey of Patronage, you are recognized by the Court as Patron. If you wish, you may relinquish your privileges to Rhaggo Bullbreaker, or to any other named individual, so long as they are of mortal lineage and a native of your world. The majority of your predecessors requested similar accommodations."

"We don't have time for this," hissed Scaela.

"Shut her up," ordered Galdur.

The thing behind the desk lifted a gauntleted hand, pointing a finger at Scaela. She was instantly lifted into the air, bound and trussed by iron chains. In an unflattering twist of irony, Van noted also that a length of golden stitching had cinched her mouth closed.

Galdur stared wide-eyed. He walked a slow lap around Scaela while she glared at him, her nostrils flaring. Coming to a stop in front of her again, he doubled over laughing.

"Amazing," he said, practically in tears. "So, I'm in charge now?"

"You are a recognized representative," repeated the suit of armor. "You may bring litigation or hear standing petitions. But first, there is a matter pending arbitration."

"Pending what?" Galdur cocked his head. "What do I have to do?"

"The representative of Malus is due payment for services rendered."

"Who?" Galdur blinked in confusion.

The entity placed its hands on the desk. "I was given to understand the incumbent had explained these matters."

Galdur looked at Van, turning up his palms and shrugging in exasperation. Together, Van and Shale pointed at Scaela.

"Well, she didn't," grumbled Galdur. "Let's hear it from you."

No response came from the person or thing behind the desk. Scaela had established a rule in case something like this happened, Van realized.

Galdur shifted uncomfortably, probably drawing the same conclusion. "Will she hurt me if you let her go?"

"It is not my purview to predict intent," said the suit of armor. "Though it bears mentioning that no harm may come to any guest of the Court during their time here."

Galdur flicked his wrist. "Get on with it, then, so she can do her job."

The entity obliged, releasing Scaela with another gesture. She dropped to her knees, touching her mouth gingerly to ensure the golden thread was gone. Rising to her feet, she stretched her wings menacingly.

"I'm sure you heard him," she fumed. "No harm may come to you *here*. We'll be back where I'm in charge soon, and if you treat us to any more of your childish antics—if you so much as speak without being spoken to—I'll torture you until your mind snaps. We'll learn exactly how many times you can come back before the spell of Vaxas breaks beneath the weight of your dying."

Galdur nodded meekly, taking a step back.

Scaela took a breath and unruffled her gown. "Would the Court please name the representative of Malus?"

"The representative of Malus asks to be referred to as Anathema," said the armor, regaining Van's full attention.

"And does Anathema want to be paid in souls, or has it invoked the amendment?"

"The amendment has been invoked," the entity confirmed. "The Patron reserves the right to refuse, as does the offering, in which event all souls held will be transferred to Malus, per the original agreement."

"Lovely," sneered Scaela, turning to Van.

Van struggled to return her gaze. "What is... the amendment?"

It was the armor that answered. "The amendment, proposed and ratified in Titan Solar Year 100256, allows the representative of Malus to nominate a living terrestrial as payment in place of the souls held, selected from among the participants in the prior year's Journey of Patronage. Once invoked, the amendment may be declined without debate, either by the Patron or by the selected terrestrial."

"Wait—what?" Van whipped his head from the judge of the Court to Scaela. "You said it was your Host of Ninety-Nine the founders made a deal with. How did Anathema end up as a representative?"

"We were at war with Anathema for half a decade," said Scaela. "The decisive battle took place almost a year ago. We lost. In other words, Malus is under new management, and as such, the Court recognizes Anathema as its representative, the inheritor and beneficiary of the contract between our worlds."

"Then, a living person can take the place of all those souls? Why?" continued Van.

"The founders balked at the number of souls lost after the first pilgrimage," said Scaela. "You see, just like the Gnosian, they assumed everyone would be sensible and refuse us. They were wrong. So, they pleaded with us again, and we offered them an out.

"We considered that in the fullness of time, some pilgrimage years would produce a poor soul yield, so going forward, we reserved the right to choose a living sacrifice instead, reasoning that some aspirant might catch our eye who would serve as good breeding stock for diaspora. Or, in the case of Ms. Chivarn… something more special."

She cast a sidelong glance at Shale for emphasis. "That, and we thought you might try to weasel your way out of things by deliberately restricting your population growth. Which you did, by the way."

Van turned to Shale, but she refused to meet his eyes, staring fixedly at the desk.

"She can just say no," said Van, pointing to the entity. "That's what it said. All she has to do is say no."

"In which case the soul of your dead little friend is forfeit," said Scaela. "Along with how many others? Oh, and more importantly, Anathema will keep right on burning through every world in creation. Mine first, and sooner or later, yours as well."

"So we just give it what it wants?" Van blurted. "Letting it take Shale doesn't solve anything. It just kills somebody else I love."

"Wrong on both counts," said Scaela. "I will explain the plan, but before I do, we should return. Our absence will have made the Gnosian surly by now, and I'd prefer he didn't wander."

"What do I call you?" Shale asked the thing behind the desk.

"Whatever conveniences you," replied the entity.

"Chivalry, then," she said. "What happens if I say yes?"

Van grabbed her by the arm. "Shale, *no.*"

She tore away from him, still avoiding his eyes. "You'll never look at me again if I'm the reason her soul burns in hellfire. What happens if I say yes, Chivalry?"

"You will be transported to Malus, whereupon the souls held as payment will be released," it said.

"I meant after that," snapped Shale. "You send me to hell, and then Anathema has his filthy way with me for all eternity?"

"It is not my place to predict intent," it repeated.

"*I'll* predict all you want me to," said Scaela. "Beginning with the fact that, if we follow the plan, none of that will happen."

"How long do I have to decide?" Shale demanded, ignoring Scaela.

"This audience was granted as a consultation," said the judge of the Court. "The representatives of Titan and Malus are henceforth obligated to settle all debts within twenty-four terrestrial hours."

"We can go," mumbled Shale, turning around and crossing her arms. She wouldn't look at Van. She wouldn't look at anyone.

Scaela turned to the First Ranger of Ikann. "Do us the honor, please, Galdur."

Galdur pointed at his chest and cocked his head in question.

Scaela wore an artificial smile, sweeping her arm across the checkerboard in answer.

"How?" said Galdur.

"Speak the name of the place you wish to go, and the Court will handle the rest," she explained. "You must do so with intention."

Van noted the twinkle of a scheme in Galdur's eye, but it quickly faded, most likely as he remembered Scaela's promise to torture him to death.

"Seat..." He hesitated. "Seat Mercura."

And so it was. They were suspended in the nowhere again, and this time, Van shut his eyes until he felt solid ground beneath his feet. Cracking an eye open, he saw they were back in the grotto.

"What happened?" Simon leapt up from where he'd been sitting—Scaela's throne, of all places. "You were gone for like half an hour!"

Scaela shooed him away. Occupying her throne again, she waited while Van explained the bizarre ordeal as best he could. Galdur was allowed to stay, on the condition he not interrupt—and with a gentle reminder that Chivalry was no longer there to protect him.

Partway through Van's explanation, Sol Starfletcher was ushered into the chamber by a pair of silent attendants. Van had no idea why the First Ranger had been summoned, and from the look on Sol's face, neither did he. But Van imagined Scaela was about to tell them.

Once Simon was caught up on their visit to the Court, he swung to face Scaela.

"I still don't buy it. If you were the representative here on Titan, and the Host was running the show back on Malus, wouldn't that have been the perfect loophole? If all the Court needs is agreement on the sending and receiving ends, why not just bring all your buddies here as soon as you became the Patron of Nemia?"

"It was the first thing we tried," said Scaela, resting her chin on her fist. "The boy skipped the part where I'd need to be a mortal born on Titan for it to work. The Court won't recognize anyone from off plane, or anything with an indeterminate lifespan. I was never legitimized. Only a seat warmer."

"Oh," Van chimed in, recalling some of the scrambled details. "It did say that, yes."

"Huh, okay," muttered Simon. "Thanks for indulging me, I guess. Obviously, we're still saying no. Shale stays. Good luck with Anathema."

Scaela pinched the bridge of her nose and shut her eyes. "There is a version of this conflict in which we all win."

Van grabbed the sleeve of Simon's tunic before he could open his mouth to refuse.

"Simon, if this has anything to do with Lilim…"

"Anathema has already invoked the amendment," Scaela explained without further invitation. "What I propose is this. Ms. Chivarn agrees to be sent to Malus. Anathema does what Anathema does, taking up residence in its new vessel. Then, it plays a nasty trick on the Court of Chivalry."

"What trick?" hissed Shale.

"Speaking through you, it will request to be sent home—*your* home, that is. The Court will then send you back to Titan."

"Why would Chivalry allow that?" Shale asked.

"Presumably because whoever created the Court had a soft spot for terrestrials," said Scaela. "Every time one of you goes off on some grand misadventure and ends up stranded in the outer reaches of the planar continuum, he always sends you back."

"Seriously?" Simon scoffed. "Whatever this Chivalry is, it can't be that stupid. It'll know she's got a stowaway on board. No way a textbook bait and switch turns the *conflux of the planes* into a revolving door."

"I think it's already happened," mumbled Van. "Twice, in fact. First with Vauna Featherfriend at Stonebasin, and then with the boy in the desert. And those are just the ones we know of."

Scaela smiled at him appreciatively.

"And why wasn't that the end of it?" demanded Shale. "Anathema got his mortal body, plus a spare. Debt paid."

"Anathema didn't *choose* either those doomed children." Scaela leaned back on her throne. "In the moment of their death, they chose Anathema, unwittingly absolving our enemy of its responsibility to the Court."

"The boy in the desert fell and broke his neck," Van remembered aloud. "But Vauna Featherfriend didn't die at all. He was perfectly healthy when I met him."

"He most assuredly was not," sneered Scaela. "That pitiful little vector of disease had been dying for most of his life. He was ready to kick off any time. Unluckily for him, it happened when he was alone with you."

"Wait," said Simon, closing his eyes and shaking his head. "You shouldn't even know about that kid. We didn't find out about him until after I scryproofed us."

"Keenly observed, Gnosian," said Scaela, her eyes flashing. "Take it as proof that what I'm about to tell you is true."

She leaned forward, her wings arching behind her.

"There are forces at work for whom the events of this year are already a matter of record. I count myself among them, because centuries ago, somewhat by accident, I was let in on a little secret. There exists a prophecy, and in it is named Van the Scribe. It was foretold that he would come here, on this day, to stand against Anathema."

She leveled a finger at Van.

"That boy alone can convince Anathema's vessel to take the steps necessary to save our worlds, and he alone can provide her with the weapon she needs to do so."

Simon spat. "If we follow your plan, we won't save anyone. All that scheme does is turn *your* Anathema problem into *our* Anathema problem. Shale would be as good as dead, and the rest of us would follow probably five minutes later. If that thing beat the Host of Ninety-Nine in five years, it'll finish off Titan in a week."

"Assuming we give Anathema a healthy vessel, that's almost certainly true," said Scaela. "Instead, I propose we give it one we've fatally compromised."

For a matter of seconds, the chamber was as quiet as the grave. All eyes fell on Shale, who kept very still, meditative, as she rolled the idea over in her head.

"Sol Starfletcher," said Scaela. "How long does your black arrow take to kill?"

The First Ranger stiffened. "Minutes. Sometimes less."

"You will use it on Ms. Chivarn, and when we return to the Court, she will agree to Anathema's demands."

"Why would that even work, though?" said Simon. "The last couple of kids Anathema died inside didn't slow it down much."

"Those children were incapable of joining fully with Anathema," said Scaela. "As are most living things, thankfully. But Ms. Chivarn is special. She can—"

"Don't call me that," Shale whispered.

"She can take the heat, so to speak. She can hold all of Anathema at once, and Anathema knows it. But to die bound to her, even for such a being, would be a true death. Anathema would be flung back to whatever ghastly plane birthed it, if not destroyed outright. Everybody wins."

"Except Shale," said Simon. "If we do this, she dies. How are you not getting it through your head that we aren't okay with that?"

"Which brings us to one last item of discussion." Scaela's sharp gaze fixed on Van, and a smile teased her lips. "Van the Scribe of tribe Dolse, might you have brought me a present?"

Van blinked. With numb fingers, he reached into his back pocket and produced the tiny satchel. Atariel the Everliving's gift to the chieftain of Mercura.

"The hell is that?" Simon glanced between the satchel and Van. "What did you do?"

At a gesture from Scaela, one of the robed attendants strode forward and cupped their hands in front of Van. Still in a daze, he handed them the satchel, and they took it to Scaela the Listener on her throne. She drew the sack open and fished out its contents for all to see—a shard of smooth obsidian, about the size and shape of an arrowhead.

Galdur's eye glistened. "That's the witch's…"

"That's right," said Scaela. "A fragment of the scythe of Vaxas—with just enough kick left, I would guess, for exactly one miraculous resurrection."

With Scaela's plan thus laid bare, another restless silence settled over the chamber. This time, Shale was the one to break it.

"Double antlers on mean snake," she muttered with detached recognition.

"No." Simon turned to her, his look of betrayal deepening. "We are not *killing you.*"

"I have twenty-four hours to decide?" she confirmed, eyes flicking to Scaela.

"Closer to twenty-three by now."

Shale crossed to the throne and grabbed the satchel from her, obsidian shard tucked safely back inside. "I don't trust you with this."

Turning on her heel, she marched past Van, who fumbled to catch the tiny pouch when she threw it at him. Without further comment, and without stopping to look back, she strode out of the chamber alone.

33 Double Antlers on Mean Snake

Simon refused to back down, arguing with Scaela for what felt like hours following Shale's dramatic exit. He shunned the very idea of prophecies and predestined encounters, demanding she take action to deescalate the situation with Gnosos, which in his mind was still the more pressing danger. Of everything Scaela had revealed to them, the only part Simon acknowledged was that she needed their cooperation. So, having nothing else to barter with, he bartered with that.

In exchange for considering her plan at all, Simon pressed her to leverage her ill-gotten authority as chieftain to make a public statement—to order the tribes to surrender to Gnosos, preventing further loss of life—but she dismissed him casually.

"One apocalypse at a time, if you please," was her only reply.

Simon tried to drag Van back into the debate, his fiery rhetoric deteriorating into a full-blown tantrum. Van had never seen his friend so desperate, shouting himself red in the face as he vacillated from denial, to anger, to bargaining, and then back to denial again.

When he could stomach it no further, Van turned and staggered toward the mouth of the cave.

"Need air," he muttered. It wasn't an excuse. His head was swimming, and he could hardly breathe. He thought he might faint if he stayed down there a minute longer.

Simon yelled after him as he left, but he scarcely made out the words. He needed time to think—time he barely had, apparently. More than that, he needed to talk to Shale before she did anything rash. But that idea scared him, too. If the devil was telling them the truth, he didn't trust what he might say to her.

Outside the grotto, the evening breeze cooled his clammy skin and cleared his head. Van walked slowly, taking the obsidian shard out of its satchel to inspect it. The fragment stirred awake, vibrating expectantly against his skin, as though it sensed its time had come. It felt heavier than Van remembered.

As much as he needed a break from Simon's company, he pitied him. To learn at fifteen that your whole worldview was a lie was bad enough. But to find out after more than a century, when a day ago you considered yourself well informed? That must be a bitter medicine to swallow. What could they do, opposed and coveted by such glacial forces? Did there exist any meaningful way to resist or outrun the unseen hand reaching from the hallowed past—through hell itself— to move them like pieces in a game? Did most people simply live out their days never realizing that the fate of the world was teetering on the edge of a razor, constantly, forever?

"If that's how the world is, then it really *doesn't* matter what we do," Van thought out loud as he walked. "Win or lose, something else will show up to destroy us in another day, another week… a few years, if we're lucky. Why not just let it burn?"

The night air offered no reply. That was for the better. He hadn't meant it. He was only trying the words on. The devil seemed to believe he had a choice, and that his choice would make a difference. He wanted to believe that, too. The problem was that the choice left him just as paralyzed. If it really was up to him, he could never condemn Lilim's spirit to a fate so horrific. And neither could he ask Shale to die.

Van returned the shard to the satchel and tucked it into his tunic, weighing Scaela's proposal against his vastly more rational doubts. If even one thing she'd told them was a lie, he would never see Shale again. The last person he loved would be gone. And, he supposed, the world would end, which some might consider unfortunate.

As he wandered the outskirts of Seat Mercura, mired in his thoughts, he found it no easier than before to find a quiet place to meditate. Remembering something he'd glimpsed when he went looking for Ghan Mudcatcher, he turned back to the cottages by the pond. This time, he walked past them, ambling toward the neighboring hamlets—in particular, the one that would have been lent to the aspirants of tribe Vaxas, on any other year.

As expected, it stood empty. An abandoned village of log cabins on the other side of a hill from the bustling Seat. The hamlet was built around what might have been a pond once, or perhaps an abandoned quarry. It was just a sinkhole now, treacherous in the night. The Mercurans had piled stones around its perimeter to prevent visitors from falling in if they strayed too close unawares.

A section of the makeshift barrier was formed of old masonry slabs, and because Shale was on his mind, Van climbed onto the nearest stone. He sat with his back to the cottages, facing the yawning pit, but he decided against dangling his legs over the side as he otherwise might have.

"Whose fields these are I think I know,
Their hearth is cold already, though,
They will not mind me stopping here,
To watch their fields at night aglow..."

This time, the dark of night replied.

"That's the rhyme you sang for her. Right before the Gnosian blocked me out."

Van looked over his shoulder. Scaela the Listener was running her fingers along the rough stone, her expression serene. He'd hoped for Shale, but instead, the devil herself now had him cornered, alone.

"Looks cozy. May I join you?"

"I don't suppose I could stop you," said Van.

She hoisted herself up and slid over to sit beside him, brushing him with a wing, but he didn't bother to move away. Fleeing was no more an option now than when Simon had suggested it. Better to simply throw himself into the sinkhole, if he decided he needed a way out.

"I thought you might like a chance to speak candidly." She gazed up at the stars. "You were censoring yourself in front of the others. I could tell."

"Forgive me if I don't consider you someone I can confide in," said Van.

"You don't still think I'm after your soul, do you?"

"I haven't decided," said Van. "Simon thinks you'll simply torture us into giving you whatever you want."

She chuckled softly. "A member of the Centus Minaré would have to be woefully desperate to resort to torture for subsistence."

Van glanced at her. "And why is that?"

"Because souls in anguish taste terrible," she said.

He narrowed his eyes. "You're kidding."

"I'm not," she said, smiling politely. "Tortured souls are rotten things. A self-respecting aristocrat dines only on the souls of mortals who died for a righteous cause, steeped in yearning and heroism. Fresh and crisp, like a grape right off the vine."

Van could only stare at her.

She sighed. "Very well. Another gesture of good faith."

She fixed Van with a gaze he couldn't look away from, her eyes churning with otherworldly light.

"Should you proceed as I requested in neutralizing Anathema, I will under no circumstances seek to acquire your soul, neither for my own consumption nor for any other reason."

The hair on the back of Van's neck stood up, and a smell like hot metal filled his nostrils. The voice that poured from Scaela's lips sounded like a multitude speaking in concert. Somehow, Van knew that voice couldn't lie, and could never break an oath—but if answered, it would bind the respondent just the same. This was the voice of a devil. Realizing it, Van considered keeping his mouth clamped safely shut.

"To be clear, this doesn't obligate me to proceed in that way." Van's said carefully. "You're only saying that if I do, you won't eat my soul."

"Just so," the legion-voice replied, Scaela's flickering eyes still a molten blur.

"And this arrangement pertains only to the choices we make at the Court of Chivalry tomorrow. It will not apply to any future occasion, nor on any kind of recurring basis," he clarified.

"Indeed."

"Alright," he said. "Yes. Fine. I agree."

She smiled. Her eyes became just eyes again, and her voice was no longer a choir.

"There, isn't that nice? Your soul is safe. Do you trust me now?"

"Not particularly," he said.

"What a shame," she sighed, pulling her knees up. "You seemed so open-minded in the beginning."

"The beginning of the pilgrimage, you mean." Van averted his eyes, his jaw clenched. "Why were you watching us?"

"Because we were curious," she said. "About the Nemian boy who was supposed to save our worlds, and about Anathema's vessel, who until recently we knew almost nothing about. Those of us that believed in the prophecy were curious, I should say. There was dissension in our ranks. Many, at first, didn't trust what was foretold."

"I don't think Simon trusts your prophecy either," said Van.

"Gnosian skepticism," said Scaela dismissively. "They distrust anything they can't explain and control. What matters is that *you* believe it, and I know you do. You wouldn't have accepted the boon of Vaxas otherwise. And without her little gift, we would be up the creek without a paddle, as the saying goes."

"Simon also said that your kind can't see those types of prophecies," said Van. "That they're only meant for flesh-and-blood mortals. Was he wrong?"

"Not specifically," said Scaela. "But he painted an incomplete picture. You see, we take things that aren't meant for us as a matter of course. And the prophecies of mortals are just memories of things that haven't happened yet."

Van locked eyes with her again, another piece falling into place. "You know about it because you're the one who ate the soul of Vaxas the Shrewd."

"Indeed," she said. "Her mind was opened to me the moment we struck our accord, and her soul is promised to me when death finally catches up to her. For now, though, it is still her own."

Van shook his head. "She can't still be alive. She would be more than eight hundred years old."

"Did you really never figure it out?" She smirked. "Brynda Blackblade? Atariel the Everliving? There has only ever been one chieftain of Vaxas. She's worn a hundred faces and had a hundred names."

Van was quiet for a long while.

"Why didn't she just tell me?" he whispered.

"I can only speculate." Scaela stretched her wings behind her. "But I imagine it was a classic case of overthinking. When simple honesty would have done the trick, she instead devised an elaborate plot to seduce you. Mortals second-guess themselves a dozen times on any given day. Who knows what went through that woman's head over the lonely centuries?"

Van frowned. "Well, it worked. For an embarrassingly long time."

"Why do you suppose that is?" Scaela watched him.

Van shrugged. "Because I'm an idiot?"

She laughed. "It would be amusing if it was that simple. But no, dear. It worked because it came from a place of honesty."

"You're making fun of me," muttered Van.

Scaela held her arms out, and the night lit up with spectral images, like a scene out of a dream—or a picture book. Confused, disjointed, but penetratingly meaningful.

Van saw a startouched girl with raven hair, no more than five years old. She looked scared, and peering closer, he saw that she was running from something—a company of thronging ghosts. The spirits of the dead chased after her, clamoring to tell her secrets of dire import that her infantile mind couldn't grasp. It was the girl from the storybook at Hemlock.

One of the ghosts chasing her was Van.

"The future was revealed to young Vaxas before she could even comprehend it," said Scaela. "Her childhood caregivers dismissed her visions as nightmares, at first, but she grew into them. When she began casually unraveling mysteries that had long vexed the greatest philosophical minds of the era, people finally started listening."

The phantom image kept pace with Scaela's narrative. The girl was Lilim's age now, but her cold, calculating expression was suggestive of someone much older, with far greater powers of deductive reasoning. The girl sat on a throne in a golden hall, rows of wise men kneeling at her feet.

"The story of Van the Scribe became her favorite. He was like a fairy tale hero to her, and later, when she was the right age, she fancied herself his lover. Theirs would be a romance that crossed the expanse of time, destined by fate itself. Knowing she would be very old when she finally met him, her vanity drove her toward magic that would keep her youthful and beautiful forever, so she could play the part of the blushing bride to her yet-unborn groom."

The image changed again. Vaxas, now Shale's age, sat alone in a lavish bedchamber. A squirming mass of animate obsidian writhed in her outstretched hands, and she stared at it, her lips parted and her eyes full of longing.

"Her obsession darkened as adolescence gave way to adulthood. She stopped thinking of Van the Scribe in a romantic context. He became something more, like a private god. Rather than praying for him, she began to pray *to* him, and still he wouldn't be conceived for centuries..."

Scaela lowered her arms, and the image dissolved. The night was dark and still again.

"So, yes," she continued. "Little Vaxas had a bit too much time on her hands, and a predilection for seeking complicated solutions to simple problems."

Van sat back, letting it sink in.

"It would have been nice to hear that from someone who wasn't a devil," he concluded. "You could just be making it up."

"I could be," she said pleasantly.

"Anathema's seen it, too, you know. The prophecy." He turned to face her again. "Which means it will have already predicted all of this, and we're doomed no matter what."

"Mmm." Scaela pursed her lips. "Anathema's knowledge is not infallible. It didn't pluck those thoughts from the head of Vaxas, and it certainly didn't steal them out of mine. Anathema's source of information about our worlds lies elsewhere, and lacks perspective. The plan will work. The more Anathema thinks it knows, the better for us."

Van considered it, shifting uncomfortably on the rough stone. His rear was getting sore.

"Why, um," he started, then closed his mouth and frowned.

"More specifically please, dear."

"Why do devils only have to tell the truth when they want something?" he asked. "You could overpower us so easily, it seems silly."

She wrapped her arms around her knees, resting her chin on them.

"Because our creators wanted us to be clever," she said, as if drawing the conclusion on the spot. "To devour someone's soul after telling them that's what you intend is surprisingly difficult. As a rule, it ensures only the cleverest of our kind survive."

"But... *why*, though?" said Van.

She smiled at him. "Why have an army of soul-eating monsters when you could have an army of terribly clever soul-eating monsters?"

It was well past midnight when Scaela left Van to his thoughts, and he returned to the cottage by the pond. Shale was nowhere to be seen, but Simon was there, sleeping fitfully. Having a nightmare, from the looks of it. As Van was well acquainted by now with the exhaustion that followed life-changing revelations, he lay down and slept until late morning.

When he awoke, the cottage was empty. He estimated they had less than twelve hours before Scaela's servants rounded them up, and they'd be forced to make their terrible choice. Had Shale even come back to the cabin last night? He needed to talk to her before it was too late, but knowing her, she would be found only if and when she wanted to be.

Pulling his boots on and stepping outside to a chilly, overcast morning, Van found himself in the mood for a bath.

His eyes strayed to the pond, its water cold and brackish. With a little patience, he could probably do better, so he ventured first to the village in search of food.

Seat Mercura was still overcrowded, but its residents and visitors seemed more reined in today. Most were sleeping off yesterday's poor choices, and those still on their feet had been up all night. Van was given porridge at a public kitchen. Still feeling peckish after devouring it, he followed his nose to a stall where a girl in a Mercuran blue dress was handing out baked goods.

Van selected an oatcake from the meager selection remaining, and the girl handed it to him with a smile. She was about his age, plain but pretty, with a full bosom. Though he didn't recall seeing her on the road, he knew she must have been with the procession. He thanked her for the oatcake, smiling politely, then stood to the side of her stall. Spilling crumbs down the front of his tunic as he ate, he considered where else he might wash before confronting cosmic evil later that day.

"Are you looking for something, cousin?" asked the oatcake girl, having noticed his gaze flitting between the nearby dwellings and public houses.

"Um," said Van, his mouth full of oatcake. "Someplay to haff a baff?"

She glanced at the dwindling queue in front of her stall. "Can you wait twenty minutes?"

Van checked the position of the sun, peeking out from behind a screen of clouds. "I suppoh?"

Shooting him another smile, she returned to her work. A good deal longer than twenty minutes later, she packed up her stall, moved it out of the street, and returned to where Van was waiting. She said she knew a place, and would show him the way herself. Vacantly, he followed her deeper into the village, where they turned off the main road into an old residential neighborhood.

The oatcake girl opened the door of a small house near the end of the lane, and beckoned for Van to follow her inside. It was a modest three-room home, with two straw mattresses and a hammock in the front chamber.

"This is… your home," Van observed.

"My family's," she corrected. "They're helping in the Seat, so it's just the two of us."

She disappeared through another door without further explanation, leaving Van alone in the front room. He stood there awkwardly for a full minute.

"You can come in," called the girl.

Stepping through the doorway, Van saw a wooden tub with a low fire already burning underneath. The oatcake girl knelt beside it, kneading a soapstone into a sponge. She had disrobed, and now wore only a towel.

"I left it heating so it would be ready for me," she said. "But I think you need it more than I do. You smell like you've been working at a forge."

Van swallowed. As nice as a bath had sounded just minutes ago, he hesitated. Really, there was nothing unusual or even unexpected about her invitation. Children and adults alike offered such favors to one another every day in communities throughout Nemia, sometimes to perfect strangers. It was a practical necessity that fostered trust and cooperation. By every standard of normalcy, Van's attitudes toward such things were the anomaly. And he really did need a bath.

He stripped down and stepped quickly into the tub, trying his best not to look at the oatcake girl. The steaming water carried a floral aroma, and he could already feel his muscles unknotting. When he settled in, the girl began diligently ladling water over his back.

"What is, um," said Van, "your name?"

"Brenda Brothmaker," she said.

Van coughed, rocking forward and sloshing water onto the floor. "Brynda?"

She giggled, easing him back down by the shoulders. *"Brenda."*

"Apologies," he mumbled hoarsely. "I'm called Van the Scribe."

"I know," she said, pressing the sponge to the base of his neck to begin scrubbing him.

He blinked. "Sorry?"

"I saw you coming and going from the hunt with my First Ranger," she said. "The Starfletcher never picked me for his party. I wasn't good enough."

She drew a slow circle on his arm with the tip of her finger. "But you were."

"I don't—" he stammered. "That is to say, I'm not. I wasn't."

A split second later, her arms were around him. She pressed herself to his back, their skin separated only by a damp towel.

"We should celebrate," she whispered in his ear. "We're blooded man and woman today, are we not?"

To Van's surprise, that was all it took for the mood to evaporate.

"Thank you, cousin," he said firmly. "But no."

She pouted prettily. "You find me displeasing?"

"Not in the slightest," he said.

She went quiet for a moment. "Then, there is another?"

"There is." He nodded.

"Lucky girl," she said, scrubbing his back again, but maintaining a respectful distance. "Or, boy?"

"The former," he said, vaguely remembering a conversation from another time, on a similar subject.

"Has she ever done this for you?" asked Brenda Brothmaker. Her tone was curious, but no longer sultry.

Van chuckled softly. "No."

She smiled. "Then I am lucky, too."

Four hours before they would be whisked away to the Court of Chivalry, Van returned to the cottage, only to find that Shale was still missing.

"Where's the lady of the hour?" Simon said, activating his spell as Van came through the door.

"I was hoping you would know," replied Van.

"Have you looked for her?"

"I've been in the Seat for hours," said Van. "I didn't see her there."

Simon scoffed bitterly. "Probably hanging out with her new best friend the devil, picking out a nice marinade to baste herself in for Anathema."

Van sat down and glowered at him. "I wish you'd stop behaving as though we aren't taking this seriously."

"Hey, don't jump up my ass because I care what happens to you two," he said. "Oh, and screw you, by the way, for leaving me in the dark about what Brynda gave you."

Van sighed. "Were you always this vulgar? Were you doing something with your spell before, to keep me from hearing it?"

Simon brooded in silence. They sat quietly together in the cabin for most of his spell's time limit, and Shale remained absent. Three hours to go.

"Well, Scaela's flunkies will round us up pretty soon," uttered Simon. "I guess we'll catch up with Shale there."

"No," said Van, standing to leave. "I need to talk to her first."

"Will you be able to manage?" asked Simon, raising an eyebrow.

Van shrugged. "I'll have to."

Or so he said, but by this point, he was out of ideas. Shale was clearly avoiding him, and he could think of no one better equipped to avoid people if they were of a mind to. With no other recourse, he found himself back at the quarry across the hill, walking a slow lap around the stone wall cordoning off the sinkhole.

"I've been looking for you," he called loudly. "If you're there, please come out."

And, surprisingly, there she was—sitting in the same spot Van had picked yesterday, her back to the world and eyes downcast. Van inhaled deeply, climbed up to sit next to her, and cleared his throat.

"You're the most intelligent person I've ever met," he began. "I include Simon in that reckoning, and my father, and Ghan Mudcatcher, and... well, everyone. I can't ask you to take responsibility for the mistakes of my people, and I don't want you to die. But neither will I ask you *not* to do it, if you think Scaela's plan will work. I want to know what you think our best chance is. And whatever your decision, I want to help."

She stared into the sinkhole, saying nothing. Van wondered if he should try again with simpler words.

"I think you are very smart, and—"

"Why don't you want me to die?" Shale spoke without looking at him.

Van blinked. "Um."

She pulled something out of her belt pouch and set it on the rock beside her. A glass bottle with its stopper undone, nothing inside but a pinch of ash.

Van steeled himself. "Because you're important to me."

"Of course I am," she said with a sigh. "All of Van the Scribe's friends are important to him."

"More important than a friend, I mean." He fidgeted, growing frustrated with himself.

"Oh?" She inspected her nails. "And what does that mean?"

"You know what it means," he said, his cheeks burning.

"I'm afraid you'll have to explain it," she said.

"That can't possibly be necessary."

"You are very insensitive to the feelings of girls, Van the Scribe."

Mustering his courage, he grabbed her by the shoulders and kissed her. She remained inert, unresponsive against his lips. Her pastel blue eyes, just inches from his, were dispassionate and unseeing. When he didn't pull away, she bit him.

"Why!" he yelled, pressing a hand to his mouth as he sucked on his lip.

"Because children aren't for kissing." She turned away again.

"You're the same age as me!" he said.

"I told you before, I've already passed the test of my childhood. This one is yours to figure out. Try your luck again once you do."

"But I can't, not without you." He spoke with a lisp around his sore lip.

"Then tell me what to do," she said, trying—and failing—to keep her voice from cracking.

"I can't ask you to die," he said helplessly.

"Then we'll run away together," she said. "Take me back to the poison swamp, and we'll escape to the Twilight World.

There's a way through somewhere in that place, I'm sure of it. We'll seal the path behind us, and you can live out your whole life there before the Host of Ninety-Nine or Anathema find another way in. My whole life too, maybe."

Van swallowed. "Is that what you want?"

"What I want is for you to be a man and tell me what *you* want," she snapped, her eyes flashing angrily.

"I..." he began, but his words died on his tongue. He sighed and started again. "The prophecy she told us about—do you think it's true?"

"Of course it's true," she said without hesitation.

Van blinked, startled. "How are you so sure?"

"Because the devil was right," she said. "The only reason I would ever serve myself up like that is if you told me you wanted me to. You're Van the Scribe. I'm Anathema's vessel. Here we are together on the eve of his conquest. If you need more proof than that, you haven't been paying attention."

Van wrapped his arms around his knees and thought hard. "How likely do you think it is that Scaela's plan will work? I'm not asking you to decide. I just want your opinion."

"Define 'work.'"

"Um," mumbled Van.

She sighed. "My *opinion* is that Scaela's plan will almost certainly result in Anathema's destruction. Ninety-nine to one in our favor, if you're looking for betting odds."

"Really?" Van stared at her in surprise. "You're that certain? How?"

"Because of Chivalry," she said. "I know how the Court works. My mother spoke of it once or twice, and I eavesdropped on her any time she discussed matters of state.

Even the rulers of the Twilight World have to treat with the Court, if they want to step between realities or cross oceans in a stride."

Van's eyes went wide.

"That's how you got here..." he whispered, then walked back over his words. "Hold on. What about you, though? Do you think we'll really be able to bring you back, after you...?"

"Ah," breathed Shale. "The version where I get to live. I nearly forgot. As odds go, I can only give that one fifty-fifty."

"Fifty-fifty?" Van's chest tightened.

"There are worse odds, considering what's at stake," she said, her eyes downcast. "Although, since it's me... perhaps I'll amend my appraisal to sixty-forty in our favor."

"Still, that's—" he stammered. "Why?"

"This isn't the first time I've been trapped in some villain's game," she said quietly. "A game I wasn't even allowed to learn, where the rules themselves want me dead. You can't outplay your opponent at their own game, so it's senseless to even try. Instead, I drag the game out, and I wait. In the fullness of time, any opponent arrogant enough will become overeager, and defeat themselves."

"Double antlers on mean snake," Van observed.

She nodded, the ghost of a smile on her lips.

"Then, what in particular makes you doubt our odds?"

"Blackblade," she said, her expression falling again. "If we could know with certainty that what she gave you was the real thing, we'd be right back at ninety-nine to one. Unfortunately, that woman is a lying harlot, so it's a coin toss."

A shiver coursed through Van. Clenching his jaw, he nodded. "All right. I've decided."

"That was fast," she scoffed. "I suppose it's only my life we're discussing."

"We do it," he said, ignoring her barb. "We follow Scaela's plan, exactly as she proposed it."

Shale finally smiled—her real, honest smile. As she stared at her lap, her eyes filled with tears.

"I was hoping so much you would say that," she said, sniffing and shaking her head. "I don't want her to burn…"

By the tiniest of measures, Van relaxed, and he tried to smile back. "The paired antlers on coiled serpent rule was one of Simon's, you know."

For the first time in a day she looked him full in the face, grinning with lunatic excitement.

"The elf might credit the rule to himself, but he only proposed it because I tricked him into doing so. I invented double antlers on mean snake, and I haven't lost since."

They assembled once more in Scaela's chambers, deep in the grotto beneath the mighty sequoias and fluttering prayer flags. Van and Shale had arrived ahead of the others, Simon filing in behind them with a fixed scowl. Minutes later, Galdur Goldeye and Sol Starfletcher were shepherded in by robed attendants, and with that, all the players were present and accounted for.

Scaela sub Bethren sum Centus Minaré greeted them with a compassionless smile, tapping her finger impatiently on the arm of her ill-gotten throne.

"Once we depart, we'll be committed," she reminded them. "Last chance for questions. Last chance for second thoughts."

Nobody spoke. Sol and Galdur stood apart from each other, Sol looking dour while Galdur grinned with smug satisfaction, still basking in the afterglow of his victory. Simon leaned against the cavern wall with his arms crossed—speechless, seemingly, for the first time since their arrival at Seat Mercura.

"Don't give me that look," grumbled Simon when he noticed Shale staring daggers at him. "It's not like I get to be a part of this."

Without a word, she crossed the room to him and pulled him into a hug.

"Uh?" Simon stood there awkwardly, holding his hands up as though he was being robbed.

"In case I'm not me when I come back," said Shale. "Thank you."

Alarmed, Simon glanced at Van over the top of Shale's head, but Van only smiled and shrugged. The sorcerer's expression softened, and hesitantly, he hugged her back.

"Of course, kid," he said. "You too."

Reluctantly releasing him, Shale returned to the center of the chamber, wiping her eyes with the back of her hand as she took her place next to Van. She leveled her gaze at the devil whose scheme she was about to gamble her life on, once more as composed as if she was merely picking a card from the hands of a street magician.

"We've all decided, then?" Scaela raised her eyebrows.

"We've decided," said Shale. "We're going with your plan."

"Excellent," said Scaela. "Sol Starfletcher, you're up."

Sol's expression was set, and for an instant, Van worried he might not cooperate, as disillusioned as the last few days had left him. But he did as he was instructed, drawing his black fletched arrow and holding it free in hand as he approached Shale.

"Do it somewhere that can't be seen," said Scaela. "And as far from the heart as possible, I would think."

"The ankle, then," said Shale, taking a knee to remove her boot.

Van swallowed hard, his throat going dry. It was the same place the desert scorpion had stung Lilim. The arrow in Sol's hand had already transformed into a viper, coiling around his forearm. Shale slipped her boot off and rolled up the leg of her breeches while Sol knelt at her feet.

"There is very little pain," Sol Starfletcher assured.

"Get it over with, ranger," said Shale.

The viper struck with blinding speed, returning to Sol's hand almost before Shale finished speaking. The bite left a thin trickle of blood where the fangs had broken the skin, and her eyelid twitched almost imperceptibly—not even a wince. Without complaint, she pulled her boot back on as Sol returned his arrow to his quiver and stepped away.

Not knowing what else to say, Van asked, "How do you feel?"

"Like I've been bitten by a venomous snake and will soon die," Shale replied calmly.

"Fantastic," said Scaela, clapping her hands together. "Galdur Goldeye, kindly draw the curtain for us."

"Me?" Galdur blinked at her, already confused.

"Did you think I brought you here just to indulge your twisted voyeurism?" Scaela snapped. "You're the representative now. The Court only listens to you."

"Oh," said Galdur. "Of course. How—?"

His mouth snapped shut when Scaela's eyes flashed dangerously. He cleared his throat and started over. "Court of Chivalry?"

Nothing happened.

"Try saying it like you aren't asking your nanny if you can have a sweet," Scaela offered.

Galdur sucked in a breath and made a second attempt. "Court of Chivalry."

The void engulfed them. This time, Van managed to land on his feet by closing his eyes and counting to ten before cracking them open. They stood on the checkerboard again, and the entity Shale had nicknamed after the place itself—Chivalry—was seated behind the desk, waiting.

Van noticed a slight deviation from their last visit. A stack of uniform parchment was piled on the desk next to Chivalry, and in its gauntleted right hand was a fine goose feather quill.

"Your punctuality is appreciated, Patron," it said. "May the Court bring forward the representative of Malus?"

Galdur, still getting used to how things worked here, didn't speak until Scaela shoved him toward the desk.

"Ah," he said, stumbling before regaining his balance. "Yes, do that."

Van had no idea what he had expected to happen, but he was not prepared for what did. Anathema arrived like the tide rolling in, a pitch black wave that stretched forever to either side of Chivalry's desk. Van held his breath, thinking they might all be swept away by it, but an unseen barrier halted its passage. Anathema crashed against the invisible boundary, a dozen paces behind the desk, colliding with the sound and fury of a thunderstorm over the ocean. It settled there, sloshing and roiling, a colossal wall of liquid shadow.

"The Court recognizes that the representative of Malus is owed payment," said Chivalry.

A sheet of parchment levitated off the stack, coming to a rest near the hand that held the quill. Chivalry wrote as it spoke.

"Thirteen thousand three hundred and twenty mortals have died in Nemia since the commencement of this year's Journey of Patronage. Their souls will be sent to Malus at the discretion of the representative."

Van's jaw dropped. The number was far greater than he'd anticipated. The fighting with Gnosos, he realized. It was going poorly—extremely poorly.

"I refuse them," boomed Anathema. "I invoke the amendment."

The voice was different here compared to what Van remembered. Unshackled by an unsuitable, deteriorating vessel, Anathema's words barely resembled conventional speech, echoing like a pack of mourns laughing in the woods at night. Like a cold wind rattling the shutters of an empty house.

"The Court recognizes the representative's request," said Chivalry, quill moving swiftly across parchment. "Has the representative chosen an aspirant?"

"They've already brought her to me," said Anathema. "I choose the daughter of High Priestess Razelle, heir of Eventide. I choose Shale Chivarn."

Van fought off a wave of nausea every time he heard the thing speak. He glanced at Shale, who seemed calm and collected. She wasn't sweating or trembling like he was now, or staggering like Galdur had when he succumbed to the viper's poison. How many minutes had passed? He didn't think Galdur had lasted even five.

"The named aspirant is marked as present," said Chivalry. "At the discretion of the Patron, Shale Chivarn will be sent alive to Malus, and the souls held will be released on their previous course."

"Sure," said Galdur amicably. "Take the darkling. We don't want her."

"Does the named aspirant consent?" asked Chivalry.

"I'd like to know what you want with me first," said Shale, surprising everyone on her side of the desk. "These people told me you're a parasite, that you would use my body as host. If they're right, I would either be dead or a prisoner in my own mind."

"Neither dead nor a prisoner," answered Anathema. "Ours would be a partnership."

"To what end?" demanded Shale.

"To any end." Anathema's waveform undulated in anticipation. "To all ends. First, you can have the boy, or we can take turns with him. Then, we will go to Eventide. We will reduce your mother's fortress and all her holdings to ash, then slaughter her and her followers for their attempt on your life. No pleasure shall be outside our grasp. No conquest beyond our reach. When we tire of Titan or our touch withers it, we will blaze across the stars themselves. We will find a new planet, and we will start again. Forever."

"There's something I should probably tell you, then," said Shale.

"Speak, beautiful daughter," called Anathema.

"They poisoned me," she said. "They planned it all out, hoping to kill us both."

Scaela lunged at her, clawing for her throat, but she didn't make it to within a pace of Shale before Chivalry restrained her. She was pinned midair again, bound with conjured chains and gagged with golden thread.

Anathema's laugh was like the crackle of a mass grave set aflame.

"They poisoned *you?*" it said. "Do you want to tell them, or shall I?"

Shale looked at Van, who stood frozen in place.

"The royal line of Eventide can't be slain by poison," she said. "We neutralize any toxin in our blood with nothing but a thought."

Van watched her searchingly, but she said nothing more. She was smiling cruelly—coldly—but he paid no attention to that. He was watching her eyes. He and Shale hadn't needed words for some time to say anything truly important to each other. Her eyes were enough—telling him all he needed to know in the private language they had come to share. He only hoped that to the others, he still looked surprised.

"Um," muttered Galdur Goldeye. "Is it too late to say I'm no longer in favor of this?"

"You do not disappoint, child," said Anathema, cackling again. "What do you say? Shall we begin?"

"I accept your offer," said Shale, facing Anathema with a girlish curtsy. "Show me the way."

At a gesture from Chivalry, Shale was lifted off her feet and sent hurtling toward the otherworldly wave beyond the desk. The dark waters parted to accept her, like a great mouth yawning open. She tumbled through the air like a thrown doll, suspended helpless for a moment. Then, the shadow-substance collapsed on her with a crash, and she was gone.

Now affixed with a signature, the parchment danced off Chivalry's desk, burning away to nothing as if held over a flame. The dark tide receded, leaving them alone on the checkerboard again.

"Oh," croaked Galdur, after several seconds elapsed in silence. "Seat Mercura?"

Scaela squirmed in her bindings, her eyes blazing.

"Seat Mercura," said Galdur, a little more certainly this time.

Van shut his eyes, and after another ten count, they were back in the grotto.

"Did we win?" asked Simon, as if startled out of a nap.

"You've killed us all," snarled Scaela, lurching toward Van. "I'll flay you alive before Anathema gets the chance to."

"No, we've won," Van stammered, retreating from her. "We trusted you—now trust her."

Van had no time to explain further. A sound like thunder shook the chamber, and just like that, Shale was back. Sol drew his bow, his arrow of blue fletching fitted to the string, Galdur following suit by pulling his twin swords.

Everyone sucked in their breath and waited, eyes trained on Shale. She stretched, catlike, entwining her fingers and raising her arms to the ceiling, palms up.

"Like a charm," she said in a voice that was not Shale's.

She opened her eyes, and Van had to shield his own from the radiant anti-light shining out of the holes in her face. Screening his vision with his forearm, he watched her leave the chamber, slowly stalking back up the path from the grotto to the Western Forest.

"Uh." Simon cleared his throat nervously. "Do we follow her?"

"May as well enjoy our front row seats to the rendering of your world into a crematorium for the living," growled Scaela, narrowing her eyes at Van.

They reached the mouth of the shallow tunnel to find Shale —Anathema—on her knees in a fit of laughter, basking in the moonlight. She ran her fingers through her hair, caressing it lasciviously, clutching fistfuls of her alabaster locks to her nose to inhale their scent. In a spasm of violence, she tore at her face with her fingernails, drawing blood and digging into flesh—which healed over again, unblemished.

"Perfect," she said, giddy. "You're so perfect."

She jerked unnaturally to her feet, wheeling around to face Van. Her eyes were different now—a familiar pastel blue. Shale's, but not Shale's.

"Do we start with you?" she crooned, but then she turned her eyes upward, seemingly distracted. "No. Something more. We tell them we're here."

She lifted her arms to the heavens, and the sky itself changed. The clouds vanished, and even the starlit night beyond was swallowed whole. There was nothing now but a throbbing, crimson stain. A wounded sky dotted with blood-red stars. The sky of all the worlds dead by Anathema's hand, their ashes drifting endlessly down.

It lasted only seconds. Shale wretched and fell forward, catching herself with her hands as she spat up bloody vomit.

"You..." she said, betrayal in her voice. "You didn't neutralize it! We could have had everything, but no. You made yourself their whore."

She looked at Van one last time, her face twisted with hate.

"This isn't—" and then she fell, face down in the dirt.

The moon and the night sky returned, washing away the tormented celestial landscape. All was still and quiet once more.

Van ran to her, the obsidian shard already in his hand, but Scaela was faster. She beat her wings once and crossed the distance in an instant, knocking Van to the ground.

"Wait," she commanded.

Scaela knelt over Shale, first checking her pulse, then prying open an eye to inspect her lifeless pupil.

"All right. It's gone," she said, straightening. "Do what you want with her."

Van crawled to Shale on hands and knees, his heart pounding as he clutched the shard. He had no idea what he was supposed to do, he realized, but the shard was squirming eagerly, and he hoped that maybe it did. He placed it carefully on Shale's chest, just above the collar line of her tunic. The shard snuggled against her skin like a larval creature seeking warmth, then burrowed its way into her, and was gone.

Van held Shale's head in his lap, waiting, and wishing he still had gods to pray to. Seconds passed. Nothing happened. Even after so much horror, Van felt sure it was the most terrifying moment of his life.

Finally, she opened her eyes—those mischievous blue eyes that could only be Shale's—and coughed. Van gasped with relief, realizing only then that he'd been holding his breath. With hands trembling, he helped her sit up.

"I win," she said weakly with a delinquent smile. She shut her eyes, then, and she slept for a day.

34 Journey's End

Van tried to keep Simon away from Shale when she woke up, insisting she needed rest, as though rising from death was fundamentally similar to recovering from the common cold. Simon ignored him, barging noisily into their cottage the minute Van informed him she was awake. Shale didn't mind. She wanted to talk, to celebrate their victory. To celebrate life.

Simon peppered her with questions, and she happily answered all of them. He made her recite the story three times over, always stopping her at the last part because it was his favorite.

"When I realized Anathema knew of Eventide it occurred to me our plan might be in jeopardy," she said, sitting on her bed beside Van.

"So, you just started winging it?" Simon smiled as he leaned in. "And everybody freaked out?"

She nodded eagerly.

"Man, do I wish I'd been there." Simon slapped his knee. *"Oh, shit! The dusken betrayed us! Who could have foreseen this!"*

Shale laughed with him, nodding along at his Galdur impression with tears in her eyes.

Seat Mercura seemed transformed. Many of its visitors had already gone home to neighboring communities throughout the Western Forest, leaving the streets largely empty. Van found the quiet atmosphere altogether more agreeable, especially with the rains receding as the seasons changed once again. In just days, it would be a new year—the First Year of the Fifth Cycle of Ikanni Patronage.

Mere months ago, the idea would have kept Van up at night. Today it seemed of little consequence. It would have been nice to attribute his quietude to some newfound maturity, some perspective earned through embracing the principals his father had raised him with. In truth, he simply didn't think it mattered much which tribe ruled Nemia. At least, not for much longer.

The aspirants, now blooded men and women, were forced to remain at the Seat. Their return home had been deferred, as the state of Nemia east of the Nym was no longer well known. News had stopped coming from the Eastern Plains, and the elders of Mercura had shut themselves away in deliberation.

Scaela told Simon she would grant him an audience once Shale came around, finally agreeing to discuss the situation with Gnosos now that the threat of Anathema was behind them. She'd informed them only that she had a solution in the works. One apocalypse at a time…

Galdur Goldeye and Sol Starfletcher were waiting for them when they reached the grotto, trading glares from across the chieftain's audience chamber. When all were present, Scaela drew the trellises back in greeting.

"Galdur Goldeye," she began warmly. "I'm relieved to see you didn't have the Court whisk you away to some forgotten corner of the planet while I wasn't looking."

"What?" stammered Galdur. "Oh. Well, of course."

Van was relatively certain the idea hadn't occurred to him.

"As requested, today we discuss Gnosos." Scaela leaned back on her throne.

"All right," said Simon, stepping forward. "Galdur's the Patron now, right? So, my thinking is we get him back to Seat Ikann, then have him spread the word to stand down. Assuming the tribes listen, that should at least stem the bleeding. After that, I need to head south, find Gnosian field command, and tell them what's going on."

"What makes you think I'll agree to help you at all?" said Galdur, his tone laced with venom.

"Did you seriously forget the whole 'torture you to death' thing?" Simon snarled, peering at him sidelong. "Count it double for me. Sol would probably want in on it, too. Am I right, Sol?"

Sol Starfletcher shrugged.

"So, you do what we tell you, or we torture you to death. That clear enough for you?"

Galdur spoke no further, glaring at Simon with his yellow eye.

"Okay, good." Simon returned his attention to Scaela. "Can we use the Court to jump us straight to Seat Ikann? That would really speed up our timeline."

"News came this morning that Seat Ikann has fallen," said Scaela. "The war is already over. Gnosos won, and is in the process of putting Nemia to the torch. There isn't a thing anyone can do to stop it. Discussion concluded."

They all stared at her, dumbfounded. Van felt small, but strangely unsurprised. He wondered how long ago he'd accepted it.

"No," yelled Simon. "We didn't do all this just to watch Nemia burn."

"You saved the world," said Scaela. "All worlds, for all we know. That was the prophecy, the very reason you came here. Frankly, you should give yourselves a well-earned pat on the back. Saving Titan from Anathema was your destiny, and you fulfilled it admirably. Saving Nemia from Gnosos was never in the cards."

"No," Simon hissed through clenched teeth. "This isn't your world to give up on. Van—"

He swung to face Van, pleading. Van saw no confidence left in his friend, the man who always had all the answers. He saw no plan, nor the faintest spark of hope. Van saw only frustration and anger, and for him, that was the end of it.

"What did you mean when you said you had a solution?" said Van, turning to Scaela.

"I made an acquaintance, before Galeena Greatmother conjured me into your world," answered Scaela. "We exchanged letters, you could say. When I told him of my plans this year, he offered to lend a helping hand. With the assistance of our new Patron, we can bring him to the Court so you can meet him yourself. If everything feels above board, the Court can send you to his home overseas, and you'll leave this doomed nation behind."

Her solution, then, was nothing more than an escape.

"How many of us can go?" uttered Van.

"A few." Scaela stretched her wings behind her. "My acquaintance is well connected, though at the end of the day, he's only one man. I don't think he can spirit away an entire village, but even I'm not callous enough to reward your efforts here with death. Your passage, at least, is guaranteed, Van of Dolse. This was always the plan."

"Shale's coming too," said Van. "She's the only reason we're alive."

Shale took his hand, glancing at him with visible concern, but he could tell she knew as well as he did that there was no longer any point in staying.

"I don't think there's much left for me here," he said to her anyway, because he needed to hear it. "As long as I'm where you are, I don't care where we go."

"You aren't the only one who can make plans," Galdur interjected. "The witch has schemes of her own. She's seen the future, remember?"

"The prophecy of Vaxas terminates with the downfall of Anathema," Scaela replied simply. "We're all blind to the future now, that woman included." A smile pulled at her lips. "Incidentally, I have a feeling you'll discover your own reasons for considering what my acquaintance has to offer."

Galdur eyed her suspiciously, but he appeared intrigued.

"What do you propose...?" he said cautiously.

"Take me to the Court, and I'll explain." Scaela kept her eyes locked on Galdur. "Everyone else can wait here for now."

"Fine," he said. "Court of Chivalry."

Today Galdur got it on the first try. He and Scaela disappeared, leaving Van alone in the chamber with Simon, Shale, and Sol. Now that Scaela was gone, Simon had to use his own magic to speak and be understood. For the last time, they talked as they'd learned to in the early days of the pilgrimage, with Simon repeating everything said once for each of them.

Van went first. "You tried, Simon. I know you did, and I don't blame you for what's happening."

Simon's expression hardened, but Van saw something like acceptance finally cross his face. He stepped toward Van, putting his hands on his shoulders just like he had on their first day on the road from Seat Dolse.

"Simon Wayde," he said.

"What, um," stumbled Van. "What's that?"

"My name," said Simon. "Use it to find me, when it's safe to. This next part goes without saying, but nobody on a devil's payroll can be good news. Whoever Scaela's bringing to the Court, don't let them convince you they're on your side. Take the ticket out, if that's what it is, and leave it at that."

Van nodded.

"You're not staying," protested Shale. "Your own people are on their way to kill you. It's an untenable way to live, believe me."

"They can't kill me," said Simon, letting his hands drop from Van's shoulders. "I know too much. And when they pick me up, maybe I can still save some lives. But if the two of you..." He trailed off, looking at Sol Starfletcher and translating an extra time for his benefit.

Turning back to Van and Shale, Simon sighed. "The Court won't let me in anyway, so this ride's yours."

"That can't possibly matter!" said Shale. "We'll just have Goldeyes tell Chivalry to jump you from where you are now to wherever we're going. Problem solved! Stop being stupid!"

"Oh, and that drink you owe me?" Simon turned back to Van. "Make it a Roche twenty-two. Fair warning, it isn't cheap."

Sol Starfletcher, meanwhile, was already dragging his feet toward the cavern exit.

"Wait, First Ranger…" Van called after him.

Sol stopped, but he didn't look back.

"Just a ranger like any other now," said Sol. "I will stay and lend my assistance to Simon of the Mists. With Scaela gone, my people will need someone to speak on their behalf when the time comes. Perhaps through her absence, our chances will improve by some small measure."

"With Scaela gone," Van echoed, not quite understanding.

Sol glanced over his shoulder. "I assume she only arranged this mechanism of escape to save herself. That you are being invited along can only be a convenient afterthought, despite whatever she may say."

When Van opened his mouth to protest, his voice failed him. *But you'll die,* he thought helplessly. The last champion of Mercura deserved better. Sol, ever observant, didn't need to be told what was on Van's mind.

"If death really is coming for my people, I won't leave them to face it alone," he said. "Before death I'll have answers, though, and those will come from the last living chieftain of Nemia. After doing what I can here for tribe Mercura, I will return to the Great Swamp of Vaxas and seek out Atariel the Everliving."

Van swallowed, watching him leave. As Sol vanished out of sight, the sound of thunder rolled again, and Galdur was back with Scaela.

"Your benefactor is waiting," she crooned. "It'll be a one-way trip this time. All aboard?"

"Count me out," said Simon. He pulled his hand away from Shale, who had grabbed him by the sleeve.

"Tell us his name," Van demanded of Scaela. "Tell us his name and where we're going, so that Simon—"

"Don't," Simon interrupted. "It's better if I don't know. That way, the Inner Circle can't get it out of me."

Van and Shale searched his eyes, but his mask was set. He was businesslike, leagues away already, and that would be their only goodbye.

"Fine," said Scaela, scanning the room. "A one way trip for three. Galdur?"

"Wait," blurted Van. "Ghan Mudcatcher. If Simon isn't going, give Ghan his place."

Scaela narrowed her eyes at him. "I will not ask your benefactor to risk himself over that doddering old man."

Van's heart sank. So, that was it. Now that Van had played his part, he had no say. He was unimportant again.

"I'll take care of Ghan," said Simon quietly, arms crossed and eyes to the floor. "I can manage that much."

"Right. Without interruption this time, Galdur," said Scaela impatiently.

"Court of Chivalry."

The grotto gave way to the void, then to the familiar checkerboard. As before, Chivalry sat behind the ancient desk. Someone new was with them—a woman, Van thought at first, but he was sure he remembered Scaela referring to him in the masculine, so he looked again. On closer inspection, the newcomer was a young man after all, with a pale complexion and shoulder-length gold hair like Simon's, but he lacked the long ears typical of an elf. Van had mistaken him for a woman in part because he was wearing a fluffy red dress, made of cotton and unadorned, like a towel with sleeves. He smiled as his jade-green eyes darted from Shale to Van.

"Van the Scribe, I presume?" he said in a silken voice.

Van nodded cautiously.

The stranger's grin broadened as he marched up to Van, his arm outstretched. Van hesitated. The joining of hands was a gesture reserved for trusted comrades as a sign of respect, or to indicate the conclusion of binding negotiations. But perhaps it was different where this person came from. Van shook his hand.

"It is an absolute honor," said the stranger. "My name is Frans Abel, and I hope you'll come to think of me as a friend."

"We don't make friends very easily," said Shale, moving closer to Van defensively. "And we aren't going anywhere with you until you tell us why we should trust you."

The man named Abel shifted his attention from Van to Shale. "Well said."

He released Van's hand and evaluated Shale, his expression equal parts fascination and pity, as if studying the markings on some exotic animal. Or one soon to be extinct.

In that moment, Van realized Sol was right. Scaela had brokered a deal with this man as an act of self preservation and nothing more, but his help came at a cost. *They* were Scaela's coin—the last of the Nemians, and the displaced descendant of dusken royalty who was briefly Anathema's mortal vessel. Rarest of rarities. Shale's eyes flashed with recognition as well, and Van already knew what she thought of being anyone's trophy.

As Frans Abel watched her, considering her question, the grifter's smile fell away. He seemed to look at her as a person —perhaps even an equal—if only for a moment.

"You shouldn't, of course," he said plainly. "You should never trust anyone. Together, we'll make sure you never have to."

Shale gave Van a wary look, but she offered no further objection. The stranger had passed her test, at least provisionally.

"Separate rooms you said, yes?" cut in Galdur, crossing his arms and glaring at them. "And on different floors?"

"Of course," said Abel, turning from Shale to beam at Galdur. "Your comfort is my pleasure."

Galdur had been alone with this man for only minutes. What could he have said to change his mind so quickly? That he would turn coat on Brynda, turn his back on tribe Ikann, and on the prospect of dominion—which was surely his aim from the start... It wasn't fair that Galdur would get to live when so many others were dead and dying. It felt wrong.

There were precious few things left that felt right, though. So, on the advice of someone he trusted, Van vowed to surround himself with those things and move forward with them in hope. Taking Shale's hand, he waited.

"As we told you, Galdur," instructed Scaela.

Galdur nodded and faced Chivalry. "Abel residence, Arbus Arkad."

Epilogue

Megalomemoria, 3rd November, 101051

~~Please be advised that with regards to~~ Okay, I'm dropping the usual format. Nobody reads these, anyway.

It's been 48 hours since the memo came. "Conflict has ended following pacification of enemy armed forces." No details, even at my clearance level. Pretty soon, people all over the world will be calling it the Seven Year War. What were we even fighting that it took us this long? If Officium Prima makes a statement at all, it will just be a round of self-congratulations after the President gives everybody on the team a medal.

The C of C is a closed file. I'm not even allowed to write the words. I'm scared just to write their names, but they've already scraped my mind front to back, so it's not like it's a secret. Is that why I got my old job back? It's a long leash, admittedly, but at the end of the day it's still a leash. Are you reading this, Mr. President? Are you watching me write it? If you're hoping I'll lead you back to them so you can tie up a loose end, you'll be disappointed.

Out West, thirteen Vans finished their apprenticeships with the Guilds last year. The year before, it was twenty. They'd all be about the right age. Would he be dumb enough to use his real name, or smart enough to know it wouldn't matter?

Wherever he is, Shale's with him, so I guess he's okay. That those two found each other might be the closest thing I've ever seen to a real miracle. I wish I'd had the time to talk to him about contraception. About a lot of things, really. Some mornings, I still wake up looking forward to that hour we'd spend together. Does a person like me have the right to find comfort in knowing they're still out there somewhere?

I have a feeling things are about to take a turn, and frankly, we could use more good guys right about now.

Maybe they're not done saving the world. Maybe, if we're lucky, they're just getting started.

Simon Wayde

MQ Overseas Operations - Chief Security Officer, Subsidia Locus

Michael Goe is an American fiction writer living in Bloomington, Indiana. He grew up inspired by masters of sci-fi & fantasy like Philip K. Dick and Garth Nix, and credits his motivation to share his own stories to a lifelong love affair with tabletop role-playing games.